*the* SILK HOUSE *series*

# Written on Silk

*Intrigue. Murder. Betrayal.*
*Not only could Rachelle Dushane-Macquinet*
*lose the man she loves, her life is in jeopardy as well.*

Book Two

# LINDA LEE CHAIKIN

ZONDERVAN®

ZONDERVAN.com/
**AUTHORTRACKER**
*follow your favorite authors*

## Three ways to keep up on your favorite Zondervan books and authors

Sign up for our *Fiction E-Newsletter*. Every month you'll receive sample excerpts from our books, sneak peeks at upcoming books, and chances to win free books autographed by the author.

You can also sign up for our *Breakfast Club*. Every morning in your email, you'll receive a five-minute snippet from a fiction or nonfiction book. A new book will be featured each week, and by the end of the week you will have sampled two to three chapters of the book.

Zondervan *Author Tracker* is the best way to be notified whenever your favorite Zondervan authors write new books, go on tour, or want to tell you about what's happening in their lives.

Visit *www.zondervan.com* and sign up today!

■ ZONDERVAN®

*Written on Silk*
Copyright © 2007 by Linda Chaikin

Requests for information should be addressed to:

Zondervan, *Grand Rapids, Michigan 49530*

**Library of Congress Cataloging-in-Publication Data**

Chaikin, L. L.
    Written on silk / Linda Lee Chaikin.
       p. cm. — (The silk house series)
    ISBN-13: 978-0-310-26301-2
    ISBN-10: 0-310-26301-8
    1. France—History—Francis II, 1559–1560—Fiction. 2. Catherine de Medicis, Queen, consort of Henry II, King of France, 1519–1589—Fiction. 3. Dressmakers—Fiction. 4. Huguenots—Fiction. 5. Courts and courtiers—Fiction. 6. Royal weddings—Fiction. I. Title.
PS3553.H2427W75 2006
813'.54—dc22
    2006032095

*Interior design by Beth Shagene*

*Printed in the United States of America*

07 08 09 10 11 12 • 24 23 22 21 20 19 18 17 16 15 14 13 12 11 10 9 8 7 6 5 4 3 2 1

Dover

Calais

ENGLISH CHANNEL

SPANISH NETHERLANDS

D. OF LORRAINE

HOLY ROMAN EMPIRE

PICARDY

Guise

Clermont

*Seine R.*

Paris

*Marne R.*

NORMANDY

*Seine R.*

BRITTANY

Chatillon

Fontainebleau

Vendome

Orleans

ORLEANS

Blois

Amboise

Chambord

*Loire R.*

*Loire R.*

TOURAINE

BURGUNDY

Nantes

*Saone R.*

SWITZERLAND

La Rochelle

Geneva

KINGDOM OF FRANCE

Lyon

BAY OF BISCAY

*Dordogne R.*

*Garonne R.*

*Rhone R.*

Albret

Nerac

GASCONY

NAVARRE

Pau

Toulouse

LANGUEDOC

MEDITERRANEAN SEA

KINGDOM OF SPAIN

S.J. CHAIKIN

## FRANCE IN THE 16TH CENTURY

(showing prominent provinces and cities for this series)

■ Huguenot center

| 0 miles | 50 | 100 | 150 |
|---|---|---|---|
| 0 km 50 | 100 | 150 | |

# Glossary of French Terms

*à bientôt* — so long, see you later

*adieu* — bye

*affaire d'honneur* — duel

*ami* — (m) friend

*amie* — (f) friend

*amour* — love

*amoureuse* — enamored, affair

*appartement* — apartment

*atelier* — shop, workshop

*au contraire* — on the contrary

*au revoir* — good-bye

*beau* — (m) good looking, fine looking, beautiful

*bébé* — baby, very young child

*belle amie* — (f) my lovely, sweetheart

*belle des belles* — the most beautiful

*bien* — good, well

*bien sûr* — of course

*bon* — (adj, n, m) good

*bonhomie* — friendly, warm feelings, camaraderie

*bonjour* — hello, good day

*bonne* — (adj, n, f) good

*Bourbon* — kingly family, of royal blood

*ça alors!* — good grief! (exclamation)

*calèche* — carriage

*capitaine* — captain, sea captain, skipper

*cercle* — group of close associates, often the Queen's

*c'est bien compris?* — is that clear?

*c'est magnifique* — that is magnificent

*chatelaine* — A hooklike clasp worn at the waist for suspending implements

*cher* — (n, m) dear, darling, cherished

*chère* — (n, f) dear, darling, cherished

*chéri* — (n, m) dear, darling

*chérie* — (n, f) sweetheart, honey

*chevalier* — the lowest title or rank in the old French nobility, also, *cavalier* or *chivaler*

*closet* — a small room, for sleeping, dressing, writing letters, reading, etc.

*coif* — stiff ruffle around the neck (period clothing)

*comte* — nobleman, count

*comtesse* — countess

*Corps des Pages* — School for Pages

*coucher* — go to sleep

*courtier* — a person expected at Court by royalty

*cousine* — (n, f) cousin

*couturière* — (n, f) designer, expert in sewing

*déjeuner* — midday meal, lunch

*demoiselle* — young lady

*diable* — devil

*dîner* — evening meal

*docteur* — doctor

*duc* — French spelling for English duke, the highest ranking noble except for a prince of the blood

*duchesse* — duchess

*duchy* — the territory ruled by a duc or duchesse

*émigrés* — emigrants

*enceinte* — expecting, pregnant

*enfant* — child

*escadron volant de la reine* — Catherine de Medici's ladies-in-waiting and maids-of-honor; forty immoral women of beauty who served her political intrigues

*El Escorial* — (Spanish) a building near Madrid, with a palace, monastery, church, and mausoleum of Spanish sovereigns

*extraordinaire* — extraordinary

*fanfaronnade* — fanfare

*faux pas* — false step

*fleur* — flower

*fleur-de-lys* — lily flower

*frère* — brother

*galant* — chivalrous man, suitor

*gloire de la France* — glory of France

*grandmère* — grandmother

*grisette* — a seamstress specializing in dressmaking, embroidery, design; usually still under training

*grande dame* — great lady

*haute monde* — upper class, fashion

*honneur* — (n) honor

*honoré* — (adj) honored

*Huguenot* — French Protestant, of Calvinistic doctrine

*joie de vivre* — joy of life

*L'Echangeur* – The changer

*lettre* — letter

*ma* — (f) my

*ma belle* — my lovely

*madame* — Mrs., madam

*mademoiselle* — Miss, damsel

*magnifique* — magnificent, wonderful

*maître* — form of address for a doctor or an advocate

*mais certainement* — but surely

*maman* — momma, mommy

*ma petite* — (f) my little one

*marquis* — highest ranking nobleman next to a duke

*marquisat* — the territory ruled by a marquis, including land estates, wealth, future title of Duc

*merci* — thanks

*merci mille fois* — thank you a thousandfold

*mère* — mother

*merveilleux* — marvelous

*mesdames* — plural of madame, or of Mrs.

*mesdemoiselles* — plural of mademoiselle or of miss

*messire* — an honorable man or a knight

*messieurs* — plural of Mr.

*mes petits* — my children

*mignon* — cute

*mille pardons* — thousand pardons

*mille diables* — thousand devils (slang)

*mille fois* — a thousandfold

*mon* — (m) my

*monseigneur*—lord, addressing someone of high rank or respected office

*monsieur*— mister, sir

*mûreraies*—a grove of mulberry trees for feeding the leaves to silkworms

*naturel*— natural, natural-looking, casual

*neveu*— nephew

*non*—no

*oncle*—uncle

*on est très ami* — we are very close friends

*oriflamme*—the red banner of St. Denis, near Paris, carried before the kings of France as a military ensign; a rallying symbol

*oui*— yes

*palais-château*— palace, castle

*pardone*—pardon

*par excellent* —archetypal

*pasteur* —Bible pastor, teacher

*père, mon père*—father, my father

*petit* —(m) little, small, young, humble

*petit noir* —coffee

*petit déjeuner* — breakfast

*petite* —(f) little, small, young, humble

*prêche* — Bible study

*précisément*— precisely

*princesse*— princess

*reinette*—young girl-queen

*salle*— hall, large room

*sale de la question* —inquisition hall

*salle de séjour*— living room

*sang-froid*—(n, m) poise, self-control, calmness, indifference

*seigneur* —title of respect for a master, lord, or landowner

*sil vous plaît*—if you please, please

*sœur*—sister

*sotte*— (f) silly, inane

*tante* —aunt

*tenez ferme* — stand firm (as in Ephesians 6:14)

*tout de suite* —at once

*trés amusant*—very amusing

# Historical Characters

*Duchesse Montpensier* — of the House of Bourbon, a Huguenot

*M. Jacques Lefevre* — translated first Bible into French

*M. John Calvin* — writer of *Institutes of the Christian Religion* (*Christianae Religionis Institutio*)

*Prince Louis de Condé* — French general, of the House of Bourbon

*Prince Antoine de Bourbon* — older brother of Louis. He later became King of Navarre through marriage to Huguenot Queen Jeanne d'Albret of Navarre.

*Prince Henry of Navarre* — son of Antoine and Jeanne of Navarre

*Admiral Gaspard de Coligny* — had Normandy and Picardy under his security

*Cardinal de Châtillon (Odet Coligny)* — brother of Gaspard and d'Andelot Coligny

*Mary Stuart (la petite reinette)* — married Dauphin Francis Valois who became King Francis II

*Charles de Montpensier (Duc de Bourbon)* — had rights to the throne that equaled, if not exceeded, those of the Valois

*Mme. Diane de Poitiers* — mistress of King Henry

*Henry of Anjou* — third son of Catherine de Medici and King Henry II (Valois)

*Duc Francis de Guise* — of the infamous Borgias family from Florence, Italy

*Catherine de Medici* — Queen and Regent of France over Francis II and Charles II Valois

*Princesse Marguerite Valois* — daughter of Catherine de Medici and King Henry II (Valois), also called Margo

*Monsieur Henry Guise* — later a duc, younger son of Duc Francis de Guise

*Anne d'Estee* — wife of Duc de Guise (Francis)

*Charles de Guise* — Cardinal de Lorraine, younger brother of Duc Francis de Guise

*Mme. Charlotte de Presney* — member of Catherine's escadron volant

*Madalenna* — Italian serving girl of Catherine de Medici.

*Prince Henry of Navarre* — son of Antoine de Bourbon and Jeanne d'Albret, King and Queen of Navarre

*Monsieur John Calvin* — theologian at Geneva

*Maître Avenelle* — the betrayer of the Huguenots

*Princesse Eleonore Condé* — a niece of Admiral Gaspard Coligny

*Messire de la Renaudie* — a leader of the Huguenots, a retainer of Prince Louis de Condé

*Ambroise le Pare* — physician and surgeon to kings, a Huguenot

*Princesse Elisabeth Valois* — daughter of Catherine and Henry Valois, married Philip II of Spain

*Montmorency family and the Constable of France* — a Catholic who sided with the Bourbons in the end

*Machiavelli* — Niccolo Machiavelli, a cunning and cruel man; he was associated with corrupt, totalitarian government because of a small pamphlet he wrote called "The Prince" to gain influence with the ruling Medici family in Florence

*Alessandro (the abuser)* — a brother of Catherine de Medici

*Cosmo and Lorenzo Ruggerio* — brothers from Florence, Catherine's astrologers and poison makers

*Rene* — a perfumer, also Catherine's poisoner

*Cardinal d'Este* — from Ferrara, Italy

*Tasso* — a poet from Italy

*Ronsard* — a poet who served the Valois Court, Chatelard

*Hercule Valois* — the fourth and youngest son of Catherine and Henry Valois, little is known of him

*Anne du Bourg* — a Huguenot man sent to the Bastille by Henry II. He was burned at the stake under the Cardinal de Lorraine when boy-king Francis ruled with Queen Mother Catherine. The Huguenots then felt betrayed and planned the Amboise plot.

*Nostradamus* — a soothsayer in the Roman Catholic Church

*Jacopo Sadeleto* — Archbishop of Carpentras

*Chantonnay* — Thomas Perrenot de Chantonnay, Spanish ambassador to France

*Alencome* — Monsieur Ronsard d'Alencome, French ambassador to the English court and spy for Catherine

# Author's Note

DEAR READER,

For this series, I have researched period texts, both old and new. Though history cannot prove whether Catherine de Medici committed all of the murders attributed to her during her years in the court of France, even historians writing in her favor cannot deny that she was, indeed, a murderess on at least two occasions, and undoubtedly on others. In view of her known acts of murder, her own letters, and reports from her contemporaries, I feel confident in this portrayal.

Sadly, it is becoming acceptable in our culture for pundits and historians to defend the villains of history and to vilify the saints. Political correctness has even invaded Christian churches, permitting compromise in sound Bible doctrine in order for tolerance to reign over truth. Scripture warns of "those who call evil good and good evil, who put darkness for light and light for darkness" (Isa. 5:20 NIV). We live in a culture that attempts to impress relative values upon us to the extent that we are becoming timid to say: "It is written."

My main reason for choosing this historical period was to bring attention to the French Huguenots who stood uncompromisingly for "It is written." They will surely receive the martyr's crown from our Lord Jesus Christ at the future Bema seat (2 Cor. 5:10). Since Christ will reward our fellow brothers and sisters of this period for their faithfulness to Him, it has been a privilege for me to write about them. I wish I could have done it better.

This series could not adequately show the several centuries of events that unfolded, but I have tried to give a sampling of the Huguenot history. In order to show more of these events through the eyes of my fictional characters, I have compressed parts of the time period in which the historical people lived.

Thank you for your wonderful letters of support and encouragement. You are loved and appreciated. You can contact me through my website at *www.lindachaikinbooks.com.*

The Lord bless and keep you in these times.

LINDA LEE CHAIKIN, TITUS 2:13

*Beloved, think it not strange concerning the fiery trial which*
*is to try you, as though some strange thing happened unto you:*
*But rejoice, inasmuch as ye are partakers of Christ's sufferings;*
*that, when his glory shall be revealed,*
*ye may be glad also with exceeding joy.*

1 PETER 4:12, 13

# A Gown for the English Queen

## CHÂTEAU DE SILK, LYON, FRANCE

BENEATH THE UPPER WINDOW OF THE RENOWNED CHÂTEAU DE SILK'S *atelier*, crimson blossoms on bougainvillea vines sprawled with languid grace along a wall that secluded the inner courtyard's garden. The wind swept through the mulberry orchard, rallying the verdant green leaves into a chorus of praise. Roses, amorously tended to by the stooped gardener, *Monsieur* Jolon, offered their fragrance to the wind's promise as it flowed over the wall, through the open balustrade to the window of the Dushane-Macquinet Silk House.

A burst of activity erupted as a scurry of voices announced the approach of horsemen. *Mademoiselle* Rachelle Dushane-Macquinet, who was unwinding a wooden spool of golden thread, looked across the atelier to Nenette, her *grisette* in training and her *amie*.

"Who is coming, Nenette?"

Nenette was already at the widow, drawing aside the Alençon lace curtains.

"A carriage, Mademoiselle. It is most dusty and ugly—ooh, but a most handsome man is stepping down. La, la!"

"You are at heart, most assuredly, a hopeless flirt, Nenette." Idelette spoke wearily from her position at the cutting table, where she was measuring pink silk for the finishing touches on the surprise birthday dress for her *mignon* sister, Avril.

Rachelle laughed and looked over at Nenette. "I think you should marry Andelot Dangeau, a most fine and honorable young man."

Nenette flushed until her freckles blended into her pert face.

Idelette, who was two years older than Rachelle, looked at her dourly. "Andelot is a most serious young monsieur; he has no thoughts of marriage at this stage of his life."

Rachelle covered a smile. She was almost certain her sister concealed an interest in Andelot.

"He wants to attend the University of Paris and become a scholar," Idelette said, slipping her gold thimble on with artistic flair.

"How do you know?" Rachelle asked with feigned innocence. "Has he been sharing his heart with you again?"

One of the other grisettes snickered, and then quickly ducked her head when Idelette gave a sharp turn of her fair head in the girl's direction.

Rachelle set the wooden spool aside on the long cutting table and stood. "Do you suppose the arrival in the carriage is Sir James Hudson at last?"

"The monsieur did look very English," Nenette said, tapping her small chin.

Idelette jabbed her silver needle into her velvet pin cushion and also stood, shaking out her dark blue skirts. "Such nonsense. One does not look very anything. How are the English supposed to look?"

"I beg to differ, Mademoiselle, but I can tell a Spaniard anywhere," Nenette piped, pursing her lips.

Idelette's mouth tightened.

Rachelle looked at her sister, sobering. Idelette had not been with her at Amboise when over two thousand *Huguenots* were butchered to the satisfaction of Spain, though Rachelle had told her family what happened there, as well as the gruesome scene Andelot had unwittingly attended.

"If it is Monsieur Hudson," Idelette continued, "*ma mère* will be most upset, I assure you. He was to arrive yesterday, as you know. In another hour it will be dusk and tomorrow is Sunday. That means Scripture reading tonight."

It was the family custom to prepare their hearts for Sunday worship with a simple supper followed by an evening of prayer and Bible reading from the secret French Bible her parents kept hidden like gold coins in a treasure chest.

"If it is Sir James Hudson, he will simply need to adjust to the household," Rachelle said, shrugging lightly. "I hope so; I can think of a hundred questions to ask him about the Huguenot immigrants at Spitalfields. I do hope *Père* agrees to open a dress shop there with the Hudson family."

"I have reason to believe he will. There is even talk of transporting silkworms and mulberry cuttings by ship to Hudson land."

"I wonder if the weather of the English countryside is warm enough."

From outside the atelier door they heard hurried footsteps climbing the flight of stairs.

"Idelette! Rachelle!"

Rachelle whipped around to Idelette. "Hide the dress."

Idelette snatched the pink dress and held it behind her as the door flew open.

Avril, who would turn fourteen in two weeks, rushed breathlessly into the room. She was almost a twin in appearance to her eldest married sister, Madeleine, in Paris, who was married to *Comte* Sebastien Dangeau.

Avril's hair was dark and glossy, her eyes a deeper shade of brown. She looked jubilantly from Idelette to Rachelle.

"The Englishman is here. He told Mère his driver became ill yesterday and that is why he is so late. He was obliged to stop at an inn overnight. He has a new driver. He is coming up now with Mère. He has a satchel with a Hudson dress pattern and he asked specifically to meet the 'Daughters of Silk.'"

Rachelle clasped her hands together and turned to Idelette.

"He has inquired of us?"

"Our reputation grows, sister, even apart from *Grandmère* — not that I wished it so."

"You see?" Rachelle took hold of her shoulders and whirled her around the atelier until Idelette burst into a rare display of laughter.

"Cease, you *sotte* sister!"

"Did I not tell you that all we endured while humoring the spoiled *Princesse* Marguerite and *Reinette* Mary would bring blessing to us in the end? See how our work as *couturières* is well spoken of, even among the ladies in foreign courts."

"I must admit you were clever to see it."

Avril, too, danced about the atelier and then pretended to offer a deep royal bow. "May news of your talents travel to royal palaces, Mesdemoiselles, except for the King of Spain's *Escorial*," she said of the place where his throne was located.

Rachelle's mind jumped soberly back to the Queen Mother, Catherine de Medici. Catherine had proposed a trip with Princesse Marguerite to Spain, and there was a real possibility that Rachelle would be called back to Court to attend the princesse. *May it not be*, she thought.

"Oh! What a *belle* pink dress! Who is it for?" Avril was looking across the room where Idelette had placed it over the back of a chair.

Rachelle glanced at Idelette.

Avril started toward the chair to inspect the dress, but Idelette caught it up and walked promptly over to her work table and laid it aside with apparent disinterest.

"Never mind. Do be serious now, all of you. We have work to do, and Sir James Hudson will walk in and think we are behaving like children—"

Voices and footsteps announced the approach of their mère, Madame Clair Dushane-Macquinet, as well as the couturier from London's famous shop on Regent Street, Sir James Hudson.

Rachelle calmed herself and was standing with shoulders back and chin tilted when they came through the doorway.

Sir James Hudson was not old as she had expected. He could be little more than twenty, lithe of body, and handsome, with dark hair and eyes, and a dapper way about him that declared a man of optimistic spirit. He was garbed fashionably as Rachelle would have expected of the son of one of London's finest draperies. His chocolate velvet surcoat with subtle cross-stitch, in what looked to be a tangerine silk ribbon, showed his penchant for originality, as did the polished carved wood hook and eye enclosures. His dress presented innovation while still being far from gaudy or flamboyant.

After introductions by Madame Clair, Rachelle nodded gravely as he smiled at her, realizing she was staring.

"*Bonjour*, Mademoiselles," he said in a friendly fashion. "I bring you greetings from your colleagues, the couturiers of fashion in London —" he bowed toward Idelette and Rachelle — "and more specifically, from my father's enterprise, Hudson and Crier Draperies of Regent Street."

Rachelle noted that Sir James Hudson used the masculine term, *couturier*, for designer, and she was not at all surprised. Indeed, in most courts throughout Europe, men were the couturiers of women's clothing, though women were hired as grisettes. But in clothing designed for royalty, or for any woman of nobility or fashion, women held little role in the origination process. This was so in the Dushane-Macquinet family until Grandmère's entry into the French court during the reign of King Francis I when she designed a wardrobe for Princesse Anne of Brittany upon the request and arrangement by Grandmère's own *cousine*, the *Duchesse* Dushane. Without their courage and foresight, the Daughters of Silk, as Rachelle and Idelette preferred to be called, would not be receiving Sir James Hudson from London. Their mère, Madame Clair, was not skilled in needlework or design, but rather in the production of cloth and of selling it both near and far to monsieurs like Hudson. Père Arnaut managed the silkworms and mulberry groves, while Madame Clair oversaw the weavers and the needs of their families.

Rachelle and Idelette acknowledged Hudson's compliment with a customary graceful dip of the head, while remaining studiously silent, as Madame Clair expected, before turning their gaze back to her.

Madame Clair was always the gracious and noble lady of the Château de Silk. Her hair, the fair color of champagne, which had been passed on to Idelette, was arranged at the back of her head. Before church service she always put on her headdress, the *coif*. This afternoon she wore a high-necked black and white silk dress with draping white lace at her still-smooth neck and wrists. The dress brought Rachelle great pleasure because she had designed it for her mère as a gift, just as she and Idelette were now working on a dress for Avril's birthday. Rachelle took special pleasure in the lace she had designed for her mère's wrists. It was a little longer than the present fashion and fell softly in pleated folds with a silvery thread embroidered throughout that complemented the black silk and softened the dark color. Rachelle had made the lace longer to help her mère hide a deformity of her left hand where, as a young girl she had lost a finger through disease after she cut herself.

*That is part of my mission as a designer,* she thought, satisfied. *I want to help women feel good about their bodies, which God designed, even parts that are not perfect.* After all, what figure was perfect since the fall of mankind? Whether tall, short, plump, or thin, a woman could look *élégante* if clothed in the right lines and colors. And if they understood who they were in Christ, as God's dear children "accepted in the Beloved," they would be élégante from the inside out.

"And so, if you will permit me . . ." Hudson was saying.

Rachelle snapped her mind to attention. Her gaze followed him across the atelier to the cutting table which had been cleared of projects, for tomorrow was Sunday. He opened his large brown leather satchel with its gold initials, J. H.

Hudson laid out several variations of a lavish gown that Rachelle learned were his own creations. She was impressed, as was Madame Clair and Idelette. After a low murmur of approval, Monsieur Hudson explained.

"*Mesdames*, it is our hope at Hudson Draperies that this particular gown be created from Macquinet silk in the color of—" he ceased speaking and looked across the atelier to the bolts of silks in variations of violet, crimson, pink, ash-colored satin embroidered in silver, straw-colored velvet, dove-colored moire worked in gold and orange, yellow, ginger, orange, russet, sarcenet, and pink cobweb-lawn striped with silver . . .

"Ah, this! This is wondrous!" He removed the bolt of rosy-pink silk and laid it on the table, then took down the silvery satin with pearlized embroidery and laid it next to the shimmering silk. He tilted his dark head. "Yes, as you say, *c'est magnifique.* Add a matching ostrich feather fan of the same pink, and the outfit is stunning."

Rachelle stole a glance at Idelette to see her reaction to the lively Monsieur Hudson. There was a glint of admiration in her light blue eyes. She had tightened her lips, though, as if finding her reaction an unworthy embarrassment. Rachelle thought again that her sister was at times difficult to understand.

"And this gown must be sewn by—" once more Hudson paused, this time he bowed toward Rachelle and Idelette—"by the renowned Daughters of Silk, *Mesdemoiselles* Idelette and Rachelle Macquinet."

Rachelle smiled her excitement with a dip of her skirts. "*Merci*, Monsieur, I am *honoré*, I assure you. You have chosen the cloth and the colors which I would have favored for such a glorious gown—though I would add ermine to collar and cuffs."

"A tasteful suggestion, Mademoiselle." He smiled at her.

Rachelle looked away to Idelette. "And you, sister?"

Idelette would have pleased even Grandmère with her grave but miniscule curtsy. Idelette always retained her dignity which came naturally for her, Rachelle thought. Idelette should have been born to royalty.

"I am honoré as well, Monsieur, but such a splendid gown. It will be most trying not to have the proper mademoiselle test the fit in person as my sister and I work. It is, well, almost unheard of. I am most curious to know for whom is this belle dress designed?"

Rachelle had wondered also. She saw Hudson exchange a secretive smile with Madame Clair. Rachelle understood that it must be someone of great renown and that the project could bring notoriety. Her heart began to pound with expectation.

The smile on Hudson's face turned the corners of his mouth upward so that Rachelle guessed he was pleased with Idelette's knitted-brow curiosity.

"When you and your sister have completed this gown, my father and I will present it as a gift to Her Majesty, Queen Elizabeth I of England."

Rachelle's heart skipped like a young unicorn dancing on the high hills. Queen Elizabeth of England!

Idelette stood in silence, and James Hudson's dark eyes seemed to sparkle with satisfaction over their breathless response. Rachelle thought that Madame Clair had known this before she brought Hudson to meet them, for she was merely smiling over their excitement.

"The Queen of England," Idelette said, shocked. "But, Monsieur, the measurements, the fittings — how can we be expected to sew such a stunning royal gown here in Lyon?"

"You need not be anxious, Mademoiselle," he said cheerily. "I have exact measurements in a sealed envelope, given to me by Her Majesty's personal mistress of the wardrobe. There is small chance the Daughters of Silk will do other than delight our beloved queen."

He produced an envelope with a gold seal and handed it to Madame Clair.

"Ah, I and my daughters are indeed honoré. The *bonne* queen is beloved by all Huguenots for her support of our cause in France, and the end of her sister Mary's horrendous persecutions in England."

"Who else is more worthy of this task than your daughters? The gowns they made for the French royalty remain the talk of women of fashion in London's highest realms."

Rachelle felt a chill run up her spine.

"It is unfortunate you will not meet Madame Henriette Dushane while you are here at the château," Madame Clair said. "She remains in Paris with my eldest daughter."

"*Oui*, Grandmère is the head couturière of our family enterprise; she is the *grande dame* of the Silk House," Rachelle boasted with affection.

"She has taught us all," Idelette added.

"I am not surprised that England's royalty has looked toward Lyon," Madame Clair said. "Through several generations we have worked to develop the finest silks and colors in the world."

"The very cause that brings me here, Madame. The letter from my father speaks for itself. We are altogether anxious to come to terms with the Dushane-Macquinet Silk House."

As Rachelle knew from past family discussions, James Hudson was here at the château to arrange the final details of an earlier agreement his family had made with her Père Arnaut, for exporting Macquinet silk to the Hudson warehouse in Spitalfields, not far from London.

"We are hoping the negotiations begun with your husband's representatives in England will come to a successful conclusion," Hudson said to Madame Clair. "The partnership to be designated Dushane-

Macquinet-Hudson, Royal Couturiers of Regent Street, has met with his approval. We are anxious that the Dushane members of your family enterprise also approve."

"Since Grandmère and her cousine, the Duchesse Dushane, are both in Paris," Madame Clair said, "we have not been able to discuss the matter of your arrival with them. There has been unexpected sorrow over the death of my daughter's husband, Comte Sebastien Dangeau."

Sir James Hudson bowed gravely. "I have heard the sober news, Madame Macquinet, and it is tragic that such persecution rages in France. Thank God such madness as this has ceased in England. The Catholics seek to depose Queen Elizabeth and place one loyal to Spain and Rome on the throne, but so far God has protected England from falling back under Rome's control."

Rachelle was pleasantly surprised by his fervency. She noted that Idelette also looked unduly pleased by what could only be taken as a confession of adherence to the Reformation.

"I have taken enough of your time during such a period of grief," he went on. "I will tell my driver to bring me to an inn and return again on Monday if you permit, Madame."

"I would not hear of your leaving for an inn, Monsieur Hudson. *Non*, you must stay the night as our guest and attend worship with us in the morning."

He did look tired and worn. Rachelle suspected her mère was quick to see this, and as always, to show hospitality.

"Madame, you are most kind. I look forward to attending Monsieur Bertrand Macquinet's exposition in the morning. I have heard him in Spitalfields and know our souls will be refreshed and taught."

"We will have early supper," Clair said. "Then our cousin, *Pasteur* Bertrand, will read the Scriptures as he does every Saturday evening. Perhaps you will care to join us, unless you're too tired from your travels."

He assured them that he already felt at home due to their kindness and looked forward to them becoming close allies.

Rachelle watched him leave the atelier with her mère. She said to Idelette in a low voice, "Did you notice Monsieur Hudson's hook and eye clasps on his surcoat?"

"Who could not! Wooden, carved into animal faces!" She wrinkled her aquiline nose and gave a shudder. "What was the face supposed to be?"

"A wolf, I think. I thought them ... well, rather unique. His taste in buttons shows originality."

"If you like your fashion reflecting the king's *palais* zoo."

"His design for the English queen certainly did not show any such novelty. It is most wondrous, do you not think so?" She walked over to the cutting table where Monsieur Hudson had left them a drawing of his gown.

Idelette followed, taking the drawing from Rachelle's hand. "*Merveilleux*, indeed."

"I'm glad he did not object to replacing the lace ruff with a soft ermine collar. I loathe ruffs! They scratch and chafe." Rachelle rubbed beneath her chin.

"I hear she has red hair and lovely white hands."

"Is she not the daughter of Henry VIII and Anne Boleyn?"

"Oui, but he sent Anne to the tower where she was beheaded," Idelette said.

Rachelle shuddered. Her memory was tenderly inflamed over the recent massacre of Huguenots at Amboise Castle. Two thousand Huguenots had lost their heads at the orders of the Queen Mother Catherine de Medici and the Guises, the *duc* and the cardinal. Although she had not witnessed it, she had heard about it afterward. Heads had been posted about the ramparts and gates with ghoulish revenge, and blood ran in the courtyard.

Rachelle had escaped that day with assistance from *Marquis* Fabien de Vendôme. Not that she would have lost her head; she had been at Amboise as a lady-in-waiting to the Queen Mother's youngest daughter, Princesse Marguerite Valois, and as such had little to do with those Huguenots who died, accused of treason against the boy-king, Francis. In truth, the Huguenots had been loyal to King Francis. It was the

Guise brothers, the duc and the cardinal, whom they had sought to overthrow.

In her heart Rachelle did not fault the Huguenots, for though they had acted precipitously, as Marquis Fabien had said to her, the cardinal was a corrupt and calculating man, devoid of the faith he claimed to represent, and the duc was cunning and powerful, with extreme loyalty to Spain, which undermined his allegiance to the royal Valois family of France. Together they had heaped high the faggots for fires of persecution throughout France against the Huguenots.

As for the Queen Mother who ruled as regent over her Valois son, she would stop at nothing with her arsenal of intrigue to protect the throne of France, first for herself, and then for her sons. She especially desired the throne for her favorite son Henry, often called Anjou. He had not yet grown to manhood, but sadly, there was evidence that he already preferred other little boys to girls.

Rachelle felt a nagging uneasiness as she thought again how she was here at the Château de Silk without ever having received an official release from the Queen Mother. Therefore, her duty to the princesse as a lady-in-waiting officially remained.

Marquis Fabien had assured her before he left that he would send a lettre to Margo, as he called the princesse, asking for Rachelle's release from Court. He had access because he was born of the royal blood from the House of *Bourbon*, and after the death of his father, was brought to Court at twelve years of age to mingle with the royal children and others in the nobility, including the Reinette Mary Stuart of Scotland. Margo was a special amie of his.

Still, Rachelle lived in uncertainty, as did her mère, Madame Clair, who quietly worried that the Queen Mother would see Rachelle's absence from Court with a more shadowy perspective than the amorous, lighthearted princesse.

THE NEXT MORNING RACHELLE seated herself on a lavender and gold tapestry-covered chair at breakfast with family members and Sir James

Hudson. She had dressed in Sunday silk and was sipping from a tall Viennese crystal glass of sweetened amber tea. The pink and white plate, scalloped with gold, held warm cakes dipped in whipped egg and fried in sweet butter. The silverware sparkled in the pleasant sunlight filtering in through the dining-*salle* windows.

Her father's cousin, Bertrand Macquinet, a pasteur who had recently celebrated his sixtieth birthday, was seated at the head of the large table taking the honored position usually reserved for Rachelle's absent father, Arnaut.

Bertrand's face was angular like Calvin's, his dark eyes sharp and bright. He was a man of bonne cheer and beloved by the family. Rachelle described Bertrand's mustache as an upside-down V that grew into his short, pointed beard. His wide-brimmed black hat, used when he went to the teaching stand as the pasteur, sat on the hall table, dusted of any stray speck, for he was to teach this Sunday morning at the local assembly. His cherished Bible in the French language was cautiously out of sight.

The young Sir James Hudson appeared to be studying Cousin Bertrand with a sharp but friendly eye. "Monsieur, I understand your knowledge as a biblical scholar was received at Geneva under John Calvin."

"An awesome man, I assure you, James. I oft felt that I should enter his presence on tiptoe, but he would have none of that. It was he who arranged for me to teach at the theological university there, which God permitted me to do for more than a decade."

Rachelle sipped her tea and remained silent, but Idelette seemed to want to convince James Hudson that their cousin Bertrand was a great man of God. Was she attracted to James? Rachelle concealed a smile.

"Three years ago Bertrand was burdened to strengthen the Huguenots at Spitalfields. They had gone through so much persecution to get there that he sailed to London to hold *prêches*."

"And now you have established a French church," James said, smiling. He looked at Idelette, then back to Cousin Bertrand. "I can see well enough, sir, how your young cousines are pleased with your service to

God, as well they should be. How did you first meet Monsieur Calvin, if I may ask?"

Bertrand's hawkish face took on a sober cast as though his mind traveled far in the past.

"That I shall never forget, young James. Monsieur Calvin was forced to flee France to save himself from the wrath of King Francis I and the fiery stake. He journeyed to Strasbourg, where I too had fled. Calvin introduced me to the great minister LeFevre d'Etaples, translator of the first French Bible. I was most taken with both of them. Eventually Calvin went to Geneva, and I was given the privilege of attending him. Then, with the help of Reformers like Beza, Calvin established the grand Reformational center of Europe."

Bertrand had come to the Château de Silk from Geneva, where he had reported to Calvin on the work at Spitalfields. He had arrived bringing Madame Clair home to the château, leaving Arnaut in Geneva to conclude the work begun months earlier.

The extent of the work was not discussed, and Rachelle had been wise enough not to ask. She understood the activity concerned the printing of Bibles in the French, Dutch, and German languages, to be secretly distributed in Europe. Cousin Bertrand was even now waiting for a shipment of Dutch Bibles that were somehow to be smuggled into Holland, a most dangerous endeavor.

Rachelle looked across the table fondly at Cousin Bertrand. She had always been drawn toward his wise and grandfatherly counsel and admired his scholarly handling of the Scriptures. With her father away and her soul tender from Amboise and the death of Comte Sebastien, her frequent talks with Pasteur Bertrand had strengthened her in the midst of so much uncertainty.

"Silk weavers, couturiers, and grisettes — the Huguenots are bringing the finest skills of their craft to London," Hudson said cheerfully. "And the Dutch Protestants? They are experts in lace, thread, buttonmaking, and all manner of delicate embroidery. I tell you Mesdames, Monsieur, England is the recipient of God's grace."

Rachelle could not restrain her growing frustration. "It is all very well and good for your England, Monsieur Hudson. And I am thankful England opens her doors to us. But it is France I think of. France foolishly robs herself. One would think the king would realize the Huguenots, the middle class of this country, are the backbone of France! Without us, there is naught but nobles on one end and uneducated poor on the other."

"Quite the fact, mademoiselle, yes, quite ... and sad for your country, of course."

"Unfortunately," Idelette said, "those of the religion have small choice except to escape with their lives and the lives of their children."

"There is a far greater loss to France than silk and trade secrets," Bertrand said. "It is the removal of God's lampstand in France. With every Huguenot family who leaves, with every burning, every arrest and torture, the light of our witness departs. I fear darkness will reign if we as a nation continue to harden our hearts against the light of truth." He looked at each of them. "France is in danger of forfeiting the greatest of opportunities from God—that of leading the way in Europe as God's torchbearer. It appears to me that the *honneur* may pass to England."

Rachelle, highly patriotic, felt an unhappy twinge. She had naught against England, but her love was with France. She feared Cousin Bertrand was right.

"England has also known her years of burnings and delusions," James Hudson said. "Until Elizabeth came to the throne, we had her sister, Queen Mary. I think we all know that history has recorded many stalwart saints burned at Smithfield through her. Bloody Mary, we call her. Many leaders of the Reformation like Cranmer, Ridley, and Tyndale—all burned at the stake as heretics."

"Ah, but England is now embracing the light," Cousin Bertrand said. "England welcomes the persecuted for His name's sake with goodwill and a haven of safety. The Lord takes notice of this and the many changes under your present queen."

*Whereas the Queen Mother*, thought Rachelle, *uses persecution to maintain her throne and appease Spain.*

Cousin Bertrand seemed to sense the heaviness at the table and smiled. "But! The Château de Silk has not rejected the light. We are all witnesses for God though we stand alone," he said, his tone encouraging.

"And the silk is a gift from our heavenly Father. For without the miracle of His silkworm, there would be no Dushane-Macquinet silk, no name of renown for the cloth. You *chère* mademoiselles know that this blessing is to be used not for our own ease, but as an open door. And so it is. Arnaut has financed much of the work in Geneva and France, and now in Spitalfields and Holland. The Bibles, the special printing of Scripture portions and books, all in fine leather and gilt edge, have been spread far and near because of our Dushane-Macquinet silk. And this will continue for as long as our good God preserves us. I will be eloquent and say that our witness, our trials and persecutions, are all written on silk!"

Rachelle's heart sounded a song of thanksgiving, knowing that eternal good was upheld by her needle and scissors, and even the feeding of mulberry leaves to the silkworms would assist her calling.

"To our God goes all the honneur," Madame Clair said. "Château de Silk prospers in order to serve our Lord's work as well as our own. And, Monsieur Hudson, although my husband is not here to celebrate the beginning of the Dushane-Macquinet-Hudson alliance, I can tell you that our desire is singular. We will support the weavers' guilds in Spitalfields by making certain they have silk."

"Silk and our own designs so they can cut and sew, ma mère." Rachelle pleaded again for her special dream. "Let there be gowns sewn in Spitalfields and displayed in a fine shop on Regent Street. Even gowns of many sizes so that they can be purchased right there by passersby. Such a dress shop with our name would be unique and successful, I am sure of it."

"We share the same mind-set, Mademoiselle," Sir James Hudson said. "'Tis a novel persuasion of great interest to the Hudson family as well."

Rachelle saw a tiny flame dance in his eyes.

He turned to Madame Clair. "Indeed, 'tis our hope you and your daughters will come to London to oversee the opening of the first dress shop. Perhaps when the gown for Her Majesty is finished? 'Tis only fitting you attend Court when the gown is presented to our queen. Hudson Manor is always open for your stay with us. My father would be delighted to meet the Daughters of Silk and to discuss all this business to every-one's complete satisfaction."

Rachelle, however, noticed a subdued response from Madame Clair. It was becoming obvious she did not want her daughters leaving France. Her heart was bound with the tragic happenings surrounding her family and the talk of a civil war between the Catholic forces and the Huguenots. No one could know how such fighting would affect the Château which had been a family enterprise in Lyon from the time of Great-Grandmère Antoinette Dushane.

Rachelle nurtured her disappointment. A glance at her sister showed that Idelette was also disappointed. She had mentioned to Rachelle ear-lier that morning that Hudson had spoken to her of the hope that they would consider going to London to strengthen the alliance with the Hudson family in Spitalfields. He did not expect all three Macquinet women to make the journey, but he had suggested the possibility to Madame Clair.

But Madame Clair merely smiled graciously at him across the table and remained noncommittal.

Rachelle met Idelette's gaze. *We will not give up yet.*

A short time later, with breakfast finished, Cousin Bertrand retrieved his French Bible, tapped it with his finger, and said quietly, as if to him-self, "Remember those who have gone before us who have endured great afflictions for His name's sake." Then with his Bible concealed inside his preaching satchel, he left the château to teach that morning's message at the local Huguenot gathering.

Idelette and Avril left soon after under the friendly escort of Sir James Hudson. As they went out the front door, Avril called to Rachelle that she would keep a place for her on the bench.

Madame Clair's tired face was due to more than worry over her recently widowed daughter Madeleine and the baby. Rachelle knew she had stayed up until after midnight to finish a special silk scarf for Madame Hershey, who would attend the worship meeting, and that she had been delayed in finishing the project due to Hudson's arrival.

As Madame Clair went to the atelier, Rachelle followed and stopped at the doorway, watching as she reached up to the shelf and brought down the scarf. She glanced over her shoulder.

"Do go on without me, *ma petite*. I shall be a few minutes late. I must finish the ribbon edging. Madame Hershey will be disappointed if she cannot bring this gift with her when she leaves worship to visit her daughter. Her coach leaves for Paris soon after the meeting."

"Ma mère? About Sir James Hudson and going to London ..."

"Not now, Rachelle. I know what your wish is, but now is not the time to discuss the matter. We will wait until your père is home from Geneva. Hurry now, or you shall be late to sing the psalter."

Rachelle silenced her defeated sigh. She felt as though Madame Clair still thought of her as a *demoiselle*. She was grown now, ripe for *amour* and marriage — at least Marquis Fabien de Vendôme thought her a woman. He had not spoken of marriage, true, but ...

"Oui, ma mère," she said with dutiful respect and did not argue. She respected her mère too much for immature tantrums. *At least she had not said a definite non to London.*

What would Marquis Fabien do if she voyaged to Spitalfields?

# The Prince of Darkness Grim

## THE BARN CHURCH

RACHELLE WALKED ALONG THE SHORTCUT THAT BROUGHT HER TO THE wagon road that ran between the mulberry orchard and the silkworm hatcheries. From there it was only a five minute walk to the fields. She glanced back toward the château, and knowing that Madame Clair was not watching from the balustrade, tightened her sash, raised her silken skirts above her ankles, and tucked the waist under the sash. She had done this since a girl and saw no reason to stop now. She smiled at herself and ran through the mulberry orchard toward the dirt road. Just as long as the Marquis de Vendôme, with all of his *sang-froid*, did not ever see her acting like a naive peasant girl!

At the outskirts of the hatcheries and farther ahead to the right, a public road divided the Macquinet estate lands from Monsieur Lemoine's hayfields. Lemoine, a Huguenot, had constructed a large, new barn that was used for Sunday worship meetings, as Protestant church buildings were forbidden by the Roman Church.

The wind came sweeping through the family's *mûreraies*, or groves of mulberry trees. Rachelle basked in the breeze, rustling her silk dress, and looked at the clouds skimming across the expanse of deep blue sky. The mûreraies provided the leaves for feeding the château's silkworms, which produced the unique filaments with which Sir James Hudson was so anxious to be associated. Rachelle was not in the least surprised that the fine quality silk, which elevated the Macquinet name among couturières across Europe, was known even in the English court of Queen Elizabeth.

Rachelle's mind drifted to the merveilleux gown that she and Idelette were privileged to create. This would bring new opportunities ... but where would they lead her?

How good it was to be home again, away from the court, away from the serpentine Queen Mother, from deceit on every hand. Home. There was nothing that could add its touch of contentment to her soul more than to be handling yards of silk in wondrous shades of blues, pinks, greens, silver, gold, and burgundy—

Burgundy. A smile tugged at her mouth. She relived the romantic moment when Marquis Fabien had surprised her with yards of rich burgundy silk and cloth of gold to make a gown for herself, just as she had for Princesse Marguerite.

Rachelle had arrived at the château from Vendôme several weeks ago, escorted by the *beau* Marquis Fabien de Vendôme. A few days later a message for the marquis arrived unexpectedly, delivered by Fabien's chief page, Gallaudet, who claimed that one of the French "buccaneer's men" had brought it to him before quickly leaving, refusing to linger in Lyon a moment longer than necessary. Did this French seaman think he was in danger?

Fabien read the message, then burned it in the château hearth while she watched, wondering what it meant. He left soon afterward without discussing its content, much to her irritation, telling her only that he would return to the château once the rendezvous was held, before he departed on a longer voyage to Florida. Fabien had refused to explain any details or even the purpose for this rendezvous—a fact she found irksome, for she felt she deserved his trust. Perhaps the time they had known each other had been too short for him to have complete confidence in her.

She knew little more than that he'd left for a location on the coast, where an ally, a French buccaneer, whose name Fabien had withheld, awaited him for a secret rendezvous. That he would return to see her again before his voyage to Florida, encouraged her. The marquis had not yet spoken to her of marriage—indeed, he seemed to step back from it, and she knew physical attraction alone was never enough for a lifetime.

His caution in that area had served him well during his years at Court, maintaining his freedom as well as his integrity.

During these last two weeks she had agonized over his safety. Any involvement with buccaneers — French, Dutch, or English — against Spain, would put him at risk by the throne.

Large leaves above her rustled, and speckled sunshine trickled onto her route. She took a turn that would lead toward a thick hedge of pink oleanders.

As the hedge came into view, she spotted an opening where she could squeeze through to cross the road. Rachelle was careful to avoid touching the pink flowers; although she found them attractive, she had heard they were poisonous.

She paused by the tall oleanders, catching her breath. How unseemly it would be to enter the worship gathering out of breath and perspiring, and with her skirts hiked up past her ankles! She laughed at herself, straightening her skirts and smoothing the folds into place. Singing came loud and clear from the large barn. *Ça alors!* She was late.

Cousin Bertrand had selected Martin Luther's hymn, "A Mighty Fortress." The words, which she knew well, were clear:

"The Prince of Darkness grim, we tremble not for him;
His rage we can endure, for lo, his doom is sure,
One little word shall fell him."

Running footsteps pounded from behind; she turned to look over her shoulder toward the mulberry grove.

It was Philippe, one of the silk weaver boys, also late for the service. She smiled until the look on his face alerted her.

"Mademoiselle Rachelle, run! Duc de Guise is riding here with many soldiers!

For a time she must have stood in shock for she realized Philippe was shaking her arm, his brown eyes wide.

"Mademoiselle! Jolon sends me! Run, he says!"

She threw her hand to her forehead. "Guise! It cannot be. Here? But why? Are you certain, Philippe? The *duchy* of Guise is in Lorraine."

"Jolon has gone to warn his wife and others in the hatcheries. He says word came from a spy that le duc is bringing punishment on heretics!"

Here? Her mind revolted against such. This was not Amboise. What cause would he have?

The words to Luther's hymn continued:

"Let goods and kindred go, this mortal life also;
The body they may kill: God's truth abideth still,
His kingdom is forever."

Rachelle whirled and looked off toward the fields and the barn ... *kindred* ...

"I must warn Pasteur Bertrand."

The boy laid hold of her, his frightened eyes imploring. "Non, mademoiselle, run. Listen — horses — "

Rachelle turned her head sharply, toward the thudding hoofbeats on the road. Yes! Horses, many of them, thundering closer.

"Look!" Philippe pointed, awe in his voice. "It is him, le duc himself, with soldiers."

Rachelle saw the horsemen above the tops of the oleanders. Swirls of dust rose about the horses. If she ran to warn Bertrand, she would run straight in front of the soldiers. She dare not attempt to cross the field toward the barn.

"Do not let them see us." She drew the boy down beside her and peered through the leaves.

The duc's soldiers galloped into clear view, the horses' hoofs beating the dirt. The steel breastplates, partly covered in leather, glinted beneath the sun's rays.

"Such soldiers, such horses, such gleaming steel — " Philippe said, and Rachelle read the fear in his voice. "Ma mère is inside the barn-church. She sent me back to the bungalow for her wrap — she said she was cold — "

Rachelle gripped her fingers on his arm to steady him. "God knows. Be strong and pray for their deliverance."

The green and white flag bearing the emblem of the House of Guise snapped brazenly in the wind. Rachelle narrowed her gaze, seeking to glimpse the faces as they rode past, then — yes, there he was! The duc himself. She would recognize him anywhere. Her muscles tensed. That arrogant face with the tight mouth and contemptuous eyes was all too familiar after Amboise.

Duc de Guise reined in his horse, unsheathed his sword, and raised it above his head. His men followed suit with an ominous clink of steel. Rachelle clenched her fists. Her heart pounded in her ears. *Non, non* —

"The sword of the Lord!"

His men answered with a rousing shout. Turning their horses away from the road, they galloped across the field toward the barn.

Rachelle grasped Philippe's arm more tightly and found him trembling. She did not want him to witness what might happen.

"Run, Philippe, warn Madame Clair. Jolon may have forgotten. Tell her I said to hide the French Bible Idelette keeps in her chamber. There are other books too. Hurry!"

Philippe, his young face pale and tense, hesitated, his fearful gaze shooting back to the barn, but she gave him a little shove. "Do as I say! Quickly!"

He jumped to his feet and took off running back toward the mulberry orchard and the château.

Rachelle watched until the boy disappeared, then turned her attention to Lemoine's field, praying urgently.

Peering through the oleander leaves, she wrestled with the horror seizing her heart.

"Do something," she told herself. "Do not just sit here. Throw yourself with abandon into the raging terror! Save your sisters and Bertrand!"

As if she could! Her bitter desperation tasted only of gall. She clenched her hands into helpless fists until the nails dug into her flesh.

Who could stop such blind hatred for those labeled heretics, whose crime was worshiping Christ from a study of the Scriptures alone?

The singing ceased. Voices of praise gave way to the shouts of soldiers and the cries of protest from Huguenots trying for reason and calm. As though the Huguenots could reason with Guise's personal inquisitors, Rachelle thought.

"Father," she wailed, sinking on her knees to the dirt, "help Your poor children! If not, who can stand this onslaught from Satan? Surely those committing such rage against us are greatly deceived and need

Your mercy. Oh! Do open their eyes that the scales of blindness might fall, like the apostle Paul who once persecuted the Jewish Christians for calling on the name of Jesus, so let these — even Duc de Guise — see the truth as it is written! Help us, Father! In Jesus's name!"

❋

INSIDE THE BARN, the prayers, the crying of frightened children, and the shouts that invaded from outside the barn, all merged into one great howl as of a funeral dirge.

Pasteur Bertrand Macquinet was told the barn was surrounded by Duc de Guise's men-at-arms soon after they heard the ominous shouts and galloping horses. Bertrand was grieved, but he was far from surprised that it was happening. The overzealous Guise was resorting to the tactics he was known for.

The doors and windows were being nailed shut from the outside before the Protestants could escape. Those few men who had gone out at once to attempt to reason with the duc's men were dying, thrust through with the sword.

Once Guise gave his order to set the building on fire, his followers would set about to obey his command without a thought of wrongdoing. They did not see themselves as murderers, but as crusaders, holy warriors preserving God's truth from the onslaught of wicked apostates who followed that *diable* Luther. Bertrand knew there was no chance he could ever sit down across from Guise, with a Bible between them, to discuss Christian doctrines from the Scriptures. To be caught with the Scriptures in French brought death.

"Father God, Your sheep are trapped. Your little lambs too. I know You have the power to deliver us. Deliver us, O God, is my plea — but like Daniel's three friends, faced with bowing to the golden image or being cast into the flames — even if You choose not to deliver us, we will not deny the Scriptures to please men or demons! Give us the grace to die for Your truth if need be. Strengthen Your servants to endure. In the name of Him who alone has secured our eternal safety, Jesus, amen."

From somewhere ahead in the barn, Bertrand heard someone shouting at the door, "Let us out, *Seigneur* Guise, I beg of you. We have women and children in here. Arrest us, but let the women and children go!"

Bertrand prayed for the men not to panic. Many were shouting, banging on the door, and pushing against it with their shoulders. He hurried to the platform with his Bible raised so that the others who remained seated would follow his example of confidence in death. He was reading Psalm 41 in a loud unwavering voice when the young Englishman, Sir James Hudson, rushed up to him.

"Pasteur Bertrand, every window-shutter is nailed fast."

"I know, I know, my son. What is your relationship with the only Savior?"

"It is well, sir."

"Bon!"

"I have found a pick and a few pitchforks. I am going to try and break through that window in the back. Be prepared to escape with Mademoiselles Idelette and Avril."

"Do what you can with His strength!"

"Pasteur Bertrand," another shouted. "We are trapped!"

"God knows, mon ami."

"Why does He not help us then?"

"Like Elisha the prophet, I ask you to remember, 'They that be with us are more than they that be with them.' Come, now, quit yourselves like men and be strong. Let us comfort the little children."

Bertrand again commanded everyone's attention and called loudly to the parents to gather closely in a circle to kneel, hold hands, and pray. Although his heart ached to see the children and women, he kept his voice and manner calm.

"Women and children, over here by me. Come! The old, to your knees in supplication! Younger men and brothers, continue to labor to break open that far window, be quick! The strength of Samson flow through you."

"It is too late, Monsieur Bertrand! There is smoke."

"Work! Let our faithful God decide when it is too late."

"Should we not pray with the old instead?" another cried.

"Pray and work!" Bertrand called. "Even now angels surround this place. If God wished to stop these merely deceived men, He can."

"Then why does He not?" came another shuddering cry.

"We are appointed as sheep for the slaughter. Nay, in all these things—tribulation, sickness, nakedness, famine, or sword—we are more than conquerors through Him that loved us. Nothing can separate us from His love, least of all suffering and death."

"Yes," Monsieur Lemoine called. "Weeping may endure for a night but joy comes in the morning. Our morning will come. We will join the martyrs for Jesus under the altar near His throne."

Bertrand stuffed his French Bible into his frock coat, and using his walking stick, made for the crying children huddled together with the older women who were trying to comfort them. Two young women with babes in their arms knelt beside the group of children and tried to sing to them. One of the babes awoke and began to cry pitifully.

Bertrand came up and gathered them around him, pulling the smallest into his arms like a mother hen. He laid his hand on the baby and prayed. He tried to soothe their fears and ease their confusion, patting the young mothers on the heads. "Be strong, *mes petits*; His grace will be sufficient for even this. He is never so close as when His own are suffering. Let us pray, little ones, let us talk to our Savior Jesus."

⁂

AVRIL MACQUINET LOST SIGHT of her older sister Idelette in the smoke and din. Nor could she find Cousin Bertrand. Drawn by singing, she came upon him.

"Oh, Cousin Bertrand. I am so thankful ma mère is not here, nor is Rachelle." She huddled close beside him, trying to sustain her courage. The shouts from soldiers outside sent fear thundering in her heart. Even now the smoke was spreading and she began to cough.

She gripped his arm. "Will it hurt very much?"

"His promised grace will strengthen you, ma petite. The many who have gone before us would bear witness if they could. What hymn do you know? Sing, ma chère, sing, and do not look about you. Remember

Peter and the waves? Do not look, keep your eyes closed and sing and pray. Imagine Jesus in your mind. Think of Him in His glorious white robes, comforting arms outstretched, welcoming you to our everlasting home."

Avril tried to sing, but coughing overcame her and the smoke made her eyes sting and water. She had memorized the new words, recently placed into the 1556 Geneva Psalter, and whispered them:

"Praise God from whom all blessings flow, praise him all creatures here below. Praise him on high you heavenly host, praise Father, Son, and Holy Ghost, Amen."

❈

AT THE REAR OF THE BARN, Idelette searched desperately for Avril. *Where is she, Lord? Oh thanks be to You, Father, that Rachelle and ma mère are not here! Your providential hand detained them both! Do not let them be ruined by grief over Avril, Bertrand, and me. Help them to carry on with new courage in the knowledge that all things work together for good to those who love You.*

She came upon a group of younger men who were breaking through a window shutter with a pick and shovel and saw the Englishman, James Hudson. He should have stayed another night at the inn. He would have escaped this moment. But if she believed that circumstances in the lives of His own are governed by God, then, was he here by providence?

"You are making progress, *Messieurs*. Have courage, Monsieur Hudson!" she called. "Do not tremble because of them. Be strong in His grace."

The young Englishman looked over at her. "Ho! Do not stray afar, Mademoiselle, we may get out yet!"

Would they? Idelette prayed as she moved on. *Give us peace in the midst of suffering.*

Flames were spreading from the front of the barn. The smoke troubled her breathing. She clasped a handkerchief over her mouth and knelt, crawling forward on her hands and knees. Even if some did escape through the window, how could she leave without Avril? What good to escape and remember all the rest of her years that she had left behind her baby sister?

Keeping close to the floor helped, but her eyes teared and she could not see. The smoke silenced her, though her words continued to the Lord of Hosts. *I am going to die ... This is my time.*

The heat was terrible now. The old were gasping, sinking to the floor, coughing — she tried to encourage them and was surprised when they tried to encourage her to remain strong and trust.

The aged Monsieur Fontaine and his wife, married for fifty years, held hands like young sweethearts as they knelt low, praying together, their silver heads reminding Idelette of halos. The last she saw of them before the smoke thickened was a strangely sweet smile on Madame Fontaine's wrinkled face.

The shutters on one window burst open. "This way, through the window, quick!" sounded a voice of new hope.

"Children to the window!" Hudson shouted.

Idelette followed his voice, believing that if Avril was to be saved, she would find her way to the window and Hudson's voice.

Idelette crept along the floor to where the children were being hoisted through the window; a breath of fresh air came against her like the touch of an angel's wing. With renewed strength she called, "Avril? Avril!"

There was no answering call from her sister, but she recognized Cousin Bertrand's voice: "This way! To the window! Form a line, send the children first!"

There was singing now. "The prince of darkness grim — we tremble not for him — "

The men below the window, James Hudson one of them, were hauling children and women through the opening as fast as they could lift them. "Run!" they were charged as soon as they got their footing. "Run toward the road and the mulberry orchard!"

"We will attempt to open the barn door," one of the young Huguenot men called from outside the window.

"Guise's soldiers will cut you down. Run for help!" James Hudson called back.

"Idelette!"

It was Avril's voice. Idelette turned toward the voice. *Merci, Father.*

Avril stumbled forward, and Idelette grasped her small, trembling sister into her arms. Clinging together, they moved in faltering steps toward the window.

James Hudson saw them. "Both of you! Come quickly, that's it, up and out!"

He lifted Avril and thrust her through the window, then grabbed Idelette before she could protest to let others go before her. "Out with you, lass! And run for your life!"

"Bertrand—and you, Monsieur—" Idelette cried.

"I'll look for him."

Idelette sank to the ground, sucking in clean air, gasping and coughing to clear her lungs, as well as her sluggish mind. She caught hold of Avril's arm and pointed toward the road and the mulberry trees lining the Macquinet estate. "Run to the trees and hide. I—I will catch up."

"But Cousin Bertrand and Monsieur Hudson?"

"They rest in the hand of God. Go sister—run."

Avril was crying now, the tears smudging the traces of smoke on her tender young face. She tugged at Idelette's arm, her eyes pleading. "Come sister, come with me—"

Idelette looked back. Flames were spreading. All the others unable to get through this one unguarded window would soon be overwhelmed by heat and smoke.

Avril was yanking on her arm. "We will hide in the bushes. There are not as many soldiers in that direction."

Idelette relented. *God be with you, Bertrand and James—au revoir.*

Idelette and Avril ran together toward the trees and bushes. Idelette glanced back again.

Guise's men-at-arms were everywhere like swarming hornets. Some on horseback and others on foot, running in every direction, as though driven by madness. Those on horseback rode down those who were able to flee like helpless sheep. Without mercy the soldiers slashed their swords, whacking them down, trampling them under their horses' hooves as they fell to their knees.

Avril tripped on a clump. Idelette struggled to get her back on her feet.

They ran on, the clods of dirt slowing their pace. "Hurry, sister—"

Horse hooves pounded in the distance. Idelette turned, still gripping Avril. *Perhaps one of us can get away.*

As the soldier on horseback neared, Idelette gave Avril a push toward the trees. "Run, do not look back."

❄

AVRIL FLED FOR THE DARK SHADE OF THE MULBERRY TREES. Tears filled her eyes. *I think Bertrand will die in the smoke and fire—and James. Poor James. He was so beau-looking—*

Avril heard another horse galloping up beside her. She turned her head to look. She uttered a cry as a sharp blow whacked against her head.

She fell, blood running down her face. She could not think; she could not move. Then, turning her face from the dirt, she saw the broad chest of a horse. Its raised hoofs coming down upon her.

❄

IDELETTE, IN HORROR, SAW Avril's fate. She threw her hands over her head and screamed. She doubled over, clenching her fists. "Beasts! Antichrists!"

Someone grabbed her from behind, a hand going over her mouth, an arm going roughly round her waist, dragging her backward. She kicked and fought with a rage she did not know she possessed. She chomped her teeth into the fingers covering her mouth and tasted his blood. She slammed her elbow into his ribs—heard his revolting grunt, all to no avail. Exhausted emotionally, her strength fell away into hopelessness.

She was being dragged away, then flung over his shoulder like a slab of beef, carried off as booty to be devoured.

❄

ACROSS THE DIRT ROAD, Rachelle remained hidden among the oleanders, knuckles bared against her teeth. The ugly sounds of terror continued until she thought she would go insane with her helplessness. She covered her ears with her sweating palms.

No doubt the duc believed he had done God a service by ridding Lyon of heretics. "Beasts, made to be taken and destroyed," he often repeated from clerics who misquoted from the epistle, 2 Peter. That was their excuse for the Inquisition!

She remembered Christ had said, "The time will come when whosoever kills you will think he is doing God service."

The sounds of madness ceased. Rachelle opened her eyes, taking her hands from her ears, listening.

Wood crackled; a gust of smoke blew in her direction. The mulberry leaves shuddered. A lone bird gave a short reluctant trill then, and as though in sadness over the evil of mankind, the bird flew away.

Rachelle peered through the oleanders to see gray smoke coming from the barn. The soldiers had ridden away — or had they?

She unclenched her fists; there was blood on her palms from her fingernails. She lifted herself from the ground, weak and damp with sweat. Keeping her head low among the oleanders, she surveyed the field as far as she could see. She squinted, able to see bodies. She was shaking now and strangely chilled.

How many dead — non, how many murdered? How many had been bound with rope and carried away for the dungeons, to be burned later?

She straightened, hearing the wind swirling through the trees, and what had earlier seemed a chorus of praise was now mournful to her ears.

*Grant me courage, Lord.* If there were any yet alive and wounded, she must go to them. Possibly her own sisters and Cousin Bertrand were among them. And poor James Hudson.

Rachelle pushed through the oleanders and walked across the road. Although she wanted to run, her feet felt heavy.

Her heart froze with fear as she made her way into the field with the smell of smoke on the breeze. The grasses rustled. She stopped in the midst of the wreckage, stunned by the gruesome sight of so many cut down, including children. For a shocked moment she could do nothing except stare at the bloody carnage. Her stomach sickened as she began to recognize friends she had known since childhood, all of them members of her church. How could this have happened?

Rachelle raised her tearstained face to the sky and felt the sun warming her damp cheeks. *I want revenge. I hate them!*

If she expected heaven's rebuke, it did not come. This patience with her anger and frustration did more to melt her resistance than any rebuke. *Oh, Father*, she prayed, anguish gushing from her soul and forming a river of hot tears that drenched her cheeks. She fell to her knees, her clenched fists slowly loosened.

*Be strong, yea, be strong.*

*Fret not thyself because of evildoers . . . For they shall soon be cut down like the grass, and wither as the green herb.*

She forced herself forward into the midst of death, running, then pausing to see who had fallen and if there were any signs of life. Onward she moved, searching, searching — afraid of whom she might find.

Here was Monsieur Lemoine who had requested Bertrand to teach his flock. He had found something more precious to him in life than appeasing the powerful. For belief in Scripture alone as the final authority, he had received a sword through his heart; his Sunday shirt now soaked crimson. The Bible had been snatched from his hand and the pages were ripped out, scattered and trampled around his lifeless body, the wind now fluttering some pages.

On she ran.

Here was Madame Hershey —

She would not be bringing the silk scarf to her daughter today to celebrate the birth of her first grandson. Her daughter would soon be mourning her death.

Rachelle blundered on, the hem of her skirt stained. She saw several little ones cut down without mercy.

A lone baby cried beneath the shield of its mother's arms. Madame Scully had died bent protectively over her baby girl.

Rachelle stooped, removing the infant from Madame Scully's embrace. It was difficult to loosen the mother's hold and Rachelle choked back sobs. Finally freeing the child, she carried her into the shade, remembering the time her birth was announced.

"I will come back for you."

She walked on, coming closer to the charred barn until she saw her — Rachelle inched forward, moaning, and slipped to her knees beside a familiar silken dress the color of an April daffodil, the white Alençon lace was now stiff and brownish red. It was Avril. Avril, at sweet thirteen, her once smiling face now lifeless and crushed.

Rachelle fell across her body and wept loudly.

❁

THE SUN'S RAYS INCHED behind the mulberry orchard. The wind sighed a mournful dirge through the tall trees.

Dazed, Rachelle sat beside her sister's body. Her gaze was fixed on the gentle face of a blue wildflower that had somehow escaped the fanatical trampling of men and horses. She became fixated on the sight. What did it mean? What, if anything, was the Lord expressing to her in this hour? The flower stood unmolested, green, flourishing, its leaves and petals waving in the breeze as though dancing. How had it survived the madness?

Rachelle stirred as a hand touched her shoulder. She opened her eyes, swollen from crying, from dust and smoke. Idelette looked down at her. Rachelle sucked in a breath. Idelette?

Idelette's hair was torn loose from her carefully arranged modest curls. There was a dazed look in her pale blue eyes. Her mouth was cut and bleeding. There were other bruises on her cheeks and neck, and blood had dried with dirt and sweat. Her belle Sunday dress was ripped, telling Rachelle the brutal facts.

Rachelle groaned and reached both arms toward her. "My poor sister ..."

Idelette wrapped her arms around Rachelle's neck and they wept as only sisters can when their hearts are entwined.

"Avril — I saw it happen — and then a soldier caught me — "

Rachelle rallied. She must be strong for both of them. She drew her sister's head upon her shoulder.

"He shamed himself, sister. Your soul remains untouched."

"Non," she whispered, "it will never be all right for me again. And Avril — "

It would be cruel to contest her now. Idelette needed silent comfort and support, anything else would feel like salt on wounds. Tomorrow would have time enough for such words.

They clung to one another until tears subsided. The chilly spring wind tugged at them. Rachelle could feel Idelette shaking from cold and shock. She had to get her back to the château to their mère. Idelette was always the strong one in her faith. *Now I must be the strong one.*

From the corner of her eye, Rachelle noticed something move in the bushes. Non, not something, but someone.

Rachelle turned her head. Sir James Hudson crawled from between low-lying branches, tried to rise to his feet, then collapsed.

"It's James!" Rachelle left Idelette to run to his side. She dropped to her knees beside him. "Monsieur Hudson!"

The young couturier from London was burned and bruised, his shirt torn with blood stains.

"I'm well — it's my leg; back there — Pasteur Macquinet — "

"Bertrand!" She jumped to her feet and pushed her way through the bushes, finding him. He was alive.

Rachelle rushed to where he lay beneath a tree, bruised and unconscious, but breathing. His eyelids flicked open and he tried to raise a hand toward her. "Avril ... Idelette ... ?"

Tears welled up in her eyes. "Rest, Cousin Bertrand, do not talk now. I am going for a wagon." She turned to leave but his fingers curled around her hand. She looked down at him and saw the worry in his eyes. She swallowed, her throat dry.

"Idelette is alive, but Avril is not."

His fingers loosened. His eyes closed. He gave a weak nod of his head. "She — will suffer no more ..."

Rachelle squeezed his hand and quickly left him. As she came back to where James lay, she stooped down.

"I'm all right," he said, nursing his leg. "Mostly bruises."

It looked like more than bruises. "You were very brave, monsieur. We are in your debt."

He looked off across the field toward the road. "Horsemen." He attempted to sit up, but Rachelle pushed him back.

She stood and looked toward the half-dozen horsemen that drew up on the road.

She narrowed her eyes and gritted. "More beasts?"

Rachelle stepped away from James and glanced toward Idelette. She seemed disoriented and was sitting with her head resting on her knees, her arms wrapped around her legs.

Rachelle stood unmoving as the sound of the horses broke the uncanny stillness.

The questioning voices around her quickly turned from dismay to anger. "Are they coming back to kill the rest of us?" someone cried.

The horses drew nearer.

*Could it be?* Marquis Fabien rode slowly forward with several men, whose faces she recognized from the last time they had been at the château.

The wind ruffled the white plume on Fabien's broad-brimmed hat and the full sleeves of his linen shirt-tunic overlaid with a vest and surcoat of velvet and gold. The horse jerked its head up, its nostrils flaring, as if the smell of battle was recognized.

Rachelle watched Fabien as his gaze inched over the scene of death and woe before him. He did not move or dismount. His knuckles turned white as he held the reins, and his jaw flexed.

His chief page, Gallaudet, turned his fair head toward him with open dismay.

Rachelle stood in silence, and it seemed the moment was frozen in time. The blowing wind, the smell of charred wood, the restless whinny of horses, the creak of leather saddles. Then, as if awakening, there was movement, voices, rage.

Marquis Fabien swung down from his mount; there came the crunch of boots, a pause, an intake of breath, and then an uttered exclamation. Rachelle's bruised emotions found solace in the possessive but tender enfolding of his fingers around her arm. He drew her closer. "You are not hurt, *belle amie*? You escaped injury?"

"Oh, Fabien, I thank our God you have come back—"

He embraced her so tightly that she could hardly breathe. "If anything had happened to you—" he whispered.

He drew her head against his chest, stroking her hair. She heard his soothing voice, yet rage was just beneath his veneer, struggling to break forth over the scene of carnage before him.

"Come, I will have Gallaudet take you to the château, while I search for any yet alive. Where are your sisters?"

She clutched his arms and turned her head toward Idelette seated near Avril's body. She felt his muscles harden like granite beneath her palms as he recognized them.

Rachelle's gaze rushed to his eyes filled with outrage as they took in Avril's disfigured face, and the blood that had smeared onto Rachelle's silk dress.

"*Who?*" he demanded in a gritted whisper. "*Who* did this?"

Rachelle trembled, hating the Duc de Guise so much that she wished to spit out his name as though it were venom; and yet loving Fabien as she did, she remained mute. What if he rode after the duc and his men? If she revealed her utter loathing, would she not encourage such revenge that he would seek the duc's life?

Her emotions made her ill and weary. She must not think of this, she must not—

The death of the Duc de Guise by Fabien's sword would bring the wrath of the whole House of Guise and their powerful alliance upon his head.

Rachelle dropped her forehead against his chest and held on to him tightly.

"Do not ride after them. Do not go. Stay with me! Please, Fabien!"

He cupped her chin, his eyes warmly searching hers, and placed a brief, solacing kiss on her forehead.

"Who led these murders against the Huguenots, Rachelle?" he asked again, quietly.

She shook her head. She was well aware that Fabien believed his own father was assassinated upon secret order of Duc de Guise at the battle of Calais.

Several others knew that Guise led this attack: Idelette, Hudson, Bertrand, Jolon the gardener, and the boy Philippe—his mother was dead. Even Madame Clair would have heard his name spoken by Philippe when he ran to warn her. Thank God Guise had not turned his men loose on the Château de Silk! He would know, of course, that the château belonged to the Macquinets. Was that why he had not done so? Was it possible he had not known they were in the barn, thinking that all Huguenots were simple peasants, heretics?

It was not possible to keep the name of Guise from the marquis for very long.

*But if—if I can delay him even for a few hours—then he may not ride to overtake him ...*

Rachelle closed her eyes and shook her head again, keeping silent her hatred for Guise.

In an act of helpless fury, Gallaudet, who stood nearby, slashed his blade into the ground. "Such murderous acts can no longer be borne, *Monseigneur*. The time has come for war in France! Your Bourbon kinsman, the Prince de Condé, speaks well. The Guise faction and the Queen Mother know only the show of force."

"They that take the sword will perish with the sword," came a weak voice from behind them.

They all turned and saw Bertrand standing with his shoulders hunched forward, one limp and bloodied arm hanging uselessly at his side. He had managed to drag himself here from behind the bushes and took several more staggering steps.

Rachelle rushed and knelt beside him. "Cousin Bertrand, you should not have moved. You are bleeding again."

Marquis Fabien threw an arm around him, gesturing to Gallaudet for a skin of water.

"And what of these helpless sheep, Pasteur Bertrand? They have perished and they did not take up the sword," the marquis said with a composed voice.

"Christ has not called us to fight but to stand firm and endure ... these deeds will not go unpunished ... the Lord has His own sword. One of righteousness and justice."

Fabien took the water from Gallaudet and held it to Bertrand's lips as Rachelle held his head to drink.

"You speak well, Pasteur Bertrand." The marquis turned to Gallaudet. "Go at once to the château and send a coach for the pasteur and the mademoiselles. Say nothing yet to Madame Macquinet."

"At once, Monseigneur."

"There are others more injured than I," Bertrand objected in a hoarse voice.

Rachelle turned her head sharply toward her sister. They did not yet know what had happened to Idelette, nor did Rachelle believe her sister wanted them to know, though Idelette was in such shock that perhaps she did not care. As Bertrand finished drinking, Rachelle took the skin and hurried to where her sister sat, like Job before the pile of shards.

"I will soon have you home," Rachelle whispered in her ear. "You are my chère, brave sister; it will soon be over, I promise you."

Idelette tried to sip from the skin but her bruised mouth was too swollen. Rachelle clamped her jaw to keep her emotions from running over again into a river of tears. She carefully dribbled the water into her sister's mouth.

"James Hudson, where is he?" Bertrand was heard asking. "God used that young *messire* to save me from the flames. He too was injured."

Rachelle had forgotten about Hudson. She looked over and saw him still sprawled where she had left him.

He must have heard Bertrand, for he called weakly, "I am over here, my dear man." He groaned as he tried to raise himself to an elbow. "'Tis nothing. Methinks I've hurt my leg. I'll survive, to be sure, think not of me, sir. Lady Rachelle has been very kind indeed. But over there — " he gestured with his hand — "Lady Idelette needs a physician."

Marquis Fabien gave James Hudson a measuring appraisal that took him in thoughtfully; he then looked directly at Rachelle. She had already sensed what he may be thinking, and she turned her gaze away, feeling embarrassed.

Fabien walked up, took one look at Idelette, then removed his surcoat and placed it around her shoulders. "I have sent for a coach, Mademoiselle," he told her gently, "and *le docteur* is on his way."

Idelette gave a nod of her head but did not speak, nor did she look at him, keeping her bruised face averted. But Rachelle could see that the marquis was aware, and that anger burned in his eyes.

Fabien caught Rachelle's gaze and searched for the ugly answer. Her eyes spilled over with tears.

His jaw tightened, showing he understood. He scanned Idelette again. "I am sorry, Mademoiselle. I will find this beast, I promise you. I do not know when, or how, but when I do, I shall make him pay fourfold, I swear it!"

He turned to go, then saw Avril nearby and stopped. He gestured to one of his men to bring his cloak from his horse. Fabien wrapped the small demoiselle inside his magnificent cloak and had one of the men carry her to the side of the road to await the family coach.

Rachelle rose to her feet, feeling the wind ruffle her hair. Her mind rode the wind back through the mulberry orchard and over the garden wall, past the roses, and through the open window into the salle where they had breakfasted that morning. The words spoken by Cousin Bertrand before he had left for the barn church came back to her, bringing a lump to her throat.

*"Remember those who have gone before us, who have endured great afflictions for His name's sake."*

How could any of them have known that he was speaking of their immediate future with such painful clarity? What began with such optimism on this Sunday morning, the most pleasant day of the week, had ended with a lament. Even Marquis Fabien's unexpected return had brought him into the circle of change, with far-reaching results for him and his followers.

In such a short time, each of their lives was affected, and nothing would ever be the same again.

The baby began to cry, and Rachelle went to it gently and reached down and lifted the bundle into her arms. She cradled the infant safely against her breast and whispered soothing sounds. *Perhaps there is hope your père is alive, little one.*

❧

THE COACH ARRIVED FROM the château and came to a shuddering halt beside the wall of mulberry trees. Madame Clair stepped down and looked across the wide field, the breeze blowing her dark skirts and high ruffled white lace collar.

Rachelle's heart beat painfully. *Oh, ma mère, this will be far more painful for you than for us.*

Was it Providence that had brought Madame Clair home just when her family, and especially Idelette, would need her? If it had not been for the delay in printing the Dutch Bibles in Geneva, and the arrival there of Bertrand, Mère would have remained with Père Arnaut and waited to return with him.

Rachelle whispered to Idelette that Mère had arrived with the coach. For the first time, Idelette stirred, showing that she was attentive to what was going on around her. To Rachelle's surprise, Idelette managed to stand and began walking across the field.

Marquis Fabien intercepted Madame Clair and spoke to her, his hand holding her arm as though he feared his words would cause her to collapse. But Madame Clair stood as queenly as any royal Valois, showing herself not only a strong woman, but one who believed deeply in the faith she so heartily promoted. She began walking with dignity across the wide field toward Idelette, who drew closer.

Rachelle watched with quiet pride. She could see from the marquis' expression that he too admired Madame Clair. Her dignity at such a time made Rachelle lift her head a little higher. *This fiery trial will not destroy us. Nothing can defeat those secure in Christ.*

RACHELLE HAD THOUGHT TO join their meeting, but now she paused, watching.

The two women, so much alike in fair appearance and serious demeanor, neared one another, with the waving grasses around their feet. Madame Clair stopped and opened her arms wide. Idelette took her last weakened steps and fell into her loving, protective embrace.

Rachelle looked on with wet cheeks. The two women stood entwined, like a Michelangelo statue, a tribute to Huguenot women.

*Strengthen them both, Father God, for hard days and late nights are ahead.*

Rachelle became aware of others moving about what had now become a sanctified field. Voices were heard, like the ebb and tide of the sea. Voices of lament mixed with anger. A voice praying, and yet another quoting a verse in a tone that spoke its preciousness at such a time.

One by one the living and the dead quietly reunited with family and friends. Rachelle, still holding the baby in her arms, felt a refreshing sense of thankful relief when she saw Monsieur Scully alive and coming for his child. The child would have one loving parent, at least.

"Monsieur," she said gently, "my mother and I will be at your disposal should you need us."

"Merci, Mademoiselle," he rasped as tears ran down his creased, tanned cheeks. He took his child, his hands trembling, and she watched him walk away. Rachelle's prayer followed them.

Soon the dead were retrieved from the field for burial. Nothing remained of the barn church except blackened ruins against a bright spring sky.

Cousin Bertrand and Sir James Hudson were helped to the coach, and Marquis Fabien walked toward Rachelle, leading his horse. He paused in front of her, muscled and virile, with hair the color of sun-ripened wheat.

His eyes softened as they took her in. "You are exhausted, *chérie*. Permit me to ride you to the château — the coach has departed with the injured."

He brought her beside his horse, but she paused and walked over to the small blue wildflower and plucked it carefully. *This will go in my Bible to be pressed between the pages and kept in memory of Avril.*

The marquis waited. She came up beside him, and he lifted her to the saddle, then mounted.

The wind blew across Lemoine's hay fields. The mingled voices of prayer and rage had ceased. Soon, a bird returned to chirp in the branches of a tree and carry on as spring demanded.

One day, time would eliminate every vestige of what had occurred here. Many succeeding generations would pass. The grass would grow green again, the flowers would bloom, and who would remember but God?

They rode together toward the road, Rachelle looking at the flower. They rode toward the Château de Silk, and to what awaited them all in the days and months ahead.

# Au Revoir, My Love

RACHELLE REMAINED TENSE AND UNCERTAIN AFTER RETURNING TO THE château with Marquis Fabien. What would be the outcome of the events which their good God had allowed to invade their lives? Why was the Lord allowing such painful trials as these? What had they done wrong? Were they being chastened? Was it satanic? Many questions ran through her mind, questions with no simple answers, leaving her downcast.

Rachelle was waiting near the rose garden when Marquis Fabien walked up. He stood looking down at her, the wide sleeves of his linen tunic and his plumed hat stirring in the wind.

"The roses still bloom; the leaves are yet green," she murmured, looking toward the bushes. "Somehow I would have expected everything to have withered after such pain and sorrow, but life goes on, does it not?"

"You need not think of it now. It is an unfair weight upon your heart to attempt to come to terms with such loss and tragedy too quickly. Grief is a necessary part of healing. All things take time."

He stepped toward her and took her face between his warm, strong hands and looked down at her tenderly. Her heart stirred to life again at his touch. As she gazed into his eyes, however, she saw that more was on his mind than having her so near. His gaze was serious and distant.

"What is it, Fabien?"

His smile was faint. "I must leave you for a while."

"Oh, but —"

"I shall return tonight. Le docteur is here now, and I think Pasteur Bertrand will recover. I have seen worse wounds. And the Englishman's leg will also heal."

He lifted her fingers to his lips, turned, and descended the veranda steps. Gallaudet came around from the side of the château leading two horses, and they rode away together. His other men-at-arms and lackeys must have remained at the stables. Where was he going?

The docteur, *Maître* Pierre Lancre, was grim faced and tight-lipped as he quickly scanned the worst of the injured, then turned back to treat them. Cousin Bertrand had a gunshot wound in his leg, burns, and multiple bruises, and the docteur spent the longest time with him. James had suffered burns and an injured leg, which meant his stay at the château would be longer than anyone had expected. Then, having already checked Idelette, who suffered from bruises and shock, he ordered a glass of wine brought to her and had her put to bed until he could fully attend her.

"I am afraid you have your hands full, Madame Macquinet," he later told Clair. "Neither of the messieurs may be moved for some time."

"Think not of that, Docteur Lancre; our home is always open in times of need. Indeed, Bertrand is part of our family. And Monsieur Hudson can stay for as long as needed."

Pierre Lancre went down the hall to visit Idelette with Madame Clair and Rachelle following.

They waited beyond Idelette's chamber door while Idelette was examined, and heard her answering questions in a low, dull voice. Rachelle watched her mère, seeing the worry in her eyes, the restrained sorrow on her pale, drawn face. Rachelle marveled that she was taking the loss of Avril with such spiritual fortitude. Perhaps it was because the crisis was still present and she could not allow herself to collapse under the devastation. There was Idelette and her recovery to think about.

While Madame Clair paced the floral rug, her lips moving as though in silent intercession, Rachelle, too, remained restless, thinking of Idelette, Cousin Bertrand, and then Marquis Fabien. He had shown himself most astute; indeed, he had been the epitome of sympathy and strength, assuring Clair of his support with anything she needed, including sending men to Geneva for Rachelle's father, Arnaut. Madame Clair had assured him that a lettre would be sent to her husband promptly. Fabien had shown such concern, perhaps because her parents knew he was a

Catholic. Madame Clair, at least, had been aware of Rachelle's interest in him and disapproved. Her words were spoken more than once; her intent clearly understood: "You cannot be united to anyone other than a Huguenot; your père would never allow it, ma chère."

She walked to the hall window and glanced below. Marquis Fabien had said he was riding toward the main village to meet someone at an inn. What it was about, he had not told her, as usual. *He retains his secrecy well*, she thought wryly. He could not easily overtake Duc de Guise now, too much time had passed — unless, horrors! — unless the duc had made an early camp for the night!

Rachelle turned from the window as Docteur Lancre closed Idelette's bedroom door behind him. A small man with a drooping mustache and shiny forehead, he looked not the slightest bit encouraged from his visit with her sister.

Madame Clair stood with outward repose. "*Messire?*"

A breath rumbled through his lips. "Madame, it is as she said . . . and as we feared. But I hasten to add that she is an otherwise healthy mademoiselle who, I am confident, will come out of this shock with a sound mind and body."

Rachelle noticed her mother's shoulders sag a little. Rachelle understood that she had hoped Idelette may have been "mistaken." Rachelle had never thought so, but their mère often saw both of them as very young.

"I see," she murmured, her saddened eyes turning downward.

Rachelle felt a desire to go to her mother but refrained, keeping her face blank as she had taught her daughters while growing up. Intimate or embarrassing situations were always to be dealt with stoically.

"Madame Macquinet," he said, "I am a loyal Catholic as you know. As such, I am horrified at what has befallen my friends and neighbors 'of the religion.'"

Madame Clair nodded that she understood and accepted his condolences.

"Such behavior as this, Madame," he spread a hand, "is barbarism. No religious cloak shall ever give respectability to the behavior of Duc de Guise. His fervency has turned to fanaticism. And I shall not defend it! Even though a man be a heretic, I cannot believe the God of heaven would ever approve of such cruel deeds by his servants. And the petite Avril—" Then the stoic Docteur Lancre was unable to finish.

He shook his head, and begging pardon, paused and recovered. He went on to discuss his remedy for shock. Idelette was to rest and stay bedridden for the next several days, then he would see her again. He spoke of something to keep her quiet and sleepy.

"And you as well, Madame," he said soberly, looking at her over the bridge of his nose, "must be given a sleeping potion."

"I cannot, Docteur Lancre, I must keep all my wits at hand. There are correspondences to write, and I must arrange for my husband to come home as soon as he feels he can—" she stopped short.

Rachelle glanced at her. Madame Clair had almost mentioned the work Arnaut was doing in Geneva, which could easily have brought his arrest, and even the fiery stake if he did not recant. Rachelle looked at the docteur, seeing he had not suspected anything, but was writing his instructions for Idelette and for herself—though Rachelle wasn't sure she was willing to comply.

Rachelle knew there was little else she could learn, and she slipped away.

The wall sconces shimmered with lamplight even during the day, for the corridor would otherwise be dim. The château, though most belle, was usually chilly in winter and spring. Even now she felt a draft about her ankles as she walked wearily across the carpet, faded from generations of wear in some places. The wear on the carpets and furniture seemed to make the château more cherished to Rachelle. It connected her emotionally to family who had been here before her with dedication to the silk enterprise.

She passed Cousin Bertrand's chamber but did not wish to disturb him now. She would see him when she visited at *dîner*. As for Sir James Hudson, it was not respectable for a young woman to venture into the bedchamber of a young man alone, even though Hudson had proven himself a Christian and a gallant gentleman.

Rachelle's mind jumped back to the duc. Everyone claims they are Christian. A prayer uttered, a ritual performed, a confession of belief, but what did it all mean when a heart remained the same, even justifying murder?

After Docteur Lancre departed and Idelette slept, Rachelle waited in the main salle for Madame Clair. Clair descended the stairs appearing tense and pale and sat in the red velvet chair below magnificent tapestries that showed a garden scene from the Fontainebleau *palais-château* in Orléans.

Rachelle knelt beside Clair and laid her forehead against her shoulder, taking solace in her mother's consolation.

"I should be helping you instead of taking comfort ... you have only so much strength to expend ..."

"Hush, not so. Your presence consoles me. There is no shame in our tears, nor to our need for comfort. We all need an encourager when the way grows so long. There is a time to weep and a time to laugh. Now is our time for tears. How can we not? My youngest, your petite sister, is lying in the antechamber covered over with white linen; and Idelette, my lily, so serious, so dedicated, and now — "

"Oh, ma mère ... Idelette, it is she who worries me the most."

"Yes. She may carry this burden for a long journey before seeing green pastures." She looked off across the salle, thoughtfully.

Silence descended. Rachelle had expected her mother to allay her fears, but she now accepted them as her own. On the tables, the candles burned and flickered. Now and then, one of the servants lost control of their feelings and a sob was heard from the kitchen area or another part of the house. They had been with the family so long, they also were sorrowing.

"We are as Job this night," Madame Clair said after a long silence. "The Lord has given, and the Lord has permitted the ruthless and the blind of spirit to take away what we cherished."

"It is as le docteur said, ma mère. It was senseless and brutal." *And I hate the Duc de Guise*, she thought, but could not bring herself to say so before her mother.

"Senseless, I say, from our human reasoning, Rachelle, but not senseless to our great and wise God. You understand that, do you not?"

She did, and yet she could not come to terms with it as her mother had, and she did not wish to add to her concerns.

"Yes, ma mère."

"Understand, this could not have happened to us unless, like Job, the hedge of safety was lowered for the spiritual enemy to get through to us."

"Yes, but why?"

"If we knew the answer, ma petite, we would no longer need to trust and walk by faith. We are tested, and like Job, we will, with God's help, come forth as gold. We can choose to say, 'Blessed be the name of the Lord.' Remember that Faithful and True are two of His names."

Rachelle sat dry-eyed and silent. She did not think she could possibly muster another tear if her heart were torn from her. There would never be enough tears to mourn Avril, or to sympathize with Idelette.

"Knowing where Avril is—helps to sustain us," Clair said, squeezing her hand.

"Yes, but our loss remains."

"In our earthly sojourn it cannot be fully mended. That is why heaven is now made dearer to us, Rachelle. And God wishes it so."

Those words, *heaven is now made dearer,* unexpectedly lit a flame in Rachelle's heart. She looked up quickly. She saw the sadness in her mother's eyes, yet it was softened, mingled with hope, even certainty. Rachelle sensed that hope of God's promise growing brighter within her own heart. Yes, heaven *is* dearer to me!

Madame Clair searched her face and must have seen something not visible before. A little smile turned her lips.

In a gesture of gratitude to her mère, Rachelle placed her arms around her neck.

They prayed together as was their family custom. Afterward, Madame Clair went upstairs to write Père Arnaut the dreaded correspondence of what had visited them in his absence. It was given to Rachelle to write to Grandmère and Madeleine, but she too went off to the task while eternal hope sprang up within.

"Make me an encourager, Father," she asked. "Let me light a candle in the darkness of fear and doubt."

Rachelle adjusted the lamp on her father's writing desk, took out stationery, and dipped her pen into the inkwell. After several attempts, she settled on the words to her grandmère and Madeleine.

❁

THE LIGHT WAS FADING RAPIDLY with the setting sun and the long day edging toward its close. Billowy clouds, the color of eggshells, with tints of lavender, hung over the mureraies.

Rachelle had finished her lettre, and the envelope sat on the burnished mahogany table by the door, ready for delivery to Paris.

The darkness settled in. Where was Marquis Fabien?

She reached to close the burgundy draperies and blinked, startled by what must have been a handful of gravel flung against the windowpane.

She was in the salle on the first floor and had a clear view of the tall hedgerow and the front courtyard. There were no horses or men-at-arms, but a movement under the hedge caught her eye. A man crouched out of sight. Their gazes caught. She tensed; he reached inside his cloak and brought out a dark book and held it to his lips. Then he made the sign of the cross and signaled that he would go around to the back of the château. He slipped away, keeping out of sight.

Was the book a Bible? Surely so. Who was he and what did he want? She drew the draperies closed, then making up her mind, she sped across the chamber, out the door, and toward the back entrances.

Rachelle stepped out onto the rear balcony, feeling the night wind chilling her. There was a landing here, railed, with steps leading down to the culinary herb garden. She held to the rail and looked below into the twilight. Footsteps rushed along the path, now and then hesitating. She waited. Then the man came out of the shadows and rushed toward her.

Rachelle stepped back cautiously.

"A thousand pardons, Mademoiselle," he gasped, "the grace of our Lord be with you! Forgive me for coming to you in this way, but two men were following me back at the inn. I was able to slip away unseen, but wish to take no chances." He gave a swift bow. "I am Mathieu, a student from Geneva, where I attend Monsieur Calvin's school of theology."

The student's sober garb was familiar to her. Many Huguenot students from Geneva on their way to hold secret meetings throughout France had visited the château as a safe house through the years.

Rachelle glanced about the darkness and saw no one else. She stepped back. "Come inside quickly, Monsieur."

He scrambled up the steps and ducked inside the antechamber, out of breath.

Rachelle quietly shut the door and bolted it. She lit an oil lamp. Now that she had a clearer view of him, she could see he had been running and hiding, for his clothes were dusty.

"You have come at a dangerous time, Monsieur Mathieu. The château may be watched by Duc de Guise's men-at-arms. They attacked the Huguenot assembly early this morning."

"I had small choice, Mademoiselle. I was at the inn outside the village, prepared to stay the night, and thinking of my supper, when two men entered and sat down across the room. Soon they began to talk. They began to boast to one another of how they had attacked a group of "heretics" who met to worship the Devil, as they said. When they mentioned the Château de Silk and the Macquinet name, I was so dismayed, I almost gave myself away. I was sent here from Geneva by Monsieur Arnaut Macquinet with a lettre for his cousin, Bertrand Macquinet."

From her père!

"Only by God's good providence was I able to flee the inn unnoticed by these two soldiers. A stranger entered and boldly confronted them, demanding to know where the duc was camped. While they were occupied I slipped away."

Suspicion sharpened her voice. "This stranger who entered, did you hear his name?"

"No, but there was another man with him who called him marquis."

Fabien! He must have been there with Gallaudet. Would he dare confront the duc? Her concerns grew.

Mathieu removed a small sealed parchment from inside his cloak. In the light of the lamp she recognized her father's handwriting.

"Mademoiselle, I must deliver this to Pasteur Bertrand."

"Oui, *bien sûr*, but he was injured this morning. He was behind the teaching pulpit when a surprise attack came. I cannot promise that he will be strong enough to read my father's message this night, as le docteur has given him a sleeping potion for suffering."

Mathieu's young face fell with disappointment.

"Is Pasteur Bertrand badly injured?"

"We believe he will recover in time."

"Then God be thanked. Pasteur Bertrand has my prayers this night. Since you are Monsieur Macquinet's daughter, I do not hesitate to tell you that the message from your father bears most important content." He glanced around him cautiously as though from habit. "The Bibles Pasteur Bertrand wishes to smuggle out of France are even now awaiting his arrival. It is crucial that he act at once."

In his condition? What would have been bonne news before the events of the morning, now presented a dilemma. Bertrand was unable to leave his bed.

She was also surprised to hear that the Bibles were already printed. On that very morning Bertrand had said that her father might need to remain in Geneva for another month.

"Mathieu, are you certain? Bertrand does not yet expect the Bibles."

"Monsieur Macquinet was able to find another printer in Geneva to do the work posthaste. The Bibles are now stored in a private warehouse at Calais, guarded by Monsieur Macquinet—"

"Calais? But he was to bring them here to Lyon."

"That was the intention, Mademoiselle, until it was learned le duc may have knowledge of the Macquinet work in Geneva. It was then decreed too dangerous for the Château de Silk. Alas, le duc has struck here anyway."

"Then—you mean my père may have expected an attack here?"

"He may have worried. Then the plan with Pasteur Bertrand was altered to bring the Bibles to Châtillon, then on to Calais, where a friendly ship awaits to bring both the pasteur and the Bibles to England."

"Are you certain my père is now at Calais?"

"He is, and that is why it is most urgent that Pasteur Bertrand go there at once to join him. The Bibles must be moved from their place of concealment and brought to England before they are discovered."

Rachelle put a hand to her forehead. Her father was doubtless taking a grave risk at Calais. A warehouse was never safe for long with so many people coming and going on the wharves, and this one stacked with crates of French Bibles, with her father as their keeper.

"But it is impossible for Cousin Bertrand to travel now. Why — it may be several weeks, perhaps even longer."

"Mademoiselle, I share your very concerns after what has happened here. If there is anything I can do — well, I am at your service, and Pasteur Bertrand's. Perhaps, Mademoiselle, it would be wise for you to read the lettre from your père, since Pasteur Bertrand is not yet able."

He handed her the envelope.

Rachelle hesitated, then sent her reticence fleeing. After all, if her father was asking Bertrand to come with all speed, then she dare not delay learning of his plight.

Mathieu looked weary and worn, and her sympathy went out to him. He had journeyed far bringing her father's lettre. If anyone had discovered it upon him and read its contents, he would have been arrested. It was fortunate that Marquis Fabien had entered the inn when he did, lest the two soldiers recognize the student's Geneva dress.

"Come, we shall talk again in the morning. I will take you to your chamber for the night."

"The Lord bless you, Mademoiselle. The students at the university have heard of the Macquinet generosity toward us. The fine linen shirts sent to us are desired alike by student and docteur."

"The shirts are by oversight of my sister Mademoiselle Idelette," she said, with a smile, followed by an onrush of uninvited sadness over Idelette's condition.

Rachelle brought Mathieu past the cook's room into a hall with an alcove having steps going up to a second floor chamber that was affectionately called the Prophet's Nook. The family had it built in the early 1500s when persecution against the first Reformers in France broke with fury. Presently it was kept ready for traveling pasteurs and Bible students out of Geneva. There was a wardrobe stocked with shirts, coats, and leggings in many sizes, and upon departure, travel currency was given.

Rachelle told him that hot water, fresh towels, and dinner would soon be brought.

*"Merci mille fois,* Mademoiselle."

"Have dinner, Monsieur, and get your well-deserved sleep. You have done your part in delivering the message. I will see to its contents." Yet, even as Rachelle spoke, she wondered what could possibly be done.

She left Mathieu and started down the steps, frowning and considering her alternatives. Reaching the alcove, she set the candleholder on the ledge and opened the lettre. Holding it near the candlelight, she read her father's brief message:

> *I am now in Calais with the cargo, awaiting your arrival.*
> *We confront several difficulties. Monsieur B informs me he is*
> *under suspicion. It is perilous for him to haul the cargo aboard his*
> *vessel as first planned. We must find other means. Also, Monsieur*
> *D's warehouse can only be used for a brief time due to random*
> *inspections. Come in haste. Say nothing of my situation to Clair.*
>
> *A. M.*

Rachelle's fingers closed about the lettre, and she gazed off thoughtfully. Now what? Bertrand could not make the journey to Calais. If she sent Mathieu back to her father with the dark tidings here in Lyon, it would compound his dilemma.

As she stood, considering, she heard the servant's voice, followed by footsteps, then Fabien's question as he entered the grande salle. She hurried across the polished floor, her dark blue skirts swishing, and paused before the archway done in tiles of pale blue with a yellow floral pattern.

The grande salle was the largest room in the château, with a vaulted ceiling and chandeliers that now were only partially lit. Large Florentine tapestries lined the cream wall facing the archway.

Fabien was waiting for her. He cut a striking figure, garbed in a rugged outfit of leather and woolen cloth. His boots were buckled, his scabbard jeweled, the hat he carried was wide brimmed and sweeping. *Was he dressed for travel?*

As Rachelle set the candleholder on a table, her reaction was one of relief. He had returned safely! She attempted to deny her suspicions, but as he turned and his eyes met hers, alarm began to creep into her heart. It grew as she came to meet him, for she sensed his deliberation.

She paused, curbing her intent to flee to the strength and safety of his strong embrace. She had known since Vendôme, and even before, that he intended to take to sea, and waited for a covert message to arrive from the French buccaneers. He had never told her just who these "buccaneers" were, but she knew he had gone to meet one of them two weeks ago, and she believed his present behavior was related to that meeting.

She lifted her chin and hurried to him, smiling, determined she would not lose him, not now; not after the struggle to win his heart. She reminded herself that no other woman had done so. She was the first, and she was not going to release him now.

"Fabien." She hurried to him and clutched his rough tunic as though she would never let him go again. "Thank goodness you are not hurt. Why did you go to the inn? I was so worried."

"Have you not had enough to worry you this day?" he asked gently.

"But you and Gallaudet — do you think you should have gone there? Word is bound to find its way to Duc de Guise. When he learns of it — "

"When he learns of it and wishes to answer for his evil deeds, he will know the man to seek."

She stared at him, her frustration growing. *If anything happened to him . . .*

"But to challenge two of the duc's soldiers! The man is afflicted with madness, surely. Why else would he go about seeking Huguenot assemblies to put to the sword? He hunts Huguenots like the king hunts rabbits!"

"He is not mad. He knows exactly what he is doing, working hand in hand with the deliberate purposes of Spain and Rome. Who told you I went to the inn?"

Rachelle read the glint of impatience in his violet-blue gaze.

"Mathieu, a Bible scholar from Geneva. He arrived a short while ago bringing Bertrand a message from my père Arnaut. The student was at the inn when you arrived. He saw you. Fabien, do you not understand?" She reached again for the rough woolen sleeves of his tunic, as though by sheer determination she could hold him forever. "Now Guise will be against you more than ever."

His indomitable manner only frustrated her. He spoke in a calm voice, "Is that why you would not tell me earlier that it was Guise's men that attacked?"

"I was afraid you would ride after him. And as I feared, you sought him out. You might have been — been injured or taken prisoner."

He seemed surprised at her intensity. "Rachelle, ma chérie — please. He is an enemy and has been long before I met you at Chambord. He is responsible for the death of Jean-Louis," he said of his father. "Now he has added more crimes to his conscience, if he has one." He gently removed her clutching fingers and brought them to his lips. There was something in his watchful gaze that was both unsettling and confusing to her wearied emotions. Did he think she was being possessive?

"Gallaudet learned that two of Guise's men were at the inn. I went there to learn from them where the duc had made his camp, but Guise had left with his bodyguard, immediately after the attack on the Huguenots, to meet his wife. He and his son Henry are staying at the bishop's palais on the road to Paris. It would be foolish for me to go there. He would demand the bishop detain me. What happened at the inn between Guise's men and me and Gallaudet was unplanned, I assure you. They drew swords first. There are several witnesses."

His gaze softened, and he took hold of her shoulders. "You have faced exceedingly sore trials today, chérie; you are overwrought and weary, as you should be. I wish I did not need to disappoint you now with the news that I must leave, but — "

She drew back, searching his face. "Leave? But Fabien!"

"Rachelle, I must. The privateers are sailing and I need to be with them."

"You cannot leave now!" She grabbed hold of him.

He quietly released his arm from her grasp and walked a few feet away, then turned to face her, his eyes determined.

"My ship waits at Calais. I have no choice in the matter, as my absence would affect the privateers and their crews."

"But you told me when we left your estate at Vendôme that you would be staying here at the château until Arnaut returns, that you wanted to meet him."

"Yes, and I meant it, but things have suddenly changed."

"Changed? Toward me?"

He was beside her in a few steps. "*Mon amour*, of course not." His arms went around her again, and his gaze searched her face. He frowned. "You make it most painful for me to leave, I assure you."

This was what Rachelle wanted to hear. She would not surrender. She put her arms around his neck. "You have not kissed me since you returned from your secret meeting with the privateers."

His eyes glinted warmly. He hesitated for a moment, then his lips met hers.

"Fabien," she whispered, "do not go away—"

"By the saints, but you do try a man! This conniving side of you, chérie, is something I have not seen before. Do you think I want to leave you?"

"Conniving!"

"*Précisément*. Did I not tell you from the day we met at Chambord that I would need to leave France for a time? I kept nothing back from you. My leaving should not come to you as a surprise. Listen to me, Rachelle—" he reached for her arms—"I received word a short time ago that a ship is ready for me at Calais. I am to meet with certain buccaneers concerning an attack on Spanish galleons arming the Duc d'Alva in the Netherlands."

Rachelle, though she had expected this moment to come eventually, had convinced herself that he would change his mind once he was in love with her. She had certainly not expected his departure now—even within the hour.

She pushed away from his arms. "I should have known. You are just like all the rest. Men declare one thing and do another."

"I have not deceived you. It is you who are beginning to sound as *all the rest*, claiming rights never spoken, nor yet committed."

She sucked in her breath, hardly believing what she was hearing. She faced him with shattered emotions, knowing only that great devastation had come upon her and her family, and he appeared to be walking away when she needed him most.

"Rachelle, believe me if there was any way to delay my departure, I would do so. It is with great regret that circumstances have moved to call me now, but—"

"Circumstances! This is your choice!"

"It is, Mademoiselle. I, and others, have been planning this for many months, and at great expense. It will save the lives of many Dutch Protestants. And may God help me for the sake of thousands facing the Inquisition."

She looked at him, realizing she had gone too far. "Oh," she said meekly and bit her lip. She turned away.

He came up to her, his fingers enclosing around her arms, caressing her. "Mon amour," he said softly into her hair. He kissed her lips, then her throat. "You take lightly how difficult this is for me after this morning's tragedy. Leaving you like this when you ask me to stay will only add to that difficulty! If I fail to keep this meeting, it will affect hundreds of men who are depending on me. I leave you in good stead with Madame Clair and Pasteur Bertrand. The crewmen wait in dependence upon me to accomplish this mission. Many are faithful Huguenots who are determined to help their brothers in the Netherlands. These men know that if we can sink Philip's galleons, we will deny the Duc d'Alva soldiers and weapons. At the same time we strengthen the hands of the Dutch Protestants standing against him. What took place today with Guise and the Huguenots is the same brutality that is sweeping across the Netherlands. You should care deeply about this mission. You must care. You must believe in what I am doing."

"I do care, believe me I do, but surely others can take your place? I only know you are leaving when it is important that you stay and speak to mon père about us, even as you said at Vendôme."

A tense moment held them.

"I have made arrangements to see that the Château de Silk is guarded," he went on. "The men have already been paid. If Pasteur Bertrand was fully conscious, I would discuss it with him, but I cannot wait for his recovery."

"That you take such fine interest in me is appreciated, I assure you." She turned her back, devastated after this horrendous day. And now, to have it end with Fabien leaving was another loss. Despite better judgment, and all her careful upbringing, she burst into ungracious tears, so weary of body and soul that she snatched up a flower vase of spring violets and smashed it.

Fabien took hold of her and held her close, smoothing her tumbled hair and speaking gently. Though comforted and mollified, she did not hear what she so desperately wanted to hear, that he loved her too much to leave her, that he would stay and wait to speak to her father about marriage.

She looked up at him. "Do you love me, Fabien?"

Such a question was considered shocking, if not deplorable, in the Huguenot culture. Her sister Idelette would not have believed it of her, but at the moment Rachelle cared not at all. Perhaps she was making an error carrying on this way, for the marquis was seeing her at her weakest moment of unflattering reality. She wanted his affirmation, his unfailing devotion, and his commitment.

His words did not come for an uncomfortable minute.

"If I did not care about you, I assure you, I would not be spending this time trying to win you over to this cause to which I am committing myself."

"You 'care' about me?"

"Did I not also say at Chambord that it was love at first sight? I also recall having said that our emotions, so strong, must be tested. Let us face the facts. We know, do we not, that my religion does not satisfy Pasteur Bertrand or Madame Clair? I can only believe that your father, Monsieur Arnaut, will be of like mind about the possibility of the Catholic Marquis de Vendôme as their son-in-law."

Rachelle felt as though a splash of cold water had struck her face.

It was true that Madame Clair had misgivings about her daughter's interest in the marquis, though she had couched those concerns in softer words. What Bertrand thought, she did not know, for he had not spoken to her about it, and as for her père Arnaut, she felt he could be convinced upon his return.

She threw her arms around him. "I will make my parents understand."

"When and if I choose to have them understand, I will prefer to do so myself."

His mild rebuke sobered her, and she drew back. "You could always change your religion," she pleaded.

"The hypocrite's solution. Is it so easy then, chérie, to change one's religion like a garment? A king would find such allegiance despicable, how much more the very One who has called Himself the way, the truth, and the life?"

She had prided herself in being the one knowing truth, and now with calm assurance he had rebuked her.

She was blundering badly tonight. Her head throbbed, her senses were dulled with pain from Avril's death and the deaths of so many of her friends, not to mention the injuries to Bertrand and Sir James Hudson.

His thoughtful gaze remained fixed upon her, and a chill went through her as she read his displeasure mixed with sympathy. It was not the look she would have expected to receive from the marquis until this awkward moment. The look silenced her. For a moment they stood sizing one another up as though they had just met — for the first time.

Rachelle's heart sank when he turned and walked to the stone hearth. The firewood crackled in the numbing silence.

"Rachelle," he said gently. "We need time; I for a mission, and you for recovery. And we must not make such an important, life-altering decision while either of us is struggling with trauma. Though what you are asking may provide an immediate sense of escape and security, it would be an error for us to enter into marriage until this present turmoil has passed."

*He thinks I am trying to manipulate him, to force him into a quick marriage.*

*Well . . . was she not?*

She rebuked herself. In a weak moment to satisfy her desire to have him, she had all but suggested it did not matter what he truly believed, that one's faith in Christ could become decoration rather than foundation.

"I think it wise we discuss this later, after I return."

She was tired, physically and emotionally. She realized that except for the brief hour in her chamber when she changed her bloodstained dress for the sedate black of mourning, she had not napped, or even rested. There had been too much to do, to think about, and thinking meant feeling.

"Where will you go to catch your ship?" she asked dully.

"Calais." He stared at the fire in the hearth, frowning to himself. "I do not have much time. Gallaudet is getting the horses ready now."

Calais . . . The name of the harbor recently won back to France from Spain began to settle in her mind. He had mentioned Calais before, but now it stirred her awake. Père Arnaut was there with the French Bibles.

"Fabien, take me with you to Calais."

He looked over at her with a scowl, then, as though he could not help himself, a brief smile, tender but ironic, broke through. She had the uneasy feeling that he did not take her seriously. "You wish to be one of my crew, do you?"

"Do be serious." She walked toward him.

"I thought I was."

"Remember that I spoke of a message brought tonight by the student, Mathieu? I told you it was for Pasteur Bertrand from Père Arnaut, who is now at Calais. Bertrand's condition renders him unable to join him there, but I shall."

"Your father is at Calais? I was told he was fully engaged in Geneva?"

"So we thought." She looked quickly around for her father's lettre which she had dropped in her haste, and finding it, handed it to him.

"Fabien, you must help us. You say you will have a ship waiting at Calais; you could bring us to England, to Spitalfields, to deliver the Bibles."

"Bibles? Are you serious?"

"It would give you time to come to know him, and he you. The fact that you would come to his aid would surely convince him your faith is genuine. Oh, do you not see? It will all work out perfectly."

Rachelle waited impatiently while he read and reread the message. She watched as his jaw flexed.

"No." He handed back the lettre.

"No? He needs your help. He could be in danger."

"Most assuredly."

"But you have a ship—" she gritted.

His eyes were a flinty blue. "It is out of the question, Rachelle."

"Then you must have an ami who has a ship? A buccaneer, as you say, a monsieur who loathes Spain and Rome—who would be pleased to help the Huguenot cause. You yourself have said the cause for which you go to sea is to harry Spain!"

"And so it is. And the answer is no, Rachelle."

He stood like a bulwark, resisting all her hopes and dreams. She wanted him and could not have him. She wanted him to take her to Calais to aid her father, and he would not. Her frustration simmered into anger.

"What you demand of me is impossible," he said.

She turned and looked at him, tears in her eyes.

"I have word from a trustworthy privateer from England that the Duc d'Alva himself may soon be on a Spanish galleon. Do you know who this man is? He leads the Inquisition in Holland. Protestants are known to have killed themselves on word of his army's approach to a helpless village or town. If I involve myself with your père and the Bibles, I will not be able to intercept the galleons. I must allow nothing to hold me down. Nothing," he said again quietly. His steady gaze met hers, and his determination, though gently spoken, was clear.

Yes, she understood.

Rachelle felt tired, her rage now gone, with discouragement rushing in to fill the vacuum.

"Rachelle, I am sorry," he said quietly. "If I could help Monsieur Arnaut take his shipment to England, I would do so, for your sake, but there is no time. Your father is a wise man. He will find another ship once he understands that Bertrand will not be joining him. I have a notion he is not a novice in this enterprise."

Footsteps approached in the outer salle. Fabien looked toward the archway.

Gallaudet stood there, fair in color and calmly unreadable, though he must have understood the emotional tension that crackled in the chamber.

"Excuse me, *Monseigneur*, but the horses are ready. The time grows short."

"I shall be there in a moment," the marquis told Gallaudet.

Gallaudet bowed his head and stepped out of sight into the outer corridor of the salle.

Fabien was leaving. Who knew if he would ever come back? A sense of panic swept over her. Everything she loved and needed was slipping through her fingers.

Rachelle looked desperately at Fabien.

He watched her, his gaze troubled, but remaining firm.

"I shall see you when I return. I cannot promise when that will be, for after we attack the Spanish galleons, we sail for the coast of the Americas, toward St. Augustine, Florida. I promised Admiral Coligny, as I told you at Amboise. I am sure your work with silk will keep you productive and give you satisfaction. *Au revoir*, Rachelle," he said softly.

She turned away refusing to answer, tears dampening her cheeks, her heart so heavy it ached. She heard him hesitate, but her escaped sob did not force him to relent. She felt his thoughtful gaze, and she had the impression that he was analyzing her. At the moment her physical fairness was her least important asset.

She heard his footsteps departing. The sound filled her soul with unbearable loneliness, and as he reached the doorway, she whirled and ran after him.

"Fabien!" She snatched his sleeve. Their gazes met, and she came to him.

Swiftly he embraced her, his kiss leaving no doubt of his internal struggle. She clung to him in hope.

As swiftly as he had embraced her, he released himself from her grasp and strode through the archway and across the outer salle to the front door.

Rachelle, her face wet with tears, followed him. "Fabien!"

The front door opened and shut firmly in haste, as though he no longer trusted his determination.

Rachelle gave a cry of defeat and stood leaning into the archway, her head pressed against the frame.

*You threw yourself at him and lost ... Lost him, and his respect. Oh, Rachelle, you played the fool!*

# A Question of Poison

ANDELOT DANGEAU BENT LOW IN THE SPANISH SADDLE ON THE MUSCLED golden bay belonging to Marquis Fabien de Vendôme, and headed toward the king's stable yard at the Louvre Palais in Paris. Behind a low rise, a thin blue reflection betrayed that he was galloping straight into a wide pool of water. Saints! Something else to thwart him. Andelot leaned forward, pressing his weight into the stirrups. A warning shout rose among the dust from a nearby group of footmen and young pages, all garbed in the colors of the royal houses they served.

Andelot felt the muscled bay tense beneath him, then rise gracefully, as though extending wings. Scaling the pool, the horse landed on steady hoofs, showing training par excellence by the marquis. Andelot grinned and leaned over the saddle, patting the strong, sweating neck. Then, irritated shouts, followed by running feet. He eased the horse into a slow prancing half-circle to face an aggravated audience.

"Ho! A thousand devils," shouted a page, who by his manner announced his authority. "Do you wish to smother us all, peasant?" He waved his cap with exaggerated indignation to fan away settling dust from his satin-housed shoulders. He strode up, golden pom-poms on the tips of his slippers bouncing. He had gleaming amber hair and wore satin with silver fripperies. His hand rested on his scabbard. As he looked up at Andelot, his belt tinkled precociously with silver bells.

Andelot noticed an emblem on the page's silver-and-green uniform: the insignia of Madame-Duchesse Xenia Dushane, the Huguenot duchesse related by blood to the Macquinet family of Lyon, the very woman to whom he had been sent.

The page's green hat glittered with a large yellow gemstone, undoubtedly a gift, showing favor from the duchesse. The silver tassels on his sleeves twirled proudly in the breeze.

"Who is this madman, the new manure boy?"

"Put him to work posthaste!" shouted a pudgy young footman, grinning. "Bring a shovel for messire."

Laughter coalesced on the springtime breezes. Andelot glanced from one young face to the other, setting his mouth grimly. He was in no mood for a jocular display after the recent terror he witnessed at the castle of Amboise, where two thousand French Huguenots — those "of the religion" — were tortured, then beheaded until blood ran deep in the courtyard. In his mind's eye he could still envision the grotesque headless corpses in the river Loire. Surely, it had aged him ten years.

He dismounted, setting his dusty boots on firm ground again. "Monsieur," he said to the Dushane page. "See to the feeding and care of Marquis de Vendôme's horse, *s'il vous plaît*, and conduct me at once to the *appartements* of Duchesse Dushane, your madame."

"Messieurs," the page spoke to his fellows in training, "this pestilent fellow nearly rides us down, choking us with dust, and then deigns to give us orders."

Andelot felt the chief page's contemptuous scrutiny upon his soiled brown cloak and serf's cap. Andelot had once been destined to serve on the Cardinal de Lorraine's personal staff, and he would have worn the special scholar's wardrobe which would have earmarked him at Court as the cardinal's favorite, but his future was altered overnight after the boy, Prince Charles, revealed that Andelot had hidden in the courtyard during the mass beheadings. There still remained the small chance that he might enter the *Corps des Pages*, but that too appeared unlikely.

*I should have gone to sea with Marquis Fabien*, he thought dourly.

"I am Page Romier, in service to Madame-Duchesse Dushane."

In a feeble gesture of appeasing the page, Andelot removed his cap from his brown curly hair and bowed his head. "Honoré. But hasten, I beg of you, for the sake of my mount to feed and give him drink.

This horse was loaned to me by Marquis Fabien de Vendôme until he returns."

"Hurrah, ho! A jest, surely. Where did you steal this magnificent horse, mon serf, eh? Not from Marquis Vendôme, I assure you, for he would have trounced you in a moment."

Laughter chortled. Andelot wrestled with his disgruntled mood. He carried a missive for the duchesse from one of the most powerful and feared men in France—le Cardinal de Lorraine—and except for short pauses to graze and water Fabien's horse, he had not rested since departing the fortress of Amboise in Touraine. His bones felt heavy with weariness, and hunger gnawed at him.

Andelot narrowed his gaze at the grinning young messieurs gathered in a half circle around him. *As though I am a court jester,* he thought, his temper simmering.

"If someone does not feed and rub down this horse," he said fiercely, "you will one day answer to the Marquis de Vendôme himself, I promise you that! He has told me to take care of the golden bay until he returns to—" He stopped. No one was to know he had left France until his absence became glaringly apparent.

"The dusty serf speaks boldly, does he not?" Romier gestured toward the pond. "Go. Rinse yourself off, serf. This is the palais of the King of France!"

Andelot watched the page turn his pristine back against him and saunter away in the direction of the main palais.

His heart thudded in his ears. *If I had a sword, I vow I would draw it now and call this pompous donkey out. Am I not wearied with being treated as a beggar all my life? It is men such as he that tempt me sorely to do all I can to become like the cardinal!*

An older man, forking hay nearby, paused, and looked the horse over while leaning on his pitchfork.

"With so grand a horse as this serf rides, think thrice about what you do, Romier," he called to the page. Then he inclined his gray head toward the golden bay. "This handsome brute I have seen before. Sure of it. He belongs to the Marquis de Vendôme, as the young serf says."

*Serf!*

A younger stable boy with a broken front tooth stepped forward and took the reins from Andelot. "I, too, remember him. He's not one to be forgotten, messire. I will see to him at once."

"Merci, ami." Andelot smiled.

Andelot watched the boy leading the majestic animal away to be pampered.

Page Romier had paused and was looking back at Andelot. Doubt now colored his lean face. He tweaked his pointed nose. "So then, if what you boast of is true, and I am not yet the least so convinced, just where is the Marquis Vendôme?"

*Hah, even if I could tell you, you would not believe me.*

Andelot walked up to Page Romier. "I am Andelot Dangeau. I have urgent business with Madame-Duchesse Dushane."

Andelot handed over a preliminary missive edged in Church crimson with *fanfaronnade*.

Romier gave him a glance as he read what Andelot knew was a directive from the cardinal ordering the page to take Andelot to the duchesse. Page Romier scowled his utter dismay.

"Why did you not tell me the cardinal sent you?"

"You did not give me opportunity."

"Are you perchance, then, blood related to the Comte Sebastien Dangeau?"

Andelot smiled with prolonged satisfaction. "Oui, I am his *neveu*. Does not le cardinal say so?"

"You speak well there. But if this is not genuine—" he shook the paper at Andelot—"the cardinal will have the forger's head."

It was time for Andelot to add a bit of scorn. "The risk, messire, will be yours, I assure you, if I am hindered from delivering this lettre as so ordered by the cardinal."

*Who is also my kinsman*, Andelot could have added. However, he did not wish to parry his opponent too far into a corner, for the truth was, that after the recent rampage of horrors against the Huguenots at Amboise, at the urging of the Guise brothers, the cardinal and the duc, Andelot's kinship with the House of Guise did not shine as wondrously as it once had when he first learned he was related to them by blood.

Romier rubbed his nose and studied him anew, seeming to reconsider.

"So be it. Upon the cardinal's insignia, I will admit you to an audience with my madame. Come, I will see you are brought to Comte Sebastien's chambers as soon as your boots are wiped."

"Did you say Comte Sebastien's chambers? Non, I must speak with Madame-Duchesse immediately."

"Madame-Duchesse is now at the comte's chambers. And, if messire does not object unduly," he said in a veiled and dry tone, "we will also shake the dust from your riding cloak."

Andelot gave a stilted bow. "As you wish. Merci."

❦

A SHORT TIME LATER INSIDE THE LOUVRE, Andelot waited in the blue and gold salle of his *oncle* Sebastien Dangeau's appartement. Sebastien had served on the privy council of the Queen Mother, Catherine de Medici, until his recent arrest and imprisonment over his involvement in the Huguenot rebellion at Amboise.

Andelot glanced about the chamber as he waited for his audience with Duchesse Dushane, recalling how he had visited Sebastien here on several occasions when Andelot was younger and attending monastery school.

He admired once more the many treasured tapestry hangings from royal French worthies of the past. The Aubusson rug was worn in a few places but retained its comely heritage. All the chairs were upholstered with multicolored brocades that had a predominance of blue with threads of crimson artfully woven throughout the heavy cloth. The low settees and various cushions for sitting were all tasseled the color of gold. The wooden arms and backs of the chairs were meticulously carved into semblances of grape clusters and vines with petite flower petals, stained pink. A long table he remembered well, boasted the royal Valois *oriflamme* adopted by the renaissance king, Francis I. He walked across the chamber for a closer look.

*I should like to live in a grand place like this with servants to do all my bidding ... and if I had not displeased le cardinal—*

At the sound of footsteps approaching, Andelot turned as a serving-maid hurried in from the back of the appartment. She must have been a maid of lower status, or a cleaning woman, for her garments were ignoble, and her hands were knobby and had pink blotches, he supposed from years of cleaning. He noticed how the woman twisted and pulled on her hands. Some inward agitation most certainly gnawed at her which was reflected in her teary eyes as well. Surely the poor woman had been crying for some time.

She took him for a person of import, despite his common clothing, for she curtsied, not once, but twice.

"Oh, Messire, I fear Madame's ladies cannot come to you now, for they are all at the bedsides of Mesdames Henriette and Madeleine, praying, as they have taken grievously ill."

Henriette was grandmère to the Mesdemoiselles Macquinet. Madeleine was Oncle Sebastien Dangeau's wife. The news was troubling.

"Ill? Both mesdames?"

"Oh Messire, I had naught to do with their illness, I swear it, Messire, though I confess I helped with the *petit déjeuner*, baking the bread. It is—*was*—the fruit. Oui, it must be the fruit, for what else could it be? I assure you, both mesdames ate of the fruit two days ago."

She dropped her face into her palms, and her stooped shoulders shook.

Andelot threw a glance toward the closed doors leading off to the other chambers. Was this news of their illness worthy of his alarm, or was this serving woman overwrought?

"Ill from eating fruit? What manner of fruit was it?"

She shook her head with a small, defensive whimper. "Just some petite apples held over from last autumn's harvest, Messire. That is all. Just some apples. Oh, it was la grande madame, as they call her, the silver-haired couturière from her Château de Silk in Lyon, who first took ill. Ah, it is dreadful. She arrived some weeks ago from Chambord to help her granddaughter, Madame Madeleine, who was *enceinte*. The *bébé*, she was born in March. We were all here. Then, two days ago, Grande

Madame donned herself in most magnifique clothes and went out by carriage to buy some gifts for bébé Joan. Afterward she stopped at the fruit market to buy some rosy apples."

The serving woman's eyes watered over again and dribbled down the creases in her cheeks. "By sunset, after eating the fruit, Grande Madame was oh so ill. Her sickness was dreadful to hear — all the night she was ailing at her stomach — oh, there was naught any of us could do to stop it. She grows weaker by the day and such a kind woman too, Messire, undeserving of such suffering. She gave me lace for a new dress — and her granddaughter, Madame Madeleine, is sick also! Madame-Duchesse Dushane is vexed. She has called her own docteur — he has come several times since yesterday."

Andelot frowned, for the illness sounded far worse than he first guessed.

"This news is most evil, Messire. Perhaps a curse is upon us? I have heard the writings of Nostradamus, warning of dark omens and curses."

"Do not think of it," he said.

The mention of such things brought to mind the chilling atmosphere of the occult at Amboise. He tried to block from his mind the secret laboratory where young Prince Charles Valois had brought him above the Queen Mother's chambers.

He paced across the Aubusson rug. If only Marquis Fabien had not left France! His authority as a Bourbon gave him open doors into the court that few others possessed. Oncle Sebastien had once been a great asset for the family, but not now. There was the duchesse, of course, but she was already doing all she could.

He felt sorry for the woman; she reminded him of the peasant woman in whose charge he had been until his tenth birthday, after which Sebastien had brought him here to the outskirts of Paris to a monastery school.

When the serving woman hurried away, he went to one of the front windows, moved aside the blue and gold hangings, and peered below to the main courtyard.

*Sick ... sick unto death ... ?*

Unrest rattled the door of his mind. There was something he should remember ... He shook his head. So much had happened recently — so much death.

The royal court was not presently in residence here at the Louvre, but they were in the process of making a move to the forest tranquility of Fontainebleau, to one of the royalty's favorite hunting châteaus. The court rarely remained in Paris during the heat of summer, due to its unhealthy air. Those *courtiers* not going to Fontainebleau even now were making plans to return to their own estates. As always, however, they remained prepared to join royalty at the snap of a finger should the king or Queen Mother call for them.

Paris kept up its hum of activity with coaches rattling in and out of the gate, and guards in almost constant patrol in the courtyard. Andelot watched the flash of red and blue uniforms, the glint of their casques in the sunlight holding his attention.

*I should have begged the marquis to let me go to sea with him. He and Nappier could teach me some swordsmanship. What good to remain here in France? My future is small. I shall never become the scholar as I had hoped.*

Andelot sighed. While others loathed the study of books, history, and languages, he was fascinated. He might yet be forced to return to the Château de Silk and work again with silkworms as he had done when a boy. What else was there for him in Paris? The Corps des Pages — ah, that was but a dream, a vague promise of the past, for Cardinal de Lorraine was now angry with him.

Andelot turned from the window, rubbing the back of his neck, frowning. Prisons ... poisons ... What was it that he should remember? There was something ... something stirring at the back of his mind, calling to him, something he had wanted to mention to Marquis Fabien before he rode out, but in the rush of departure he had let it slip from his mind.

He had last seen the marquis not long after Amboise. Marquis Fabien was returning from Vendôme where earlier he had agreed that Comte

Maurice Beauvilliers should first bring Mademoiselle Rachelle for her safety.

Fabien had visited Andelot secretly at night and informed him that he was returning to Vendôme and would be taking Rachelle home to the château. He expected to remain there in Lyon until a message arrived from a certain French privateer, whereupon a meeting of the brotherhood of privateers against Spain would take place in some locale near the coast of La Rochelle, a Huguenot stronghold.

Andelot believed the meeting would have occurred by now. The marquis could even be on his way to Calais to cross the channel to England, where a privateer of the English queen had arranged for the marquis to buy a ship.

Was it too late to join the marquis? The bay would surely get him there, but was there time? What would the marquis do if he showed up with a sword he could but clumsily wield? *Perhaps I could help the cook or serve the marquis in some way.*

Across the chamber, the fire glowed in the hearth. The wind from off the river Seine, which ran beneath portions of the palais with its prison, remained chill and damp.

His boots made no sound as he walked toward the warmth. The red coals hissed and glared at him. Was the illness of Grandmère and Madeleine the beginning of a judgment from heaven that would soon scourge the whole of Paris?

He recalled from his studies at the monastery school how great sicknesses in the past had struck many kingdoms, leaving uncounted masses dead. There were so many bodies, the authorities had been forced to burn them in great fires in the village squares. At the time, traveling monks on pilgrimages across Europe spoke out as prophets, attributing the plagues to judgment sent by the saints for failure to worship and give to the Church. They had urged more reverence for relics and the need to embark on pilgrimages to burial sites. They carried bags of saintly fetishes on their donkeys, which they sold for blessing and protection.

Andelot reached beneath his tunic and removed a small, well-worn cross and kissed it. He had received the object years ago from a traveling monk passing through Paris on his way to the Holy Land on pilgrimage.

This cross was special. The monk had told him it was prayed over and anointed with holy ointment from the eternal city of Rome itself, the city built on seven hills. The cross would protect him from plague. Andelot kissed it once more to make certain before replacing it inside his tunic next to his skin. One could not be too cautious, having entered the chambers where sudden sickness had struck its curse.

He frowned back at the sizzling coals. Yes, it was wholly possible that a new plague was breaking forth. Voices were sounding in protest against the blasphemous teaching of Luther, Calvin, Beza, and against that wicked city, Geneva. Judgments were pronounced on France for not doing enough to silence the devilish teaching of these heretics and their followers.

Andelot ran his fingers through his brown locks and shook his head. These pronouncements heightened his uneasiness after what he had witnessed at Amboise. The flames of religious rhetoric crackled with devilish propaganda. Whom should he believe?

Frustration drove him back to the window again, this time drawing his gaze in the direction of the wharf with its many shops.

*Yes, the quay . . . what was it about the quay he wanted to remember?*

*Ill since Thursday . . . five days ago . . . very ill, the maid had said — due to last autumn's apples.*

*Odd, that. Apples? Could one become this sick on apples?*

A priest strode across the courtyard with a rolled parchment in hand and his robe swirling about his ankles, drawing Andelot's mind to the night before when the cardinal had sent for him to appear in his chamber. After handing him the scarlet-edged missive to deliver to Duchesse Dushane, the cardinal had risen from his chair behind the desk and faced him with a thin curling smile, his almond-shaped gray eyes showing amused contempt.

"So! You are a child full of pranks at heart. You hid under the vines tumbling from a cherub planter to spy on the beheadings of the rebel heretics! Such puerile behavior. Non! Do not try to explain that you were trapped. Such a tale is preposterous."

The lashing words had stung and remembering them again now brought a burning heat to Andelot's face. It was no good to blame the incident on Prince Charles Valois, for Charles was a boy, whereas he himself was a young man. The cardinal had proceeded to lecture him with scorn.

"Nonetheless, I make it my family duty to secure your future, though not in the capacity I had first thought. There may be opportunity for you as a family page, but I will not have you in my inner circle, not with such lack of wisdom as you have shown yourself capable. Perchance I may arrange for a position for training in the Corps des Pages if someone will sponsor you, but, henceforth, all will depend on your obedience and loyalty. Take heed, Andelot; your future success depends entirely on my good graces. The first action you will take is to end your injudicious friendship with Marquis Vendôme, a growing threat to our family house. Refuse me and there is no room for your future in the House of Guise or at Court."

Andelot stared out the palais window. He jammed his hands in his pockets.

The rustle of a skirt brought him back to the present. He turned.

An older woman of stalwart proportions and dignity to match, stood in the chamber leaning on a strong black, jeweled walking stick. He guessed the stick weighed enough to teach an enemy a desperate lesson if she so wished to use it. Andelot had heard that until her recent fall, the duchesse was particularly fond of riding, and even hunting with the king's royal party. Her shoulders were wide and straight beneath a gown of rose silk looped with pearls, with sleeve cuffs and a high collar of stiff cream lace.

He bowed from the waist. "Your Grace."

"I am told you bring us tidings from Amboise?"

"Oui, Madame." And he hesitated, for while it was bonne news, it was also exceedingly dark for Sebastien.

"Comte Sebastien Dangeau is not dead as once we all believed, but alive."

The duchesse's intake of breath prompted Andelot to hasten: "Unfortunately, Madame, he was arrested and is in the dungeons of Amboise."

# Andelot's Nightmare

"SEBASTIEN IS ALIVE?" THE DUCHESSE PLACED HAND AT HEART AS THOUGH stunned.

Andelot bowed to the Duchesse Xenia Dushane and stepped forward, handing her the scarlet-edged envelope with the religious seal.

"He is, Madame. I bring a lettre from le Cardinal de Lorraine."

The news she was about to receive was indeed dark.

"Ah ... I see."

He read nothing in her voice that suggested dislike of the cardinal, and yet he sensed the stiffness in her mood.

He watched her carry the correspondence across the chamber to Sebastien's large desk, where even on a sunny day, one had to kindle lamps to penetrate the shadows that loitered in the palais chambers. Were shadows on his mind today? Wherever he looked his thoughts confronted them.

Andelot stood unobtrusively, steeling his emotions, waiting for her to hammer him for details, but the silence continued. He looked across the chamber at her.

The duchesse sat on the plush blue-and-gold-fringed chair by a window, and for several minutes after reading the cardinal's lettre he could have sworn she had forgotten he was there.

Andelot's compassion grew as lines of dismay deepened on her face. Despite her height and strong shoulders, she seemed to him to be frail and vulnerable. Several times she breathed deeply and shook her gray head as though her burdens were too much to carry. He suspected they were, and that she relied upon her Huguenot faith for the assistance she needed. He knew little about her private doings, but since there was no mention of any Duc Dushane, Andelot perceived that he must have passed on. But then, he had not heard of the duchesse having sons or daughters.

She sat staring out the window, leaning the side of her face against her hand, her elbow on an armrest. Just as he thought she had indeed forgotten him, her attention returned. She looked squarely at him, and a sober resolve reflected in her eyes.

"So then. Comte Sebastien will soon be brought to the Bastille as a traitor to His Majesty. He will also face the inquisitors at the *salle de la question*."

The words struck Andelot like a doubled fist in his stomach.

He had expected painful news but not this!

She shook her head, dropping her forehead against her hand. "God's mercy be with us, and His strength with Sebastien. This will be dire news for Madeleine."

Andelot forced his emotions into abeyance. He stood, hands gripped behind him.

"Le cardinal informs me Sebastien was caught in the woods near Amboise while bringing word to the Huguenot chief Renaudie that the rebellion was known to the king and Queen Mother. Le cardinal also insists to His Majesty that Reformational Geneva was behind the plot to overthrow his rule, and that Monsieur John Calvin himself financed the soldiers with gold."

She used her walking stick to push herself up from the chair, an impatient gleam in her silvery eyes. "It is no great surprise to me that Cardinal de Lorraine would make so groundless a charge against the Reformer. Monsieur Calvin knew of the plot—of course he did. The bulk of the Huguenot soldiers came from Geneva where they had fled for their lives—to where the cardinal could not order the faggots set aflame beneath their feet."

"Madame, who knows who may be listening even in these chambers?" he suggested, though he dare not silence a duchesse.

"Monsieur Calvin did not approve of the rebellion." She banged the tip of her walking stick on the floor. "He warned the Huguenot leaders involved at Amboise that if they went through with their plans, blood would be spilled on both sides. He was clearly against the rebellion."

"Oui, Madame, he would not sanction rebellion against the king," he hastened, avoiding words to the contrary. Andelot could not help wondering how it was that the duchesse apparently knew what John Calvin may have spoken to the Huguenot chiefs. That she declared she had known about the rebellion beforehand was dangerous. He feared what the Queen Mother would say if she or the cardinal knew. But the duchesse seemed impervious to any risk to herself as she limped about on her dazzling black walking stick, its jewels glimmering in the lamplight.

The Huguenot leaders had planned to make a Bourbon prince of the blood the regent instead of King Francis. It was then that Catholic spies in London, favorable to the rule of the Guises, learned of the plot and alerted Duc de Guise. The duc had persuaded the spy to confess all to the Queen Mother. This unveiling helped the Guises set a trap which led to the slaughter of thousands at Amboise. Andelot had heard from Fabien that Duchesse Dushane had warned of a betrayer, Maître Avenelle, among the Huguenots. Avenelle, once a Huguenot himself, had renounced his Protestant beliefs, then disclosed the plot to rid France of the Guises whom the Huguenots considered as naught but Spain's legates and proponents of the Inquisition, rather than true Frenchmen.

"The bloody massacre at Amboise," the duchesse said passionately, shaking her head. "Marquis Fabien wrote me about it, as did the cardinal, but from quite opposite viewpoints, I assure you. Such diabolical carnage is unthinkable!" She looked across the chamber at him. "Marquis Fabien informed me you witnessed this wicked deed."

He found he could not talk of it without revulsion and nausea. "Oui, Madame. I was there, hiding as it were, and could not escape the scene until it was over." As he thought of the deaths, the carnage he had witnessed in the square at Amboise flashed across his mind, and the cries of the Huguenots echoed. He could still hear the whack of the ax and feel the chilly March wind rustling the vines around him where he hid in the courtyard.

She must have gleaned his deep aversion to discussing it, for she gave a short nod, and much to his relief did not pursue the matter.

"The marquis mentioned in his earlier correspondence to me that you are a bon ami?"

"Oui, Madame. We are very close friends."

She nodded. "He speaks well of you." Her lips tightened. She looked down at the correspondence in her hand. Her voice lowered. "Sebastien will soon be brought to the Bastille."

Andelot cleared his throat to restrain the emotions welling up within his soul. He had a deep affection for his oncle Sebastien, who had been good to him through the years.

"Marquis Fabien tells me I can trust you, Andelot. Even so, this missive from the cardinal—" she shook it at him—"also confirms you are now in his service." Her narrow silver brows inched upward in question.

Andelot felt the heat of embarrassment. The pressure of two masters, each demanding loyalty, squeezed his heart.

She did not wait for his explanation, giving rise to the thought that she had not truly expected one. His frustration wheedled him, but again he held back his emotions.

"Le marquis told me he will soon be leaving France for a time," she said, a note of thoughtfulness in her tone.

*So Fabien confides in the duchesse. If he trusts her allegiance with the cause that pulsates in his blood, then so will I.*

He shifted his stance. "Madame, you do seem to be aware of the affairs of the marquis. Yes, he is now in league with certain French and English buccaneers—allied against Spain's shipping." He added quickly, "There is also an eventual plan to aid Admiral Coligny, to reinforce an earlier colony of his in a place called Florida. I believe it is named Fort Caroline."

She looked grim, drumming her long fingers with gold rings set with emeralds and sapphires.

"And the small colony is at peril from the well-equipped Spanish garrison called St. Augustine. Ah, Andelot, I believe Marquis Fabien plays a dangerous game, as I am sure you are aware."

"Oui, very dangerous, Madame. Marquis Fabien is intent upon taking his ship to England where English buccaneers await him."

"The marquis warned me to leave Paris for my estates in Orléans," she said several moments later. "I believe the Guise brothers, the duc and the cardinal, hope to learn the names of those at Court who may have been involved in the Amboise plot—if there were any at Court so involved." She looked at him with eyes as frosty as a winter's morn. "My assessment of why Sebastien remains yet alive in the dungeon is that it enables our enemies to force him to betray his associates. Do you agree, Andelot?"

"Oui, Madame."

He had heard from Fabien that Duchesse Dushane was a private ally of the Huguenots, and known as a woman of some authority within the inner echelons of Court life. She was one of those privileged few of high title who belonged to the Queen Mother's afternoon cercle. Accordingly, the duchesse possessed knowledge of the happenings at Court that had proven to be desperately important to her friends. On a number of occasions she had warned the Huguenot nobles of danger. Marquis Fabien's Bourbon kinsmen, Princes Louis and Antoine, in particular, had been warned of murderous plots hatched against them by enemies at Court—all for power, for the House of Bourbon had legal claim to the throne—and so the House of Guise and their allies at Court wished to destroy them.

What had the cardinal written to the duchesse besides giving her the austere news that Sebastien had been charged with duplicity in the plot?

"Madame-Duchesse, may I be so bold as to urge you to heed Marquis Fabien's request that you depart for your estate in Orléans? And if Sebastien is not released from the Amboise dungeon, would not his wife and newborn be better in the protective company of her parents at Lyon?"

"Your concern is well taken, Andelot. Under varied circumstances, I too would heartily agree with the marquis. Unfortunately he was not aware of the grief that has befallen us with this sudden illness. Henriette cannot be moved just now, nor Madeleine. The maid told you, I believe, of this illness?"

"She did, Madame. I hoped it was not as dire as she described."

She heaved a sigh. "It is le docteur's opinion that cousine Henriette should not leave her bedchamber until she gains strength enough for the arduous journey. And Madeleine — well, perhaps; but she has begun to worsen, having been stricken a day later than her grandmère Henriette."

She heaved herself up from the chair using her walking stick and moved over to the window. "And I am becoming too old and set in my ways to flee before the baying hounds. The news of so many men dying needlessly at Amboise has been disheartening, and the news of Sebastien, more personal and crushing, especially to Madeleine. I dread to inform her — and coming so soon after the birth of their first *enfant*!" She shook her head. "Ah, so great a trial. God's mercies and extended grace are much in need. We will all need greater strength and unfettered faith in His purposes for us and for France as well. We must lean upon the grace of God." She bent toward him, favoring her stick.

The lamplight sparkled on the ebony cane. *Lean upon the grace of God.* She, in her weakness, was kept from stumbling, for her confidence in Christ was not misplaced. Andelot contemplated her steadfast faith.

"The decision to leave cannot yet be made," she continued. "Madeleine must decide when she awakens. I will show her the lettres. We will discuss her ability to travel with le docteur. As for me, I will remain here with Henriette, regardless of the medical decision for Madeleine." She gave him a measuring glance. "I am surprised you did not go with Marquis Fabien."

"Oui, Madame. I had considered joining Marquis Fabien's voyage," he admitted boldly, straightening his shoulders. He was pleased he had gained muscle in recent months.

"He was against that idea?"

"I cannot say, for I did not approach him on the subject, Madame. I fear my expertise with the sword is lacking. Not that he would refuse me for that cause alone. However, there was an opportunity here in France that I desired far more than going to sea and visiting the Huguenot colony."

*What he does not know is that the opportunity is no longer available to me.*

"Perhaps it is well you did not go, Andelot. Though Marquis Fabien has not said so in his lettre, I suspect he has more on his mind than financing a voyage to reinforce a colony for Admiral Coligny. However—" and her expression grew troubled as she studied him—"remaining in France may yet prove as full of risk for your future as taking to the seas."

She might have heard through her many spies that he was, in some way, related to the Guises. Perhaps she knew something of the cardinal's dire plans for him.

"Marquis Fabien walks a dangerous line as well, Madame."

"Assuredly. And if he sinks a galleon, he will hear the angry wail of revenge all the way from Madrid to the ear of the Queen Mother. I suppose he made up his mind to take to the sea upon thinking Sebastien dead. I cannot envision him leaving if he knew Sebastien were to face the inquisitors."

"I believe you are right, Madame. He was told by his own Bourbon kinsman, Prince Condé, that Sebastien had been killed with the Huguenot seigneur, Renaudie, in the woods. The marquis also thought that Mesdames Henriette and Madeleine would return together to the Macquinets at the Château de Silk, and that Sebastien's wife and newborn would be comforted there."

"It will be a grievous trial for Madeleine when she learns that her husband lives only to face the inquisitors. She will want the company of her family at the Château de Silk. It is unfortunate this sudden illness that plagues her and her grandmère interferes with any hope of immediate travel to Lyon." A stalwart look of resignation settled into her countenance.

Andelot tore his gaze from the walking stick. He bowed lightly. "Just so, Madame."

"Very well, then. Wait here until I call Romier to take you to the dining hall and then to your barracks. You need food and rest. I will call for you again this evening after I speak to le docteur. I must also decide on whether to try to intercept the marquis with the news of Sebastien."

*Ah—food, rest, and sleep!*

"Merci mille fois, Madame-Duchesse!"

ANDELOT WALKED WITH THE page, Romier, across a courtyard toward the barracks located behind the main palais.

The Louvre, built by Philippe Auguste, stood on the grassy margin of the river Seine with the palais walls and bastions surrounded by a moat. It was here at the Louvre that Andelot had first met Marquis Fabien. Fabien had been in the royal company of the Dauphin Francis and Mary of Scotland when he had come to Andelot's rescue. A group of pages, all sons of the nobility, had decided to teach him he was naught but a peasant, more suited to wiping muddy boots than keeping their company. A page was threatening to toss him into the moat when Marquis Fabien approached with a warning: "Andelot is related to me by marriage. As such, anyone who touches him henceforth will have me to contend with."

After that, no one in the Corps des Pages troubled him again.

The dining area in the barracks had its own pantry and a large cooking area. Together with the buttery, the room encompassed the whole left wing of the barracks. The area was raftered with dark beams, its walls darkened from generations of cooking. The cookery was rich in pewter, iron, and copper. The canopied fireplace took the whole of the right wall, and on the other side a long, low table with benches worn to a smooth polish.

Preparations for *déjeuner* were underway. The savory aroma of meat on a spit told Andelot how hungry he was. He would eat and retire to a bunk for some sleep before the young men in training would arrive from their duties. There were several hounds licking out greasy cooking pans by the buttery. A precocious cock wandered about in search of tidbits of ground corn, looking as if it dared the hounds to chase it away.

"Something to wet our throats," Romier said to a serving boy, who looked to be eight or nine years old. It was not unusual to see even younger children working long hours in the barns, stables, cooking area, and laundry rooms.

"Leon, fetch that lamb joint to the table — there's a good lad — and draw us a pitcher from the ale cask. Set out cups and water in the basins."

Andelot washed, then took a place at the bench. The aroma of broiled lamb browned and dripping with melted fat wafted to him. The bread was cut in generous slices, and Andelot's cup was filled with ale. He dipped a chunk of oven-warmed bread into his bowl of lamb's broth floating with onions.

As he devoured his meal he consoled himself, musing over the possibility that once he moved among the blooded nobles as kin to the cardinal and the duc, matters would change. There would be no more Romiers to wink and chuckle because he looked like a serf. He frowned and gnawed the lamb bone.

The door flew open and several pages hurried in, their boyish faces flushed with dread or excitement.

"News from Amboise! Riders have just come. There was a rebellion by the Huguenots against the king. Comte Sebastien Dangeau was one of them. He has been arrested and will soon be sent to the Bastille. The others are dead. There was a great slaughter ordered by the cardinal and Duc de Guise."

Romier pounded the pages with questions, but they had no more information to give.

"You are certain of all this?" Doubt marked Romier's lean face. "Ah, but it cannot be!" Romier doubled a fist and struck his other palm. "Renaudie was a noble messire."

"Do not permit the royalists to hear you speak thus," said one of the pages.

Andelot got to his feet. "It is true. I was there and saw the horrors. It is the cause for which I have traveled here to Paris. I have come straight from Amboise to bring this dark word about mon oncle Sebastien to Madame-Duchesse Dushane."

They turned to look at him. The fiery cauldron brewing in Romier's eyes made Andelot wonder if he should not have held his tongue altogether.

"You were at Amboise? With the Guises?" Romier asked.

"I was there, not with the Guises, but with Marquis Fabien de Vendôme."

Romier said with a tinge of regret, "It is so, messieurs. He rode in on a golden bay. The stable attendants vow the horse is the marquis' best stallion."

Andelot felt a touch of pride over being trusted with the marquis' horse.

There was a moment of studied silence.

All eyes were upon him now.

Romier drew Andelot aside to the table. "Sit down and finish your meat. You have journeyed far if you come from Amboise. Make known to me the failing of the Huguenot uprising. And how is it Duc de Guise captured Monsieur Renaudie?"

Romier appeared to know more than he had first let on. No one among the pages had even mentioned that the seigneur of the rebellion had been Renaudie.

Romier's gaze had lost its coldness.

Andelot calmed himself, and ignoring the pages who loitered around the table, removed the one weapon he did own, a long-bladed knife given him by the marquis, and sliced a hunk of yellow cheese. He looked evenly at Romier as he cut into it. Andelot told of the slaughter of the Huguenots at Amboise, but emphasized that the beheadings were ordered by the Queen Mother, Catherine de Medici. He could see the alarm brewing in Romier's face.

"Why did you not tell me this when you first rode in? I would surely have paid heed to you!"

"You were slow to listen and quick to mock."

Romier waved an impatient hand between them. He leaned forward, jabbing a finger in the air toward Andelot. "You are most certain Comte Sebastien is not dead?"

"He is alive. And will be brought before the salle de la question for his Huguenot faith."

Romier groaned. "If only this had not happened now. Surely the marquis would have done something to save him? He is related by marriage. He is also an ami of the king. I have heard they knew one another since youth. They were schooled together here at the Louvre."

Andelot knew he must be more cautious with his information. He had made several errors already, due most assuredly to his weariness. He believed he could trust Romier, but voices carried in the large room, and there were many pages loyal to the House of Guise.

"The marquis does not know of Sebastien's capture. When they departed Vendôme, it was believed that Sebastien had been killed."

"Ah!" Romier dropped his forehead against his palm and lowered his voice. "Why not turn to Admiral Coligny? My madame has confidence in him."

"The admiral is aware of Amboise. He has called upon the Queen Mother and King Francis to grant a religious colloquy to discuss the reasons for Huguenot rebellion."

"Mon père fought under the admiral, and he is a brave seigneur," Romier said. "If he will bring the Huguenot cause before the king in this upcoming colloquy, then we are well represented. But it will not help Comte Sebastien."

Silence settled over them.

Andelot frowned, musing over the unsolvable problems.

Finally Romier shook his head. "There could be no more evil news for Comte Sebastien's wife than this that you bring to her now, Andelot."

"It pains me well, I assure you, for as I have said, Sebastien is mon oncle."

Romier scowled. "Madame Madeleine is not fully capable of understanding her husband's plight now. It is the strange sickness that has come upon her. She is often not aware. I overheard le docteur tell my madame."

"What did he say?" Andelot asked.

"That he suspects poisoning."

Andelot stared. "Poison?"

"But, yes — from spoilage. There could be no other cause than the bad fruit, for both the grande dame of the Château de Silk and Madame Madeleine became sick. Only they ate the apples."

"Apples ..." Andelot repeated, frowning at his mug of warm ale.

Bad fruit, yes; spoiled, perhaps. Perhaps the little worms were in the apples, and they ate them and did not recognize the fact until — non,

non, that is all wrong. Why, he had seen much spoiled fruit eaten by goats and they had seemed well enough — certainly they did not become poisoned. He pushed his mug away, feeling light-headed himself. He was weary, exhausted, that was all. Sleep, he needed sleep.

He pushed his chair back and stood. By this evening when he met with the duchesse again, his optimism should have returned, though there was little reason to think so.

He excused himself from Romier and was shown by a lackey to the rear grounds of the Louvre where the barracks of the Corps des Pages were located. A small bunk invited him. He removed his boots and settled to the bunk. He shut his eyes and threw an arm across his forehead to blot out the daylight from a nearby window.

Was there not something he wanted to remember, something that required attention? *What was it?* he pondered, while succumbing to the warm, comforting arms of mothering sleep.

❦

ANDELOT WATCHED THE BOY, *Prince Charles Valois, open the door, peek inside, then beckon him to follow. Andelot felt himself floating through passage after passage. Where am I? Amboise ... the palais of Amboise. They stopped before a giant menacing door.*

*Charles sneered at him, took hold of his arm, and drew him into a large shadowy chamber.*

*"Come, peasant, this way," Charles hissed.*

*Andelot heard Marquis Fabien's voice, whispering chilling tales of Catherine de Medici in his ear. "Soothsayers abide wherever she resides. Cosmo Ruggiero came with her from Florence. He never leaves her but for short periods. Cosmo the astrologer, the alchemist, puts dead men's bones in the fire, stirs up powders and perfumes. He draws her horoscopes and makes petite wax figures in the likeness of those who have stirred her enmity. They are to suffer pangs as their wax similitude's melt into the flames. Cosmo is a purveyor of poisons for Her Majesty. He and his brother handle herbs and roots fatal to life. There on the quay near the Louvre they have their shop."*

*Andelot, as though in a trance, followed Charles into a small writing closet built into a turret.*

*"Behold a secret stairway." Charles grinned. He opened a narrow door built into the stone and pointed upward.*

*Andelot peered past him toward a flight of steep stone steps. Charles held the candle which flared in a draft.*

*"This way, peasant, hurry!"*

*Andelot found himself on the stairs rushing upward, with Charles's cackling laughter gaining distance on him. "Hurry, hurry, hurry —"*

*Charles stopped before a door at the top, removed a golden key, and entered. Andelot stepped up into a laboratory with a bunk, a chair, and a desk, upon which lay an ancient manuscript. The writing was in Latin with zodiac chart illustrations. To one side was a drawing of a woman named Semerimus and a ziggurat that wound up into the clouds.*

*"What say the stars, peasant? Can you read them?" Charles mocked.*

*Andelot stared at a cabinet against the wall. He saw many vials and sealed packets, dried herbs and powders. On one of the sealed packets was written*: For Her Majesty. White powder. Very strong. Sprinkle on flowers, book pages, and inside gloves. Death within days.

*Suddenly Charles wore a mask of fear. "Maman is coming. Flee!"*

*Andelot bolted for the door and darted with Charles down the outer steps and onto a ledge. The wind lashed and rain whipped his face. A blinding streak lit up the gray, rushing Loire flowing beneath him crammed with Huguenot bodies choking the dam. He was losing his balance on the ledge, as the martyrs beneath him made room for him to follow —*

*"Saints preserve me!"*

❊

ANDELOT SAT UP, HIS heart thudding, sweat upon his neck, his hands grasping at the bunk frame.

*Poison.*

The sun had set, and only a vestige of twilight peered in through the window.

From the corner of his eye he caught a movement at the doorway. He turned his head. It was Romier.

"My madame sends word. You are to see her now."

Andelot rushed behind a curtain to pour a bucket of water over himself. Shivering, he proceeded to dry off and change into the fresh garments from a pack roll that Romier must have laid out for him. Andelot expressed his gratitude to the page while he hurriedly dressed to keep his meeting with the duchesse.

Torchlights blazed at the entrances to the palais as Andelot crossed the courtyard. Guards stood with plumed helmets, shining silver and bronze, their boots polished and gleaming.

Reaching Comte Sebastien Dangeau's chambers, Andelot was met by Duchesse Dushane. Her face was strained.

"Andelot, I report grievous news. Le docteur is with my cousine, Madame Henriette, now. He tells me she is dying and he cannot save her." Her voice cracked and she turned — quickly, holding a handkerchief to her mouth.

Andelot saw her shoulders shaking beneath her gown.

He was at a loss to know what to do in the presence of so great a titled lady, overcome by sorrow. Should he try to comfort her? Put an arm around her shoulder? Lead her to a chair?

He merely stood with head bent. Suddenly he thought of Rachelle and her sister Idelette, and the Macquinet family at the Château de Silk. How bitter this news would be for them. Grandmère was beloved, and her death would be a severe loss to the family.

Duchesse Dushane was in control of herself again, dabbing her handkerchief at her eyes and cheeks. The thought was pressed that sorrow, death, and loss came to all, both poor and great. In the end, whether peasant or king, death came. Watching Madame-Duchesse weeping, helpless against the grim reaper, with jewels twinkling on hands growing old, caused his soul to cry, *Who then can gain the victory over death and the grave?*

"Is there nothing then, Madame, that can be done?"

She shook her silver head slowly. "Non."

Andelot could not explain the agony that seemed to come to him from nowhere, stooping his youthful shoulders.

*Is there nothing then, O my soul? Nothing but death and loss? Oh! Pity then the moment that gives the crying enfant life!*

"If only Henriette's daughter, Clair, and her granddaughters, especially Idelette and Rachelle, could be here to say their au revoir. How dismaying that they are not," the duchesse said. "Even Madeleine — in the very next bedchamber, is too ill to rise and go to her grandmère's bedside."

Andelot paced around the chamber as her words broke through his concerns. The duchesse was now sitting and seemed to be struggling to bring her feelings under her usual firm grip.

*Dare he suggest what was on his mind? Why not? It was fair to Rachelle, a granddaughter so firmly attached to her beloved grandmère.*

"Madame? I would ask that you send me at once to the Château de Silk. I will bring the Macquinet mesdemoiselles here."

"Yes, I thought of that, but there is not time enough, Andelot — she is most ill."

"S'il vous plaît, Madame. I have a horse, the marquis' horse! He races like the wind. If the marquis knew the urgency, he would have me use his stallion to accomplish this feat. It would mean much to the Macquinets, I assure you, if they but knew the shortness of time, Madame."

She looked at him with a sympathetic expression. "And what is your determined interest in all of this?"

Andelot hastened: "You see, I was raised at the Château de Silk in Lyon by a nurse until mon oncle Sebastien came and brought me to Paris where I was placed in a monastery school. I remember well the dignified woman the Macquinet Daughters of Silk so affectionately called Grandmère. I should feel it my duty to do my utmost to see Mademoiselle Rachelle has one last meeting with her grandmère — to kneel beside her bed and pray."

She appeared to take control of her emotions once more and walked over to the desk using her walking stick.

She was now the Duchesse Xenia Dushane, in command by right of blood title. "Yes, you must try to bring Rachelle, at least, to say *adieu*. It is appropriate and most telling of you, Andelot."

He felt the color rise up his neck to warm him. This great lady approved of him.

"I will send my chief page with you." She rang a small gong and Romier, who had waited outside the door, entered.

He bowed. "Your Grace?"

"Prepare my fastest horse. You will ride with Andelot to Lyon tonight."

"*Tout de suite*, Madame-Duchesse!"

# The Summons from Paris

THE DAY AFTER MARQUIS VENDÔME'S DEPARTURE, RACHELLE WAS convinced her life was over. The future that lay before her was arid and hopeless. She wished she had never seen Fabien, and forgetting her own willful part in what had happened, blamed him for her troubles. She forgot that she had eagerly wanted him, and instead she hated him for leaving her and for his failure to commit himself to marriage. She refused to accept his reasoning that time was needed, or that her family would resent her marriage to a Catholic. Why had he not seen fit to discuss this before? Why had not she?

Rachelle mulled over her problems. Added to her sorrow was grief over the death of her petite sister, Avril, and the violation of Idelette. There seemed no solution to her misery. Even so, her thoughts returned too often to Fabien.

*I was a fool to fall in love with him*, she thought again.

As time passed, however, she began to awaken to her own accountability. Perhaps she had tried too hard with him? She recalled what her eldest sister Madeleine had once advised her when discussing the marquis: "Men can be elusive creatures when you try to catch them. Doing so may take the relationship to an early grave, especially before they have fully made up their own mind about a woman. If she moves in quickly to stake her claim, a man may reconsider — and even step back. Dealing honorably requires your patience, but this will enable you to tell the difference between a man who will not commit himself to you, and the one who will take his commitment to you seriously — for a lifetime — but will not do so hastily. The marquis has been taking his time and has avoided many potential traps. He is, however, a most problematic *galant*. He wishes to possess—but does not wish to be possessed. I would strongly advise you to not pursue him until he chooses to be caught."

"You seem to know much about him."

Madeleine had shrugged. "Do not forget I have seen him grow up at Court. He is Sebastien's *neveu* by marriage. I have seen the belle mesdemoiselles—many of them from high nobility—trying to capture him. They all have made the same mistake; selling themselves too cheaply, making themselves too easily caught—and probably not worth having."

"Is it all but a game then?" Rachelle had asked ruefully.

"Not a game, but the prelude for a most serious relationship that must endure through every joy and tribulation. I advise, chère sister, that you make yourself a desirable treasure he struggles to win, not the other way around."

Thinking of the last scene with him, Rachelle's frown deepened. She winced, remembering how she had pleaded and run after him, literally holding on to his sleeves. She felt a hot blush stain her cheeks. *How could I have acted so? Because I love him!* But that love, her sister would say, must be tempered with wisdom and dignity.

It was awful to think that she might appear to Fabien to have fallen into the footsteps of Madame Charlotte de Presney, who had plotted to corner Fabien in the garden.

Rachelle thought about her tendency to ignore obstacles and risks that stood in the way of her desires. She preferred to avoid thinking of them, or if she did acknowledge their presence, she would tell herself that they would be easier to deal with if left for the distant future. And now she had surely set her heart upon Marquis Fabien de Vendôme while ignoring some serious obstacles. Though his place in her heart was as solid as the architecture of the Louvre, she began to wonder if he might have been but a secret dream of a wide-eyed damsel desiring a prince of her own.

Rachelle forced her mind, as well as her heart, to confront the staggering issues that stood between her and the marquis, and they were more numerous than she had previously thought. First, his religious loyalties disturbed her family. In practice he was not blindly loyal to Rome, but was that enough for her parents and Grandmère? He attended daily Mass at noon when at Court; whereas true Huguenots went to the Bastille dungeon and then the fiery stake before compromising the greatest truth recovered from Scripture: of justification from all unrighteousness and every sin by faith alone in Christ's finished work on the cross once for all.

Secondly, there was his royal Bourbon bloodline. No matter what Fabien told her of his freedom to choose the woman he wanted, was that truly so? She knew so little of what his Bourbon relatives expected of him, though she was most certain that the Bourbon princes fully expected him to marry a princesse from one of the royal houses of Europe, or at least a woman of high nobility. Rachelle's own heritage was far from peasantry, and she was proud of the reputation of the Macquinets among other couturier families on the continent, but she did not have the blood of kings' daughters. Grandmère's cousine was Duchesse Xenia Dushane, but that did little for Rachelle, who would not inherit the title. In contrast, the Bourbons were in line for the throne of France after the Valois, and it was no secret that Valois sons were in weak health. What would a marriage alliance with Rachelle Macquinet bring the Bourbons other than a name in silk?

Fabien would most assuredly have a light and debonair retort, but the serious truth remained: if Fabien must win over her Huguenot family, Rachelle must win over the princes of the blood!

She wondered seriously for the first time how far he would be willing to go in denying obligations to his bloodline. Fabien's near relatives, Prince Louis de Condé and Antoine de Bourbon, the King of Navarre, would have great sway over him. Thus far, they had not meddled. Perhaps that was due to his youth. Strange, how she often thought of Fabien as mature. As for wisdom, he did seem to have his share. He had avoided a mistress and an illegitimate child, the sinful bane that touched the indulgent nobles like a plague. It was so common that something must be said for a young man, of his virility and status, to have avoided it. Did that not speak eloquently for his self-discipline, his spiritual convictions? As for the Bourbons' show of apparent indifference to his marriage, that could change as quickly as an announced engagement.

As she stared into the icy reality confronting her, Rachelle wondered how she could have possibly been so naive. For all practical purposes, it was not even possible for their relationship to become more than a brief romantic interlude.

Her stomach tightened. Oh, to just discover at the last moment that she was a secret princess! Or perhaps have Duchesse Dushane unexpectedly leave her title to her — *La Duchesse Rachelle Dushane-Macquinet!*

She laughed derisively at herself, then just as quickly tears came to her eyes. There were no secret princesses on either side of her family, and one was not likely to spring up with the daffodils. Non, reality was oft bitter and hard as the death of Avril and the cruelty to Idelette, and there was no simple solution to her love for the marquis. She had best face the truth. She was not a silly dreamer like her grisette maid, Nenette, who waited for a comte to ride up on his stallion and take her as his comtesse.

Rachelle had understood that it was a risk to fall in love with the marquis — and she had lost.

THE WIND ROSE WITH unexpected fury before a rainstorm moved in and pelted the windows of the château. Rachelle lifted her dark blue skirts and sped up the stairs clutching her father's urgent lettre. It was late, the house silent now but for the noise of the torrent of rain. She must alert her mère to Arnaut's dangerous dilemma. There was little time to lose. On the landing, curling her fingers around the glossy banister, she thought of the marquis. He would be soaked to the skin before he and Gallaudet reached the inn where the rest of his men waited. Would they stay the night there or ride on? Knowing Fabien, he would brave the wind and rain.

She narrowed her gaze, furious with herself for allowing his situation to trouble her mind. "I hope he drowns," she gritted and flounced along the corridor where the Venetian glass wall sconces glimmered like heavenly light through a prism. After a moment she stopped outside Clair's chamber. The lamps were yet burning and sending a wedge of waning light beneath the door. She tapped lightly.

Nenette opened the door. The rims of her eyes were pink, showing losing bouts with tears.

"Is she asleep, Nenette?"

"She is awake, but Mademoiselle Idelette is asleep," she murmured.

Rachelle knew her mère had brought Idelette to her chamber tonight to sleep, that she might watch over her and comfort her.

She entered the chamber, which was decorated in soft tones of ivory and lavender, and glanced toward the large bed recessed into the wall. The filmy curtain with lavender lace trim was drawn closed on one side.

Clair must have heard her entry, for she came around the side of the curtained bed. Seeing Rachelle, she walked toward her, her dressing gown of silvery-blue floating behind her. Her golden-gray hair was undone and hung in a long braid across her shoulder. She looked exhausted but her light blue eyes were awake.

"Rachelle, ma chére, I thought you would be in bed by now. I was preparing to come and bid you a night's rest. Idelette has finally fallen asleep."

Rachelle joined her mother in an alcove near a window with the draperies pulled closed against the pummeling rain. Though they were alone with no one untrustworthy to overhear, in a low voice, Rachelle swiftly explained why she had come, and then handed her mère the lettre.

Clair stood and paced slowly as she read of her husband's dilemma.

"I must write Arnaut of the worsening danger to him and to us. Calais is alive with Spanish loyalists. If this lettre had fallen into the hands of the soldiers at the inn and taken to Duc de Guise, I have little doubt but that he would have ordered the arrest of us all this night." She turned to Rachelle. "How did the student escape their notice at the inn?"

Rachelle controlled her emotions as she spoke. "We have Marquis de Vendôme to thank for his swift action. I tried to keep from him the knowledge that Duc de Guise was behind the killings, but he discovered the truth. He and his page, Gallaudet, rode to the inn where the student was about to be questioned by two of Guise's soldiers. Fabien and Gallaudet challenged Guise's soldiers, demanding to know where the duc had made his camp for the night, enabling the student to flee. As they argued, the soldiers drew swords and a duel ensued. The two soldiers were killed."

Once again Clair was placed in the uncomfortable position of indebtedness to Marquis Fabien, as she had been several weeks ago when he had escorted Rachelle home from his estate at Vendôme. Rachelle had been unchaperoned while there, which raised a frown on her mother's brow. Later, feeling embarrassed by the incident, Rachelle commented to Idelette that her possible death at Amboise had seemed less threatening to her family than her perfectly innocent stay in a private chamber at Vendôme. "I assure you there was a strong bolt on the door," she had quipped to Idelette.

"Where is le marquis now?" Clair asked.

Rachelle concealed her dire grief mingled with anger, lest her mother see just how deeply she cared for the marquis. "He has departed once again, as usual. He claims that urgent business has developed, and he regrets his inability to personally thank you for your hospitality."

"He has left then?"

Her mother did not know of Fabien's buccaneering plans and showed her bewilderment.

"Oui, he rode out several hours ago and will not be back — not for a very long time. He is voyaging to England."

*How disappointed Mère would be had she seen my shameless pleading for him to stay.*

Rachelle again thought of how great a lady her mother was, while she herself lacked patience and self-sacrifice. Why was there such a difference between herself and her mère and Idelette? Rachelle blamed it on her spiritual waywardness. *If only I were as dedicated to God as they are, I should be most different in my temperament.*

"The marquis is going to England?" Clair looked at her.

Rachelle realized her mistake. Her mother would disapprove of her journey to London to work for a time with the Hudsons if the marquis were staying in England also. Rachelle needed to show she was not enamored with him.

"He will not remain in England for long, I assure you. I believe he mentioned to Cousin Bertrand that he is sponsoring some of the expense of bringing supplies to Fort Caroline, in the Americas."

"Florida? Ah, oui, your père spoke of the colony to me as well, some time ago. I did not know the marquis was an ami of the Huguenot admiral."

Rachelle decided to keep silent and not rush to reinforce Fabien's reputation by aligning him with the devout Huguenot, Admiral Coligny.

Clair again studied the message in her hand, and her elegant features tensed. "Arnaut must be warned with all speed. Bertrand cannot travel to Calais anytime soon. The student, Mathieu, was it? I shall need to send him to your père come morning. Have you seen to his needs?"

"Oui, he is well settled for the night with food and clothing."

"A lettre must suffice to your père. How did Mathieu arrive, by horse?"

"Non, on foot from the inn. I did not see a horse."

"Then a horse will be given him, and I shall see to his expenses. I wish I might go to your père myself, but—" she shook her head and looked toward her bed—"it is not wise to leave your sister now."

Rachelle would have asked to go to Calais in her place, but she saw no weakening in her mother's stance.

Clair's eyes softened, and she laid her palm against Rachelle's cheek in a gesture of motherly endearment. "You need your sleep, ma petite. Go to your rest now, try not to worry. Our burdens are very heavy, but it will not always be so. He will lead us through this darkness."

Rachelle nodded, trying to offer a small smile for her mother's sake. *Do not betray your feelings now.*

She walked to the bed and gently moved aside the curtain to look in on her sister. Idelette had taken the sleeping medicine and was in deep slumber. The sight of her bruised face tugged at Rachelle's heart. She narrowed her eyes as smoldering anger leaped to renewed flames.

*It is not in me to forgive so easily. I loathe Duc de Guise! I should not be robbed a moment's rest if the marquis ran him through with a sword!*

THE NEXT MORNING CLAIR'S family bid adieu to Mathieu, who would leave for Geneva with a new wardrobe, money for his journey, and some extra for his Bible training, as well as Rachelle's own horse, which she had presented to him as a gift. Mathieu was overwhelmed with Macquinet brotherly love and vowed he would rather die than fail in his service to the Lord Jesus.

"If it would help to bring the Bibles to Spitalfields, I would swim across the channel with them."

"May the Lord provide a drier conveyance," Cousin Bertrand said weakly from his bed, his humor intact. They had all laughed, one of the first times since the attack. It had made Bertrand's prayer as Mathieu knelt inside the chamber one that came as close to joy as Rachelle remembered.

Avril's funeral was held on estate property, and Bertrand insisted on being carried to the graveside on a litter to conduct the service. The only one who did not attend was Sir James Hudson because of his injured leg. He stated that if a second person were carried to the family cemetery on a stretcher, it would discourage even the most stalwart.

This was but one of the funerals that took place in the village district outside of Lyon that week, for there were many, most done in haste. Rachelle had heard, with a cautious glance along the back roads, that many of the Huguenots expected the Duc de Guise to return. There would be other villages and other attacks against the heretics. Some believed it had been merely by unfortunate chance that the duc had ridden this direction on a Sunday morning and found an "unlawful assembly of worshipers who would not attend Mass," and therefore had to be killed. But after what Mathieu said about the two soldiers at the inn, Rachelle did not believe so. Some found the stark reality of planned persecution too difficult to accept. They would not believe that evil reigned in the minds of their fellow citizens who would turn on them if the right happenstance stirred them up. Rachelle had heard it over and over again. *Not here. It can never happen here the way it does in other towns. The Duc d'Alva will never come to France.*

"He does not need to come," Rachelle had quipped the afternoon of the funeral when neighbors came to pay their respects. "The King of Spain has his legates: le Duc de Guise and Cardinal de Lorraine."

Several of the neighbors were not Huguenots and looked at her sharply, and Madame Clair smoothly intervened with a change of subject and a firm glance in Rachelle's unrepentant direction. She had left the grand salle after that, and when everyone had gone home, her mother had sought Rachelle in the garden. It was a pleasant spring day after the rains, and the flowers were in bloom with birds trilling.

"Ma chére, you must guard your tongue. You are becoming cynical and too sharply spoken."

"I see no reason to be corrected in speech in order to not offend them. Can they not handle the truth?"

"Truth must be spoken in love."

Rachelle knew as much. "I am sorry, ma mere, if I embarrassed you, but I care not what they think."

"You must care. They are our neighbors. We must live together in respect of one another and in peace, if we can. Remember, 'as much as it lieth in you, live peaceably with all men.'"

"I suspect that some of them knew the Duc de Guise was riding toward this village and deliberately withheld the information. They come here not because they grieve for our great loss, but as spies."

Clair wore a pained expression. "You may be right, but the Lord has not given us the sword of judgment, Rachelle. That sword is rightly His alone. The duc will one day answer to Christ for the deeds done while upon this earth. We show our faith by turning our sufferings over to His hand."

Again, Rachelle knew these things, and yet she had not made her heart's peace in surrendering.

"I have often wondered how Stephen could be stoned to death as the book of Acts tells us, yet forgive his tormentors. 'Lay not this sin to their charge.' Sometimes I think if it were me, I should pick up the heaviest stone and hurl it back!"

Clair smiled, then sobered. "Ma chére, such an attitude as Stephen bore can only come from God's indwelling Spirit. How else could he do as Christ did on the cross?"

*But Avril is dead!* she wanted to scream.

Her mother's self-control continued like a running stream. "Stephen was filled with the Spirit. Our old sin nature wants to fight back. But we must not yield to it, but to our new nature. Yield yourself to God—yield your anger to Him. If not, I fear you will be the worse for it."

Her mother's eyes, so full of sympathy and concern, brought tears to Rachelle's. She turned away and nodded briefly, letting a rose rest on her palm as she looked down at its fragile petals.

*Avril is dead; Idelette has been raped; how can she be this trusting except by God's strength?* Some women went to pieces over the death of a child. Some became bitter and blamed God. But now the bitter cup had come upon them, and Rachelle knew she wrestled with truth the way Jacob wrestled with the angel in Genesis.

❋

THE NEXT FEW DAYS passed quietly. One morning, Rachelle approached Cousin Bertrand's chamber with a tray in hand, heavily laden with *petit noir* and warm buttery rolls.

There remained many reasons for encouragement. Cousin Bertrand was recovering his strength sooner than Docteur Lancre had thought.

For Rachelle, the greatest of comforts in these days was when they all gathered in Cousin Bertrand's chamber in the evenings after *dîner*, before they retired, to listen to him read the Scriptures in French. In the past, this had been a time she had taken for granted. Too often her mind had wandered to other issues important to her. Now, their time together seemed nearer to the One who held the family in His hand.

Bertrand had chosen the book of Acts for the family devotions, for as he said, it held great examples of the sufferings of early Christians, and this was a balm for the church's sufferings in France. Bertrand would close his reading by turning to 2 Corinthians and enumerating the apostle Paul's sufferings, where he had been beaten and stoned; gone thirsty, hungry, without sleep, without adequate clothing, and so much more for Christ's sake, and for bringing the message of the only Savior of lost mankind to a persecuting Roman Empire. Paul's dedication and suffering inspired Rachelle.

*My Savior Jesus, enable me, the least of all, to be faithful to Your name.*

Now as Rachelle came to Bertrand's door and tapped, Siffre opened to her. He was a gaunt elderly *chevalier* who rarely smiled, though his eyes shone with a pearl-like luster. For some reason, just looking at Siffre always drew a smile from her.

"Bonjour, Siffre."

"Bonjour, Mademoiselle," he said stiffly.

"I have brought Cousin Bertrand his petit noir."

"With much thick cream and sugar, Mademoiselle? He will not drink his morning brew without it."

They went through this every time she brought the pot to Bertrand, so it had practically become a game. "Oui, Siffre, with cream and sugar."

"Very well, Mademoiselle, merci. I will pour him a cup."

Rachelle looked past Siffre to Bertrand upon his bed. She was pleased to see the ruddy color had come back into his thin cheeks. It was said that before rising in the mornings, he always reached over to his bedside for his Bible to read some verses. "If I do not fill my mind with the living Word in the beginning of the day, then it is soon filled with thoughts from the spiritual enemy who plots our failure and ruin."

"Rachelle, ma petite, come, come, sit beside the bed. I am heartily ashamed to be lying here like a lazy hunting dog past his youthful days."

Rachelle smiled and sat upon the arm of the winged chair done in royal blue tapestry. "I should live so long as to see you lazy," she said, laughing. "You were up too long yesterday, Docteur Lancre says so. He fears your fever will return."

"I am stronger this morn than yesterday. This afternoon I shall rise and make my bed and lie down no more until the darkness settles, the way God intended." He focused his sober gaze upon her. "Tell me, how is our beloved Idelette?"

She set her jaw and froze her smile. "Ma mère says she is recovering well. The bruises are fading, except for her lip. Unfortunately Docteur Lancre believes she may have a scar at the right corner."

*But is she recovering as well as ma mère says?*

Rachelle's own conversations with Idelette did not suggest so.

Bertrand nodded soberly, accepting the truth beneath the casual words. What else was there to say of the delicate and troubling matter of her sister? While Avril was removed from the earthly scene of suffering, Idelette had to continue carrying burdens no one else could help her bear.

"And the young James?" he asked, taking the cup that Siffre gave him and sipping the steaming brew. "A little more cream next time, s'il vous plaît," he commented as usual.

"Docteur Lancre says he will fully recover the use of his leg. He is most anxious to be walking again so he may return to London."

"Then the young James best rouse himself posthaste because I fully intend to leave for Calais within a day." He took a bite of the roll. "And a little more butter next time, s'il vous plaît."

*Calais?* She straightened with interest. "Then you truly intend to join Père Arnaut? Docteur Lancre will not be pleased. He insists you must convalesce for another six weeks at least. So Mère told Père in her lettre of last night."

"The bon docteur, he means well, but he is idealistic. Six weeks? Non. Time is short, life is short. One must get on with one's calling. There is no time to be planting posies."

"But Cousin Bertrand, how can you manage such a long journey?"

"I shall manage. Siffre will be with me. I shall be as comfortable in a Macquinet coach as here upon this bed. And accomplishing much more, I assure you." He waved his buttered roll. "If I stay lounging much longer, ma petite, I shall become fat and lazy."

She leaned forward. "Then let me go with you. I can be of much assistance, I promise you. Père Arnaut may need me on the way back to Lyon, or we may wish to stop in Paris to bring Grandmère and Madeleine and the bébé back here to the château. They will need my assistance on the journey home. You know ma mère would go to Paris tonight if she could, but she does not feel it wise to leave Idelette, and Idelette refuses to go to Paris. Ma mère can hardly get her to leave her chamber to walk in the garden."

"Do you wish to go to Calais because le marquis may yet be there?"

She stood quickly. "I admit that my head was once turned by le marquis, but no longer."

Her vehemence caused his brows to lift. "Is that so?"

"What feelings were between us were short-lived. It is over, and I am satisfied that it is."

His sharpened gaze studied her. She felt her cheeks flush.

"Clair will be pleased to hear of it. She fears you will be hurt by involvement with such an important young man of esteemed background and title."

She walked over to the bedpost, taking hold of it, and faced him, determined. "My plans differ from his, I see that now. I have my amour for silk, for becoming the couturière who follows Grandmère." Rachelle tightened her fingers around the post. "Marriage is impossible for varied reasons. He is of the royal blood, as you know."

"Yes," he said, watching her.

"I was unwise to take seriously his mild flirtation with me at Court." She threw back her shoulders. "I will learn to forget him. I have my part to do in creating the famous gown for the English queen."

"Your mind accepts the facts, I see that, mignon, *bien*," he said gently. "For he admitted he has altered his viewpoint since Chambord and Amboise, where he first met you. Attractions come and wane. He has come to see that he is not seriously inclined toward taking on a wife and family in the foreseeable future."

Her breath caught, then her fingers tightened around the bedpost as her temper climbed. *Attractions come and wane, do they?*

"He spoke to you of me?" *Fabien had not mentioned that!*

"Oui, he is of an uncertain mind concerning his future, and that of France. He may be right about a civil war," he said thoughtfully, his fingers pinching his short, pointed beard. "Let us hope Messire Beza is correct when he speaks of a religious colloquy that will bring rights to the Huguenots to worship freely. Both he and Admiral Coligny are working together to convince the Queen Mother to hold such a colloquy at Fontainebleau this year. I must see the admiral at Châtillon about this while en route to Calais."

Minister Beza had recently come from Geneva and was in close contact with Monsieur Calvin, but at the moment a religious colloquy was the furthest matter from her mind. *So Fabien had altered his thinking about marriage in general since Amboise, had he? Was that another reason why he had left France?*

She did her best to hide her inner turmoil. Was she convincing Cousin Bertrand? She believed he worried more about her steadfastness of faith than he did Idelette's. Idelette's sobriety and studious nature impressed the family and the local assembly of believers, while Rachelle with her enthusiasm for adventure and risks, was watched with mild concern — mild, that is, until she had shown up from Vendôme escorted by the dashing marquis, who retained his loyalty to the Roman Church, even if he loathed Cardinal de Lorraine and called him "lecherous and dangerous."

"I find the marquis an interesting young man," Bertrand said, surprising her. She had expected him to notice as much ill about him as he could in an attempt to discourage her.

"I found that we shared many of the same thoughts on several important issues facing France. That he wishes to join the buccaneers harassing Spain is noteworthy and not altogether displeasing to me, I assure you. Even so, if Clair knew, I suspect his action would further convince her of his unsuitability where you are concerned. She wishes you to marry from Geneva, as you are aware, to one of Calvin's promising students."

Rachelle stared at him, not hearing what he said about Geneva students and marriage, for she and Idelette had long known this. She moved closer to his bed. "But how did you know of his interest in the privateers?"

Bertrand looked as calm as ever. "He confessed this to me."

"The marquis?" She was surprised that he would ever admit his plans for buccaneering to a dedicated pasteur like Cousin Bertrand. Had Fabien then also told him of the Spanish galleons heading for the Netherlands with soldiers and supplies for the infamous Duc d'Alva, and that a joint venture of French, Dutch, and English privateers were planning to attack? That the marquis might not have disclosed that much, and since she retained loyalty, however strained, she would not ask Bertrand anything that would unmask Fabien's secret plans.

"The marquis has long planned to join the French buccaneers," she said. "He mentioned it to me at Chambord, insisting Spain receives her wealth to fund the Inquisition with the gold her treasure galleons bring King Philip from the Americas. I cannot see the marquis confessing this venture as something he feels ashamed over. Since few would ever suspect him of becoming a buccaneer, how is it that you suspected?"

His thin smile convinced her she was right.

"I did not suspect, ma chère; it was Siffre."

"Siffre!" This surprised her. She turned to look at his valet, but he had left the chamber.

"Siffre happened to be out walking in the garden as he does late every evening before taking to bed. He saw a stranger arrive some weeks ago bringing a message from a French buccaneer to the marquis. The messenger thought he was alone when he told him that the privateers had news of the Duc d'Alva's galleons bringing soldiers and weapons to the Netherlands. Siffre came to me about it. He knows the wish of your père that I watch over his household in his absence, ma petite. It was equally clear that while the marquis was coming and going these past weeks, that you and he spent a certain amount of time together. Both Clair and I have seen the lively flame that dances between you."

Rachelle remained silent. None of that mattered now. It was over.

"He is a most difficult seigneur to understand at times," Bertrand said, musing. "He declares himself a Catholic, yet he embraces many of the ideas of the Huguenots. In regard to the Guises, he discerns the dark direction in which they are leading France. He is to be commended for such insights. And more importantly where our family is concerned, is his personal faith in Christ. I told him this, but I am grieved to say that the marquis has not satisfied me in this matter, and though I think he is a Christian, on several critical issues of doctrine, he avoided an answer."

"He can be contrary," she said. "I am certain he knows and understands. He has given me some insightful answers. He has also discussed matters very thoroughly with Andelot." She was irritated Fabien had not satisfied Bertrand when she was certain he could have done so. *Why had he not?*

"Andelot Dangeau ... ah, oui, I remember him, the fatherless boy, the unclaimed neveu of Sebastien?"

"Oui, but he is a boy no longer. He has grown up. And it is now said that Andelot is blood related to the Guise family."

"Most curious. I also discerned something else in my talks with the marquis, something that worries me, mignon. There is some matter harassing him other than Spain; oui, some little foxes that eat at him, and of these he also would not tell me."

She could have told Bertrand plainly of the fox in particular that goaded him. It was Duc de Guise, and Fabien's hatred for him, and the belief that the duc, and perhaps the cardinal, had Duc Jean-Louis de Vendôme, Fabien's father, assassinated.

She did not speak of this however.

From somewhere behind her, Siffre cleared his throat. "*Pardone*, Messire Bertrand, but Nenette says there is a young monsieur here to see the mademoiselle, with the name of Andelot Dangeau. He has come from Paris with a lettre from Duchesse Dushane, and the monsieur says it is important"

Andelot! For one of the few times in recent days, Rachelle's smile arose genuinely from within the well of her heart's affections. He was just the young monsieur she wanted to see, for if anyone could make her feel sane and more optimistic again, it was her petit ami from childhood. Wholesome Andelot, with his winsome smile and warm, easy manner. She had not seen him since Amboise.

Excusing herself from Cousin Bertrand, she left the chamber and sped down the corridor, past Nenette and to the stairway. Nenette followed close behind. "He is most beau now, wait till you see him, Mademoiselle."

As Rachelle descended the stairs, she was met by two serving women on their way to announce Andelot's arrival to Madame Clair. They drew aside, parting the way for Rachelle, who hurried down, Nenette still nimbly following. Rachelle reached the bottom and crossed the wide floor under the cascading light from torches on the high stone walls, her mourning dress rustling stiffly.

Andelot Dangeau stood in the doorway, another monsieur beside him, whom she recognized as Duchesse Dushane's page, Romier. Both men wore grave faces. Had the news of the Guise attack reached them? They bowed, hats in hand.

"Andelot." Rachelle managed a smile despite her apprehension and extended her hand.

Andelot advanced. He was fine looking, with brown hair and eyes. "Mademoiselle Rachelle, it is a lamentable message I bring from Paris, and now I have learned the bitter news of what has befallen you here. My condolences over your family's loss of petite Avril."

*There would be ample opportunity to discuss these details with him later.*

"Merci, Andelot mon ami, it is most tragic, all that has come upon us these weeks. What news do you now bring?"

"I shall begin with a happy surprise. Sebastien is alive."

Rachelle caught his arm. "Alive! Oh, Andelot, but how can that be? And does Madeleine know? Oh, wait until I tell Madame Clair! This is a gift from heaven amidst all of the storms!"

His smile was genuine, yet she caught the flicker of sadness in his eyes. "Oui, I was sent to Duchesse Dushane with the news only some days ago. Your sister, Madeleine, will be shocked when she learns."

"When she learns Sebastien is alive? But you say you come from Paris, how is it that she does not yet know?" Her voice tense and cautious.

He pushed the lock of hair from his forehead and changed stances. "Well, she is ill, you see — and Madame did not think it wise yet to tell her that Sebastien is in the Bastille." His voice lowered as though the words were too heavy to speak. "He is to be sent to the salle de la question."

Rachelle stepped back. She searched his eyes and saw the pain, saw his gaze fall to the floor. He fidgeted with his hat.

"The salle de la question," she whispered. Silence wrapped around her. Her hand formed a fist. "Better to be dead!" She closed her eyes tightly trying to bring her emotions under control.

"Duchesse Dushane requests that you come to the Louvre palais," he whispered. "Your grandmère and sister need you; they are both very ill. Madame and her private docteur are caring for them."

Rachelle looked down at the envelope he extended, as though it were poison, as though whatever news written there would come to pass if she took hold of it.

"What kind of illness?"

"The duchesse has explained in the lettre. Would Madame Clair offer you her coach for your ride to Paris? There is no time for delay, we should leave this hour."

She raised her eyes to his and read what was left unsaid. "I shall come." He nodded. An overwhelming sense of loss descended on her like a bleak, smothering blanket. Grandmère — Madeleine!

She took the envelope, holding it to her heart, and turning away, she started for the stairway to be alone in her chamber.

Her mother was coming down the stairs, the two servants waiting beside the banister as if they suspected more dark tidings.

"Bonjour, Andelot," Clair greeted, looking wan in her mourning gown, but her head was held high. "What news do you bring from my *tante*, Duchesse Dushane?"

Rachelle did not wait to share the lettre with her mother, knowing Andelot would discuss all he knew with her. She ran down the corridor and entered her chamber. Away from sympathetic eyes, she tore open the envelope with shaking fingers and read Madame Xenia Dushane's words of explanation about the sudden illness that had first taken hold of Grandmère, and then Madeleine. As though in a trance, Rachelle stood without moving, reading and rereading the concluding words the duchesse had written with an irregular handwriting that betrayed her tears.

*Rachelle, if you wish to see your grandmère once more in this valley of the shadow of death, make all haste to fly to her side. Her hours are swiftly declining. May our sympathetic Savior who wept at*

*Lazarus's tomb for the unhappiness of Mary and Martha uphold you as you cling to His faithful promises to be with you in every trial.*

Rachelle gripped the lettre. She moved with uncertain steps toward the chair.

Tears flooded her eyes and her throat cramped.

Grandmère — dare she think it? Even say it? After enduring the loss of Avril, not her beloved Grandmère!

The damsel Nenette, who had followed softly, came up beside her and laid a hand on her shoulder. "Oh, Rachelle — Mademoiselle, what has happened?"

Rachelle, overwhelmed, moved past her and collapsed on her knees beside her bed. With hands at her bosom, she wept before her Savior's throne of mercy.

*Oh, Father God, I come to You in the name above all names, that of Your beloved Son, our Savior, Jesus Christ. Oh, I beg of You, heavenly Father, do not take Grandmère home yet. I must see her one last time. Oh, sustainer of our every breath, have mercy! I cannot bear losing her without a last adieu — I know she will be ushered into Your presence, for Christ has secured deliverance of her precious soul! But, oh! For me her departure will be heavy! And Madeleine — oh, Father! She has just given birth — what would the bébé do without her — and Sebastien! Oh, poor Sebastien —*

✻

EVENTUALLY RACHELLE BECAME AWARE of Nenette's weeping, and opening her eyes, saw the girl also kneeling, hands clasped. Nenette, like Andelot, had been raised without parents by one of the women who worked in the silkworm hatcheries before being cared for by a nurse on the estate. Nenette had found favor in Grandmère's sight and was brought to the Macquinet château to enter training as a grisette. She had gravitated toward Rachelle, and soon, Nenette had become her personal maid.

Rachelle moved closer, placing her arm around her, drawing Nenette's head down on her shoulder, and sadly stroking her tumbling red curls.

"We must have courage, Nenette," she choked, her throat dry from crying. "This time we live in was given us by God. We must accept it."

"Oh, but why should Grandmère die now? She is most kind, and we need her—"

"Yes, we need her. Oh, Nenette! It will not be the same for me without her, not ever! I was so looking forward to telling her of the gown for the English queen."

"Ah, oui!" Nenette dropped her face into her small hands.

Rachelle stood. "We must rise, petite amie. I must go to Paris. We need to pack some of my things, get my hooded cape, and my French Bible."

Nenette raised her swollen eyes, horror written there. "The Bible? Non—oh, do not, Mademoiselle!"

"Oui." Rachelle stood firmly to her feet. She tossed back her wealth of autumn-brown hair, her thoughts far away at the Louvre. "I will. No one will stop me from reading it at her bedside! I want it. Go and bring it. Hurry."

Wide-eyed, Nenette stumbled to her feet. Groaning her dissent, she nevertheless rushed to unearth the hidden Scriptures from a carved wooden box in the wardrobe.

Rachelle took it, pushed it beneath some garments in her brocade satchel, and closed the latch. Nenette had grabbed her hooded cloak, and Rachelle, snatching it, hurried from her chamber.

As she came down the stairs, Madame Clair was still discussing matters with Andelot near the front doorway. Rachelle squared her shoulders and looked at her mother. Their gazes met evenly.

Clair sighed, and closing her eyes, gave a nod.

Rachelle walked briskly toward Andelot.

"Is the coach ready?"

"Oui, it is out front now," he said.

Rachelle turned quickly to her mother and they embraced.

"Be careful, ma chére; this I do not like—it worries me—this sickness. Do be careful."

"I will. What of Cousin Bertrand? He intends to start for Calais tomorrow—"

"Today," came the firm voice, and she and Clair turned to see Bertrand leaning on Siffre's arm, coming slowly but steadily down the stairs. "Andelot? My bag, s'il vous plaît."

Andelot in a few strides was at the stairs. He took up the bag and aided the pasteur across the hall to the doorway.

Clair, with calm repose, met him. "Are you sure, Bertrand? It is a long journey."

"Not too long, when it is this important. Have you a word for Arnaut?"

"As ever, my prayers, my amour. Tell him we are finding God's grace sufficient. That we will stand firm."

Bertrand planted a brief kiss on her forehead and came toward Rachelle, who lingered just outside the open door on the veranda. "I shall accompany you to Paris first, then on to Calais."

She gave a nod of assent and hurried ahead toward the large coach where Siffre waited to help her in, as the driver, Pierre, stored the baggage.

In a few minutes they boarded the coach-and-six, with Siffre riding horseback between Romier and a guard, and Romier leading the marquis' golden bay on a tether. Rachelle steadied herself as the coach moved down the graveled sweep and on to the road to Paris.

# A Matter of Apples

THE MACQUINET HORSES WERE MAKING GOOD SPEED ALONG THE ROAD to Paris. Rachelle sat across from Andelot on leather-lined seats with stuffed cushions while Cousin Bertrand was arranged with a blanket by the window, his legs on a stool.

"Well, Andelot, the mademoiselle tells me you were surprised by information that you are related to the House of Guise," Cousin Bertrand said. "Tell me, will you be pleased to be elevated to the court?"

"I do not know, Messire Bertrand, I swear it. At one time I was most pleased, for I had heard my tutor would actually be the grand Monsieur Thauvet. But now, matters appear to have reverted back to where they were before I was brought to Chambord to meet the cardinal."

Rachelle was surprised to hear that. "Oh, why so, Andelot?"

"Cardinal de Lorraine was disappointed with me after the Amboise massacre, and now he demands I give up my friendship with Marquis Fabien."

"Ah? You are a particular ami of the marquis?" Bertrand asked, studying him.

"He is a seigneur worth knowing, Pasteur."

"Is he now? And he considers you the same, does he?"

"Surprisingly, Messire, he has befriended me from the time I first met him at Court. But then, he befriends many who are not of the blood, or even titled."

"He must," Bertrand said wryly, "if he has joined the rowdy buccaneers."

Rachelle moved uneasily and glanced at Andelot, who looked as though he may have said something wrong.

"Surely your new kinsmen will secure a merveilleux education for you with the best of tutors at Court," Rachelle said, changing the subject from Fabien, "even if you do not have Scholar Thauvet."

"Thauvet," Bertrand said, "the instructor of princes and dauphins?"

"Le marquis also had Thauvet," Andelot said, a hint of defense in his voice.

Bertrand smiled thinly, amusement in his dark eyes. "One wonders what the famous marquis may have thought of the renowned Thauvet."

"It matters not so much that I have him, as long as I enter the university. To become a scholar, Pasteur Bertrand, is my foremost wish, but — " Andelot shrugged — "that is now uncertain, even though I was told that my père, Louis Dangeau, is not a Dangeau at all but — " he stopped, glanced at Rachelle, then said again — "not a Dangeau. Then ... there was my mère, not a pristine lady, so I was told."

"Oui, I remember you telling me when we journeyed to Amboise — Oh, how long ago it seems now. A thousand years, Andelot. So much has happened to us."

"Oui, and not all bonne news, I promise you." He leaned back, playing with his cap.

"This sickness of your grandmère and Madeleine is curious," Andelot said, musing. "I would wish to discuss my concerns with Marquis Fabien if he were here. I wish he had not gone to Florida. Two years, such a long time to be away when we need him."

Rachelle struggled with her emotions. She tried to relax into the comfortable velvet cushions, but her fingers were tautly bound together in her lap.

"But you are here, Andelot, and I am grateful for your concerns for my family."

His comely face darkened with embarrassment, but she was accustomed to his responses and overlooked them.

Bertrand tapped him lightly on the shoulder with the tip of his new walking stick. "This sickness, Andelot, tell me about it."

Andelot leaned forward, his eyes troubled.

"I do not know how to say this, Pasteur Bertrand, but I have grievous concerns about what may have caused Grandmère and Madeleine to become so ill. It is the cause for which I wanted to ride back with you, so we could discuss it without upsetting anyone." He glanced at Rachelle, then back to Bertrand. "That is, Pasteur, if you will permit my conjecture? It is not my purpose to disturb Mademoiselle Rachelle, but —"

"Do speak, Andelot," she said.

"By all means, speak your concerns," Bertrand added. Alerted, Rachelle sat up, paying close heed.

"Does it not seem most odd that both your grandmère and Madeleine should become sick after eating fruit?"

There was a strained moment of deliberation. Bertrand studied him. "Fruit?"

"Oui, the apples. How could a single apple each, make them ill to the point of death?"

For a time she could not fathom his words. "What have apples to do with this?"

"Are you saying, Andelot, that Grandmère and Madeleine ate apples, and le docteur blames this for their illness?" Bertrand asked.

Andelot's fingers inched their way around the brim of his hat. "That I do not know, Pasteur. I have not spoken with le docteur. I thought Duchesse Dushane mentioned in her lettre that it was the apples which made Grandmère and Madeleine sick."

Rachelle shook her head. "Non, she said nothing of that, how could that be?"

"How could it be indeed?" Andelot said and glanced from one to the other.

"But I thought they both had the fever." Rachelle was growing confused.

"A fever, oui, but from eating apples. *Extraordinaire?*" He shook his head.

"This proves most interesting; do go on," Cousin Bertrand said.

Rachelle listened, her tension building as Andelot told them what had happened to Grandmère and Madeleine: Grandmère's trip to the market, the basket of apples bought there and served with their after-noon déjeuner of goat's cheese, bread, and lamb's broth.

"Madame's page, Romier, mentioned that he had overheard le docteur mention the possibility of poison."

"Poison!" Rachelle sat upright.

"You are sure of this?" Bertrand asked. "Page Romier is trustworthy?"

"Oui, though he did not mean poison as we think of it now; he meant bad fruit, but when Romier said it, genuine poison was the word that struck me cold."

"As it should. Go on, young monsieur."

"Later I had a dream that made me remember the time I entered the Amboise laboratory above the Queen Mother's chambers. And then I realized what had been troubling me for so long." He paused. "Poison," he said in a quiet voice. "A poison made into a white powder."

Rachelle's skin became chilled as Andelot related his experience with Prince Charles Valois in the laboratory of one of the Ruggerio brothers from Florence.

"I wish I had thought to discuss it with Marquis Fabien before he went to sea, but so much had happened. There were zodiac drawings and occult arts. But it was most clear that her men from Florence are skilled in apothecary and poison making. The packet of powder was left with instructions for the Queen Mother."

When he had finished his tale, she hesitated, pondering, fear clutching her heart.

"You are suggesting Catherine de Medici gave poison to Grandmère and Madeleine?" Cousin Bertrand asked sharply, leaning toward him. "Why would she do so?"

"That is the question, Pasteur Bertrand, why? Even if Sebastien seemed a risk to her plans, now that he is in the Bastille facing execution, why would she want to poison his wife?"

"And Grandmère, if it is true," Bertrand said.

"It cannot be," Rachelle said, "neither Madeleine nor Grandmère pose any threat to the Queen Mother. Not only so, but how could she have poisoned them both, and at almost the same time?"

"Oui, that is so. But my suspicion remains that she poisoned the apples," Andelot said.

"But how would the Queen Mother even know Grandmère would wish to buy apples?" Bertrand said.

Andelot sighed. "I have considered that difficulty many times over since leaving Paris for the château."

"The Queen Mother would need to have the poisoned apples at the market and have them prepared to sell to Grandmère," Bertrand said. "How would she know Grandmère would come to that fruit stand?"

"Yes, well ..." He ran his fingers through his wavy brown hair and then leaned back against the seat. "Oui, you must be right, Pasteur Bertrand, for it would be most difficult for the Ruggerio brothers to deliver such poisoned apples. They would have had to wait until they saw Grandmère leave the Louvre and then follow her."

"You admit that is most unlikely," Bertrand said.

Andelot looked dissatisfied, but in the end, gave a nod. "I suppose having that dream when I did, and remembering the laboratory, made me think so. My suspicions must come from the horrors of Amboise. I begin to see sinister plots where there are none."

"Maybe. Then again, Andelot, maybe not. Let us not rush to dismiss your theory until we know more of the details. It has been said by reputable messieurs that Catherine de Medici has not recoiled from using poison in the past. Let us hope it was not so where Grandmère and Madeleine are concerned."

*Poison ... the Ruggerio brothers ... Catherine.* Rachelle shivered.

She pondered Andelot's words, and though she did not trust the Queen Mother, the idea of poisoned apples seemed too difficult to have arranged, unless the fruit had been delivered to their apartment in the Louvre. From what Andelot said however, Grandmère had bought the apples herself from a market stand.

Still, Rachelle could not shake the thought completely from her mind. From the thoughtful frown on Cousin Bertrand's face, neither could he.

As the shadows of twilight settled over Paris, the Macquinet coach clattered down the damp cobbled streets past the Hôtel de Clugny, the Hôtel de Sense, and toward the Louvre palais. A few days had passed since leaving Lyon. Soon the Louvre came into view, on the grassy margin of the river Seine, with its walls and bastions inside a moat. The wall surrounding the Louvre had four gates, each with its smaller postern gate and tower. The southern gate, opposite the Seine, was the strongest, low and narrow, with statues of Charles V of the Holy Roman Empire and his wife, Jeanne de Bourbon, staring solemnly down upon all those who passed by, as though confirming the absolute and united rule of sword, state, and church. From there, Rachelle could see one of the oldest churches in France, dedicated to St. Germain, Bishop of Paris.

The coach passed through the gates, bells jingling on the handsome horses. In the center of the inner court stood a round tower, which could be defended from a raised embankment or rampart. The tower was ill famed for its oubliettes, or dungeons, under which the river flowed, bringing no comfort to Rachelle.

They drove up to the entrance to the prized appartements and single chambers awarded by royalty to certain members of the higher nobility and those serving the throne. The marquis was said to have a chamber that he was obliged to occupy at certain times of the year when he was called to Court. Refusal to join the king's entertainments when called could bring royalty's displeasure and even an appearance before the throne to answer for slackness. Most of the nobility, fearing charges of treason, came dutifully, but others were so delighted to be at Court, they only returned home to their estates at a birth or a funeral.

Sebastien, as a former member of Catherine's privy council before his arrest, had been awarded a choice appartement. Rachelle wondered how much longer her sister Madeleine would be permitted to retain occupancy. Most likely the Queen Mother would soon order Madeleine to depart, if she had not already done so.

Rachelle wondered what her sister's plans would be now that Sebastien was known to be alive and on his way to the Bastille. Madeleine would hardly wish to return to the Château de Silk now, but would rather wish to remain in Paris and work for his release.

Rachelle thought that, had the marquis not left, he might have appealed directly to King Francis on account of Sebastien. *And if there was a chance of pressing his friendship with the king, what then? If he learned Sebastien was to be hauled before the salle de la question . . .* Rachelle narrowed her gaze thoughtfully and glanced at Cousin Bertrand. Was there the slightest chance to intercept the marquis at Calais?

*Not that it matters to me, but to Madeleine and Sebastien — and bébé Joan.*

Perhaps Duchesse Dushane would take Madeleine into her own spacious quarters when the Queen Mother told her to vacate the appartement. As a duchesse she had special rights at Court and was treated with deference despite her association with the Huguenots, for the persecutions raged mainly against the serfs and middle class of France. Even Admiral Coligny, a staunch Huguenot, was welcomed at Court and indeed had audience with King Francis and the Queen Mother.

Rachelle comforted herself with the thought that the Father above would give them new and far more glorious chambers in which to abide in comfort and everlasting joy. When she recalled the future blessings promised the redeemed in Christ, she knew how tawdry were the much sought after glories of earthly kingdoms, destined to be governed by the great stone made without man's workmanship, whose righteous rule would cover the whole earth.

*"Seek those things which are above, where Christ sitteth on the right hand of God."*

Where had she read that verse in Scripture? And only recently too. She must find it. Idelette had often told her that since the French Bible was forbidden and they may not be able to possess it much longer, they must discipline themselves to memorize more of it.

---

RACHELLE, WITH COUSIN BERTRAND and Andelot, was escorted into the Louvre palais by Page Romier.

With heart beating quickly, she went through the corridor and up the marbled steps, entering the blue-and-gold *salle de séjour* of Comte Sebastien and Madeleine.

She stood, breathless, taking in the familiar furniture with silver tassels, the heavy blue brocade coverings, and draperies on the windows. Even the musty smell of ancient furniture and the Aubusson rug, walked upon by kings, struck her with the sensation that she may be too late.

Too late. What could be more heartrending than those simple words?

Andelot had spoken to one of the ladies-in-waiting who had left to announce their arrival to Duchesse Dushane.

The duchesse came from one of the interior chambers, and Rachelle was struck that she looked weary and older than during their last meeting at Amboise. Rachelle curtsied and the duchesse caught up her hand.

"Your Grace?" Pasteur Bertrand inquired.

"You have come in time."

"Is there any improvement, Madame?" Rachelle asked.

"I fear there is not. Le docteur is with your grandmère now."

The duchesse noticed Bertrand's bound arm in a sling and that he used a walking stick.

"What happened to you, Pasteur Bertrand? Were you thrown from your horse?"

"Ah, Madame, I see you have not received Clair's correspondence."

"Non. Has something of import occurred?"

"Unfortunately so, which leaves me with the difficult task of explaining."

"I am in no state for more troubling events, I assure you. But come, we will talk in the next chamber while one of my ladies brings pastries and petit noir." She turned to Romier who stood near the door. "Romier, do help Messire Bertrand."

"I can manage. Merci, Madame," Bertrand said. "I am feeling much stronger. I intend to leave first thing in the morning for Calais."

"Calais? It seems you have more than one venture to tell me about, but at least permit Romier to help settle you comfortably on the divan."

She turned to Rachelle who waited anxiously with only one matter on her mind. The duchesse's eyes softened.

"Do not hesitate to go to Grandmère, for she is becoming weaker."

"Oui. Merci, Madame."

Rachelle went past her through a door into Grandmère's bedchamber. Ladies-in-waiting stood or sat about near the chamber wall. One lady sat on a brocade chair near the bedside. Rachelle did not recognize her, but she appeared of high title. A docteur was there, and she thought he might be the famed Ambrose Paré, royalty's own physician-surgeon, who had removed the wood splinter from the eye of Catherine de Medici's husband, King Henry II, after the accident during a friendly joust that had taken his life.

The docteur beckoned her forward. The ladies moved away to grant Rachelle privacy. Their faces wore sympathy, and many looked tired from long hours of vigilance.

Rachelle approached the bedside and slipped to her knees on a little padded brocade stool. *Could this gaunt face belong to her sprightly grandmère, who once had twinkling dark eyes and roses in her cheeks?*

*Ah, death and sickness! How it decays the body and turns it to dust!*

Rachelle took the limp hand between her own and held it against the side of her cheek. *Grandmère, do not leave me. You are the one who understands me best.*

※

OUTSIDE THE BEDCHAMBER IN the main salle, Andelot stood watching through the doorway. Had the sight not been so sad, it would have been a tender and lovely painting, he thought. The gracious Rachelle kneeling with her belle skirts spread about her on the floor, her luxuriant auburn-brown hair in curls on one shoulder, holding the grande dame's fragile hand.

*I think I am in love with her,* he mused, *but who am I to think I could ever have her?*

Andelot said his own silent prayers as he had been taught. He wished he could send for the bishop, but he dare not; such would not be permitted. He noted the absence of ceremonial candles and incense. There would be no last rites, and none of the ceremony that attended the dying of a Catholic noble or monarch.

Later, he saw Bertrand coming out of another bedchamber that he assumed must be Madeleine's. Andelot took a risk and walked up to him.

"Monsieur, should we not call for the bishop?"

"Grandmère does not take last rites." He put a hand on Andelot's shoulder. "You see, it is Christ alone and His promises we trust for eternal deliverance from the just retribution of our sins and weaknesses."

"But, I thought — Ah, well, I see. If I may, I should like to go in and say my prayers."

"We will both go in, Andelot. I am certain Grandmère would be pleased by your presence."

A few minutes later, when Andelot entered Grandmère's bedchamber with Bertrand, the docteur came up beside Bertrand as though he might know him. Perhaps he did, for it was said that Docteur Ambrose Paré was a Huguenot.

"She is conscious but cannot speak without effort. I believe she knows who Mademoiselle is. She tires easily, so we must not overwhelm her."

Andelot kept back, kneeling some feet behind Rachelle who remained at Grandmère's bedside, holding her hand. Pasteur Bertrand stood at the foot of her bed.

"Grandmère?" Rachelle whispered. "It is Rachelle! Can you understand?"

⁂

GRANDMÈRE HEARD RACHELLE'S VOICE as though from a distance. She tried to turn her head and focus upon her beloved granddaughter. There was something she must tell Rachelle, something most important. *If only her mind were more alert to speak the danger — yes, that was it — the danger — danger — the gloves — Rachelle, ma chérie, the gloves! Tell Xenia! Tell Madeleine! Rachelle, do not wear the gloves that wicked woman gave to the three of us —*

"Do not be fearful, Grandmère. Do not become overwrought," Rachelle whispered, trying to soothe her, but Grandmère did not wish to be quieted. She was dying, but she had little to fear, for Christ had triumphed over the sting of death. *The sting of death is sin. But thanks be unto God who gives us the victory through Jesus Christ our Lord.*

Grandmère prayed again as she had done upon every awakening when her mind became briefly clear. She tried to squeeze Rachelle's fingers and direct her gaze toward the belle red box sitting on the stand where the gloves remained after she had removed them — *when? Yesterday — a week ago?*

Grandmère remembered she had gone out to shop, to the market-place. She had felt full of hope and joy. Madeleine's daughter was doing so well, and Madeleine too. And then, when she had returned here to the Louvre, she fell suddenly and violently ill. Her breathing became difficult, as though she were being slowly smothered. The following night was passed in a burning fever with a terrible weariness in her limbs, and by morning she had lost control of them. She could scarcely breathe and the pain in her chest worsened. She had wanted to warn Madeleine, but by then her speech had deserted her as well, and she was not remembering things. Then Xenia had come with the best docteur, a Huguenot, Ambroise Paré, the king's surgeon. Grandmère remembered little after that.

In rare moments of consciousness she had known there was something she must tell the ladies in attendance. They were all in danger; *yes, that was it. Danger!* She remembered the gloves, but her mind was failing her again, and she could no longer express her fears —

*Gloves*, she said, *remember the gloves? But could they hear her? Was she even speaking aloud?*

The Lord Jesus was her solace and calm expectation. *Though dumbness seals my lips, You know, O Lord.*

Nothing escapes the Lord's knowledge, no, not the suffering of those who rejoice to bear His name among His enemies. *Fear none of those things which thou shalt suffer . . . Be thou faithful unto death . . . and I will give you the crown of life.*

Her aging body would turn to dust, but her life was not ending. He to whom she belonged had triumphed over death and the grave. Would it matter that she had so briefly tasted the cup of suffering? Soon now ... soon, the anguish would be forgotten, the ecstasy of seeing the Lord of glory would be hers. No one could take that away—not a persecuting cleric, nor even a king.

# The Belle Red Box

RACHELLE WAS RESTING HER HEAD ON GRANDMÈRE'S SHOULDER. ANDELOT saw Bertrand speaking to one of the ladies-in-waiting. She left the bedchamber. Now what? Perhaps he should not have been surprised when some few minutes later the lady returned and handed Bertrand a bowl with several small rosy apples. Bertrand walked over to the docteur who listened in silence, head bent, attentive, chin in hand. They spoke for some time; the docteur took the apples and quietly placed them in his satchel. Andelot felt pleased with himself.

Grandmère was trying to speak once more. Rachelle, too, noted it and raised her head. Andelot saw a note of recognition in Grandmère's eyes and Rachelle leaned close, putting her lips to her ear.

"Grandmère," she whispered, "can you recognize me? Can you squeeze my fingers?"

Andelot felt compelled to move up beside Rachelle and kneel. Bertrand, too, had come up and stood with the forbidden Book open in hand. A short time ago Andelot had wanted the bishop, but now he was glad the bishop was not present to observe. Even at this emotional moment he could not keep from making curious glances toward the forbidden Bible in French, as though he half expected to see a serpent slithering from among its pages.

Should he say what troubled him? Yes! This was no time to be timid. He leaned toward Rachelle and whispered.

"Ask if it was the apples that made her sick."

"Poisoned apples, Grandmère?"

Grandmère made a throaty moan. Then — "Non, non —" came her weak voice. Rachelle exchanged glances with Andelot and Bertrand.

Andelot agonized, listening, watching her lips, while Rachelle kept her ear close. Bertrand, too, bent over Grandmère, laying a hand on her forehead. "It is me; Bertrand, Grandmère. Were you poisoned?"

Andelot looked down to see Grandmère's fingers barely taking hold of Rachelle's. With a great effort and drawing of breath, a word slipped through in garbled syllables.

"Gla — glu. Glau —" Grandmère's voice struggled.

Andelot heard Rachelle's quick intake of breath.

He glanced at her. Did Rachelle understand? What could it mean . . . if anything?

Bertrand continued to quietly pray, his voice calm and confident. *"Though I walk through the valley of the shadow of death, I will fear no evil: for thou art with me . . . Into thy hands I commend my spirit . . . Today shalt thou be with me in paradise . . . "*

Andelot frowned and gave him a sharp look. A strange irritation goaded him. *What gave him such confidence! Who does this man think he is to take so much authority upon himself? See how he gives confidence to Rachelle and Grandmère. Who gave you this authority — not the bishop, not the mother Church. It is She who has been given all authority! Yet look at him with that forbidden Book, as though he has access to the living God of heaven!*

Andelot was hardly aware as the docteur came swiftly to the bedside to attend Grandmère.

Andelot stared at Bertrand. As if he felt the intense gaze, Bertrand turned his silver head and looked straight down at him where he knelt.

Bertrand's dark eyes flickered with what Andelot took as firm confidence.

Embarrassed by his own hasty indignation, Andelot lowered his head and fingered his heavy silver cross, saying a prayer.

Andelot felt his neck and ears burn. *What came over me?*

The ways of the so-called Christian Reformers were known to him. He held much respect for this Huguenot family, and for that matter, he even felt *bonhomie* toward Bertrand. It was as though something dark had taken hold of him that he could not explain.

He heard Rachelle say: "I understand, Grandmère."

Grandmère sighed and her breathing softened.

Andelot stood and looked down at Grandmère, then drew back from the bedside toward the window, his mind active. Grandmère had meant to say something important to Rachelle with those syllables, and he believed Rachelle had understood.

If not the apples, what was it that had made her deathly ill?

Madame-Duchesse had come to the bedside to kneel, praying words that Andelot had never heard before. It took him a minute to understand she was saying words from the French Bible, but were they the words of the true Bible the bishop owned in Latin?

Nevertheless, they were pleasant words in French and he liked them.

*"My sheep hear my voice, and I know them and they follow me: And I give unto them eternal life; and they shall never perish, neither shall any man pluck them out of my hand."*

Who spoke those words? Jesus?

Several minutes passed, and then the docteur spoke: "It is over, Madame, Messire. She has departed from this world."

Grandmère was gone. *Wherever she went, she would not return to inhabit that poor, aged body again*, Andelot thought, glancing over to the bed.

Muffled crying sounded, coming mostly from the ladies gathered along the far wall. Andelot was about to leave the chamber when he noticed a change in Rachelle. She stood, looking intently about the chamber. He could see by her narrowed eyes that she knew something. She looked determined, even angry. He followed her gaze to a chest of drawers. On top of it sat a pretty red box with the initials in gold: *C M*.

Rachelle stood staring at it. Andelot's gaze dropped to her hands. They were clenched.

*C M*, Andelot mused. *Catherine de Medici, bien sûr!* Andelot stared at the red box. He saw Rachelle move over to the chest, her rigid back toward him.

"Messire?" the docteur's voice interrupted.

Andelot turned quickly, nodded, and was about to leave the chamber when Rachelle brushed past him entering the main salle, carrying the red box in her hand.

He swiftly followed.

❧

ONCE IN THE OUTER chamber, Andelot saw that Duchesse Dushane and Rachelle had entered a private chamber. He followed and spoke to one of the ladies.

"It is urgent I speak with the duchesse and Mademoiselle."

"Madame and Mademoiselle will not speak to anyone now. They are in grief."

"It is most urgent. Go now and tell her so, s'il vous plaît!"

The ladies looked at one another in bewilderment, and at last the woman went to inquire. In a moment she returned and stood aside the open door. "They will see you now."

Andelot followed her through a second chamber into a small sitting room. Rachelle held the red box and was standing before the duchesse who sat in a large cushioned chair, her head leaning back wearily.

"Andelot," said Rachelle, "where is Cousin Bertrand?"

"He remains with le docteur."

"Call him, if you please. He must hear what I have to say."

Andelot bowed toward the duchesse, for he had noticed her looking thoughtfully away from him to Rachelle. *Had he given away his feelings for Rachelle?*

A few minutes later, all were seated except Rachelle, who stood facing them.

"This box came from the Queen Mother," she said. "I was in her royal chamber when she handed it to me, along with two others. It was this box that Grandmère was trying to draw to my attention."

"Caution, Rachelle," Cousin Bertrand admonished. He looked at the duchesse. "Madame, you are certain we go unheard?"

❧ 144 ❧

"All of my ladies and pages are trustworthy, Messire Bertrand, but you speak wisely in asking. I am sure there are no listening tubes or closets connected to this chamber. That is why we meet here. Sebastien went over it inch by inch when he came here several years ago with Madeleine. And Madeleine is very cautious about such things. I believe she checks every chamber at least once a year."

"Bon. Then, the box came from the Queen Mother?"

Andelot stood, restless.

"I believe Madeleine received one also," the duchesse said.

"As did we all—except Idelette," Rachelle said, "which seemed most unusual in itself, for Idelette did most of the dressmaking work for the Reinette Mary Stuart. The engraved boxes were bestowed before we—Grandmère, Idelette, and myself—left Chambord. Grandmère came here to Paris for the birth, as we know; Idelette returned to the Château; and I was called to Amboise in service to Princesse Marguerite.

"The Queen Mother said the boxes were gifts for our *par excellent* work on the silk gowns."

"But Madeleine was not involved in the gown making at Chambord," Duchesse Dushane said.

"The Queen Mother stated that Madeleine's box was in celebration of the coming birth of Sebastien's first child. She made it most clear it was to be opened only after the successful birth."

"Are you saying, ma petite, that you think Grandmère was poisoned?" Bertrand asked, his tone quiet, but blunt.

Andelot looked quickly at Rachelle. He saw her mouth tighten. "Oui," came her firm reply.

"But not by the apples?" Andelot asked.

"Non."

"Nevertheless, I have asked the docteur to make a test on the apples," Bertrand said.

The duchesse frowned. "This is quite difficult to believe, Rachelle. Why would Catherine wish Grandmère to die? But nonetheless, proceed with your hypothesis."

"You may think me mad, Madame, but I, along with Andelot, believe that Grandmère was poisoned, and I now believe that the poison was inside this box. Madame, we are all witnesses as I open it."

Andelot looked from Rachelle's taut face, to the duchesse, who looked shocked. Bertrand merely looked grave and thoughtful.

Rachelle lifted the lid — *it was empty*.

Andelot refused to be disappointed, but Rachelle fell silent and stared in bewilderment.

Madame sighed.

"I would not have been surprised had you found poison," the duchesse said. "It has been done before, though even the mention of it could put us in danger."

"Is that not expected?" Bertrand said, making his way to the fire. "The marquis warned me to be aware of the Queen Mother. He does not trust the upcoming colloquy to be held at Fontainebleau this fall. I confess the thought of poison crossed my mind. I have discreetly mentioned this to le docteur. He will consider an autopsy upon Grandmère, in strictest secrecy, you understand."

"If not in secrecy, there is no telling what may become of those who meddle," the duchesse said darkly. "I know Catherine de Medici very well, and le docteur knows the secrets of this infamous court, I assure you."

Rachelle retained a thoughtful silence. Andelot, watching her, was not satisfied with the empty box, and he did not think she was either.

"Mademoiselle, was your box also empty?"

Rachelle shook her head. "The boxes themselves were gifts, but mine had a jewel inside. I have worn it on two occasions and received no ill effects."

"Madame, do you know what this box contained?" Bertrand asked the duchesse.

"*Mais certainement.* A merveilleux pair of gloves from Catherine's special maker on the quay," the duchesse said.

Rachelle looked up. "Oui, and that is what I thought Grandmère was telling me, *gloves*. But I expected them to be inside the box."

Bertrand turned from facing the hearth. "Tell me, Madame, can you recall whether or not she may have worn them?"

"Oh well, bien sûr, I remember distinctly that she had them on when she returned from the market—"

Andelot raised his gaze sharply, as did Rachelle.

"Ah …," Bertrand murmured, frowning.

The duchesse's voice had suddenly gone flat as the implication of her own words appeared to have left her shaken.

"Gloves," she reiterated.

Rachelle nodded. "I am most sure she tried to say the word *gloves*."

"Just so," Andelot agreed. "Not apples, but gloves. The apples were eaten at about the same time as the poison was working, for several hours, through her skin."

Rachelle sprang to her feet and took a turn about the chamber. "Poor Grandmère. If only I had been here! I should not have taken refuge at Vendôme but come straight to Paris!"

"You could not have stopped what took place," the duchesse said. She clenched the handkerchief she held upon her lap. Her face was pale.

Rachelle sank onto a rose settee, head in hand. Andelot walked up beside her.

"Why did I not receive a pair?" Rachelle cried, as though it were unfair that Grandmère should be poisoned while she went free.

*She loved Grandmère more than anyone in the family*, Andelot thought, at a loss to comfort her.

Bertrand walked over to Rachelle, laying a kindly hand of encouragement on her shoulder. "If you did not receive gloves, perhaps it is because you are yet useful to Madame le Serpent. We must see to it that you do not return to Court." And he looked at the duchesse for her confirmation.

"I shall do my utmost, Bertrand, but as you know, it is the Queen Mother who decides such matters. Perhaps with Sebastien arrested on charges of treason, she will have no further interest in the Macquinets."

"May God grant it, Madame, but I have my doubts."

"We must consider that we still have no proof of poison."

Andelot, however, was convinced.

Bertrand looked at Rachelle. "You say Madeleine also received the same gloves? Then chère ladies, you must find them! For her illness is most likely caused by the same devilish means."

"Madeleine!" Rachelle sprang to her feet as though a burst of energy flowed through her and fled from the sitting room in a direction that Andelot guessed must be her sister's bedchamber.

The duchesse heaved herself to her feet clutching her walking stick. "Cher God in heaven," she whispered as a prayer. "Yes, yes. Madeleine's gloves were sitting in plain sight on her vanity table for the last week. I remember now. She had mentioned them to me when I came to see bébé Joan. Saying something about how they were too large."

"Then give thanks to God they did not fit," Bertrand said. "The shortness of the time she wore them may spare her life."

The duchesse turned toward Andelot, her eyes bright with worry. "Andelot, this way, we may need you."

She limped with her cane as rapidly as she could, and Andelot followed.

Madame called to her maid of honor as they passed the outer chamber.

"Madame Sully, detain le docteur should he try to depart just now. I have something important to ask of him."

"Oui, Madame-Duchesse."

Andelot followed the duchesse to the door of Madeleine's bedchamber without restriction. Her ladies were keeping silent vigil and candles gleamed. One of the ladies-in-waiting was blotting Madeleine's pale face with a cloth. They moved aside as Rachelle swept in and begin to search the vanity tables and bureaus.

Duchesse Dushane walked over to the bed and looked down upon Madeleine.

"How is she?"

"She sleeps most soundly, Madame. Le docteur gave her more medication."

Andelot's heart was as heavy as a satchel of rocks. One look at the once belle Madeleine Macquinet-Dangeau and he feared her trek was not far behind Grandmère's. Anger boiled in his stomach, bringing with it a hideous fear of the tall Italian woman in black. Why had she done this?

Duchesse Dushane dismissed all the ladies-in-waiting, and though surprised, they departed into the antechamber. She looked across the room at Rachelle, who was still searching with frantic determination.

"They are gone," Rachelle cried.

"They must be there. I saw them on that very table next to the gold filigree box."

She turned and looked at the duchesse. "Who could have taken them?"

"The ladies would never steal from her, or from me."

"I was not thinking of that, but perhaps they removed them."

"Or," Andelot said uneasily, "would she have given them away because they were too large?"

The duchesse sat down heavily.

"Let us ask the ladies-in-waiting." Rachelle hurried to the door of the antechamber and went inside.

Andelot heard her questioning them. A few minutes later she returned, walking slowly, thoughtfully.

"They know nothing about the missing gloves. Mademoiselle Richelieu says she remembers them on the table beside the box, but that was on the day Grandmère became ill. She has not seen them since. The others say the same."

The duchesse groaned.

Rachelle went back to the bureau and searched again, but then threw up her hands. "It is no use. Someone took them."

"Perhaps your sister put them away somewhere before she became ill," Andelot encouraged.

Rachelle did not appear convinced.

Andelot watched Rachelle near the bedside of her eldest sister. She kneeled and prayed, then followed the duchesse out. Andelot went back to the sitting room where Cousin Bertrand waited. He was holding up well, though his face was drawn and lacking some color. Andelot explained that the gloves had disappeared.

"What is this about a poison laboratory at Amboise?"

Andelot told him of his ill adventure there at the fortress with Prince Charles Valois and the astrology chamber near the Queen Mother's bedchamber.

"There were many poisons, Monsieur; I saw them myself," he said in a hushed voice. "And there was a certain powder in a vial with a written note. *Sprinkle on garments or inside gloves*, or some such words of that nature. I cannot recall all, but I fear some of that diabolical poison was used in the gloves."

"I believe you may be correct, Andelot. Astrology, the black arts, and poisons." Bertrand shook his head with grief. "I hear it is even at Rome as it is here at Court. For your sake, you must promise to say nothing of what you know to anyone at Court, especially to the Guises."

"Of that, Monsieur, you may be certain."

Bertrand regarded him evenly. "Let us hope so, Andelot."

"Just so, Monsieur, but what of you? What of this long journey to Calais you mentioned to Mademoiselle Rachelle? Will you yet go?"

Bertrand gave him a hard, thoughtful look. "Do I take a chance with you, Andelot?"

"Monsieur?" He wrinkled his brow, uncertain what he meant.

"Rachelle trusts you implicitly. From what I hear, so does Marquis de Vendôme, whom you are able to call your ami. The duchesse too appears to welcome you into her confidences. You are here with us now, hearing us speak of poison and betrayal. And yet I am told from other reliable sources that the cardinal looks upon you as a possible favorite, that he intends to enter you into the university for a high position in the state church, perhaps to follow his own steps and one day receive the red hat as a cardinal after him. And shall I take you into my confidence about why I go to Calais and London?" Bertrand arched a silver brow, his dark eyes measuring him.

Andelot did not know what to say. He was accustomed to the Huguenots taking his friendship for granted, speaking freely in his presence, even as he did in theirs. The thought of betrayal after the slaughter of Amboise was hideous to him. He realized, however, this was not well known to Pasteur Bertrand, a theologian from Geneva who would be considered a bon "catch" by the inquisitors.

"Monsieur," Andelot said, "I confess that I do not know the reasons for your going to Calais or to London, but I suppose it has something to do with propagating your Reformational beliefs. But that is not why I wish to go to Calais with you. It is to try to warn Marquis Fabien that Sebastien is facing a cruel and monstrous death, and perchance the marquis can delay his voyage and appeal to his ami, King Francis."

Bertrand watched him, and his dark eyes glimmered. "That is one of the reasons why I go."

Andelot found that he somehow wanted this older monsieur to trust him. "No longer, Monsieur, am I deemed the favorite of the cardinal, for as I mentioned in the coach, I have offended him while at Amboise. They say I have their blood, that mon père Louis was a Guise cousin disowned by the family, and that Louis was adopted by Sebastien's family, the Dangeaus. But I am not esteemed enough to be in a position to know the plans of the cardinal."

"Then if you accompany me to Calais, your advancement at Court through the bon graces of the cardinal will be at further risk."

"I shall be fully disowned if the cardinal learns I brought the marquis word of Sebastien's arrest."

Bertrand seemed aware. "Do you wish to serve the cardinal?"

Andelot hesitated. He was sure the way to this man's friendship was through integrity.

"Monsieur, I think you know that I am not a practicing Huguenot; therefore I am not averse to studying in the church universities. I had hoped to become a great scholar like Thauvet. However, I do not wish to be a practicing priest."

"You walk a narrow path, Andelot. You must be careful where it leads you."

"Just so, Monsieur. And yet, learning may yet enable me to discover where this narrow path you speak of leads to in the end."

*And just where will it lead me?* Andelot wondered.

"Your dilemma weighs heavily upon you, as I can see. None can choose the path your feet will tread except your own will and heart. My advice is to pray much about your decisions. Look to His counsel and His working in your soul. His Word will guide you if you surrender your desires to His purposes. I can tell you from experience to be most cautious in dealing with the House of Guise."

"Monsieur, if I intended to please only the cardinal, I would be far removed from this chamber."

"Unless you were a spy."

Andelot, stunned, stared at him. "A spy!"

But Bertrand's thin smile and burning eyes assured him he did not think it so. "If for no other reason than your amorous feelings for the mademoiselle."

Andelot felt his neck begin to burn. "I have other reasons, Monsieur Bertrand. I assure you upon my honneur, I would never betray the marquis. And if he were here now he would swear it so!"

Bertrand put a hand on his shoulder, his gaze sober and frank. "Do not be angry because I test your fealty, Andelot. As a Huguenot pasteur, and an ami of the hated John Calvin, I must be cautious of those I hold in confidence."

"You speak well, Monsieur. It is true, what you say. I hope one day you will know I can be trusted."

Bertrand's eyes softened. "I feel strongly that the hour will come. It may interest you to know that I have decided to make certain it will come. So you wish to be a great scholar, do you?"

Again, Andelot was taken off guard and stared at him. "That is what I hope to become."

"Then perhaps there are more ways to accomplish that hope than you now realize. But come! We have no time to lose. I tell you this; I go to Calais to intercept the very one you say is a true ami to you, to the Macquinets, and to Sebastien."

Rachelle and the duchesse had returned to the sitting room, and Bertrand looked over at Rachelle who was speaking in low tones to the duchesse. "Matters have changed," Bertrand said. "I see them in a clearer light than I did only a week ago at the château. I begin to think the marquis, who appears to have earned everyone's confidence, including Madame's, may be the seigneur we need to save Sebastien."

Andelot felt his hopes revive. "Then we shall try and intercept him at Calais?"

"As you say, we shall try." He looked over at Rachelle. "I think it wise that Rachelle join us."

Andelot had not expected Pasteur Bertrand to suggest it, but he knew she wanted to go for her own reasons.

"When would you wish to leave?" Andelot asked.

"If we hope for success, we must not delay. I would leave this night."

Andelot agreed. "With the help of Madame and Page Romier, it can be arranged, Monsieur."

"Bien, do all you can. I shall speak with Rachelle while you ready matters for travel."

A short time later with the duchesse and Rachelle informed of Pasteur Bertrand's plans, Duchesse Dushane promised all the assistance necessary, including fresh horses. She would stable Fabien's golden bay until Andelot returned, for he had told her that he feared the grand stallion had been ridden too strenuously in recent weeks. The truth was, he did not want to see the marquis' scowl should his favorite horse look worn upon his return.

With matters settled concerning their plans, the duchesse called her servants to gather supplies and ready the horses. Andelot joined Bertrand and Rachelle for a light meal with the duchesse and learned that Rachelle agreed to go on to Calais and leave her sister Madeleine in the care of her ladies and the duchesse.

"I want to be the one who tells Père about Avril and Grandmère," she said. "Madame Clair would approve, I am sure."

Andelot was sure this was the primary reason she wanted to go, but he guessed there were other reasons as well. This dampened his spirits, for he was not ignorant of the flame that burned between Rachelle and Marquis Fabien.

She sat across the table from him, and as he watched, he was struck again by how she had changed since Amboise; he had first noted the difference at the château when he brought news of Grandmère. At first he thought it was his imagination. She had been through much turmoil, as had they all. But now that he had been around her for several days, he could see Rachelle truly had changed.

The once tender brown eyes were now like hard, flashing jewels. Her face, too, carried a new determination he did not recall seeing in the past. This worried him. He wondered if she dreamed of revenge. Andelot had no spiritual problem with revenge, though Pasteur Bertrand rejected the idea. Andelot did have fears for what might happen to Rachelle if she tried to enact the revenge she wanted. Would the marquis notice the change when he met her again?

He was aware of some matter that had arisen to build a barrier between Rachelle and Marquis Fabien, some chill which held her in silence whenever his name was mentioned. *Should I not be content to have it so? Maybe this will give me opportunity.*

Andelot smiled and relished his choice cut of roast pheasant and chestnuts.

After the meal, as they prepared to depart, the duchesse informed Rachelle that she would write the unhappy lettre to the Château de Silk of Grandmère's passing and explain Bertrand's wish for Rachelle to accompany him to Calais.

The duchesse came to Bertrand.

"Our good God go before you, Bertrand."

"Your servant, Madame. I suspect our paths may again cross, perhaps at Fontainebleau at the colloquy in the fall."

"I shall be there in full support of our cause, I promise you. You are always welcome at the Dushane estate. Au revoir."

Rachelle dipped a curtsy. "Merci, Madame, for all your care for Grandmère and Madeleine." She kissed her hand, and turning, swept from the chamber with Bertrand following.

Andelot bowed as the duchesse turned to him.

"Your Grace, I bid you adieu."

"Godspeed, Andelot. Do tell the marquis we need him desperately to intercede on behalf of Comte Sebastien."

# The Privateers' Expectation

## CALAIS

Marquis Fabien's arrival at the medieval town of Calais was bittersweet. It was here that the French forces under the command of the Duc de Guise defeated the English and won him the title of the great Le Balafrey, and it was near Calais in an earlier battle that Duc Jean Louis de Bourbon had been left to die, cut off from reinforcements by the same scheming duc.

Calais had long been the port of passage across the channel to England. The *citadelle* was the name given to the line of defense around the *Pas de Calais* with fortifications dating from the thirteenth century. Though there were complaints from merchant ship captains that the old port was a den of pirates, to Fabien this was a most fitting port to wait quietly with the other privateers for word from spies on the movements of Spanish galleons.

In spite of the sea air, the day seemed warm and muggy. Fabien entered one of the gates with Gallaudet and his men-at-arms, all heavily armed. The town was surrounded by ancient walls, which were encircled with canals that formed a moat. Here, generations before, Calais had faced starvation under siege by the English King Henry rather than surrender. There was a French tribute to the seven burghers who had offered to surrender their lives if the king would permit the rest of the French populace to flee the city. If Fabien could think of anything good to say about that monarch who had invaded France so long ago, it was that he had not slaughtered the people of Calais and had also spared the lives of the seven brave burghers.

"Such ordinary and reasonable acts now seem magnanimous, Gallaudet," Fabien said as they rode into the town, the horses' hooves rattling over the ancient cobbles. "It seems rare this day when kings and ducs mind burning women and children alive in a place of simple worship."

"Just so, Monseigneur."

They went toward the Place d'Armes, the main square in the town center with the thirteenth-century watchtower. From the lookout, a guard searched the horizon, alert for approaching enemies.

Fabien noted that many of the new inhabitants of Calais were Huguenots fleeing persecution from other areas of France. They had brought with them their valuable weaving skills, and he saw many shops producing all manner of intricate lace and cloth. Should they need to flee farther to escape fiery faggots, the next place of refuge was across the gray channel to what had become, under Queen Elizabeth, Protestant England. He knew that many Huguenot *émigrés* of French middle class were settling in Spitalfields, where they labored in the growing industry that produced lace, silken cloth, and many goods that gave them such a fine name among the English.

"Monseigneur, look — silk weavers." Gallaudet gestured across the square to some shops with magnificent displays of lace.

As Fabien viewed the various weavers, skilled craftsmen, and couturières, a dark mood settled over him. He narrowed his gaze upon a haunting image of Rachelle when he saw a French woman carrying a bolt of lace along the wooden walk between shops.

*Do not think about her.* He noticed a certain monsieur who followed her into the lace shop. *Could it be?* He bore a marked resemblance to Bertrand, except he was younger. *Monsieur Arnaut Macquinet?*

After settling their horses and baggage at the hostel near the quay, and leaving some of his men there, Fabien took Gallaudet and Julot Caszalet, a relative to Sebastien, and went down to the harbor where ships of all sizes and from many regions were at anchor.

The smell of the sea, the wind, the lap of water against the hulls, all awakened him to a new world that beckoned with far more enticement than did the velvet and pearls, the smothering ambition, and the many ruses of the French court.

His ship was waiting; this first sight wove its romantic spell of enchantment upon his mind. Here was the *Reprisal*, as he was wont to name her, lulling peacefully at anchor, her guns now sleeping but fully capable of taking on a Spanish galleon. She was top of the line, bought from one of Queen Elizabeth's closest plotters, and with her secret consent. Fabien had paid a king's ransom for this, one of the more advanced English ships of this day. Even so, had it not been for his meetings with the queen's privateers: Captain John Hawkins, Sir Martin Frobisher, Sir Francis Drake, and others, he might not have gotten this particular vessel.

As Fabien boarded, he was greeted with fanfaronnade by the crew, but to protect his identity from reaching the throne of France, his family ensign would not fly until at sea but would be replaced by a flag of piracy when intercepting ships from Spain.

This was a British capital vessel equal to other ships of the line, heavily armed, and maneuverable. The experienced crew had been handpicked by Nappier who would serve as *capitaine* while Fabien learned the secrets of mastering his own vessel. Fabien's own men, eager to board Spanish vessels and fight their enemy hand to hand with swords, would have to learn the ways of the sea from the skilled crewmen. The ship's cannons would be in the hands of gunners hired by Nappier. As for navigation, though Fabien believed he could assist Nappier with charts and sextant readings, he would need to trust Nappier's experience.

The crew respected Fabien. He was sure it gave the corsairs satisfaction that they would be serving under a Bourbon and a genuine marquis on whose buccaneering vessel they would sail to attack the despised leaders of the Inquisition. In the process they would take their booty from Spain's galleons. Fabien had already decided he cared very little if the stolen wealth from the Caribbean was taken away from Spaniards who lit faggots under the feet of Huguenots and Lutherans.

These corsairs knew little of Fabien's own skills with the blade except through the praise of Nappier, and some believed Nappier boasted of this to give pride and confidence to his men. "It is always wise to prove one's self," Fabien had told Gallaudet. "And it gives me pleasure to show them that a noble is not always a fop who just happens to be born wealthy and of royal blood."

Fabien looked upon Nappier with genuine affection and trust. Nappier had left the sea and worked himself up in the Royal Armory, becoming the chief master swordsman. Fabien had met Nappier at the armory at a time when Fabien's impressionable youth had demanded a masculine image to admire. From the time he turned thirteen at Court, he had heard Nappier's tales of buccaneering exploits. Nappier had won his affection and respect, and Fabien had hired him in order to acquire his skills with the sword, both the rapier and the short broad blade.

As the years had passed, Fabien learned of Nappier's contempt for King Philip's Spain and had talked buccaneering to him until Fabien, coming into maturity, had agreed to one day sponsor a ship with Nappier and handpicked members of his former crew. After the Amboise massacre, Fabien felt it imperative that those privateers wishing to aid the Dutch against the Duc d'Alva should move forward without delay.

Fabien knew enough to survive buccaneering ventures for he had gone on several short, secretive voyages when younger and out of school for the summer. Away from Court, it had been easy enough to get his way. The only kinsman who had known about these brief escapades, and who looked the other way, was his favorite Bourbon cousin, Prince Louis de Condé.

Condé had served as one of the principle soldiers of the Huguenot army during the past religious wars in France. Dashing adventurer that Condé was, he merely smiled at Fabien's secret ventures, and no one had been the wiser except perhaps Sebastien, who had for reasons of his own, affected ignorance of Fabien's youthful ventures.

Privateering against Philip's treasure galleons from the Caribbean region of the Americas had been one of Nappier's favorite endeavors, and he was just as eager now as in the past.

"Ah, the ship! It is the best I have seen, Monseigneur," Nappier told him on the tour that morning. He rubbed his big hands together, his eyes sparkling like polished black pearls. "We will give no quarter to the persecutors, eh? We will board and fight with the blade!"

"I am anxious to destroy Spain's supply lines, Nappier, I assure you."

The sun was beaming down upon the gray-blue water and glittering like schools of silvery fish. With great delight Nappier brought him around the grand ship showing him all that was his.

"Ah, she is a grand beauty, she is. She will serve us well," Nappier boasted.

Fabien placed hands on hips and looked up. She had the usual three masts, but her main mast carried additional furls of canvas.

"Topgallants, they are, Marquis Fabien. The new system first used by Hawkins. They can be struck when needed for extra thrust."

"Another reason why I had wanted this ship," Fabien said.

The *Reprisal*, at 120 tons, was built with a fine projecting beak and a square transom stern in which two cannons were mounted on either side of the rudder. From the sides she carried the full complement of two rows of guns.

Nappier brought Fabien to the captain's cabin. It looked comfortable and was fitted with an adequate bunk, a writing desk, and several chairs. Some maps were tacked to the dark oak-paneled walls. His sea chest had been brought in, and a stack of leather-bound books were placed on the floor.

Later that night by lamplight, while his ship gently creaked at its moorings, Fabien thought about Rachelle's father, Monsieur Arnaut. Fabien did not want to involve himself, but once he had seen him near the lace shop, he could not dismiss the man's dilemma from his mind. He found himself struggling with his conscience. How could he leave Arnaut on his own, in danger, with none to help? He would not take the monsieur and his cargo to England, but he could protect him while he was in Calais awaiting transport for his Bibles to the Huguenots at Spitalfields.

He sent for Gallaudet and ordered him to the vicinity of the lace shop on a clandestine mission.

"Discover all you can about how matters progress for him, but do not identify yourself as the page of the Marquis de Vendôme." Fabien was well aware that his association with the band of buccaneers would place him in dire straits with the French throne, not to mention Spain. How his actions would be perceived by Rachelle's father was questionable. It may not be easy to smooth over his association with them, though Fabien needed no justification in his own mind for fighting Spain's inquisitors, nor for defending the privateers in so crucial a task as defending their realms.

Several more days passed as restlessness stalked the privateers. Fabien called for a meeting in one of the warehouses on the dock.

Capitaine Pascal, reminding Fabien of a lean, hungry wolf anxiously lying in wait, paced incessantly, his tall calf-length boots squeaking. The Dutch Captain Williams looked at him derisively. "The cat's hungry for his rat. Sit down, Pascal. You make us all nervous."

"Something has gone wrong, I swear it; I feel it in my bones. Where is now the news from Plymouth, I ask you? Come, come, Messieurs, you know as well as I that we should have heard by now." His eyes scanned the large empty warehouse where three oil lamps hung along the walls. A storm was brewing and the wooden structure creaked. The pilings beneath the wooden wharves groaned like chained ghosts.

The twelve capitaines with their first mates scowled.

"There is naught to do but wait, Pascal," Nappier said. "Patience is the price of our coming victory."

"Maybe there is a spy among us, eh?" Pascal looked about at each of them as though to sniff them out.

Fabien, lounging by the door, shifted his gaze from the window where rain splattered through a broken pane, to his fellow Frenchman, Pascal. He had known the young corsair for several years now, having met him through Nappier. Pascal could be trusted. He had sworn fealty to the Bourbons and held a particular liking for Fabien. But Pascal had a disposition that cultivated suspicions, which usually came to naught.

A spy? Fabien glanced about at the privateers and rejected Pascal's unhappy mood over the delay in taking to sea. There was not a man in the group that would side with Spain, no, not for a treasure galleon of booty from the Caribbean. He had heard from Nappier that each capitaine had firsthand knowledge of the ways of the inquisitors.

Nappier waved an arm and stood from the chair where he sat. "Spies, bah! You speak riddles, Pascal. Each of us here tonight is itching to sink the Spaniards' innards."

"Aye," said the Englishman, Captain Tuvy. "D'ye be goin' insultin' us, Pascal? A spy, 'e says! Ye'll be accusin' me next of harborin' papists in me 'old."

"Bah, he says, and I say, why have we not heard from Plymouth? Matters, they have gone most injuriously, Messires."

"The weather has worsened," Fabien said. "From the feel of the wind, the storm comes from the north. There is most likely a delay. Patience is called for, Pascal."

Pascal placed his hand at his heart and bowed. "Marquis de Vendôme, I beg of you, the Spaniards may have spotted the spy bark off the coast of Spain and sunk her. Or what of the English ambassador at Madrid?"

"What about 'im?" growled Tuvy, his eyes narrowing over talk of the English. "Are ye now accusin' 'im? Next thing I knows, ye'll be accusin' me queen. And methinks I won't be puttin' up with that, Pascal."

"Your prickly nerves goad us all, Tuvy," Fabien said. "Pascal does well to wonder about the bark."

Pascal's smug smile in Tuvy's direction brought a scowl.

"Methinks, my lordship Vendôme, that all ye fancy Frenchmen ban' yerselves together at the chagrin of the blessed English. But I 'asten to add, me lordship, that I in no ways be accusin' ye of unfair leadership in this matter. Nay, not for a paltry minute."

"You are wise, Messire," Fabien said smoothly, running his fingers along his handsome Holland shirt with wide sleeves. "The wage I offer you and your blessed English crew can only come through fancy Frenchmen."

Pascal's lips spread into a wide smile. "The English never bathe is what I hear."

Tuvy scowled. "That 'asn't a rodent's hair to do with this. As for 'is lordship, I supports 'im. I never spoke against it."

"The blessed English, he calls himself, Monseigneur." Nappier also goaded Tuvy with a grin. "We did not think your controlling Calais all these mournful years was anything but curses to us."

The Frenchmen laughed; the English privateers scowled. The Dutch looked on with forbearance at the French and English self-indulgent bickering.

"Enough, Messires," Fabien said. "We are all in this enterprise together now. It is cursed Spain who looms as the intolerant tyrant over all our countries. We all have one mind: to cut off the head of this viper by sinking its galleons and denying Alva his soldiers and weapons."

"Ah, your lordship, 'tis sprightly said. Why, you're a bristling one to be sure, and I means it from the bottoms of me blessed heart! The first one of us over the side and onto a Spanish deck gets to keep a few papist heads to 'ang in 'is captain's cabin!"

Laughter erupted.

Fabien turned to Nappier wanting to make certain the Frenchmen knew that he was not usurping Nappier's authority as capitaine of the *Reprisal* just because he was their seigneur. He oft found his high position a hindrance, for he had never been one who needed to press subservience from his men. He preferred the company of men like Nappier and Andelot—whom Fabien considered a refreshing change from the haughty nobility. Like his kinsman, Prince Louis de Condé, he also could cavort with soldiers and privateers and find acceptance among them.

"But not indefinitely," Fabien said. "I know through contacts in the French court that the army of Duc d'Alva desperately needs more soldiers, foodstuffs, and weapons. He will either risk his precious galleons or journey by land. If he goes by land, it will slow him down considerably. He is aware that Dutch forces under William of Orange are lying in wait. Do you agree, Henrich?" he asked of the Hollander, a muscled, flaxen-haired man with hard blue eyes.

The Hollander wore a stern face. "Lord William waits, as you say, Monseigneur, and if your Admiral Coligny could raise a few thousand more of his and Prince Condé's Huguenot soldiers to join his forces, we could meet Alva and smash him and his papist inquisitors."

Fabien was not as optimistic, but the Hollander's point was well taken. Fabien spoke, "What do you think, Capitaine Nappier? Is it wise to send one of us across the channel to Plymouth to see the reason for the delay?"

The privateers perked up their ears and regarded Fabien, then Nappier, with interest. They knew he had been Nappier's protégé with the sword, but the comaraderie between monseigneur and serf impressed them.

"It may be wise, Marquis," Nappier said, pacing about and relishing his place of authority among the buccaneers. "I say, the longer we keep our vessels here, the longer suspicious eyes put us at risk as the days pass. Let us be clear on one matter, Messires — " he turned with a sweeping glance to all capitaines in assembly — "Calais is indeed in the hands of France again, but she crawls with Spaniards and spies. We may hope our presence here is yet undiscovered, but if a Spaniard recognized any of us and sent a message to Madrid, it could delay the sailing of the galleons to our loss."

It was soon agreed to allow Pascal to slip away before dawn to Plymouth, the nearest English port from Spain, and make contact with friendly spies. It was hoped their man on the French bark, loitering in safe waters off the coast of Spain, had by now received the message from the French ambassador's page, a secret Huguenot. The page was to send word by longboat to the bark's capitaine, who would promptly sail for Plymouth. If all worked according to plan, the word they awaited from Plymouth could only be delayed by rough weather.

The meeting ended and the privateers slipped away one and two at a time, melting into the darkness of the wharves.

The rain had ebbed when Fabien stepped onto the wharf, putting on his cloak and settling his wide-rimmed hat. The lamps on the vessels at anchor glowed in the darkness. Several of his men emerged from the shadows; Gallaudet came forward.

"What did you find out?" Fabien asked.

"It is as you thought, Marquis. Monsieur Arnaut Macquinet is here. He is being secretly shielded in a small antechamber connected to the Alençon lace shop. I asked around and learned the shop belongs to the Languet family, all Huguenots. They do much trade with the French weavers at Spitalfields. No lettres have arrived for him from Lyon or

Paris, I was told. Then he knows naught of what befell his family at Château de Silk."

"I did not think he would, Gallaudet. Correspondence is slow. And I am in no frame of mind to tell him his petite child is dead and his middle daughter forced. This tragedy should be broken to him by one closest to his heart. He must wait for the lettre from Madame Clair. Let that suffice. So far we have kept the incident silent here. Tell the men the matter must not be broached by any of them, or they will know my extreme displeasure."

"Just so. I will warn them again. Would you have me contact Monsieur Arnaut of your wish to see him?"

"Non, not yet. But have Julot watch over him when he goes out of the shop."

Fabien was awake at the first hint of dawn. Dressed in leather breeches and a loose linen tunic open at the neck, he was enjoying his petit noir and watching Capitaine Pascal's ship, le *Fox*, leaving Calais harbor on its way across the channel to Plymouth. The ship's lights were out, and the dark ghostly image, barely silhouetted against the horizon, slipped quietly out of port as faint ripples reflected the dawn.

The storm had passed and a morning star gleamed.

Rachelle came to his mind. That she had tried to manipulate to get her way bothered him. He leaned against the ship's rail and watched the brightening horizon. He had insisted on his freedom, and doubtless she was hurt and angry.

The situation they had brought upon themselves was not one easily overcome. He was young, and Rachelle younger still. Dark days were looming over France, and love, if it were genuine, must be rational enough to confront the winds of trial. Much stood against them that he had merely set aside in the beginning, including his position, their allegiance to different bodies of Christian doctrine, and the times in which they found themselves placed by God.

Life and love and passion were not for the fainthearted. Life itself offered little comfort from the cruelties that abounded. Love, if it were to prosper between them and grow, must know how to give and forgive; and passion without a marriage commitment was but lust, empty of valor and without endurance, as in the Scripture he had read while at Vendôme: "Charity endureth all things."

⁂

"Ho! Monseigneur Capitaine!"

Nappier strode across the deck of the *Reprisal* toward Fabien, with the plume on his hat swaying, his hand on the jeweled scabbard that was a gift from Fabien when Nappier served at the Royal Armory in Paris.

"We do not need to wait for Pascal's findings. This arrived just now from Plymouth. The messenger is with the cook eating now."

Fabien broke the seal and read the short message: *Proceed to planned rendezvous with all haste; the quarry has ventured from its pond.*

He glanced up and saw the gulls wheeling in an updraft. "The wind is favorable. When is the soonest we can sail?"

"Tomorrow morning, Marquis; the capitaines will need to take on foodstuffs."

"Gallaudet! I need you with me. We have to pay a visit to Monsieur Arnaut."

Fabien stepped to his cabin to get his scabbard and belted it carefully. He grabbed a dark tunic from a hook and shouldered into it. Snatching his hat, he strode out and across the deck to the gangplank with Gallaudet rushing behind as though he were accustomed to unexpected action from his seigneur.

"What are we about, Monseigneur?"

"We will pay a short visit to Monsieur Macquinet. He must be warned of the spy Julot noticed loitering near the Huguenot shop. Now that we are departing, we can no longer act as his secret bodyguard."

"The galleons were spotted then?"

"They were. We sail for the rendezvous point off the coast of Holland. We shall wait there to surprise them. Are you in a warm, mellow mood to greet le Duc d'Alva's new soldiers, Gallaudet?"

"I am overflowing in bonhomie, Monseigneur."

# Hearts at Conflict

THE COACH-AND-SIX CARRYING COUSIN BERTRAND, RACHELLE, AND Andelot entered Calais at sunset. Silvery clouds tinged with pink, gray, and lavender loitered over the channel waters between the continent and England.

*More rain?* The roads were slippery and muddy all the way from Paris. Rachelle longed for a warm bath and a bed, either at an inn or the Languets' house, but she dreaded the moment when she and Bertrand must tell her father about Avril. She thought perchance the lettre, written to him from Madame Clair, might have arrived by now. If so, it would be most *naturel* that he would wish to rush home to Lyon to comfort his wife. *Might they be too late to contact either her père Arnaut or the marquis?*

Rachelle prayed earnestly.

The carriage wheels and horse hooves clattered down the mistenshrouded street. Here in the Huguenot section of Calais, Rachelle's first sight of the lace and couturière shops scattered along the crowded way brought her some cheer. One of these lace shops belonged to the Languets, a family originally from Alençon, whom the Macquinets had done business with for years. Persecution had driven them from their château to English-controlled Calais to set up their lace shop, exporting to London.

Calais had been reasonably safe for Protestants, but matters had changed since it was now under French rule, due to Duc de Guise's military victory over the English several years earlier. Now, even Calais could not promise to remain a haven for Protestants in France. Already there was a movement from the bishop to close Huguenot churches. Should persecution break out, they must look across the channel to England's Spitalfields.

The Macquinet coachman helped Rachelle and Bertrand out onto the carriage block in front of the Languet lace shop. He then brought the coach around the corner to the hostelry to board their horses for the night, followed by Andelot, Romier, and the guards who had escorted the coach from Paris.

Mist swirled around her as she lifted her dark-hooded cape, fixing her gaze on the exquisite lace shop. Even her weariness could not smother the rise of *joie de vivre* which soon swept through her as she gazed under the shop awning at a lace display arranged in several new patterns and crochets, with variegated colors, including shades of pink and rose. Some were feathered with gold so that when it was sewn to sleeves, necklines, skirt loops, or hems, it would fall in soft draping folds.

"C'est magnifique. I must look inside. I have yet to see any lace this wondrous. I should buy at least one bolt to take home to the Château de Silk," she murmured to Cousin Bertrand. "It will please ma mère and may even cheer Idelette." Idelette was always entranced with lace of any kind. Some of this particular lace on the gown for the English queen would make it all the more belle.

She glanced to Cousin Bertrand's alert figure in black, his dark eyes flashed under his white brows. His attention was directed to the upper story window with open shutters and draperies pulled back. Figures moved about the chamber.

"Ah! It appears we are in time, Rachelle. We best make our entrance through the back way. I believe Arnaut entertains a surprising and unexpected guest. Come, as I recall most clearly, there are steps to Monsieur Languet's door."

Rachelle had forgotten that Cousin Bertrand had been here in the past when traveling to Spitalfields, often smuggling French or Dutch Bibles to ministers. Burning at the stake awaited any who printed, distributed, or even possessed a Bible in the French language. He would often say, "We must be willing to lay down our lives if called upon to do so. We, and we alone, are the torchbearers, and we must be about our Father's business. If the Reformation fails in France, then I fear all is lost for us as a great nation in Europe. We must *tenez ferme* as the Word tells us: stand firm in the battle now raging, for it will affect generations to come. We must persevere to be useful and not hide in fear. For what is our life? It is but a vapor. What we do, we must do while it is yet light."

Rachelle was sure she did not have the same courage as Cousin Bertrand and her père Arnaut.

She followed him across the cobbled way and around the shop through a narrow alley into a small stone court with high rock walls. A vine bearing some manner of purple flower rambled along the top of the wall and spilled over a lattice archway. She passed through the archway into an even tighter court where pots of geraniums grew alongside a steep double flight of stone steps that wound upward to the back entrance of the house.

Rachelle did not recall the Languet family very well, for she had been a child when they had left Alençon for Calais, but she did remember an older husband and wife and a married son. All the family members worked on their lace while secretly aiding Huguenot ministers like Pasteur Bertrand.

Rachelle climbed the steps and waited for him on the porch, hoping the exertion would not stress his still-tender injuries. He made it to the door with only moderate difficulty and used his stick to beat three raps on the door, followed by two and then three more.

A moment later the door opened by a small serving woman with cautious eyes.

"Bonjour, Thérèse, it is I, Bertrand Macquinet. My cousin Arnaut is here, I do presume?"

Her sallow face broke into a smile. "Oui, oui, Messire Bertrand. Come, come, they are all in the salle now. Your bonne arrival will be most pleasing. Messire Arnaut has been wondering of your absence."

Rachelle's heart sank. Bertrand, too, apparently picked up the hint. "Then there has been no correspondence yet received from the Château de Silk for Arnaut?"

"Non, Messire, no lettre has come for anyone."

Rachelle glanced at Bertrand. He met her gaze with a slight drawing of his brows.

"Then we have much news to pass on, Thérèse. Announce us, s'il vous plaît. This is Mademoiselle Rachelle, Arnaut's daughter."

Thérèse dipped a curtsy, her faded face producing a smile, and opened the door wider, beckoning them inside to the small foyer where a flower-strewn rug graced the floor. There was another door to the right, and voices came from there. Footsteps approached, and she turned to see Arnaut Macquinet in the doorway. He was a rugged man, broad-shouldered beneath his sage-green coat of brocade satin, his square face handsome with a cleft in his chin. A slash of chestnut brows matched graying chestnut hair that once had been darker than Rachelle's own wealth of auburn-brown.

A look of surprise and delight broke on his face as he first saw her, and then his cousin Bertrand standing in the foyer.

"Père!" she called with a catch of both joy and sadness in her voice. She had not seen her father in over a year, and she ran to him, relishing the fatherly hug that left her feeling safe and loved once more. "Oh Père, how happy to be with you again—"

Her voice failed on that unfinished note, for as she raised her head from his shoulder and looked up, her gaze fell on Marquis Fabien. He stood in the chamber Arnaut had just come from, his expression holding the same hint of surprise that must have shown on her face.

Arnaut, who knew nothing of her relationship with Fabien or that she had even met him, turned to Fabien. "May I present my daughter, Rachelle; Rachelle, this is Marquis Fabien de Vendôme."

Rachelle recovered. Determined this time to rebuild her dignity, she retained a cool, almost unreachable demeanor and offered a curtsy. "Monseigneur," she murmured distantly.

His eyes hardened perceptibly as he scanned her. "Mademoiselle," he said as distantly, bowing.

"Le marquis is here on business, Rachelle, and whatever are you doing here with Bertrand? Surely your mother did not come also?"

"Non, mon père. I came alone with Cousin Bertrand and Andelot Dangeau; you remember him, of course?"

He smiled indulgently, his arm still around her. "But yes, of course I remember your *petit* beau, Andelot."

Rachelle covered a wince. Her father made it sound as though she and Andelot had always been secret sweethearts. Arnaut turned to the quiet figure of Bertrand standing a few steps away, looking sober, as though he too understood the task before him.

"I had begun to think mon cousin that you had returned to Geneva and would not come to Calais," Arnaut said cheerfully. "Then you did receive my message."

*He certainly does not know what happened at the château.*

Rachelle glanced toward Fabien. He was watching Bertrand and Arnaut. Evidently, she thought, the marquis had not told her father anything of the events of recent days at Lyon. *Had Fabien discussed the message she had shown him about the Bibles?* He wished to avoid any involvement in the dilemma. *But then, why was he here?* Her father could not have sought the marquis because he was not aware of his presence in Calais. Had Fabien changed his mind about taking the Bibles to England?

Rachelle retained her poise and felt most pleased with herself. A glance at Fabien found his gaze on her. Their eyes met and clung for a moment as she miserably felt the heat begin to stain her cheeks. She lifted her chin as she had seen the sophisticated ladies at Court do and turned her head to Arnaut.

"Le marquis is here on business."

"Ah?" Bertrand's white brows climbed. "I was told by Andelot that you have your own ship."

"I do, Pasteur Bertrand, but urgent business calls me away from Calais."

"Perhaps we can continue our discussion in Languet's study," Arnaut said. "Messires, if you please?" He extended an arm toward a door that led into another room. "Rachelle," he said, "Thérése will take you to the guest room to rest and refresh yourself before dinner."

She was to be excluded from the men's business dealings, but she was accustomed to this and knew better than to push herself before her father. He had always taught his daughters to keep to their work as couturières and grisettes and leave the risk taking to the men in the family. Little did her beloved père know all the horrendous experiences she had come through since she last saw him, and by God's grace, she had survived to grow stronger.

"Mon cousin, you have injured yourself?" Arnaut asked, as he noted Bertrand protectively favoring his right arm and shoulder.

"I tell you aforehand that I bring news that will test your soul, mon cousin Arnaut."

Rachelle stood tensely on the top step, looking after her father, an ache in her heart as she realized the agony he was about to face. After Arnaut and Bertrand passed into the next room, she moved her gaze across the room to Fabien.

He watched her evenly.

She met his burning violet-blue eyes with new determination. Now was the time to reclaim her shattered reputation from the humiliating rags of their last meeting at the château. There would be no more falling at his feet and begging for morsels of his favor.

She waited for him to walk to where she stood by a banister, her hand resting on the newel. She had never seen him dressed this way before — in rugged leather breeches, boots, and a dark loose tunic with full sleeves. His rapier was housed in a jeweled leather sheath, and he carried a wide-rimmed hat that also appeared to be of sturdy leather embellished with silver.

"You mentioned having come here from Paris. What were you doing at the Louvre when you were secure at the château with the guards I trusted?"

It was as though he were bracing himself for another emotional duel about why he should not leave France or her.

She arched a brow. "My reasons, Marquis, are my personal concern. Like you, I have matters that include no one except myself, and I feel no obligation to explain them for your approval."

Her grave dignity appeared to further exasperate him. His steady gaze sent the skin on the back of her neck tingling.

"I have no desire to detain you from your beloved ship for even a moment, I assure you," she continued. "I did not come to Calais to locate you, if that is your concern. I came to see Père Arnaut. Had I known you were here, I should have delayed my entry until after your departure."

The marquis knew nothing yet of Sebastien's state in the Bastille, or that they had journeyed here with the hope of securing Fabien's help in appealing to the king. Nor was she prepared to speak to him of Grandmère's death, for her emotions would weaken her before him when she needed to be strong. It was wiser to leave the distressing news of Sebastien for Bertrand or Andelot to tell.

Rachelle retained an attitude of cool indifference, though her heart ached for the handsome man who stood before her, as unreachable as she.

His eyes sparked blue fire. He regarded her gravely. "You are not only a beautiful woman, but an exasperating one."

Rachelle lifted her chin. "Then I shall remove my exasperating presence from your affairs, Monseigneur, and so I beg your leave." With élégante demeanor, she turned with the practiced air of Princesse Marguerite and began to ascend the stairs. "I bid you adieu."

She heard his small intake of breath. She had taken only one step when his warm fingers took possession of her arm, detaining her.

Her heart raced. She turned toward the warm glitter in his eyes, which did nothing to soothe the moment between them. He drew her down the step until she stood before him.

"You are deliberately trying to frustrate me."

She trembled. "I should inform you, Marquis, that I do not know what you intend by those accusing words." Her eyes fought his. "And I request that you release me."

His eyes narrowed, and in defiance he pulled her closer until she felt the rough tunic beneath her palms; she resisted her desires, knowing her only chance of winning him was to convince him he could lose her. She turned her head away, afraid he would try to kiss her, knowing she could not resist him for long. Already her heart was thudding from his nearness.

Footsteps from the stairwell brought the moment to a swift conclusion. His hand dropped, and he stepped back as Thérése appeared above on the landing. "Oh, I do beg your pardone, I did not know you were with company—"

Rachelle tore her gaze from Fabien's and turning on her heel, slowly ascended the steps, as though untroubled. Little did he know the weakness in her knees.

She had left him looking after her, but when she reached the top she did not turn to see if he was still there. She was sure he was infuriated.

She had survived their first dreaded meeting since Lyon, and she hoped she had been elevated in his mind. Even so, what had changed? They remained estranged, two contrary wills warring. Her heart felt no more comforted now in her pretense of indifference than when she had thrown herself unwisely at his feet.

Once in the small chamber where she could refresh herself, she sank against the closed door and placed her palms to the sides of her head.

*I will not think of him!*

❋

MARQUIS FABIEN STOOD GAZING at Rachelle as she ascended with her head high and her back straight. She looked more belle than ever, though she wore but a simple traveling cloak of blue with a fur collar. Her dress was also plain—the color of mourning, it covered every inch of her skin and throat. Her thick auburn-brown hair lay tumbled about her shoulders from traveling. He had accidentally touched it, and even now, his senses could feel its softness on his hand. Her paleness, due to so much recent sorrow, touched his heart, but her defiant eyes when he had caught hold of her, left him infuriated.

*"Mille diables!"* He breathed, feeling angry and turning on his heel, his boots sounding on the hardwood floor. He snatched up his cloak and strode to the back of the house and down the steep stone steps to the small court past the geraniums.

"Gallaudet!" he demanded.

The lithe, muscled page, fair of head and calm, appeared at once.

"Where have you been?" Fabien demanded with impatience. "Do I need to shout for all to hear?"

"Non, Monseigneur. I beg pardon. I was just—"

Fabien waved a hand. "Never mind. We are returning to my ship."

"Now? But I thought Andelot Dangeau wished to see you and—"

Fabien's steely gaze met Gallaudet's.

"Just so!" Gallaudet said.

Reaching the street, Gallaudet turned and went for their horses and began to round up the Bourbon men-at-arms loitering about an eatery.

Fabien looked back toward Languet's shop. A strange fury burned in his belly so that he realized he was apt to make a fool of himself if he remained in his frustration.

Rachelle was behaving most unreasonably. First, she had pleaded with him to stay; now she refused him with cool disinterest!

He was using sound judgment in leaving France. A year's absence would do him—and her—good. His feelings were getting out of hand —impossible to make sense of. He would not marry her.

*I will not think of her!*

❈

THE *REPRISAL*, MOORED AT the docks, was being loaded, sharing her narrow berth with storm-battered ships from the sea routes. Several tall-masted ships were arriving, fine ships, carved and gilded, sliding through the water, with gulls wheeling in their wake.

The workers on the wharves swarmed noisily. Fleet schooners maneuvered between the ships, unloading their massive holds, hauling off casks of Spanish olive oil, cloves, and cinnamon from the Caribbean. French wine and crates of delicate Bruges lace were waiting on the docks to be loaded as workers staggered beneath iron-hooped bales while horse-drawn wagons added to the chaos.

"Marquis Fabien! Wait!"

Fabien heard the familiar voice shouting behind him and halted his horse. He turned in the saddle and looked over his shoulder. Andelot was clinging precariously to one side of the step-bar of a wharf taxi-wagon, waving at him with a free hand.

Fabien's temper eased at the sight of the young man he had all but adopted as his petit frère, though Andelot, no more than five years younger than Fabien, was swiftly becoming a comely young messire to be reckoned with. Fabien had long ago guessed that Andelot was infatuated with Rachelle, but he had paid scant attention. Now he no longer thought the notion amusing and measured Andelot more seriously as the taxi-wagon rattled closer.

Fabien swung down from the saddle and turned his reins over to a lackey who led the horse off to the wharf hostler. Fabien watched as Andelot jumped from the wagon and trotted up, breathless and grinning.

"Marquis! But it is bonne to see you again, I swear it. I meant to speak with you at Languet's shop, but I was too late. I came just in time to see you riding away. Are you soon to sail?" His eyes searched the harbor. "Which fine ship is yours, Monseigneur?"

"How did you escape the eye of your kinsman, the cardinal? I would have wagered you to be under his supervision and ready to leave for the university by now. Or would you be pleased to sail with me?" Fabien threw an arm around his shoulder and walked with him toward the ship. But the unexpected thoughtful gleam on Andelot's face told Fabien that he might be taken seriously.

"Sainte Marie! But you have indeed changed, Andelot, mon bon ami."

"I vow, Marquis, you surely entice me to abandon Paris, for I am much dispirited. There is to be no university, for Cardinal de Lorraine has disowned me."

"So soon? Then you have a tenfold reason for rejoicing," Fabien said. "What is the cause?"

Andelot glanced at him cautiously. "You are the cause, Marquis. He demands I give up my friendship with you and the House of Bourbon. There will be no Tutor Thauvet, no great university. I was to first have entered the Corps des Pages, but now the door will be bolted tight against me."

"Since I appear to be the stumbling block, mon ami, I will take oversight of your schooling myself."

"Ah, but I did not mean to suggest—"

"I would have suggested it sooner, except for your call to Chambord to meet your unexpected new kinsmen, the Guises. As for the School of Pages, if I were at Court, I would sponsor you and place you under the training of Gallaudet. But as I am not likely to be at Court for a year or longer, you need to be placed now. Let me consider what noble house you would do well under. In the meantime, you will come aboard to see the *Reprisal*."

"The name is most bonne, Marquis, and very telling!" Andelot grinned. "And you are most generous, a better ami no man could have. I have been thinking that I should like to sail as your valet."

"I do not need a valet aboard a buccaneering ship."

"A cook, then."

"Non," he said gravely. "The food will be terrible enough without your assistance. Andelot, mon ami, you have the heart of a scholar, and a scholar you shall be if I have anything to say about it. Besides, I want you to keep an eye on the mademoiselle's safety."

"Mademoiselle?"

"There is only one," Fabien said, looking at him gravely.

"Ah, oui ... Mademoiselle Rachelle."

There was an uncomfortable silence as they walked until Andelot asked, "What did you think about the gloves, Marquis?"

Fabien turned his head. "Gloves?"

"She did not tell you?" Andelot sounded stunned.

Fabien stopped on the wharf. "Tell me what?"

Andelot stared at him, a frown deepening over his brows. "Nor about Oncle Sebastien either?"

"What about him? He is gone, since the massacre of Amboise."

"Ah, Marquis Fabien, then there is much I need to explain and tell you. It concerns the reason we have accompanied Pasteur Bertrand here to Calais. If this was only about him and his cargo of forbidden books, neither I nor Mademoiselle Rachelle would have need to come."

Fabien again grew sober. "Come, then. We best talk in my cabin."

Fabien and Andelot continued along the wharf with Fabien frowning to himself and wondering why Rachelle had not shown more reasonableness with him. So her affairs were her own?

They stepped onto the gangplank, sloping up to the *Reprisal*, and despite the mood that pervaded, Andelot was enthused over all he saw as they walked around the deck and then into the captain's cabin.

"A ship that will make a name for itself, Marquis, I can feel it. I think I should give you this blessed cross the traveling monk gave me a few years ago. It comes from Rome, from the Vatican. The pope blessed it." He reached inside his tunic. "If you hang it in the cabin it will bring protection in case you run into a storm or come up against a Spanish fleet."

"I think you better keep it. You may yet have dealings with the cardinal from which you need to be delivered. He may be pleased to see you wearing it."

Andelot nodded thoughtfully. Fabien opened his cabin door. He smiled. "Duck your head, the doorframe is low."

"Marquis Fabien, sometimes I do not think you truly are a Catholic."

"Now why would you think that? I have said as much before, many times."

"True, but—"

"Even Mademoiselle Rachelle believes I am, as does her Huguenot cousin, Bertrand. It is the reason the Macquinets are cautious of me, I assure you."

"If you are leaning toward Geneva, then you ought to tell them, for her parents and Pasteur Bertrand would warm to you."

"And that would please you, mon ami?"

"Bien sûr—" He stopped, looked at him, and turned his mouth wryly.

"What will you have to refresh yourself?"

"A cup of ale, s'il vous plaît."

Fabien grimaced. *Ale, the petit noir of serfs and slaves*. He opened the cabin door. "Gallaudet! Tell Percy in the cook's room. Make it ale."

Gallaudet returned with cups and a foul appearing ceramic jug. Fabien gestured with disdain. "This, what is it?"

"Ale, Monseigneur. As you said. It is the jug Percy gave me."

"I wager he does not think his time worthy of washing jugs?"

"He says washing the jugs will ruin the brew, Monseigneur."

"Did he! Can anything ruin so disgusting a brew? Then again, perhaps that is why it ferments."

Gallaudet smiled and poured. He bowed, handing it with smooth deference to Fabien. "Monseigneur."

He and Andelot raised their cups.

"To the owner of the *Reprisal*! Happy hunting, Monseigneur!"

Fabien returned the bow. He toasted. "Devastation and ruin to Spain's galleons!"

"So be it!" Gallaudet said.

"To the bottom of the sea!" said Andelot.

Fabien took a mouthful, then pushing open the cabin door, rushed to the rail and spat it out.

***

FABIEN PONDERED ANDELOT'S DARK news of Sebastien's imprisonment. The salle de la question! That Sebastien would be brought before the inquisitors overshadowed all else. He was alive, yes, but for how long?

"The Cardinal de Lorraine said this, you are certain, Andelot? Sebastien will face questioning by Rome's inquisitors?"

"It is so, Marquis Fabien. It is most diabolical. The cardinal called me to his chamber at Amboise and informed me. He was most calm. Then he entrusted his own missive to me to deliver to the duchesse."

Fabien opened the cabin door again to allow the breeze to circulate. The cramped space of the cabin and the low ceiling were tiresome and gave him a feeling of being caged.

*It will be better when I am at sea*, he repeated to himself.

"The news of Sebastien is a double-edged sword," he told Andelot.

"Everyone is hoping and praying, Marquis, that your bonhomie with the king will influence him to show grace to Sebastien."

"With the duc and the cardinal's control over Francis through their niece, Mary?" Fabien shook his head. "I should have better success invading a dragon's lair than altering the young king's mind to oppose the will of the Guise brothers. Even so, I will do all in my power to see Sebastien free of the Bastille."

He would also write to his own kinsmen, the Bourbons, but with Prince Condé also having been secretly involved in the Amboise plot, there was no assurance that even Condé's position as a prince of the blood would prevail for Sebastien. Even now the Guises would be plotting to strengthen their influence over King Francis, and were not above getting him to move against any Bourbon prince in line for the throne.

"I am sent by Duchesse Dushane to receive your lettre and deliver it to her. She will take it to the king if she can get past Cardinal de Lorraine whom they say is never far from him."

"The cardinal fears that those of a different mind other than he and the duc may gain the king's ear."

This cast a shadow upon his plans. If it had not been for the Spanish galleons that were even now on their way toward the Netherlands ...

Fabien leaned against his desk and folded his arms against his chest. He stared intently out the open door where he could see the gray waters of the Calais port and hear the cry of gulls. Sebastien's imprisonment was not the only unsettling news to arrive while the *Reprisal* was on the verge of departing. Andelot had told him of the death of Rachelle's grandmère, the beloved grande dame of Dushane-Macquinet silk. The strange circumstances surrounding her death convinced him of cunning mischief instigated by the Queen Mother.

He rebuked himself for having risked Rachelle and her family, permitting her to get the key to the listening closet at Chambord before the Huguenot rebellion. If the Queen Mother had given poisoned gloves, it could only be because she discovered Rachelle had dared to enter her royal bedchamber to take the key.

But then, why was Rachelle spared? He frowned. He could think of but one reason: Catherine planned on using her in the future.

Fabien turned his gaze on Andelot who stood near the door.

"Did le docteur suggest Grandmère was poisoned?"

"Non, but would he dare if he suspected the Queen Mother?"

"A fair question ... A perilous thing to do, even with undeniable proof. Ambrose Paré is the best of physicians, a Huguenot. Would he say anything? But then, to whom would he report it? To the young King Francis? Hardly."

"Duchesse Dushane has requested an autopsy. Le docteur will tell her what he finds privately."

"And the gloves?"

"They are missing. Does it not appear suspicious that neither pair were found?"

"If the Queen Mother's spy, Madalenna, had not been away at Fontainebleau, I would have suspected her of slipping into Madeleine's chambers and removing them," Fabien said flatly. "However, Catherine has some equally devious spies, including several dwarves. Were inquiries made of her ladies-in-waiting?"

"Mademoiselle Rachelle did so, but no one appears to know anything."

Fabien had Andelot explain once more what he had seen that day with Prince Charles in the astrologer's chamber at Amboise. Fabien had known even as a boy about the Queen Mother's involvement in the occult. There had also been many whispers about Catherine in her younger years when she was married to Henry before he became king. It was said that she had poisoned the dauphin, Henry's older brother who held the birthright to the throne, to bring kingship to Henry.

"I was in the chamber with Grandmère and Rachelle during the last minutes of her life, Marquis. We both heard her try to say the word *gloves*."

"And that was to the question of whether she had been poisoned?"

"Yes, at first we thought it was the apples — or at least I did."

Fabien's anger blazed. "How did Mademoiselle Rachelle accept the death of Grandmère?"

"Bravely, Marquis. Oui, most courageously. It is her way. But I have noticed a new firmness in her, a new determination I do not recall from the past. She believes the Queen Mother took her grandmère's life, and if she could, Marquis, I swear she would seek revenge."

Fabien stood with hands on hips scowling at his desk. Revenge was not like Rachelle. She had recently been hurt deeply by circumstances that shocked her innocence and left her unsettled and anxious. But now that her father was here, Fabien believed she would receive the support she needed.

He also thought back to her willingness to enter the Queen Mother's bedchamber for the key to the listening closet, and agreed with Andelot. She had been through so much recently that it was unfair to hold her to account for her recent behavior.

Gallaudet leaned in the doorway. "Monseigneur, pardone, but a visitor wishes to see you posthaste. Monsieur Bertrand is here."

As Gallaudet spoke, an unexpected shadow fell across the doorway.

The tall figure in the dark scholarly robe with a white coif and a very wide-brimmed black hat used by the Geneva ministers stood outside the door. "Bonjour, Capitaine."

"Welcome, Pasteur Bertrand. But Nappier, who is an ami, and the finest swordsman I have had the privilege of training under, is presently the capitaine of the *Reprisal*."

"Ah, then, most interesting. So you are a swordsman, are you?"

*Now why is he here, and what does he want?* If it had anything to do with the French Bibles and a voyage to England, he would have to disappoint him, even as he had to disappoint Monsieur Arnaut earlier that day at Languet's lace shop when telling him he could not take him to England. Surely Arnaut would have told this to his cousin Bertrand. Fabien trusted that after his order to Julot, the spy would no longer be prowling about Languet's shop.

Bertrand entered and Andelot quickly pulled out a chair.

"Merci. I shall get straight to the point, Marquis de Vendôme. Arnaut is taking Rachelle at once to Paris in order to be with his eldest daughter, Madeleine. The news that Sebastien lives brings glad tidings, but Madeleine will need to be encouraged over his imprisonment. The attack on our own Huguenot assembly resulting in the death of his little one, Avril, is weighty. He is strong in the Lord, however. Arnaut will come through this trial, for we are not so unwise as to think suffering and tribulation will circumvent Christ's own. This world was no friend to our Savior, and He has forewarned us that it will treat us as it did Him.

"Andelot assures me, Marquis de Vendôme, that you are most sympathetic to the Reformation cause. As such, I will need your confidential help to bring my cargo to Spitalfields. Your assistance in this matter is of great import."

"Pasteur Bertrand, I wish I could help you, but as I already made clear to Mademoiselle Rachelle at the Château de Silk when we discussed this matter, as well as to Monsieur Arnaut this afternoon, my time will not permit. The *Reprisal* sails tomorrow."

"Ah yes, you favored me at the château by telling me about these notorious Spanish galleons."

Fabien still wondered why he had told Bertrand and not Arnaut.

"What I did not explain, Pasteur Bertrand, is how your fellow Protestants, including William of Orange, are counting on us to eliminate those crucial Spanish supplies. There is only one possible way I can see the dilemma of delivering the Bibles can work." Fabien leaned back against his desk gravely: "Since I fully understand the importance of your mission, I am willing to take you and your smuggled Bibles to England, but only on the condition that it will not impede our attack on the galleons—which unfortunately, would require your presence during fierce battles, endangering your very life and limb. Afterward—assuming we survive intact, I would then be willing to take you and your cargo to England."

Fabien waited for the full impact of his words to hit Bertrand. He was confident Bertrand would decline, probably with a frown over Fabien's brutal mission, and then seek to obtain other passage.

"We are making for the Netherlands' coast tomorrow," Fabien continued. "While the wind is in our favor. You understand."

Bertrand wore a challenging smile. "Ah, I accept your offer, Marquis Fabien. I too wish for the defeat of Spain's cruel conquests, whose wealth from the Americas allows them the luxury of great armies to crush the Reformation in the regions they control. The tender shoots of the Reformation are seemingly defenseless against the boots of the Inquisition, or as Rome calls it, the Counter-Reformation."

Startled, Fabien regarded the minister, wondering at his boldness. "Let me get this clear, Pasteur Bertrand. You would join forces with privateers, some of whom, shall we say, may not have legal articles from their respective kings or queens to attack Spanish shipping?"

Bertrand stroked his short, pointed beard. "Précisément. Let us say also, that ministers do not have legal articles from the same kings and queens to bring Bibles printed in French, German, or Dutch into their realms. There is no freedom to own Bibles, nor to preach from them, nor to build Huguenot churches." Bertrand offered his grim smile. "So then, Marquis, it is settled? I ask for no special treatment aboard your ship, except that I should like to take my loyal servant Siffre with me. I yet need his aid in working my shoulder bandages."

Fabien tried one last ploy.

"You will need to have your cargo hauled across England to Spitalfields — no easy task, Monsieur."

"Also true, but I have done so before. The Lord has not failed me in any of these past difficulties, and I think His sufficiency will once again provide for my particular need."

"Monsieur Bertrand, you do fully understand, do you not, that of necessity, I shall become for a time a buccaneer giving no quarter to the Spaniards?"

"It is fully understood, Marquis. Let us hope the kings of Spain and France do not fully understand," he said wryly. "While I do not agree with such actions unless war is sanctioned by just cause of provocation — I shall not weary you with my reasons now."

"And you are willing to go on this venture, knowing I cannot take you to your destination until this issue with Alva is met, and bested?"

"Précisément."

There was silence.

"Bien! It is settled." Bertrand pushed himself up from the chair. He smiled at Andelot who had listened with keen interest.

"Adieu, Andelot. I plan to return to France from England in the fall to attend the upcoming colloquy. I shall see you again."

"I shall very much hope so. Adieu, Monsieur."

Bertrand walked to the door, replacing his black hat and straightening the bit of stiff white ruff around his collar. Fabien was struck again at how much he resembled Monsieur John Calvin.

"Siffre waits on deck," Bertrand said. "Duchesse Dushane has sent Romier, her trusty page, and several guards to aid in the loading of my prized cargo. We shall proceed with the matter at once, Marquis. Merci."

The skirmish was lost. Fabien had relented. He now worried that this man of character, whom he had a strange liking for, would meet the face of trouble, for the wharves were a hotbed of spies. The last thing he wanted was for the godly Bertrand to be caught and arrested on heresy charges to join Sebastien in the Bastille.

"One moment, s'il vous plaît, Pasteur Bertrand. Just where is the warehouse that keeps your treasure?"

"On the southern end of the wharf. Warehouse twenty-three. I have the key. You need not trouble yourself. I realize you and your capitaine are busy loading your own supplies."

"Anything can go awry. I would not risk your going there. I think it far wiser to wait until dark, whereupon I will speak with Romier about working with Gallaudet and my men-at-arms to take care of the matter."

Fabien thought Bertrand looked relieved, or perhaps he was merely exhausted. Fabien's conscience awoke and smote him. *Bertrand was in his sixties, recovering from the great trauma of only a few weeks earlier.*

"While we wait for nightfall, I will have you and your serving man — Siffre, is it? — shown to a cabin so you may settle in. I am afraid your space will be very cramped, Monsieur."

"I have slept in far less desirable places. Merci, Marquis Fabien."

By agreeing to Bertrand's presence aboard the *Reprisal*, Fabien had just opened a door that allowed him to become even more entangled with the Macquinets, and for the Geneva pastor to become more involved with him.

Fabien stood with arms folded across his chest, head tilted, watching as Bertrand walked down the gangplank with Gallaudet, and an older monsieur that must have been his servant, Siffre.

"Why is it that I feel that Pasteur Bertrand's boarding at such a time as this is something he had planned for?"

Andelot said, "It is because you would not carry my silver cross, Marquis, so God has now blessed your voyage with Pasteur Bertrand."

Fabien narrowed his gaze, thoughtfully watching Bertrand until he was no longer in sight.

From below on the wharf, a voice shouted, "Monseigneur Vendôme, pardone, have you seen Andelot?"

Fabien recognized the young page, Romier, garbed in the green and silver and a scabbard with the duchesse's coat of arms. He called out from his cabin door, "What do you want with him?"

"Monsieur Arnaut and his retinue will soon be ready to leave for Paris. Their coach-and-six will be waiting beside the street. Monsieur asks if Andelot is returning with them. Monsieur wishes to be on the road within the hour to go to his ailing daughter at the Louvre."

Fabien turned toward Andelot who was scowling, a frown on his brow.

"I could be of help to you and Bertrand on the voyage," Andelot said hopefully.

Fabien smiled. "Is it truly for the smell of the sea and battle you would join us? I think not, mon cousin. And yet would you come with me to Coligny's colony in Florida with no taste for battle? Knowing the wrath of Spain for the Protestant corsairs?"

"We will claim it was our duty to France, to His Majesty, Francis."

Fabien smiled wryly. He knew Andelot excelled in the spirit of learning, was content with his books, his love of languages, his religious studies, and a curiosity about John Calvin he would not admit to.

"You have another calling, mon ami. There is a better future for you in the Corps des Pages than on a buccaneering ship." And should something go wrong on this mission, he did not wish to have Andelot's blood on his hands. "It is enough that I stir the wrath of your kinsman. If you also follow me, you will make him your full enemy. Cardinal de Lorraine does not spare any for pity, not even you. Andelot, there are but a few minutes. There are lettres I must write before you leave."

Andelot called down his intentions to Romier while Fabien went to his desk for parchment, ink, and quill.

He was still writing when Andelot came back across the wooden deck and through the open door. At last he signed his full Bourbon name of nobility and used the appropriate seal with the coat of arms of Duc Jean-Louis de Bourbon, now his own except for the title of Duc, as that was carried by Prince Antoine de Bourbon, the King of Navarre. Fabien stood from behind the cramped desk and handed Andelot the two lettres.

"Give one to the duchesse, and the other to Duc Bellamont. The rest they will take care of." He threw open his sea chest and took out a leather money bag and placed it in Andelot's hand as he protested.

"Marquis Fabien, I should not take this — "

"You will need it. It should hold you over until matters are arranged with the pages. Stay in Paris. Stay, and learn. Be the voice of reason where fanatics walk. Hold in your heart a love for the truth — especially the truths God has revealed to us in the Scriptures."

"Tell me, Marquis Fabien, have you read the forbidden French Bible?"

Fabien lifted a brow. "I read it when I was twelve — a translation by Lefèvre d'Étaples."

Fabien placed a hand on Andelot's shoulder, the ring once belonging to Jean-Louis de Bourbon catching the waning sunlight that slanted through an open shutter.

*It may be that one day in the future, your knowledge will do us both very well, Andelot.*

The silence that followed was broken only by the hurrying footsteps on the deck. Romier appeared, twitching his nose as he doffed his hat toward Fabien.

"Pardone, but the Macquinet retinue is waiting. They just sent a man to ask again for Andelot."

Andelot appeared to have finally failed in his words. He placed the marquis' lettres under his tunic.

"Adieu, Marquis Fabien. When the *Reprisal* fights for Holland against Spain, it must be the best ship on the sea." He grinned.

Fabien smiled. "Adieu, mon ami Andelot."

Fabien walked with him to the gangplank and watched as he went down to the wharf and ran toward the Macquinet coach, which was parked in the distance near wagons, taxis, and horse-drawn carryalls.

Fabien gazed at the coach, but he did not see either Arnaut or Rachelle who remained inside. He could go down to say adieu, but with the tension between him and Rachelle, what could be accomplished?

A half dozen men-at-arms on horseback waited nearby with another horse that Andelot was to mount. The coach-and-six moved out slowly into the street followed by the horsemen. Andelot turned in his saddle and lifted his hat in a salute. Fabien did the same. A few minutes later the small caravan rode out of sight. They would soon be on the road to Paris.

Fabien stood as the dampness, the smell of the port, the sounds of the gulls, the movement of the ship beneath his boots as it shifted within its moorings, all bespoke a very different world than the one to which Rachelle and Andelot were returning. A strange emptiness beat within his heart. He set his jaw, determined not to look back, and turned away from the wharf.

He crossed the cabin and sat down at his desk to study the map of the region in and around Holland, moving aside other papers, maps, and leather-bound books.

Some time passed before he noticed the air from the open door was colder, and the daylight was dimming. He lit the candle that was shortened from late-night study. Outside his window gray fog was starting to swirl across the deck. It would be a perfect night for loading Bertrand's forbidden treasury as well as for silently leaving the Pas de Calais under wraps of misty darkness. If all went as he and the privateers had planned, in not too many days hence, they would rendezvous with Duc d'Alva's galleons near the Netherlands.

# The Long Road Home

RACHELLE RETURNED TO PARIS WITH HER FATHER, MONSIEUR ARNAUT, to find Duchesse Dushane smiling as she stood to greet them in the Louvre salle of the Macquinet apartment. One look at Madame's face lifted Rachelle's spirits.

"Madeleine is recovering?"

"Many thanks to our God—she is! Oui, Arnaut, your daughter Madeleine is awake from her feverish slumber, and le docteur says she is on her way to a slow but certain recovery."

With joie de vivre, Père Arnaut bent over her hand and thanked her for the care she had given his daughter when neither he nor Madame Clair could be with her.

"May I see her now, Madame?"

"She will be most thrilled, Arnaut. The bébé is with her. You shall see your first granddaughter. Le docteur is here as well. I am certain you will wish to discuss matters with him after you speak to her."

Rachelle was pleased about Madeleine's progress, but her thoughts soon strayed to Grandmère and what the docteur might have learned from the autopsy. After a short visit with Madeleine in order to not over-tire her, her father came out of her chamber and told Rachelle he would speak alone with the docteur.

Some time later the docteur came out and bowed to her, then departed. Rachelle swiftly entered the salle where her father stood staring through a window toward the river Seine. He heard her entry, and turned.

His face was tired, the lines of prolonged strain deepening around the corners of his mouth.

"What did he say about the manner of poison that was used?"

"There is no proof of poisoning, my daughter."

"No proof," she protested, walking toward him. "But the gloves."

He squeezed her shoulder with understanding.

"There was probably an abscess of her lung," he said quietly. "Le docteur now believes Madeleine's illness was not related to Grandmère's."

Rachelle closed her eyes in a moment of frustration. "Then what made them both so violently ill at the same time? Madeleine had many of the same symptoms, but she did not leave the gloves on for as long, whereas Grandmère wore her pair during her shopping. Mon père, it was the gloves I tell you, the gloves from the Queen Mother. I shall never be convinced differently."

"The gloves," he said patiently, "are not to be found anywhere in the appartement. Without them we have no proof of poisoning. It is merely suspicion."

"But others saw the gloves. Madame Dushane saw them, the ladies-in-waiting—"

"There are no gloves now, ma petite."

"What does Madeleine say?"

"Madeleine claims she may have been ill before trying on the gloves. She had not been well for several days."

Rachelle shook her head and sank to the rose settee. "I will not accept this, mon père. I have no doubt in my heart that it was her—Madame le Serpent! And I for one will not forget that she took Grandmère from me when I needed her most in my life!"

Pain came to his eyes. He swept up both of her hands into his and held them tightly. "My daughter, pay heed to what you say. I do not want you upset about the Queen Mother like this. It is dangerous. The ears of others, ami and foe alike, are apt to hear. It may easily reach the royal chambers. I have already lost one daughter—" His husky voice caught, and he squeezed her hands tightly. "I do not want to lose another, not by illness nor by her determination to discover evidence of some evil deed."

Rachelle threw her arms around him. "Oh, mon père . . ."

He hugged her tightly. She heard him struggle to restrain his tears. She had always loved him for his ability to be emotional, quite unlike the restrained and sometimes wry Cousin Bertrand. Both men were so different in their outward display of feelings, yet they were the two strong masculine forces in her life.

Then there was the marquis. His strength of purpose, like granite, seemed to exist on an altogether different plane.

"Promise me, daughter, that you will not say anything rash that could wing its way back to the Queen Mother. She has many spies, some are easily recognized, but there are others we would never suspect. We must be ever vigilant."

A chill went up her spine as she met his grave eyes. *It was fear that had silenced the poisoning of Grandmère and Madeleine.* The gloves had vanished, and with them the proof that they had been treated with poison. It seemed that neither the docteur, nor anyone else, would dare make a charge against the Queen Mother. And as long as the docteur would not affirm that poison had taken Grandmère's life, then it mattered not what Rachelle said, nor whether her father agreed with her. No recourse remained, for who dare accuse the Queen Mother?

As footsteps came across the chamber floor, softened by the thick Aubusson rug, Rachelle and Arnaut turned. It was one of the ladies-in-waiting, a golden-haired young woman with sleepy eyes. Rachelle knew little about these servants, or to whom they swore fealty, but she took for granted that they were loyal to Madeleine and the duchesse. After her father's brief warning, she wondered if anything was as simple at Court as it appeared. She was learning that a life at Court did not especially please her, and that those who were here had driving ambitions that seemed to exceed those of the serfs and other villagers she knew in Lyon.

"Messire Macquinet, Madame requests you and the mademoiselle be taken to your rooms to refresh yourselves before you join her for dîner tonight."

"Merci, mademoiselle. One moment, s'il vous plaît."

After she left, Rachelle felt her father's gaze and sensed he might be worrying about her in ways he did not for Idelette, or even Madeleine.

"Ma petite daughter," he said gently, his voice low. "Whatever befalls us, be it fair or dark, must first pass through the hands of our God who is faithful and true." He put his arm around her shoulder and walked her toward the door." Madame Xenia's suggestion is a welcome one," he said, calling the duchesse by her first name. "A little rest and quiet will do us well. We have yet much to discuss with her, not only about your sister, but Sebastien."

The words "hands of our God who is faithful and true" echoed in her mind for days afterward, giving Rachelle much to ponder. She knew these principles were taught in the Scriptures, whether or not her mind and spirit were able to grasp all the implications. Though she clung tenaciously to the truth that God could be nothing other than wholly faithful and true, consistent with His unchanging character, the sting of disappointment shouted unfairness, and she struggled to overcome thoughts of revenge.

*I know Grandmère was murdered and that Madeleine could have died as well, but for the grace of God. If I could find those gloves, I could prove it, even if it meant risking my own safety. How many more will she poison for her selfish ambitions?*

In the days after returning from Calais, her father made plans to transport Madeleine and bébé Joan to Lyon where Madame Clair waited anxiously, writing several lettres asking for news. Poor Mère was anxious to be with Madeleine, and yet she was fully needed at the château to care for Idelette and Sir James Hudson, whom she claimed was "becoming like a member of the family. His bon cheer is a welcome relief, and he apologizes for the care he requires. I assure him we give in the name of our Redeemer who gives to us all things freely. He marvels that I can say these things after losing Avril. I tell him I did not lose my youngest daughter. I know where she is — and it is a far better place than France is becoming. I long for your return ..."

Arnaut was of a mind to send Rachelle home to the château to be with Idelette and allow their mother to come to Paris. Madeleine was doing well under the docteur's care and, as Rachelle had expected, she wished to stay in Paris where her husband, Sebastien, remained incarcerated in the Bastille. Rachelle saw improvement in Madeleine as she fought to renew her strength. It was when she held her bébé to her breast that she would say what burned in her heart.

"I must regain my strength. I must live for Joan. Sebastien and I must both live. Oh, Rachelle, if the Lord does not help me, what shall I do without my husband? I do not want to lose him. I wish we could escape France altogether and begin a new life at Spitalfields. Cousin Bertrand seems to think it a place of God's refuge."

Rachelle paid scant attention to these words of leaving France, deeming them the utterances of a fearful mother and wife fighting to survive.

"Madeleine, tell me; what could have happened to the gloves you and Grandmère wore?"

Madeleine, with dark hair and eyes like Rachelle, moved uneasily on her pillow.

"They did not fit me. One of the women must have taken them away."

"And Grandmère's as well?"

"I do not know. Rachelle, I do not like to think of it."

Madeleine still claimed she did not believe the gloves were poisoned, but that some bizarre sickness had struck them and claimed Grandmère's life due to her age. Rachelle sensed this was preferable to Madeleine because the alternative was so starkly wicked she did not wish to consider it.

"If only I could free Sebastien, then we would go away."

"Where would you go?"

"Anywhere but France!" She looked down with furrowed brow upon the sleeping Joan.

Rachelle shook her head. "This is our home, our beloved country, ma *sœur*."

Madeleine sighed wearily. "You might think differently if it were your Marquis de Vendôme in the Bastille."

Rachelle, seated on the edge of the huge bed with its pale green canopy, straightened her back.

"He is not my marquis and never shall be. He told me so at Calais."

Madeleine looked surprised, then repentant. She was the protective older sister again and reached over to squeeze Rachelle's clenched hand.

"I am sorry, Rachelle; I did not know. I was afraid something like this might happen. Many mademoiselles have tried to capture him and failed—where you succeeded. And though he is young and adventuresome, he may yet decide to settle down and marry. The Bourbon family, however, will never—" She stopped abruptly.

Rachelle stood and changed the subject. "Even if Sebastien were released, how could he leave Court?"

"What? Do you think he will ever be one of the Queen Mother's counselors again? It does not seem possible."

Rachelle said no more on the matter.

"Have Père and Madame Xenia been able to gain an audience with King Francis yet? The lettre from Marquis Fabien is possibly our only hope." Madeleine cupped the head of her bébé and studied her sleeping face with tenderness.

Rachelle loathed disappointing her. "Non. The cardinal claims the king is ailing again." She added with cheer, "But we not will give up."

❀✲❀

DURING THOSE UNCERTAIN AND trying days and nights, while Rachelle remained with her sister, their father worked tirelessly on behalf of Sebastien, obtaining lettres of request for pardon from many tolerant Catholic nobles in good grace with the Queen Mother and the young king.

Duchesse Dushane traveled to her estate near Fontainebleau in Orléans to also seek an audience with King Francis that she might deliver the marquis' lettre to either him or Mary, but she also was foiled.

"The ever watchful Cardinal de Lorraine has forbidden her an audience," said Rachelle. "Rather than turn the lettre over to the cardinal, who might burn it, it remains undelivered. She expects to try again with the Queen Mother."

"Then I shall go to Fontainebleau myself," Madeleine said, her dark eyes bright with desperation.

Rachelle laid a hand on her arm. "You are not strong enough and you know it. Let Père and Madame continue to work at this."

In a last desperate attempt, Rachelle wrote to Princesse Marguerite Valois pleading with her to intercede with the Queen Mother, but there was no reply, not even from the usually generous Marguerite. Only later did Rachelle learn that Marguerite was in one of her moods of depression because there was talk again of her marrying Henry of Navarre, and this time the talks were growing more serious.

A few days later, Rachelle knelt before Grandmère's open trunk, rearranging her sewing equipment and preparing for the inevitable journey home to Lyon. She was not eager to depart, for she wished to locate the glove makers in Paris, but she'd delayed, waiting for Andelot to have a free day from his training in the Corps des Pages. He had, upon their return from Calais, given lettres from the marquis to the duchesse. The duchesse had, at the request of the marquis, called for the master of the Corps des Pages and introduced Andelot, giving him the marquis' lettre of recommendation. Andelot was accepted into the school, but to protect him from the ire of the cardinal, Andelot would not wear the Bourbon colors and coat of arms of the marquis, but the green and silver of the duchesse.

Rachelle's jaw set with determination as she perused the familiar sewing items for the first time since Grandmère's death, packing only those that would be important to other generations in the Macquinet-Dushane family. She handled the special needles, the gold thimble, and Grandmère's *chatelaine*. She had brought these with her, intending to do some creative sewing for Madeleine and the bébé.

"Now it is all over," Rachelle murmured to the empty chamber. "How little we knew at Chambord that we would never again work together as Daughters of Silk."

*But was it over?* her conscience asked in the stillness. Rachelle considered all the rigorous training she had undergone since a small child and how it would be lost if she failed to apply what Grandmère had entrusted to her. She and Idelette were the recipients of family trade secrets. The work they had such affection for would continue as long as they pursued it and passed on what they knew to their own daughters and the next generation of silk growers, weavers, designers, and grisettes.

She held the gold thimble in her hand as though clasping a ruby.

It was not over. Had not Princesse Marguerite and the Queen Mother already said the Macquinets would make Marguerite's wedding trousseau? The Queen Mother ...

Rachelle clutched the gold thimble in her fist.

*I am a Macquinet Daughter of Silk, and I will go wherever my work takes me, as Grandmère taught me.*

Later, when Rachelle had the trunk ready for traveling, she left the chamber and met her père Arnaut, who approached with a lettre in hand.

"Daughter, your mother has written requesting you to come home, and I am in agreement with her and the young James Hudson. He is getting anxious about the gown for Her Majesty of England. He must have it cut, sewn, and garnished in four weeks so that he may leave for London. His father wrote of his urgent need for James to return."

Fortunately, Madame Clair had written that she wished to come to Paris to spend time with Madeleine and petite Joan when Rachelle left. She had yet to see her granddaughter and was most desirous of doing so.

Locating the glove makers would need to wait. Remembering the gown and the work to be done brought Rachelle an unusual sense of purpose. It was almost with relief that she agreed to go home to the château, home to her silk, and show Idelette the belle new lace she had brought from Languet's shop in Calais. She wondered how her sister was recovering. There had been no correspondence from her, but only from Madame Clair.

Rachelle believed that her mother wanted to come to Paris now because she expected Sebastien's death. Madeleine would need her more than ever.

Meanwhile, Arnaut and the duchesse continued their endeavors to gain Sebastien a pardon from the king. Secretly, Rachelle did not entertain much hope. Sebastien must answer for the charge of treason against the king and also for heresy.

On the following day, Rachelle left by coach for Lyon, escorted by two of the duchesse's guards. She smiled and waved at her father through the coach window as the horses trotted across the court and through the main gate past the Seine. Soon they were on the road to Lyon and home — home to her silk, to the task at hand, to create a belle gown for another queen, a Protestant queen who opened her gates to persecuted Huguenots from France.

As the long journey of several days began, Rachelle settled back in the leather seat and closed her eyes. She would think about nothing except silk. She must devote herself entirely to the gown until it was finished. But even while she pictured the silvery dress with pink feathers, the burning violet-blue eyes of Fabien haunted her and brought a familiar feeling of loss to her stomach. She tightened her mouth and stared grimly out the window at the passing Paris scenery without actually seeing it. *Where is he now? Will he think of me at all?*

He would be gone for a year or longer. An eon compared to the time they had known one another.

*Only one amour burns in his heart at present, and that is the desire to fight the treacherous, persecuting Spaniards.*

<hr />

### THE BASTILLE

EVERY PART IN HIS BODY SCREAMED WITH PAIN. Was it he — Comte Sebastien Dangeau — who was screaming, or was he hearing others?

Screams filled his mind and ears day and night. The pain never stopped. He was somewhere in the torture area of the cavernous dark dungeons below the Bastille where torches weaved their serpentine shadows on dank stone walls. Rats crawled, cockroaches watched stealthily. The stench was putrefying. The sound of fires hissing in the hearths and chains rattling convinced him he was living a demonic nightmare from whence he would awaken to the fresh wind and sunshine of a Paris afternoon. There was no escape. The only true escape was death — into the arms of Christ.

Here in the torture chambers, the lowest acts that could be inflicted upon a man or a woman were practiced on murderers, traitors to the king, and those of the religion.

Sebastien was on the rack again; had he ever left it?

Somewhere a fire blazed, with an array of red hot pincers, tongs, and pokers, ready as needed for wretched victims. All the while he heard religious chants, saw various men in robes with long sad faces walking slowly about in the shadows of the dank stone walls, offering the crucifix for kissing.

Sebastien's throat was parched. His lips were blistered, his tongue so heavy he could hardly speak. He had long abandoned hope for a dribble of water. Death would come soon with blessed release. The jasper walls of the Father's house were waiting, and angels would welcome him in the name of the One who had conquered death, Jesus. How precious that name—his only hope.

His Presence was there amid the excruciating pain. The pain was as unbearable as his mental anguish: the temptation to succumb. Wonderful relief was promised if he simply did as asked.

The anguish in his knee was unrelenting. He had fainted so often that he could not be sure he was awake or dreaming. His left hand had been crushed in the iron glove. He could not even remember how long ago his knee had undergone its ruin. An hour ago? A week, a month?

At first they had not tortured him. They hoped for his cooperation in giving the names of every Huguenot at Court who might have been privy to the Amboise plot under Seigneur Renaudie. Weeks went by in the filthy cell until the day they led him away after he refused to recant. That had been the beginning. Accused of treason, of concealing enemies of His Majesty, he had been questioned for hours, and days.

"I know nothing ... I was not involved ... I know no one at Court disloyal to the king ... I am loyal to King Francis ..."

Then a different inquisitor arrived, wearing robes. He began asking Sebastien in an exceedingly kind voice if he wished to see his belle wife, Madame Madeleine, and his newborn daughter named Joan.

Other robed men stood around him with lamentable faces holding candles and crucifixes.

"Would Comte Sebastien Dangeau prove his loyalty to the mother Church by kissing the blessed crucifix? By undergoing all religious ceremonies? By attending Mass?"

This question was repeated … and repeated …

"Would Comte Sebastien Dangeau confess his heresy, repent, and attend Mass to prove his total submission to what is absolutely required for salvation?"

The lead questioner with large, sad brown eyes took a handkerchief from his robe and touched the tears away from the corners of his own eyes. "You must remain on the rack, Comte Dangeau. It is the only way. But that is the beginning. There is the thumbscrew, the red hot spikes and pincers, the slicing of the tongue in two, the maiden coffin of spikes—but messire, why go through this when your well beloved Madeleine has given proud birth to your first child? Do you not wish to see them? What you must do to gain your release is as nothing. Recant your heresy, and attend Mass daily. Do so and you may walk from here free to rejoice at the bedside of Madame Madeleine and your daughter. If not, Madame will join you here for like questioning."

Sebastien heard little of this, so great was his pain. Salty sweat dripped onto his eyes; his blurred vision tried to focus.

"Messire Sebastien, he that has suffered in the flesh has ceased from sin. No suffering for the moment is of apparent value, but afterward, when your soul is saved because of it, and the soul of Madame Madeleine, and your enfant daughter baptized—the anguish will prove to have been of utmost deliverance. You will see—unless you fail to understand the truth and embrace it, proclaiming heresy."

Sebastien shut his eyes. He gritted his teeth so hard he tasted blood.

"God, non, God help me!"

"He will help you, messire, once you recant the diabolical lies propagated by Calvin and Luther. The bébé may also be taken away, messire, and raised apart from heresy in the monastery. But you and madame will never see her again. What will you do? We have no more weeks to delay, messire. Shall I give the order to send guards to your appartements in the Louvre palais for your wife?"

"Non, non, I beg of you, not my wife, s'il vous plait, not Madeleine —"
Tears ran down his cheeks.

"You know what you must do, messire."

Sebastien wavered; for a moment the peace he had known at various times came again, and he felt new strength refreshing his spirit.

But then . . . He thought of Madeleine on the rack; Madeleine, with all her tenderness, and his mind was filled with a rush of terror.

*If I had only to think of myself, I might endure to the end, but I must live to see my wife and bébé escape to England. If I die, Madeleine might be arrested and brought here — unthinkable!*

Sebastien heard his own voice coming like the wail of a sick creature: "I — I will do all you say, Monseigneur — oui, all you say."

The man in religious garb smiled benignly. "You are becoming a wise man, Comte Sebastien." He lifted a hand toward the guards and nodded to the other robed men.

"Release the ratchet, loosen his chains, feed and water him, bathe him, and tend his hand and knee. There is cause for rejoicing; Comte is now prepared for the religious ceremony. I will send word to Cardinal de Lorraine."

*Wherefore let them that suffer*
*according to the will of God*
*commit the keeping of their souls*
*to him in well doing,*
*as unto a faithful Creator.*

1 PETER 4:19

# The Announcement

THE SCARLET BLOSSOMS ON THE BOUGAINVILLEA VINE ALONG THE WALL
of the garden held tenaciously under the gusts sweeping down from the
hills and through the grove of mûreraies.

The château did not welcome Rachelle home as the haven of security
and purpose as it had in the past, not without Grandmère. Less than a
year had passed since Rachelle and Idelette first left with Grandmère
as her grisettes in training for Paris and then on to Chambord Palais
to work on gowns for the Reinette Mary Stuart-Valois and her sister-
in-law, la Princesse Marguerite. Less than a year ... but for Rachelle,
it seemed that more had happened to alter her life than in all the earlier
years combined.

How could one's life change so drastically? Like gusts of wind that
rushed unexpectedly to shake, to tear, to leave scattered in ruin! Why
did God permit it? Her family was serving the Lord! Why had not the
pain and loss come to the wicked?

Her conscience smote her. Cousin Bertrand would look at her with
his brilliant dark eyes and tell her she was distrusting God's purposes:

"'The Lord hath his way in the whirlwind and in the storm,' the
prophet Nahum told us. But would ruin prevail? Non. And the winds
came, and the storm beat upon that house, and it fell because it was not
founded upon a rock.

"The rock is Christ, Rachelle. Though the mountains shake, though
they be carried into the midst of the sea, He is our solid foundation. He
said He was going away to prepare a place for His disciples, and would

*come again to bring us to where He is. For we look for a city which has foundations, whose builder and maker is God."*

Rachelle drew in a breath and pushed open the wide, lattice double doors into the spacious atelier, and went to her work as she did each morning after her petit déjeuner.

It was in this chamber that several generations of Dushane-Macquinets had jealously guarded family silk secrets for what at the time was called the "new cloth," although silk was hardly new in the distant East from where the silk filaments had first made their way into Europe by the caravan trade route called the Old Silk Road.

No one discussed Grandmère's strange death, though she was certainly in their minds and hearts. Perhaps, Rachelle thought, they knew they would be overcome by a host of emotions once they began to discuss the petite silver-haired grande dame. Only once did Rachelle, unable to keep silent, bring up the gloves.

"They were poisoned somehow, I am almost certain. Andelot agrees with me, and though the duchesse is cautious, even Cousin Bertrand is suspicious."

Madame Clair's look counseled the wisdom of silence. She later took Rachelle aside, and with her hands on her forearms, said gently: "Such talk will not help any of us now, ma chère. Your sister Madeleine is still at the Louvre. I shall be going there to be with her when I settle on travel plans. We must guard our tongues. We dare not risk the attention of the Queen Mother with Sebastien in the Bastille."

Rachelle noticed more pronounced lines at the corners of her mère's pale blue eyes.

The warning was the same as that spoken by her père Arnaut, so Rachelle thereafter hid away the suspicions inside her heart. She might conceal them, but she would not forget, and if the opportunity ever came, she would continue to seek the truth.

During the days following her return home and after her mère left for Paris to help Madeleine, Rachelle threw herself into her work. Her days were fully occupied with completing the gown for James Hudson before his departure to England.

"You are very talented," he said, shaking his dark head and grinning. "Wait until my father meets you and takes a look at your design book. Several of your gowns are stunning. I especially want to try out the one with bell sleeves. Who knows? We may start a new fashion trend in London."

"I should be thrilled. The sleeves should be done in very light and airy material with a delicate gossamer thread of gold or silver woven into it. What do you think?"

"Yes, we'll name the gown 'La Rachelle.'"

Rachelle laughed, one of her first in many days. The work on Queen Elizabeth's gown was progressing so well that James, as she had taken to calling him at his request, was delighted, and made his plans to return to England within two weeks.

Idelette did not join them often. When she did her sections of the project, it was usually in the evenings, alone. Not even the bolt of new lace Rachelle had brought back from Calais from the Languet family had returned Idelette's enthusiasm as Rachelle had hoped. Idelette admired the lace and made her comments, but that was all.

Afterward, Rachelle had encouraged her to come out of her solitude, but her sister preferred to keep to herself. Rachelle prayed this would soon change.

"I am embarrassed by the marks on my face," she had explained to Rachelle. "Look at my mouth. It is revolting. The gash is healing, but when I eat it feels swollen and bleeds easily."

"Chère, you are so brave. Take courage. Within another month or so you will not even notice."

"Unless it scars ..."

"I will show you a few beauty tricks to help hide it until it fades. I learned them from Princesse Marguerite."

Idelette groaned wearily. "Ah Marguerite! Will she marry King Philip's son or the Huguenot, Prince Henry of Navarre?"

Rachelle remembered what the Queen Mother had told her about a visit to Spain. She shuddered. She hoped she would forget all about having to attend Marguerite during that time. *It is one thing to seek for an answer to poison gloves, but quite another to travel with Madame le Serpent to Spain with its dreadful Inquisition.*

"Marguerite loves but one monsieur, Henry Guise — the son of the duc." Even speaking the name of Duc de Guise was difficult for Rachelle without her voice interjecting the loathing she felt.

"Marguerite will never be allowed to marry him. A Guise for a son-in-law would threaten the Queen Mother's sons coming to the throne."

Some days later inside the atelier, Rachelle sighed and rubbed the frown away from between her brows. She walked over to the long table where the silvery-pink gown was spread upon the long working table, shimmering in the light that beamed in through the windows. Her project for today was to meticulously sew the small pearls on the bodice. James had told her the Hudson family received the pearls without expense from a wealthy English merchant who wished to please his queen. The one stipulation was that Queen Elizabeth know from whom the pearls had come.

Rachelle's mind drifted. James Hudson had once said the English queen had beautiful hands. "She is exceedingly vain of them, they say. She likes to display them on her lap without gloves to the foreign courtiers and ambassadors so that they will return to their respective courts and tell how pretty her hands are."

Rachelle smiled to herself. What woman did not feel gratitude for something lovely about her outward appearance? Rachelle was pleased with her thick and shiny auburn-brown hair that the marquis found so much to his liking. She was grateful there was something about her that the apparently immovable Marquis Fabien could be moved by — but could not own. She was satisfied in having stood her ground in Calais, refusing to melt at his touch. Let him have his beloved ship — his true amour. She glowered and curled her lip derisively. *His wondrous love, a ship! Well, la, la.*

She snatched up her needle and put on Grandmère's gold thimble. Her frustration and anger subsided as quickly as it had risen its ugly head. *Oh Fabien, that you might want and love me more than anything else in this cold, heartless world ... as much as I want and love you.*

She fantasized his unexpected return, bending on one knee, clasping her hand between his, and begging her pardon. His violet-blue eyes would sizzle with desire. *"Ah, marry me, ma chérie, there is no one else like you, I vow it. I want you more than ships, more than Spaniards' heads dangling from my cabin wall."*

She laughed sourly at herself. "Get on with your work. You are as silly as Nenette."

She must not delay. It behooved her to impress the English queen with the Dushane-Macquinet-Hudson enterprise, that the queen may smile upon the Hudson family and give their business special favors in London and at the English court.

Rachelle readied her own sewing equipage and began the tedious work of attaching the pearls, using a pair of pince-nez to magnify her vision so every prick of her needle, polished with beeswax, was precise. She was hard at work when she heard the doors open. She glanced up to see Sir James Hudson enter with his usual smile. In the days following her return from Paris, she had found him both comfortable and safe for her wounded heart.

"Bonjour," he said, using one of the few French words he could say correctly.

Rachelle was thankful she and her sisters had learned English when children, at Père Arnaut's insistence, otherwise James's amusing attempts at communication would have ended in hilarious disaster. He knew it as well and often laughed at himself.

Leaning on his crutch, he joined her at the table, as he had each day since her return. Thankfully, his leg was not broken as was first believed, and his injury was now thought to be a slow-healing sprain.

"How you will manage on your own on such a long journey, I cannot imagine," she said. "If only your père were not ill, you might stay a little longer. Nenette will be sad to see you go," she said with a twinkle in her eye. For it was no secret that her grisette had become attached during his stay there.

"I daresay that if Pasteur Bertrand can make it to Spitalfields, then I, a hearty young Englishman, surely can. I'm glad Nenette will miss me, at least."

"We shall all miss you. But I am sure you will be most delighted to be home in London again."

"What was meant to be a two-week visit to Lyon has become two months. I can't say I'm disheartened. I've come to know the Macquinet family as true friends," he said. "I only wish the circumstances had been happier." She tried to mask her feelings of loss as he continued.

"I wish you and Idelette were coming to London with me. After all, this gown is mainly your work, and your sister's."

"And your design," she said with a firm nod. "I admit I would give much to be at St. James Court when you present this gown to Queen Elizabeth."

"You should be there, Rachelle."

The friendship that bound James Hudson to her family had seen such sorrow, suffering, and loss that they had dispensed with most formalities and called one another by their given names. She did not mind, though, for even Andelot addressed her as Mademoiselle Rachelle.

"Perhaps someday I shall come to England, if not with Père Arnaut, then with Cousin Bertrand. His work, as you know, demands travel between the two countries."

"Then *someday* is as much as I can possibly hope to receive now. I tell you, Rachelle, this gown will dazzle many great ladies at Court and make your name and Idelette's a topic for fashion. You will find it a necessity to come to London."

"And do not forget your own," she said with a smile. "The ladies will surely desire a Hudson design after your queen wears this one."

His dark eyes twinkled. He had a pleasant smile, and though he could not be said to be as dashingly beau as the marquis, he was handsome enough for any woman, and his love of silk and designs made him interesting.

During his stay he had looked over her sketchbook of designs, complimented her talent, and offered suggestions. In the weeks since her return as they had worked together on the queen's gown, the time had gone by quickly. There were no emotional demands placed upon her, and he never once intimated strong romantic interest, which made it easy to be in his company throughout the day. She found she could talk to him as easily as she could Andelot. She did see him watching her on occasion, but always, he behaved as an ami. Perhaps he was wise enough to know her heart was already bound, and any attempt to crash the boundary would end with more harm than good.

At least James appeared to be content to have it so. He was one of the most patient men she had met.

When the gown was at last finished and packed as carefully as a shipment of gold, he made arrangements for his journey to Calais where he would catch a ship to England.

"I'll look up Pasteur Bertrand at Spitalfields when I get back. I'll do all I can to have him convince your parents he needs to bring you and Idelette with him on his next return from France."

On the morning James Hudson departed from the Château de Silk, Idelette did not come down to bid him adieu for she claimed to have a headache. James produced a lettre addressed to Idelette, his expression showing compassion and understanding that she had chosen to remain in her chamber.

For once he wore no smile. His dark eyes were somber.

"Please see that your sister has my lettre."

She took it from him. "Oui, bien sûr."

His smile returned. "Good-bye, Rachelle. Merci for your kind hospitality these months. The Lord keep you all in His care until we meet again, with hope, in London."

She smiled and watched him walk with his crutch to the carriage. The box with the belle gown for the queen was stored inside with greater care than James received.

He grinned and called back to her as the driver, with a steadying arm, helped him step up and into the carriage. "Next time you see me I'll be as fit as these horses."

She laughed. "I will not be surprised."

"Good-bye again!"

"Au revoir. God speed. Give our greetings to Bertrand."

"I shall. Adieu, Rachelle, adieu, Nenette!" He waved to Nenette who lingered behind on the porch. Rachelle watched from the front veranda with her grisette until the coach was out of sight. She would miss James. The château felt a new silence.

Weeks later, one of Duchesse Dushane's horsemen arrived after a long ride on the route from Paris to Lyon to deliver a message from Madame Clair. Rachelle opened the lettre quickly and read. Breaking into a delighted smile, she then hurried inside and dashed up the stairs to find Idelette.

"Sebastien is free, sister. Listen to this—" she waved the message —"it just arrived by the duchesse's carrier." Rachelle read aloud:

> *My daughters, we have long waited for some bonne news after all that has occurred recently! Your brother-in-law, Sebastien, was released from the Bastille today. He is ill and recovering, but alive, pardoned by the king, and after recovery, will be in service again to the Queen Mother. Needless to say, we have all laughed with joy and also wept many tears in our reunion, but thanks to our God, Sebastien lives to be with Madeleine and his daughter. Your père is the most pleased I have seen him in months, but sober-minded as well. He and Sebastien have spent much time together alone, speaking of the fiery trial. Your père is considering another trip to Spitalfields when Monsieur James Hudson arrives here.*
>
> As ever, your mère.
> Jeremiah 29:11

Rachelle tossed the message into the air, laughing, and met Idelette in the middle of the chamber. They held each other, laughing and crying at the same time.

Afterward, Idelette brought out her French Bible from its secret place and sat down. She found the Scripture verse that Madame Clair had listed.

Idelette read aloud: "For I know the thoughts that I think toward you, saith the LORD, thoughts of peace, and not of evil, to give you an expected end."

Idelette stared across the chamber to the window, seeming lost in her musings. "I hope I can depend on such a promise as this."

Rachelle walked up to her and placed her palms on her shoulders. "Oui, bien sûr," she said gently. "You are loved, ma sœur, by God, by all of us."

Idelette remained silent.

A LONGER LETTRE FROM MADAME CLAIR came within three weeks, keeping them informed of Sebastien's recovery, their sister Madeleine's improving health, and the growth of petite Joan. There were inquiries about Idelette and about matters at the château.

Madame Clair went on to write that she was aware that by the time her lettre was received at the château, the gown would probably be finished and Monsieur Hudson would be on his way back to England, stopping along the way in Paris to meet with their père on some business matters concerning Dushane-Macquinet-Hudson.

Idelette went on winding purple and gold thread onto smooth ash wood spools, while Rachelle read the last sentence of the lettre aloud: "Our God took Grandmère to be with Himself, but He sent a balm for our wounded hearts by blessing us with a granddaughter."

Rachelle looked across at Idelette. Her bruises were healing, but discoloration remained, and there was a certain wariness in her attitude, or was it worry?

Rachelle folded the lettre, putting it aside. "I wonder what Joan will be like when she grows up? I know Madeleine has turned fearful about a future for her here in France."

Idelette's mouth tightened. "I understand Madeleine's concerns for petite Joan very well, believe me." Then she stood and went off by herself again.

Later that day, Rachelle noticed Nenette shaking coins from the pink jar on the hall table.

"La, la, whatever are you doing, Nenette?"

Nenette looked over her shoulder.

"It is at the request of Mademoiselle Idelette." Nenette held up a sealed lettre. "She tells me to see that the messenger-rider is paid extra to deliver her message posthaste."

Rachelle saw that it was addressed to Madame Clair at the Louvre. Feeling uneasy, she glanced toward the empty stairway.

Nenette pushed her unruly red curls from her neck and back under her lace coif cap. "I am worried about her," she whispered.

Rachelle was grim. *Something was wrong. Idelette seemed frightened.*

As the next weeks passed, Rachelle's concerns kept her in a state of mental turmoil, neither did Idelette's silence encourage her. Then Madame Clair's third lettre arrived.

Rachelle watched tensely as her sister read the lettre in silence. Then a look of relief crossed her pale face.

"Père and Mère are both returning here to the château, not that I wished to take them from the side of Madeleine. I was hoping Madeleine would come also, but Mère says Madeleine will not leave Paris no matter the consequence ..." She read on to herself, then added, "There is no further news on Sebastien's health."

Rachelle was not surprised that Arnaut and Clair were coming home if what she suspected about Idelette were true. Their parents would rally to Idelette's need, just as they had for Madeleine.

Idelette read on in silence for another moment, folded the lettre, but did not hand it over to Rachelle as she usually did. Rachelle respected her sister's privacy, realizing their mère must have written some personal admonitions for Idelette alone.

Idelette looked at her soberly, then sighing, she stood up from the settee. With shoulders back, her face so pale and young, she licked her lips. "There is something I have not wished to tell you, sister. I find it shameful to even speak of it, but Mère tells me I must be honest with myself and others, and that it is not my shame, but even so ... But I think you already understand anyway."

Rachelle nodded in silence, hands clasped tightly on her lap, and she looked down at the toes of her slippers.

With a toneless voice, Idelette admitted what Rachelle had already guessed: she was pregnant.

Rachelle had never told her about the night Marquis Fabien and Gallaudet had ridden to the inn — that they had learned the identity of those who had led the attack on the barn. Rachelle suspected that one of the two soldiers they dueled from Duc de Guise's group was Idelette's attacker. Perhaps one day if Idelette ever wished to discuss the matter, Rachelle would tell her.

Idelette went up to her bedchamber, closing the door. Rachelle knew better than to run after her with sympathy in her voice. Idelette had always been more isolated in her feelings than either of her two chatty sisters, Madeleine and Avril, and was closer to their mère.

Rachelle pushed open the wide double-lattice doors to the atelier and sought comfort amid the familiar bolts of silks and velvets. An emotional stillness settled over her.

No wonder Idelette had reacted stiffly when Rachelle mentioned how Madeleine, when worried about the future of her daughter, Joan, spoke of leaving France. Idelette, too, would have a child, but her child, whether a daughter or son, was less likely to have a secure future. Her child would have no loving père to smile proudly when born. And Idelette would receive no encouragement from a supportive husband. She might long for a man's strong arms around her to let her know they were together as she went through the pangs of birth. Instead, she had known only selfish, lustful brutality.

Rachelle's heart beat faster as she walked about the room, touching the familiar, but receiving no solace.

"You were once the cheeriest chamber in the château. You were the heart of Macquinet silk, of its daughter couturières and grisettes in training. And now!" she whispered vehemently.

The atelier, with its treasures, had become gloomy. Alas, how the needles that once smiled, and the cutting instruments that once purred with busy satisfaction, were silent. The bolts of silks and brocades shimmering like liquid jewels sat adorning the long velvet-lined shelves. The intricate laces from Alençon, Bruges, and Burgundy were all in their proper place. She and Avril had wound those very bolts of lace with great care onto the waxed ash spindles. Rachelle looked about, painfully aware of deep wounds and losses.

"They might as well be wrapped with horse hair."

Yes, everything appeared the same but nothing was the same. Rachelle's gaze took a survey of the half-finished gowns and frocks, then stumbled at Avril's pink birthday dress.

She thought of all the lessons on the careful cutting of patterns, the secret flawless sewing — even the discussions between her mère and grandmère with Père Arnaut over the correct way of feeding the mulberry leaves to the silkworms. How they had argued over the care of the cocoons! But beneath it all, bonhomie had reigned supreme. She thought of Père joking with Grandmère, for he had looked upon her as his mère because his own had died when he was a child. How Mère would laugh at their antics and tell Arnaut to stop teasing Grandmère.

Yet Grandmère had enjoyed it.

She thought of the benign prattle and competitive girlish bickering between her, Idelette, and Madeleine before she married Sebastien, over who would be allowed to work with Grandmère on a special design.

Now, for the first time, Rachelle understood Madeleine's willingness to leave France in search of a new dream . . . Because the first dream was now an old dream that had perished.

And now — one ruthless rape and Idelette was with child.

Her sadness boiled into rage, and she began to tremble. What right had the Duc de Guise to ride here from his duchy in Lorraine robed in self-righteous judgment and heap abuse upon so-called heretics? Yet, while the duc rendered his justice in the name of God, his own followers raped and pillaged? The "Sword of the Lord," Guise had declared himself.

*Non*, Rachelle thought, *but murderers, with eyes full of adultery.*

She tried to focus her mind on the problems at hand, but each time she collected her thoughts, fresh gusts of fear and rage struck her. In a burst of outrage she hurled her pincushion across the room at the mannequin. The blank form without a face of compassion stared back, unmoved by her demonstration as the pincushion landed silently on the floor and the mannequin's white periwig glistened in the sunlight like a deceptive halo.

She walked over to the window, resting the side of her head against the frame and fingering the lace curtain. There must be some way out, some reason for these severe testings that were shaking her to the core of her soul. God had not abandoned them. She would never believe so.

*"It is never so dark that God cannot deliver."* How often had she remembered hearing Cousin Bertrand say that?

She pressed her palms to the sides of her temples, closed her eyes, and tried to focus on the Lord's wisdom and unending love. What had

Cousin Bertrand said in the lettre he had secretly left for her in Calais before he had gone away?

Rachelle went over to her table and desk and rummaged through her drawer where she kept some special things meaningful to her, things she liked to read during a break from her work. There were verses copied down from the family Bible and some lettres. She found the one she wanted and skimmed Bertrand's words until she came to where he had encouraged her with the story of Lazarus becoming sick and dying while the two distraught sisters, Mary and Martha, sent urgent word to the Lord to please come:

> *"Come quickly, come now, Lord!*
>
> *Yet He told His disciples, 'I am glad for your sakes that I was not there.'*
>
> *"And ma chère Rachelle, remember how the Lord permitted his disciples to pass into a great tempest of the sea ... 'and his disciples came to him, and awoke him, saying, Lord, save us: we perish. And he saith unto them, Why are you fearful, O ye of little faith?'*
>
> *"And remember, ma chère, the apostle Paul went hungry, was shipwrecked, imprisoned, beaten, and stoned, yet he wrote: 'Nay, in all these things we are more than conquerors through him that loved us.' He was persuaded that nothing that touches us when our pathway leads into a dark valley shall be able to separate us from the love of God that is in Christ Jesus."*

# Entrapments

## FONTAINEBLEAU

CATHERINE DE MEDICI WAITED RESTLESSLY INSIDE HER STATE CHAMBERS at Fontainebleau for her spy Madalenna to return from the errand given her earlier that day. Catherine's mind, like a restless bird soaring to and fro and unable to find a perch of rest, mulled over one more time how the duc and the cardinal were meddling with the Valois throne of France.

The chamber, haunted by the remnants of past kings and with gold and blue frescoes and silk and brocade draperies of gold, was now occupied by the Queen Mother, who paced incessantly on the ivory carpet of crimson floral, her stiff black gown and her coif in contrast.

That accursed family! For too long the Guises had plagued her life. She despised them. *The fanatical self-righteous duc! The lecherous hypocritical cardinal! If only I dare poison them.*

She felt a small shiver run through her. She dare not use poison again. There were whispers ... She must avoid being recognized during her walks near the wharves to her secret apothecaries, the Ruggerio brothers, from Florence.

Catherine often disguised herself, and when in Paris, would leave her appartements in the Louvre by a secret way and walk to their shop on the wharf. She enjoyed being in disguise, and afterward would loiter in the marketplace to hear what the Parisians were saying about the Queen Mother. She took perverse enjoyment in this secrecy as she also did in her listening devices at Court. "That Italian woman," the Parisians called her, "the foreigner." It was clear they did not think well of her. But the Duc de Guise, ah, the wondrous le Balafrey, as they called him!

Their brave military general and hero. Some even said that if Francis was King of France, then the Duc de Guise was King of Paris.

No. She dare not attempt using poison on either the duc or the cardinal lest she be suspected. There must be some other way. An assassin, yes. And how Machiavellian to have the assassination blamed on some irate Huguenot. She chuckled. Ah, yes, her time would come. She must have patience. And if not a hapless Huguenot, then perhaps the formidable Marquis Fabien de Vendôme?

She began her rapid pacing as her thoughts jumped to the problem at hand.

Upon successfully eliminating the Huguenots at Amboise, the duc and the cardinal had convinced her son Francis to summon the Bourbon princes of the blood, Louis de Condé and his brother, Antoine, the King of Navarre, here to Fontainebleau to answer for the Amboise rebellion of March.

Catherine sealed her lips tightly. This was a bold and audacious move on the part of the Guises against royal blood. Foolish Francis could not see that Mary's oncles were using him to strengthen their own hold on the throne!

She was going to need all of her subtlety in the weeks and months ahead to counter the intrigue the Guises were weaving to gain control of France. If they were successful in removing the Bourbons, who were next in line for the throne after the Valois, what would be their next move? Le duc was even now scheming to have his son, Henry de Guise, marry her daughter, Princesse Marguerite.

I will not allow it. If there is to be no marriage with Spain — then there will be one with Henry of Navarre!

Her lip twitched involuntarily. Not that she cared about the Huguenots, but without her little Huguenots at Court, there would be practically nothing to keep the Guises from storming the palais and seizing the throne.

She drummed her fingers along the top of the tallboy. How to prevent the duc and the cardinal from ruling France through her inane son Francis and his wife — that Mary Stuart? Catherine sneered at the thought of Mary's coquettish ways. What an error to have ever allowed

Francis to take the niece of the Guises for his queen. *Did I not have the foresight to oppose it? Ah, but Henry, my husband, insisted because of his lust for Diane de Poitiers. Poitiers, that witch! I would have poisoned her if I could have gotten by with it, but Henry would have suspected. He knew enough to blame me secretly for the death of his brother, the dauphin.* It was Poitiers who had wanted Francis to take Mary as his queen, and Henry had done as his aged mistress desired.

Catherine thought of her rival, Diane, whom she had tolerated for twenty years until Henry was killed in the joust. Afterward she had gotten even for the woman's disrespect to her all those years.

*And I will rid myself of Mary Stuart as well.*

Ah, that would demand all of her wit as a student of Machiavelli, the protégé of Lorenzo de Medici, her father, back in her youth in Florence, Italy. Machiavelli had written:

> *A prudent Prince cannot and ought not to keep his word,*
> *except when he can do it without injury to himself; or when*
> *the circumstances under which he contracted the engagement*
> *still exist. It is necessary, however, to disguise the appearance*
> *of craft and to thoroughly understand the art of feigning or*
> *dissembling; for men are generally so simple and weak that he*
> *who wishes to deceive, easily finds dupes.*

Catherine nodded. She had learned her political lessons in the de Medici palace in Florence — and in her oncle Clement's Vatican.

She had duped them all here in France, playing the Huguenots against the Guises, and the Guises against the Huguenots for as long as it served her purpose.

She heard the pattering of footsteps and turned. It was the Italian girl she had taken with her from Florence when Catherine's uncle, Pope Clement, brought her to France in his own papal ship to marry Henry Valois. Madalenna was her slave, just as the dwarves she kept.

Madalenna's dark eyes, seemingly empty, stared at her.

Catherine frowned impatiently. Sometimes the girl seemed deaf and dumb! "Well? Have you anything to report?"

"Oui, Madame. La Reinette Mary is on her way to see her oncle, Duc de Guise, in his private chambers."

"Is she! Ah! The petite *fleur*! And is she belle and sprightly in her chère petite ways to bring a smile to her scheming oncle's face?" Catherine curled her lip.

"She seemed well, Madame."

"Saints be praised. And what of our even more saintly cardinal? Is he at his most devoted prayers, or waiting with le duc to scheme against me and my royal house?" Her voice ascended in anger.

Madalenna moistened her lips. "Le cardinal waits with le duc, Madame. They both await Reinette Mary."

"Go, then. Continue to watch. I want to know immediately if anyone enters the private chambers of my son, the king."

"Oui, Madame!"

As soon as Madalenna left, Catherine walked through her bedchamber with the gold initials *C M* emblazoned on the wall. She entered her private closet and unlocked a small, secret compartment. *So, Mary is on her way to see her two oncles.*

Disguised listening tubes had been installed in the compartment through the ingenuity of Rene and the Ruggerio brothers. She had used this mode of spying for years and had even managed to spy on her husband, King Henry II, when he was in the company of his mistress, Diane. Catherine patiently brought her ear near the tube for Duc de Guise's chamber. She did not need to wait long before his voice could be heard—

"Ah ma chère Mary, the king's summons has been delivered to Antoine de Bourbon in Navarre."

"Will Antoine come, Oncle?"

"He will have no choice. He must come and bring Louis with him, or stand in rebellion against the king."

"What should Francis do, mon oncle?" came Mary's soprano voice.

Catherine ground her teeth under her breath. *Do? Do? I will tell you what a king would do. He would not permit your oncles to rule him through you!*

The Duc de Guise spoke: "The House of Bourbon ... a danger to our house ... they must be removed ..."

His voice lowered, and though Catherine slowed her breathing, straining to catch his syllables, the conversation was garbled.

Catherine listened in a trance. Then she heard the words that most filled her with hatred.

"And what shall I do, continue to spy on Catherine?" Mary asked.

"Yes, watch her. Report back to me her movements. She cannot be trusted. She is too friendly with the Huguenot Admiral Coligny and the Bourbons."

The voices faded as they must have moved across the chamber. A moment later Catherine replaced the plug on the listening tube and closed the secret compartment. She stood in chilled silence. Too friendly with the Huguenots, was she? What did that fool Guise know about what she was doing? She was merely leading them on for the appropriate final kill! *We shall also see about our little Bourbons Louis and Antoine! So they needed to be removed? We shall see, my fine arrogant Duc de Guise!*

Catherine sat down at her desk and wrote a brief message to Sebastien to come to Fontainebleau.

❀

A HANDSOME COACH-AND-FOUR RATTLED along at a fast clip across wet cobbled streets on a gray twilight evening traveling away from Paris and the Louvre, far away from the infamous Bastille where Sebastien had been recently imprisoned; away from its putrefying stench, from its pain and human suffering. *Forward! Onward toward Fontainebleau château-palais in Orléans. Make haste, for the Queen Mother has called for you, race past the king's royal forest for hunting his stags — past the gardens and trees, see the gray doves fleeing safely to the hills. Ah, do not look back, Sebastien, do not remember your months in the dungeon and underground torture chamber. One* faux pas *and you will be taken there yet again. Watch your step when you are at Court, keep your facial expression submissive and benign, do not let them guess how you plan your escape from France with Madeleine and Joan.*

He grasped hold of his emotions. His frenzied mind pointed ahead: *there — you see it at last. Fontainebleau, palais of French kings and queens. Ah, how the massive structure gazes out upon the less fortunate in complacent satisfaction, like Mother Babylon boasting to her foes: "I sit a queen and am no widow. I shall never see sorrow."*

Comte Sebastien's elegant attire, his elaborately equipped coach, his uniformed footmen and pages, including his newest page in training, his neveu, Andelot, all announced him as a nobleman of prestige and authority as his entourage swept past the villagers on the country road leading away from Paris.

And so he was, at least outwardly.

*I am Comte Sebastien Dangeau, a member of the privy council to the Queen Mother, Catherine de Medici,* he repeated to himself, trying to subdue his trembling, but the reminder of his freedom did little to strengthen his bones. He scoffed at the noble impression he was making on the poverty-burdened serfs and shopkeepers eyeing him as some great one as he drove past.

*I am powerless, and I know it.* His weakness reached down to the deepest crevices of his soul.

His useable hand trembled; his crushed hand felt pain anew, but he knew the suffering was mostly in his mind. Though it had been over two months, lingering images jabbed their fiery pitchforks into his mind.

Fontainebleau, fifty kilometers from Paris, was looming closer, the door to his luxuriant chambers would soon open to him like a lover's embrace. "Come out of the stormy persecution. Are you not a courtier of renown once again?"

Fontainebleau, isolated in the pleasant countryside of Orléans, with its old oaks and pine trees, with the river Seine nearby and the moonlight reflecting on its waters, was a hunting lodge, a château, and a palais. But among the stately forest trees, the trill of birds, and the innocent eyes of the doe — there were also loathsome dungeons where the condemned were kept without hope. Sebastien felt his heart quicken in nervous fear. No matter how he struggled to overcome these emotions, they returned to haunt him.

His fellow Huguenots had met such horrifying deaths back in March at Amboise. He shook his head. They were dreadfully forsaken, though not of Christ. Even in their sufferings, they had called out, saying His Presence was near.

*I need to depend on Christ more. When this fear overtakes me, I must remember Him. He is there to help, as Madeleine reminds me.*

The sudden unbidden tears springing from Sebastien's eyes surprised and angered him. Men were not to show such emotion. The salty drops poured down his cheeks. He brushed them away in a gesture of self-loathing, feeling his rough skin with deep creases. He shut his eyes and pulled his pristine handkerchief from beneath the lacy cuff of his blue and burgundy coat.

His conscience flogged him yet again: *I am a coward. I surrendered to the inquisitor's wishes while better Huguenots than I died in faithfulness to Christ.*

The carriage lurched in a sporadic gust. Twilight settled, making the coach darker. From outside, he heard his smartly uniformed coachman shout at the peasants to scatter. They always gathered outside the gates of the royal residences seeking coins. Sebastien heard the long whip hiss and snap several times, clearing a path.

His thoughts continued to race along with the drumming hooves.

He moistened his dry lips.

He knew he would never recover from his injuries. The pain in his twisted knee relentlessly taunted, *Remember the Bastille? You may be taken there again. The dungeon waits if you refuse to comply.*

Memories, like leering demons, stirred from dark corners of his mind. *You will go back there one day. Remember the red-hot pincers that tear at the flesh? How the inquisitors carve out tongues, poke out eyes, cut off feet, hands, arms? Remember?*

*Therefore, be wise; do not risk your good favor with the king by even a suggestion that you intend to escape; do not let the Queen Mother know you have concern for heretics, lest she question your sincerity in attending Mass at noon each day.* Recurring pain served to remind him of how near he had come to being burnt at the stake for heresy. He had trained his mind to avoid the brutality of the past.

Though Sebastien concealed things he would not discuss even with his wife, Madeleine, he could not easily hide his mangled left hand. At least it was his left hand, and he was able to cover it in a black velvet glove.

Those brutal scenes he had been forced to watch as part of his punishment came alive again, carved with vivid terror across his mind. He could not destroy those stark images, nor could he rid his nostrils of the stench. He leaned his head near the small coach window and thrust the shutter open, feeling sick.

His handkerchief, always perfumed with sweet musk, offered no refuge. He still smelled the rotting, unburied corpses that were ofttimes left to torment the prisoners. He leaned out the window and sucked in cool, fresh, rainy air.

The coach bounded through the gates of Fontainebleau, but the groans from his mind pursued him.

He looked over his shoulder, back toward the road, as though expecting to see a grayish apparition following him, pointing a bony finger of accusation for his willingness to escape the dungeon by recantation while they had endured for the name above all names. He saw only the royal guards, dressed in spotless crimson, gold, and black, their swords glimmering, receiving him into their habitations.

The driver brought the coach to a stop in the courtyard of Fontainebleau. Sebastien heard the horses snort and whinny as his lavishly garbed footman opened the door and bowed.

Sebastien stepped down, swayed a little, and was swiftly steadied by Andelot Dangeau, who, with a guard, had ridden ahead of the coach on the marquis's golden bay, while other pages rode behind, at the tail end of the procession.

Andelot had evoked the scorn of the Cardinal de Lorraine over his actions at Amboise with the boy, Prince Charles. Whether or not the cardinal intended to continue his remoteness toward Andelot was questionable, and troubled Sebastien. He was secretly pleased to have learned that Andelot was now excluded from the cardinal's personal league. Sebastien knew the cardinal treated the boy-king Francis in a cynical and overbearing manner. Why would he treat Andelot differently? He hoped the cardinal's aloofness would persist.

Sebastien blamed himself for ever having brought Andelot to Chambord to meet the duc and the cardinal. He should have delayed, making excuses until the cardinal lost interest and forgot about his kinsman. Now, though presently Sebastien's page, Andelot could yet become caught in the inner circle of the Guise coalition. Thankfully Andelot seemed content and was not seeking to win back the cardinal's favor, due, no doubt, to Sebastien securing the scholar Thauvet as his tutor, as the marquis had written and paid handsomely to acquire. If the cardinal discovered it was the Bourbon marquis sponsoring Andelot at Court, there would be trouble. Thus far, the cardinal had paid no heed. Scholar Thauvet was one of the most learned men at Court, and also a secret Huguenot. Did the marquis know of Thauvet's forbidden faith?

Sebastien felt the chill of drizzling rain hurling against him. He drew his cloak, heavy with silver embroidery, around his slumping shoulders. He was not an old man, but recently he had been mistaken for Madeleine's père, though he was but ten years her senior. His sufferings in prison had aged his body and in two months' passing, his once dark hair bore streaks of gray.

In a badly limping stride, he made his way across the wet courtyard, attended by pages and liveried footmen, all at his call.

An ostentatious young monsieur was loitering near the orangerie, and Sebastien saw that it was his sister's son, Maurice.

Comte Maurice Beauvilliers ambled forward, wearing a peacock-blue gilded cloak, slashed black hose, and a sombrero hat with an ostrich feather dyed crimson.

"Mon oncle," he stated, "I must speak with you. It is urgent."

Sebastien paused. "Be it so, Maurice? I am late for audience with the Queen Mother."

"I know you are about to see her. That is why I have waited here enduring this most miserable rain and cold. I must present a petition to her, mon oncle, and you can do so for me most easily, I assure you."

Sebastien felt a rise of impatience. Maurice was spoiled by his mère, Comtesse Francoise Dangeau-Beauvilliers, who schemed day and night to advance Maurice's favor and importance at Court. Sebastien believed she could have helped her son far more if she had not given him his every wish.

"Ma mère Francoise, your sister, has written this lettre to the Queen Mother, mon oncle. Do see that she has it."

Maurice handed over a sealed parchment. Sebastien took it reluctantly. He loved his sister and neveu, but their intrigues now seemed to him, after such sober days, as unwise.

"What does she petition?"

Maurice smiled, lifting the pink rosebud from his sleeve and smelling it. "I want Mademoiselle Rachelle Macquinet to return to Court that I might marry her. I am madly infatuated, and I must have her."

Anger sprang up in Sebastien's chest. The request was selfish and frivolous. "Do not be a fool, Maurice. I have no time to worry about my young sister-in-law coming to Court. She is content at the Château de Silk. Let her be. She has lost petite Avril and her grandmère in so short a time." Pushing the lettre back into Maurice's hand, he brushed past him and went on his way.

***

ANDELOT DANGEAU WATCHED SEBASTIEN enter the royal hunting lodge-château of Fontainebleau, escorted by royal guards in red and gold livery to the receiving chamber of the Queen Mother, Catherine de Medici.

What new bedevilment awaited?

Andelot had overheard the exchange between Sebastien and Maurice over Rachelle, and his frown grew deeper. Maurice stood one hand on hip, his cap with an ostrich feather cocked arrogantly to the side of his curly dark head. His jewels and rings glittered in the torchlight that flared from the courtyard, and his satin finery irked Andelot so that he glowered at him. Maurice did not favor him with a glance of recognition, but took a gold box from his belt, opened it, removed a bit of snuff, and with practiced elegance, applied it to each aristocratic nostril. Afterward he turned and looked at Andelot standing by the golden bay.

"So you wear the finery of the House of Dangeau. It is no secret to me, serf Andelot, that your wayward ami, le marquis, is footing your bills and paying the scholar Thauvet to turn you into a philosopher."

"Wayward, Cousin Maurice? Why do you speak so of le marquis?"

"Tut, tut, do you take me for one who is ignorant of his bent for sword and ship?"

Andelot cast a quick glance about them; most of the other pages were loitering in idle talk. "Do not speak so loudly, I beg of you!"

"Always his defender, are you not? Well, no wonder, when you are laden with bags of silver from him—and that best of horses." He nodded toward the golden bay.

"He is not mine," Andelot said shortly. "I am caring for him until he is reclaimed by his rightful seigneur. And for what cause should it offend you if my seigneur, the marquis, has opted to sponsor me? What page at Court is not sponsored by some seigneur?"

"It offends me not, as long as you remember your place, Andelot. Do not think because le marquis befriends you that you shall have your way with Oncle Sebastien. And as I have said before, do not call me cousin."

Andelot itched to feel Maurice's chin beneath his knuckles. "Greatness, mon comte, is not gained by demand, but by worth. One higher than you has commanded that I call him cousin, yet I refuse."

"Le marquis again! He may find upon his return from harassing Spanish galleons that the king may call him traitor! Then I shall make my own plans for bringing Mademoiselle Macquinet back to Court. Do not forget that my mère is Comtesse Francoise Dangeau-Beauvilliers, and she has access to Princesse Marguerite and the Queen Mother. You may tell that to Oncle Sebastien who appears to favor you above me!" And he walked off.

Andelot stood glowering after him.

Duchesse Dushane had in the meantime come to Fontainebleau, and Romier, her chief page, strolled up, his bells jangling. "Well now, Andelot, the other pages have come to me with a wager that the golden bay is not the true horse of Marquis de Vendôme."

"We have discussed the golden bay at the Louvre. He is the marquis's horse and you know it as well."

Romier wiggled his long nose. He put a placating hand on Andelot's shoulder. "I do know it, mon ami, but our fellow pages tell me they will only believe you are speaking the truth if you agree to a race through the woods. The golden bay against all of our horses. What say you?"

Andelot was in a tired mood. The Corps des Pages had been harassing him for weeks, and after Maurice's insults, he itched to even the score. He looked from Romier's haughty face with its aquiline nose to the challenging faces of pages from the various houses of the nobility, all watching with little smirks and refusing to accept him into their elite camaraderie.

"Though the golden bay wins the race, how does that prove it is Marquis Fabien's stallion?"

"It does not, but they wish to race anyway."

Andelot turned his mouth dourly. "Very well. I shall race any and all, but each one who races will have to give one silver coin to the winner."

"I will see what they say."

The pages huddled together. Romier returned a minute later looking pleased. "They agree. When can you race?"

"In the morning, after our duties are performed for our seigneurs."

"Well enough; tomorrow then. We will meet at the stables."

Andelot watched as they all walked away laughing among themselves.

*I will laugh last and best.*

# A Great Discovery

THE MORNING WAS COLD AND BLUSTERY. IN THE DISTANCE, FONTAINEBLEAU was visible through the trees, a stately backdrop against a worsening sky which threatened to overcome the weak sunlight on a frosty morning.

Galloping hooves broke the hush as Andelot raced down the road from the royal stables, assured that he could stay in the lead on Marquis Fabien's dazzling golden bay. He laughed at Page Romier and the other pages far behind on their stable horses, followed by the group of young lackeys. He snatched his fine feathered hat and waved it mockingly at them to catch up, then crammed it back down on his head.

On Andelot's left, the land was mostly marsh, the haunt of wildfowl. The powerful stride of the golden bay frightened a raven which gave a raucous squall and glided out over a pathway, swooping among low-hanging branches that held shadows against the light.

The faint patter of October rain had turned into a drizzle. The spirits of the pages were becoming as damp as their uniforms and standards.

Andelot glanced over his shoulder. He was still several lengths ahead of Romier when, deciding to take a shortcut, he turned his horse off the road from Fontainebleau into a thicket where dark branches interlaced overhead. An angry shout from behind reached his ear. The pages admired his tenacity but dared not follow. Superstition, mingled with religious beliefs, lurked in the hearts of many who nurtured old tales from medieval history, which declared the woods a habitation of wicked beings, and even heretics. At times they were not certain which was worse, a cloven-hoofed demon, or a follower of Monsieur John Calvin. The ecclesiastics said they were the same. To question the difference might bring the charge of heresy. But Andelot had no time to worry about cloven hooves, nor the definition of heresy, for on this splendid morning, despite the foul weather, he wished to forget the troubles brewing over the Bourbon princes' involvement in the Amboise rebellion as well as recent talk concerning Marquis Fabien. More than once he had heard mentioned the word *corsair.* That Maurice hinted of swords and buccaneering ships did not bode well.

On the road, the pages reined in their horses to a nervous but proud prance, as Romier paused and turned his horse to dash after Andelot.

Andelot rode the marquis's stallion past trees and bushes. Ahead the few remaining oaks stood, reaching a web of dark branches mingled with fir, beech, and pine.

A stream ran dark and sullen in the cloud-shrouded land, merging clumps of dark woodland thickened. Andelot turned in his saddle to see Romier not far behind on the duchesse's best stallion, a mottled brown. Andelot smiled to himself, for Romier feared superstitions about the woods as much as the others who had not followed.

Darkness deepened and lightning flashed as they raced forward, the drizzling rain whispering through the dark fir trees. Suddenly Andelot pulled his reins, the horse dug in its front hoofs, slowing to a halt. Romier was not far behind and was too cautious to ride past, even if it could gain him distance in the race. He rode up beside Andelot. From the scowl on his face, Andelot could see he understood his reluctance.

There was some sort of skirmish ahead, and the smell of a campfire hung on the moist air. Distant sounds of alarm set their stallions to a nervous prancing, and they held them steady. "Easy," Andelot whispered to the bay and leaned over to stroke the sweating animal.

Romier tugged apprehensively at his glove. "Fighting here?" he asked softly. "We had best turn back to Fontainebleau."

Andelot shook his head, still poised to listen. What reached his ears over the wind was not the sound of battle but the voices and cries of women and children.

"Trouble," Andelot said. "Let us see what it is."

"If there is trouble among the serfs, let it be their trouble, not ours."

"Shall we not see at least? It is the cry of women." Andelot moved the golden bay cautiously forward. Romier followed reluctantly, fretting his displeasure.

The jingle of their royal harnesses and the plod of horse hoofs over damp mossy ground went unnoticed as they threaded their way through the trees. Andelot began to see the signs of trouble ahead. At a place where several trees had fallen in some past windstorm, he saw a number of unarmed serfs and women and children clustered around a campfire. A shouting argument was underway with a Dominican cleric. The Dominican was not armed, but several of his guards were, and they apparently waited for the cleric's word to arrest a Frenchman.

"Huguenots," Romier whispered. "Come along, Andelot, this is not our battle. Keep your distance from the Dominican if you wish to avoid wrath."

"Non, we must do something, else they will be taken away. After Amboise I cannot bear the sight of such things. Let us use our authority."

Romier looked at him as if he were mad. "Authority — *what* authority?"

"Look — they are about to be arrested. Who knows the ill fate they shall suffer for meeting here like this?" Andelot kneed his horse forward.

"In the name of Cardinal de Lorraine, stop!"

Surprised, all eyes turned toward Andelot. He was pleased he had taken care today to wear a fancy cloak over his tunic and a fine hat with the colors of the House of Dangeau. They spotted him on the powerful golden bay and stared, aghast.

Seizing the moment, the Huguenots broke and ran in all directions. Andelot watched an older monsieur, who must have been in charge of preaching, hurry through a cluster of trees. He clutched a book, which he hid swiftly under a fallen log before running on and disappearing into the misty shadows.

The angry cleric demanded, "Who are you, sire, to interrupt the business of the Church? These were heretics — holding an unlawful gathering."

Romier rode up grudgingly, giving Andelot a glower. He hastened to smile upon the cleric. He bowed low in his saddle and removed his crimson hat with a wet feather.

"Ah, Monsiegneur, forgive, I beg of you, this intrusion," he said soothingly. "My ami is hasty in practicing his chivalry. He mistook you for the raiders of the poor peasant farmers and wished to prove himself worthy of honneur, being a kinsman of . . . er, le cardinal."

"Le cardinal? By all the devils, what rank folly is this?"

"I assure you, Monseigneur, we did not realize you were arresting heretics," Romier said, smiling pleasantly at the cleric.

The cleric looked at Andelot. "You are related to le Cardinal de Lorraine?" His eyes raked him over.

Andelot did not doff his hat, in keeping to the role of a Guise. "I am a Guise, Monseigneur. I go by the name of Andelot Dangeau *Guise*." From the corner of his eye, he saw Romier's sharp glance.

"Ah? If you are related to le cardinal, how is it you would interfere in the arrest of heretics? I have had my eye on them since this summer, but they are slippery as wet fish. They move their place of meeting from week to week. The cardinal will not be pleased by this. One might think your intervention was planned."

"Not so. Monsieur Romier and I were having a race. We decided — that is, I decided — to take a shortcut through the woods back to the stables at Fontainebleau."

The cleric studied Andelot for a moment, taking in the form of a lad who was progressing in strength and wit, and appeared to find his guile-lessness endearing. Then he glowered as if thinking of the heretics who had escaped him yet again. His black brows furrowed.

"And what will you do about your transgression, Sire Andelot Dangeau Guise?"

Andelot shifted uncomfortably in the saddle and glanced for help to Romier, but Romier for once was speechless as they stared at one another. Andelot sought to recall what he knew about transgression. Sin he understood, but transgression was yet another word.

"Would you repeat, Monseigneur?"

"You have made it possible for a nest of heretical cockleburs to escape. Could you, Sire Andelot, be bent on heresy, in spite of your kinship to the House of Guise? Even among them, I have heard there are one or two."

Andelot smiled. "I could hardly be a heretic. I may enter the training of the Church once I graduate from the company of Monsieur Thauvet. And I assure you, I do not even know what the Huguenots read in their forbidden literature—"

Romier interrupted quickly, as though he thought Andelot was not sufficiently repentant. "Monseigneur, I assure you the lad," he said of Andelot as though he himself were twice his senior, "is, as I explained, anxious to fill his studious mind with acts of chivalry. May his transgression be pardoned with an indulgence from the Church."

The cleric rubbed his chin thoughtfully. His eyes took in the golden bay stallion. Andelot tensed.

"The horse is not mine," he said swiftly.

Romier seemed to grow exuberant at the apparent success of his intercession. "Let him pay twice the indulgence."

"Twice!" Andelot turned to him indignantly. "With what do I pay twice? When but once is beyond my allowance?"

"Silence," the cleric demanded with such awesome thunder that Andelot felt the lightning of doom crackle over his head. For the first time he measured the weight of his error.

*What if I have to explain all this to Cardinal de Lorraine?*

In the silence that followed, nothing moved but the wind rustling dead leaves overhead, and drops of rain on his hat and back. The golden bay snorted unhappily and pawed the mossy, sodden earth.

"Messire Andelot," the Dominican said. "See that you are at Saint Catherine's in the morning. The price of your indulgence shall then be determined."

Andelot sighed within. "I shall be there at dawn, Monseigneur."

"Then you may take your leave."

Andelot lowered his head in deference, turned his horse, glared at Romier, and rode off, Romier swiftly behind him. Some distance away at the stream bank, Andelot held his mount.

Romier's face was flushed with exasperation. "You ox! You have blundered us both into this. You had better pray this incident does not reach the cardinal. For if he hears of this venture and calls us to account ... every move I make for the Huguenot duchesse will bring me under suspicion. And you had no authority to call yourself a Guise as yet."

Andelot gave him a dour look, then turned his horse in the direction they had just left. He stood in his stirrups to peer back into the shadows. He could see nothing.

"Now what do you think you are doing?" Romier asked.

"I wonder if all the Huguenots escaped?"

"You would do well to concern yourself with *our* escape. Do you not know the Dominican may return?"

"The old preacher left his book under the logs."

"Let it mold! I ride to Fontainebleau to appeal to madame for safety. Perchance I can foil the Dominican with a worthy gift for Saint Catherine's from the duchesse. She is most generous in these matters when it comes to safeguarding her own."

"Go then," Andelot said. "I will see the book for myself."

Romier looked at him with incredulity. "If the writing is found on you, Andelot, not even the duchesse will be able to save you — especially after the Dominican suspected you of deliberately aiding their escape. You may call yourself a Guise all you wish to no avail. And your call to meet him at the church is anything but a trivial matter, I assure you."

"Have you no curiosity to know what these Huguenots are reading behind locked doors and in the shadows of the woods? I have often wondered how the Scriptures would sound in our own French tongue."

"I have heard them before. The duchesse has a French Bible, but she is wise enough not to bring it to Fontainebleau under the nose of the cardinal and the Queen Mother. Come, Andelot, ami, do not meddle. Let the viper remain asleep and you will not be bitten."

"What harm can one glimpse do? Since I am to be a scholar, I would see for myself what they are studying."

Romier shook his head, and turning his stallion, rode off.

Andelot watched him disappear among the birches, then turned his horse in toward the meadow where the Huguenots had been meeting.

He tied the horse a short distance from the spot and walked to the fallen trees, now more in shadow as the sun drew to the west.

The Dominican appeared to be gone, and Andelot listened carefully. The rain had mostly ceased, except for a few last drops dripping from the branches.

The campfire still smoldered in the dampness, and the smell of smoke lingered.

*It was a mistake for them to have made the fire, and they should have gathered deeper into the woods.*

The horse snorted, shaking its mane as though bidding him not to stray any farther, yet Andelot felt an inner tug-of-war. Why this curiosity? A stronger prodding urged him forward to see for himself, to understand what was driving men and women to risk their lives in order to read the unauthorized Bible in French. What held such compelling power over them? What manner of souls were Calvin, Luther, and Beza to encourage men, women, and even children to risk their lives?

Moving from the shadows to the cluster of decaying logs, Andelot removed his glove and ran his hand into the place where he had seen the old preacher hide the book.

Despite the chill wind, he felt the sweat on his brow. His hand touched the book. He lifted it free and slid it inside his tunic. He looked about. He could not stay here in the open, but there was a place near a stream that he had seen previously along this path. There were boulders, overhanging tree branches, and a rocky cleft where he would be safe for a time as he read.

He mounted his horse and rode, reaching the location as the rain started up again.

With the bay tied under a sheltering tree, Andelot walked through shrubs growing close to the rocks until he climbed a short distance into the boulders. There, under an overhang, he spread a saddle blanket on the rock. His gaze skimmed the slope through which he had ridden. He sat watching for a while until reassured he had not been followed by a lackey serving the Dominican. He removed the forbidden book from under his tunic.

He opened it. His eyes fell to the writing, and he stared with excitement.

"It is the Bible ... It is in French," he murmured in awe. The preface declared the translation to come from the original Hebrew and Greek, not in Latin, and put painstakingly into his own language.

*Beware, Andelot, you know the penalty for studying any portion of the Bible in what is considered the vulgar tongue, whether it be English, Dutch, or French. It is heresy to translate the Scripture into the vernacular, and no less a crime to possess it, or to read it.*

Andelot had seen the cardinal order the burning of many hundreds of Bibles on the streets of Paris, calling the translation into French, "black arts." The poor chevalier who owned the bookshop was arrested and put to the screw because he had refused to name those individuals who had brought the Bibles from Geneva or his neighbors who had purchased one from his shop.

Andelot knew that in 1408 the Church decreed no one, on pain of being burned, could translate Scripture into French, nor even speak it, but only in the sacred tongue of Latin. Why Rome had declared Latin sacred Andelot had not attempted to ascertain in order to avoid the appearance of doubting the glorious decree.

He supposed the Church had the law against translation in order to protect the Holy Scripture from apostates. In making such a law, however, they had placed the Bible under the lock and key of Latin clerics, so that very few could gain access.

Andelot turned the pages carefully, his fingers trembling. As his gaze fell upon the words, a sense of awe crept over him.

*I feel as if I am walking into a holy place.*

A blast of chill wind struck against him and stirred the pages. He drew back against the boulder looking cautiously at the sky. Afar off in the mountains, he saw lightning flash, followed by a rumble of thunder. He looked down at the Bible. The wind blew the pages back, and he saw that it had been printed in Geneva.

He heard the rain pelting.

Nevertheless, he would read the words for himself.

*The Gospel of Saint Matthew.*

His gaze dropped farther down the page.

*"Now the birth of Jesus Christ was on this wise..."*

As he read through the gospel of Matthew, the midday sun behind the clouds crept lower in the sky. During a lull in the rain, a squirrel scampered across the leaves into the forest.

*"Therefore whosoever heareth these sayings of mine and doeth them, I will liken him unto a wise man, which built his house upon a rock... And the rain descended, and floods came, and the winds blew, and beat upon that house; and it fell not: for it was founded upon a rock. And every one that heareth these sayings of mine, and doeth them not, shall be likened unto a foolish man, which built his house upon the sand: And the rain descended and the floods came, and the winds blew, and beat upon that house; and it fell: and great was the fall of it."*

The afternoon wore on, but in his mind he was journeying back to the hills of Judea, sitting on a grassy plain listening to the majestic voice of Jesus echoing in his ears. For the first time, he had read the gospel of Matthew in his own language. There was so much more here about Christ that he had never heard.

*I never knew His words were so wonderful.* His heart burned within as he read in detail about His miracles, His teaching, His crucifixion and resurrection.

*"Then the eleven disciples went away to Galilee, into the mountain where Jesus had appointed them. When they saw him, they worshipped him...*

*"Then Jesus came and spake to them, All power is given unto me in heaven and on earth. Go ye therefore and teach all nations, baptizing them in the name of the Father, and of the Son, and of the Holy Ghost: teaching them to observe all things whatsoever I have commanded you: and, lo, I am with you always even unto the end of the world."*

Andelot sat, unable to stir from the wonder that enveloped him.

The sun was low in the west, and he would not get back to his quarters at Fontainebleau until dark. Sebastien would wonder where he had been. One look at his face as he walked into the chamber and he would know something had happened to him. Andelot now possessed a new tenderness in his soul for the person of Jesus Christ. A passion to know more burned within. The very thought of being able to read the remainder of the New Testament made his heart beat faster.

"Lord Jesus, You are more wonderful than I thought You to be!" he said aloud. He looked up at the darkening sky again, but this time he felt only love and joy. His fear was replaced with gratitude, for now he understood that when the Savior suffered and died on the cross, He paid Andelot's debt of sin. He bowed his head, giving thanks and surrendering all that he was and ever hoped to be to Jesus, the Son of God, who said, "And lo I am with you alway."

He closed the Bible and stuffed it inside his tunic. The old preacher would miss this prize worth more than gold. But Andelot could not think of parting with it until he had at least read it through once. The preacher would likely come back for it when he believed it safe, but find it gone.

*I could write him a note and tell him I have it. I might arrange a secret meeting with him. No doubt he could teach me much. But I must return to Fontainebleau to write the lettre. Oui, that is what I will do. I will meet this preacher for myself.*

As ANDELOT RODE BACK through the black woods toward the glimmer of light at Fontainebleau, he remembered he must appear before the cleric early in the morning at Saint Catherine's. How could he pay for his indulgence?

*I shall go to him and say, "Paid in full, Monseigneur priest, with the blood of Jesus, and guaranteed by His bodily resurrection from the tomb!"*

Andelot laughed with joy and began to hum, though he had no hymn to sing, for there were none, except the chants he knew. There was the hymn that Martin Luther wrote, he had heard Rachelle and Idelette singing it at Lyon, but he knew not the words. Something about a mighty fortress … a bulwark never failing? He shrugged and began making up his own hymn. The melody did not bring a shower of light bursting in the dark, but his heart was full of joie de vivre and the words came naturally —

"Jesus, you have set me free,
Opened my eyes so I shall see.
Your words will I cherish until I die!
What a wonderful day when I found Your book
Hidden in the nook.
Just one look, and now I know . . .
You will never let me go . . . Your words have told me so!"

AT DAWN THE NEXT day, the morning being soggy after all the rain, and as mist floated below a still-darkened sky, Andelot rode to the monastery located far from houses and farms. He carried a small bag of coins and wondered what the cleric might say if he knew some of the money he would bring for the indulgence had come from Marquis Fabien. And Romier had pitched in some coins after Andelot had complained, "If you had not so charitably told him I should pay for an indulgence, and even twice, I might not have this irksome debt at all."

"Saints! See how you make excuses for your blundering? It was you, mon ami, who transgressed into the Huguenot gathering. Did I not warn you against it?"

"You did, but since you are serving the dedicated Huguenot duchesse, you should realize that it was not a transgression. Listen, Romier, one day soon I will trust you with a secret that will change your entire life."

"Ha! That, I must see. And what is this merveilleux secret?"

"You must wait for the appropriate time, then I will show you."

Romier tipped his golden head and looked at him askance. "You bluff, but I shall wait, and see. Here — some more coins. I shall make amends for tolerating you — you are reaping what you well deserve."

When Andelot arrived at Saint Catherine's, the Dominican cleric was working behind his desk, a candle burning. The rain had started again, beating gently against the window. Andelot noted how weary he looked, as though he had been up all night in a vigil of sorts. There were dark circles beneath his eyes and his brow was furrowed. Andelot felt a wave of compassion for him.

The cash box sat on the desk before him with a list of standard fees for indulgences.

*Why is it a transgression to help the Huguenots escape, when the words they had met to read are but Scripture?*

Andelot laid the bag of coins on the desk.

The cleric raised the bag from the desk. "It is sufficient; you may go in peace."

Andelot looked at him for a puzzling moment, remembering something he had heard once about the Reformer Luther from Germany. Was it not this, paying of money for transgressions, that had troubled him to search the Scriptures? Go in peace. Was acceptance with a holy God obtained through paying money?

Andelot wrinkled his brow. He was about to question the cleric, then thought better of it. If he wished to rouse more suspicion, this was the way to go about it. He bowed and quickly departed.

For days afterward he thought about the Dominican and felt sympathy for him as he recalled the dark circles beneath his eyes and his worried brow. Could the Dominican, so religious, ever obtain the peace he claimed he could give to other transgressors?

THE ROYAL PALAIS OF Fontainebleau had long been a favorite residence of French kings. The older Fontainebleau had been a hunting seat from the twelfth to the sixteenth centuries when King Francis I assembled the finest Italian artists and sculptors of the Renaissance to restore the palais. Now it was one of the most treasured of royal châteaus.

Though Andelot's days were mainly spent in long hours studying Greek, Latin, and the works of Erasmus, he still felt privileged to be here at Court with Comte Sebastien. Andelot relished the beauty of the palais-château and the large evergreen forest, for Fontainebleau was situated in the heart of the forest.

The wind was fresh and clean, and he was pleased to be away from the stench of Paris that sometimes grew unbearable. He mentioned this to Comte Sebastien on their arrival, and Sebastien agreed, but then grew most sober.

"With the palais situated in the forest, flourishing with game, there is grand prospect for the court to indulge in all their favorite pursuits: hunting, riding, shooting, eating, and drinking too sumptuously, and of course — " his voice dripped with disgust — "intriguing one against another. Do not set your heart on vain pursuits, Andelot. Pasteur Bertrand would tell you the same. And favor with the king is like a mist on a hot summer morn. So soon it vanishes and none remember."

Andelot thought this a strange admonition from Sebastien; he had recanted all that he claimed he had once held to be solemn truth to save his life and return to Court. All he had lost had been again showered upon him: power and glory amid luxury, sprinkled with religion — but it was now accompanied by Sebastien's apparent scorn. It was not lost on Andelot that his oncle now went to Mass each day and sat in the conclave near the royal family while Cardinal de Lorraine officiated. Andelot also went, and though he had a growing understanding of Protestantism, for him the Mass had never been a problem as it was to the Huguenots. Even so, Andelot had to admit that since Sebastien's release from the Bastille, the things he had once esteemed now appeared to weigh on him like chains around his ankle. Andelot loved his oncle, and his worries for him grew. He sometimes acted suspiciously. Andelot had seen him with a map of England, going over every inch of it with a strong eyeglass. Was he thinking of Marquis Fabien and his travels, or something else?

One night after Andelot had been at Fontainebleau for two weeks, a blustery wind brought an unseasonably strong storm crooning eerily about the château cornices on the side of the palais where Sebastien had his chambers. Andelot was seated in the outer antechamber used by the pages. The large candles on his desk burned with clear, unwavering light as he read.

Scholar Thauvet had assigned Andelot's reading and thesis before returning to Paris for some weeks to lecture at the Paris university. Andelot placed the book to one side of the desk, which was piled with other leather-bound manuscripts and papers. He glanced over his shoulder into the sitting chamber to make certain unfriendly eyes were not watching. He found the chamber empty; all was quiet except the wind.

Though this alcove was private, used by Sebastien's chief page, there were two other doors leading from the alcove into other chambers. One of these was Sebastien's private bedchamber and writing closet; the other was a sitting chamber with a hearth, where a fire of pine crackled.

Andelot remained cautious. Many were the times when some high-placed official serving one of the noble families would enter the sitting chamber from the outside corridor without knocking and commence to order Andelot about as though he were naught but a common lackey. He found these interruptions most annoying.

Cautiously, he pushed aside the works on Erasmus that Thauvet had given to him to study and slipped the French Bible out from under the stack before him. He could keep the Bible with his books, for no one paid attention to what he was reading except his tutor who was still in Paris. Andelot had removed the outer covering from one of his worn, private books and placed it over the French Bible to conceal it.

It was not that he intended to keep the old pasteur's Bible. Andelot had tried on several occasions to make contact with him in the forest by leaving a carefully worded message in the logs where the man had concealed the forbidden Book, but he must have suspected a trap for there had been no reply.

The wind blew noisily with a whine. Andelot found the place in the Bible where he had stopped the night before and continued the epistle of Paul, the apostle to the church at Rome. This lettre to the Romans seemed an excellent place to start since the Vatican was at Rome.

*"Therefore we conclude that a man is justified by faith without the deeds of the law."*

As Andelot considered the text, he was startled by footsteps swiftly crossing the outer chamber floor. The wind had muffled the sound of the front door opening. Before he realized it, the Cardinal de Lorraine's secretary stood beside his reading table looking down at him. Andelot looked up at the towering shadow that bent over the desk. His heart shuddered within like a tower on a crumbling cliff. The gaze he met belonged to Monseigneur Jaymin, a cleric who was close to the cardinal.

*Help, Lord!*

"Ah, Andelot, Andelot ... and where is your seigneur, Comte Sebastien?"

Andelot noticed that Jaymin carried an official paper in his large hand. The man's knotty knuckles were the first thing Andelot had noticed when they had met.

Andelot closed the cover on the Bible to give the impression he had been studying Erasmus and stood quickly. "Comte Sebastien has gone out, Monseigneur. Shall I give him your message?"

"On such an evening as this? It will soon be raining. I would think he might wish to be sitting by his fire reading. Sebastien and his nightly promenades," he said with a friendly laugh. "And he with his troublesome knee."

Andelot smiled, trying to calm his thudding heart and hoping he did not sound breathless. "He does like his strolls, Monseigneur."

Jaymin was of an angular body, with a shiny scalp and large doleful brown eyes over a hawk nose. Andelot, who was a little shorter than Marquis Fabien, and by no means small, only reached Jaymin's chest. Jaymin's height was somewhat of a jest among the pages, for they said that while the Queen Mother kept dwarves, Cardinal de Lorraine kept giants.

"I am surprised you did not attend your seigneur on this promenade."

"He excused me. I had my studies."

"Ah yes, ah yes." His gaze dropped to the book on the desk with Andelot's hand resting casually over it.

"A wise man, Scholar Thauvet. You are most blessed to have him as your tutor. He will join us soon I understand. The cardinal is most interested in how his services to instruct you were incurred." He smiled.

Andelot tensed. He dare not mention Marquis Fabien. He delayed and then said, "Incurred, Monseigneur?"

"Scholar Thauvet is sought after by the most noble of families. He is paid handsomely. And therefore, le cardinal merely wondered how it is that Sebastien incurred his services for you, considering."

*Considering that Andelot, though said to be related to the Guises, was no longer of any interest to the cardinal—why would Thauvet agree to become his tutor?*

*It was wise not to mention Sebastien either.*

"Grace has indeed been thrown over my shoulders as an undeserved mantle, Monseigneur. It was not Comte Sebastien who arranged for Scholar Thauvet, but Duchesse Dushane. She did so, I believe, because I was raised on the estate in Lyon of which she is an owner ... And she had taken a kindly interest in me. She knew how disappointed I was when I offended the cardinal who had first thought to send me to the university."

*I am doing well. I can see the change in his eyes. He no longer looks so suspicious.*

"The cardinal will be pleased. He has rethought his discipline of you, Andelot. You are a kinsman we must not forget, and though the cardinal has been most taken up with other affairs of state, he tells me to assure you he has not forgotten you." He smiled, showing strong, even teeth.

"Merci." He bowed his head. *I wish he would forget me altogether.*

"The cardinal wishes to know what Scholar Thauvet is having you study here at Fontainebleau?"

Andelot kept his palm on the book. "Oh. So many subjects, Monseigneur. All most interesting. I am studying and preparing to write a paper on Erasmus."

"Ah! The English Oxford scholar. A borderline Reformer, is he not?"

"Erasmus? Oh, I ... do not read him so."

"He promised a more accurate Greek version of the New Testament. He went on from Oxford to Rome to study for the work."

Andelot smiled. "Rome ..."

"And Erasmus made a new Latin text as well, did he not?" Sebastien's full voice came from behind them. He entered the chamber from the outer hall door.

"A Latin text to remedy the errors in Jerome's," Jaymin said, turning toward him.

Sebastien removed his hat, and Andelot hurried to take his wet cloak as well.

"It is beginning to rain." Sebastien limped over to the hearth to warm himself.

Andelot kept an eye on both men as he took away the comte's things and went to pour his small glass of wine. Sebastien was not the manner of man one would easily notice in a chamber where the strong presence of the Duc de Guise and Cardinal de Lorraine were gathered, or even the cleric, Jaymin. He was unassuming, a man of quiet speech, seldom speaking unless spoken to. Yet he was alert and shrewd and underestimated. Was this the reason Catherine de Medici had chosen him as one of her chief counselors? He no longer worked to seek personal power as the Guises and others. Sebastien worked to maintain security for those he loved, and after Amboise and the Bastille, he avoided controversy. His hair, now marked with gray, was smooth and thick, cut in a bowl shape, shaved to just above his ears, with a short fringe cut straight across his forehead. When he showed himself at Court, however, he wore a black collarbone-length wig that was intricately waved. His eyes were large, the prominent feature of an otherwise unassuming but pleasant face, with a wide jaw. When at home with Madeleine, he wore the somber, darker colors of the Huguenot leaders like Admiral Coligny and the great French theologian Theodore Beza. But at Court, as he was now, he wore clothing of finest satins, velvets, and dyed leather, embroidered with gold or silver.

"Ah, so you are acquainted also with Erasmus," Jaymin said, joining Sebastien at the hearth and accepting the goblet that Andelot served in silence like any expert page.

"You may have forgotten, Jaymin, that Scholar Thauvet is an ami. He would become most bored with me if I did not know something of the great theological concepts to discuss with him." He raised his goblet toward Jaymin.

Jaymin smiled and raised his goblet. "To His Majesty, King Francis II." He drank, then sighed with satisfaction and looked into the firelight.

"One wonders if the Bourbon princes will toast to the king. They will have ample opportunity."

"They are being summoned then? The Queen Mother had not made up her mind as of this morning."

"But the king has," he said with a touch of superiority. "Le Duc de Guise has aided the king in drawing up a royal summons. The envoy will leave in the morning for Navarre. If Princes Louis and Antoine de Bourbon do not come to Fontainebleau, they will be in rebellion against the King of France."

Andelot returned to his desk. From the corner of his eye he saw the book. Sebastien and Jaymin were once more discussing Thauvet and Erasmus. Andelot picked up the book to push it under a pile of manuscripts and papers.

"The cardinal will want me to report on your progress, and what you are reading, Andelot," Jaymin said. Leaving the hearth again, he walked to the desk, hand extended for the book that Andelot held.

"I could wish, Andelot, you would remember to keep my chamber door open as I requested," Sebastien said, unusually cross. "The warmth from the hearth needs to reach my bed. The cold is most trying upon my bones."

Andelot, gripping the book, moved quickly away from Jaymin's outstretched hand to do as Sebastien ordered.

He stepped toward Sebastien's chamber doors, opening them. He hoped his face was unreadable as he started to turn back when Sebastien snatched the book from his hand and opened it.

"So!" Sebastien limped to one of the stone walls in the sitting chamber where the firelight from the torches cast weaving shadows. The wind whined, and the draft caused the fire in the hearth to sputter.

Andelot stood with his hands behind him, shoulders back, firelight sparkling on his black and white uniform.

Sebastien snapped off some questions about Erasmus while appearing to read from the book, demanding Andelot answer while Jaymin watched Andelot's struggle with amusement.

Momentarily stunned, Andelot looked at Sebastien with the torchlight spilling down upon his graying head, his shoulders a little stooped.

Something was happening between them, and all he could do was follow where Sebastien led. His respect for his unassuming oncle ascended.

All at once his Greek struggled forth to reveal what little he knew.

Sebastien scowled. "Has the duchesse hired Thauvet at much expense for naught?"

He paused as Andelot shrugged.

"Louder," Sebastien commanded, lifting his eyes toward the ceiling as though bored. "Have you been neglecting your studies because Thauvet is not yet here?"

Andelot's stumbling discourse burst forth in French, larded with a tint of Latin.

Sebastien groaned deeply, then snapped in Greek: "The vulgar tongue is forbidden. You shall neither pray in it, nor sing chants in it, nor quote Scripture in it. Understood?"

Andelot nodded. "Yes, Seigneur Sebastien."

Sebastien snapped the book shut and laid it carelessly on a table. "You shall see me in my chamber first thing in the morning. Your schedule must be changed to include an extra hour of study in Greek."

"Just so, Monseigneur." Andelot went back to his desk, pulled out his chair, and sat down. *How could Sebastien possibly have known about the Bible? He is shielding me.*

Andelot pretended to resume his studies while watching from the corner of his eye.

They were conversing again about the Bourbon princes. Jaymin, standing by the hearth, casually reached inside his cleric robe and handed Sebastien a parchment.

"For the Queen Mother's signature, Sebastien. Count Crussol will need it in the morning when he rides to Navarre to present it to Antoine de Bourbon. Spies have informed us that Louis and his wife are there also, visiting."

"Yes, bien sûr, I shall see to it first thing in the morning." He walked with Jaymin to the door. "Does the Queen Mother know the Bourbons are being called to answer for Amboise?"

"Is there anything of import happening at Court that the Queen Mother does not know? She has more spies than Chantonnay," Jaymin said of the Spanish ambassador.

Jaymin departed, and Andelot stood abruptly to face Sebastien. Sebastien limped to the main door and locked it, then slumped into a chair by the fire, head in hand. He groaned.

"Andelot, you were a fool to bring that Bible here!"

Shocked, Andelot stared down at him. "But how is it you knew?"

"I knew from the beginning. I am the bigger fool for allowing you to keep it beneath the very nose of the Cardinal de Lorraine. I saw you reading it, and the way you were reading did not convince me you were studying Erasmus. I searched when you were out and found it. I should have burned it, but I could not."

"Burn it!"

"Would you burn the Book—or your fleshly body? I have seen Huguenots burned—I have smelled them. There has been enough loss in this extended family. Do we need to lose you to the flames?"

Andelot stared at him, more worried now by his ashen look than about the discovery. He dropped to one knee beside the chair, feeling the heat from the fire.

"Mon oncle—Monseigneur, I beg your pardone. Not because I am sorry I read the words of God. I give God thanks daily that I have them. I am repentant because I should not have brought the Book in here, where it was possible to implicate you. I should have been more careful and kept it in the forest, even as the Huguenot pasteur did."

Sebastien gave him intense scrutiny. "Where and how did you come by this French Bible, Andelot?"

"There were Huguenots meeting in the woods when the Dominican from Saint Catherine's came upon them with armed men. I saw the old pasteur hide a book under some logs before fleeing. Afterward, I came back for it. I have tried to contact him, but to no avail, and so I still have it. There is naught like it, Monsieur Sebastien. To read the Scripture in one's own tongue—to read all of the New Testament for the first time, and in understandable French—it is a great honneur."

Sebastien blotted his pale forehead with a kerchief.

"You know the penalty that could be pronounced upon you should this be found in your possession?"

"I tell you, Monsieur Sebastien, that when Père Jaymin reached for the book—I could feel the scorching flames rising about my feet. Your quick distraction at that very moment saved me."

"So you are one of us now. That is worthy of thanks. But to be a Huguenot will mean your life is at risk."

"I do not know if I am of the religion. I have merely begun to learn, and to read the words . . . But to have the Bible and read it does not mean I cannot be a bonne Catholic."

"Jaymin is suspicious. I saw the curiosity in his eyes. Why do you think he came here? Yes, to bring me the paper, but also because the cardinal is watching you."

"I could see he remains suspicious."

"Jaymin is shrewd. A kind man, but wholly dedicated to the cardinal. He will grow even more suspicious now." He began to push himself up from the chair. "We must burn the Bible. I deplore such action, but we must take no chances."

Andelot was horrified. *Burn it?* But he had just found it. He had not even read all of the words yet.

"Monseigneur, I beg of you, give me at least time to return it under the log for the Huguenot pasteur. He may never be able to own another copy." *Nor will I*, he thought miserably. "I will go now," he said. "On the golden bay I can be there in a short time."

"You do not realize how dangerous this can be for you, for us. Monsieur Jaymin may have decided to put a watcher on you."

"Then let me hide it here in my quarters until there is a way for me to take it to the forest."

Sebastien frowned, staring at his black-gloved hand, then studying Andelot, as though his comeliness and youth were being weighed.

"I see how much this means to you. Even so, this is dangerous, Andelot. If you will not permit the thought of burning such a treasure, you must hide it as though it were a chest of rubies and return it to the tree hollow tomorrow. For I tell you the truth, if you are caught with it, I will not be able to save you from your folly. And if it is known that I have permitted it, I will not be able to save myself this time."

Sebastien pushed himself up from the chair. His eyes were firm. He was again the monseigneur and Andelot the page. "Conceal it as best you can."

Inside the bedchamber, the Bible sat on the table disguised as a work of Erasmus. He would need to give it up. *There is only one way,* he thought, *to memorize the words. For my memory is secure, it cannot be confiscated, and I can recall the words whenever I choose, even in the company of the cardinal. Yes, perhaps the best way to carry portions of the Scriptures about without fear of arrest is to memorize them.*

❋

SEBASTIEN WATCHED ANDELOT RETRIEVE the Bible. His eagerness for the Word had touched Sebastien's heart, and he could not bring himself to give the command to put it on the coals.

He put his good hand to his damp forehead. The mortifying memory of bowing on his good knee to Cardinal de Lorraine and recanting tore at his heart. Madeleine did not know he had done this; how could he ever tell her? Many other brothers had not weakened in the Bastille, nor at Amboise. They had gone on to greater suffering, to eventual release by merciful death—whereas he had accepted release through compromise.

Would God forgive him? He believed so, otherwise he would not be saved by grace alone through faith in Christ, but by his own work of enduring suffering to the end. He believed, however, that there would be a great reward in heaven for those who were martyred for the sake of Christ. Whereas he, Sebastien, though eternally secure in Christ, had lost his crown.

His sigh came very deeply. *Sebastien, you are the worst of cowards. Did you see how the fiery passion for the truth glowed in Andelot's eyes? He has a great hunger for the words. How could I order him to throw the Bible in the hearth and reduce it to ashes?*

What if Jaymin came back tonight with guards and insisted the chamber be searched? Non, Jaymin would not act that boldly, that brutally. He suspected, yes, but he would not rip the mask from another's face. He would wait and watch. Jaymin was a strange one. Although loyal to the cardinal, yes, even his closest ami and ally, Jaymin had sympathy for heretics. He would not find joy in discovering Andelot's forbidden Bible and hauling him before the cardinal. He would do so because he believed strongly in Rome's teaching; but he would not enjoy his task.

Sebastien lifted from the desk the official paper Jaymin had left for him to present to the Queen Mother and read the royal summons that the Guises had arranged for the young king to sign.

> *You doubtless will remember the lettres which I wrote you touching the rising which happened of late at Amboise, and also concerning mon other oncle, Prince de Condé, your brother, whom many prisoners vehemently accuse of involvement; a belief which I could not at first entertain against one of my blood.*
>
> *I have decided to investigate the matter, having resolved not to pass my life in trouble through the mad ambition of any of my subjects. I charge you, mon oncle, to bring your brother to Orléans whether he should be willing or not, and should the said prince refuse obedience, I assure you, mon oncle, that I shall soon make it clear that I am your king.*

Sebastien chewed his lip. They would be fools to leave the safety of the Huguenot kingdom of Navarre and enter this cockatrice den! This was surely the Guises' work.

He began to pace. And now, what will you do for the Bourbon princes? How could he face Marquis Fabien when he returned if he should fail to at least warn his kinsmen that they were being invited into a trap?

*What could he do?* He limped on, hardly noticing the growing pain in his knee, so deep were his thoughts.

So here he was at Court, counselor to the Queen Mother, who kept a poison closet for political opponents, who trusted astrologers more than she trusted Scripture — did she even know what was in the Book? Which of them did? Sebastien recalled what the Huguenot leader Coligny once told him, how shocked he had been when reading the Scriptures for the first time in his own tongue to discover that many of the teachings of the Roman Church were not taught in the Bible.

Thus far, Sebastien had managed to walk the thin gray line of compromise. No simple task, as he had assured Madeleine, forcing her to keep her French Bible back home at the Château de Silk. He was thankful, however, that with the raging tide of persecution sweeping across France, they had survived thus far. He had staunchly held to his task of avoiding mention of certain convictions, though he now avoided the word *convictions*, and spoke instead of "understanding," since it left room for accommodation. He had learned to keep his thoughts of John Calvin and Martin Luther behind a bolted door. He would not open that door, for reason argued that should he open it again, he may need to answer for it.

His plans to escape to England with his family must not be discovered. Not even Madeleine knew of his decision, but he knew she would be joyful at the prospect. Her worry was great over raising Joan in safety as a Huguenot.

The pine smoldering on the hearth sent off a pleasant scent and a comfortable warm glow. Even so, Sebastien's shoulders sagged from the long day's ordeal, and he wished for little more than a chair beside the burning coals.

His thoughts remained upon the trap set for Prince Louis de Condé and Antoine. He dare not send a message to Navarre, not now. It would be safer to send word indirectly through Duchesse Dushane. Yes, he would contact her tonight. That was as far as he would go to risk himself.

Then there was the Marquis Fabien . . . If only it were possible to warn him about the danger to his Bourbon kinsmen, but Fabien remained at sea. Just today, Spanish Ambassador Chantonnay had angrily registered a complaint of an attack upon a Spanish vessel. There was no proof to incriminate the marquis, but if Fabien did not cease his warring and return, he might find himself an object of the Queen Mother's wrath. Though Sebastien noticed she appeared to be looking the other way of recent days. He wondered why.

# The Wiles of the Enemy

Duc de Guise's forces took elaborate precautions throughout Fontainebleau and Orléans for the arrival of the Bourbon princes: Louis de Condé and Antoine de Bourbon, Marquis Fabien's nearest kinsmen. Sebastien had heard that not so much as a table knife remained to the town's people-at-arms. Guise, a shrewd military commander, made certain no men-at-arms loyal to the Bourbons were concealed in any of the houses or on the streets masquerading as peasants.

Warnings were delivered to Antoine de Bourbon at the small Huguenot kingdom of Navarre from several Huguenot nobles, including the duchesse: *Caution. Do not venture forth from your kingdom of Navarre.*

Sebastien worried, but was helpless to affect the course of action. From the Queen Mother's council chamber he could look out and see the pikemen, their metal glimmering. The duc's soldiers were stationed all along the route and out of sight in the woods.

Noontide came with the expected prominent arrival of the Bourbon princes to meet the king and defend themselves against questions of treason. Sebastien brought Andelot to stand with the chief pages from the various noble houses while he, as a chief counselor to the Queen Mother, took his position near the royal dais. He wore a collared cloak of black over a white satin waistcoat and dark hose. He must remain as cautious as a fox in such serpentine company. They believed him loyal; they must continue to think so — the very reason he had not risked sending a message directly to Louis as he had done before the debacle at Amboise. There were spies watching him, of that he was certain.

Duchesse Dushane was also under suspicion, but she managed to stay aloof of anything that would connect her to Guise's enemies. She did not come today, but pleaded "skeleton pain."

There was a shuffle near the royal entrance and every eye turned toward a double door carved with the arching vine of the royal *fleur-de-lis*, overlaid in gold. The door swung open and four plumed guards in red and white formed a promenade through which King Francis, the Queen Mother, and Reinette Mary Stuart-Valois entered the audience hall. Sebastien and the courtiers bowed as the royal threesome took their elevated chairs.

Sebastien could smell a rat, could sense the restrained atmosphere of malicious glee emanating from Duc de Guise and those surrounding him. He had the boy-king Francis under his control, so the decisions being issued under the royal seal were, for all practical purposes, put forth by the duc and the cardinal. But the Queen Mother caused Sebastien's curiosity to bristle. Why was she permitting the two Bourbons to be arrested when she needed them to oppose the Guises? Sebastien did not doubt for a minute that Catherine de Medici also had some scheme loitering in the shadows of her mind. Though Sebastien knew most of her endeavors at Court, he had not been able to discover this one. She seemed to be cooperating with the duc.

The duc strode up and down the royal carpet, his short gold-trimmed cape fluttering. There was the energy of self-assured victory in his every step as he smoothed his short pointed beard with one jeweled finger. The cardinal entered through a thick Genoan velvet curtain embroidered with the oriflamme. His lustrous crimson-and-white robe rustled softly, and as he neared the duc, the fragrance of perfume came to Sebastien's nostrils. The jeweled cross hanging across his chest reflected a beam that streaked across the side of his face.

"The Bourbons are on their way," he told the king and Queen Mother. "They have sent chamberlains ahead to announce their approach."

"They have come alone?" the Queen Mother asked.

It was as he thought. The princes were to be arrested. The written admonition to not fear coming alone was given to mislead them.

Duc de Guise leaned toward King Francis and spoke in a low voice, but Sebastien overheard.

"Remember, sire, when they arrive, we are all to remain silent."

"Monsieur Comte," said the Queen Mother. Sebastien stepped toward her with a small bow.

"Madame?"

"The Prince de Condé and the King of Navarre are aware that you are related by marriage to another Bourbon kinsman, le Marquis de Vendôme. They will think the better of our meeting should you greet them in the name of the marquis and escort them through the gates with peace."

In the name of the marquis! Sebastien felt the stinging lash. Betrayal!

She smiled at him, her prominent eyes amused as she read his dilemma. She knew he retained a certain loyalty to Prince Condé despite his words to the contrary. She knew that back in March he had slipped away from Amboise castle to warn Condé that Catherine knew about the Renaudie plot. It now gave her pleasure to have him betraying Condé rather than warning him.

Sebastien's heart thudded with the indignity. He struggled with the tentacles of his hatred for her, gasping emotionally to not let his soul sink into the morass of darkness. He heard her soft chortle. She loved to watch those whose loyalty she doubted flounder. Did she know his service to her was a ruse?

His rage must remain masked. If she knew, then what might she do to Madeleine and Joan? Ah yes, he knew she had tried to poison his beloved! He would not admit this to Madeleine or Andelot or the Macquinet family. He could not allow their suspicion and fear to put him at risk, for she might guess that he knew.

As though his crushed hand were molded to his heart's emotions, he felt it throbbing.

Duc de Guise broke the trauma. He turned with a thrust of his shoulder to the Queen Mother. "The Marquis de Vendôme is now a common corsair, Madame, striking against Spain's treasure galleons." He turned to King Francis. "Sire, I well understand how you and the marquis shared bonhomie while being tutored at Court together when growing up, but this is no time for sentimentality. The marquis has brought the anger of Spain upon us. King Philip is enraged over the loss of his galleons."

"Monsieur le Duc," the Queen Mother said, "do let us keep our minds on the Bourbons we must deal with now."

"Before you bring the Bourbons here to meet with the king, come and warn us," Cardinal de Lorraine told Sebastien.

*Warn them?* What need was there to warn them? What could two unarmed men accomplish when the palais was thick with armed guards?

It was the Bourbons who needed to be warned that they had fallen for an evil ruse. Louis and Antoine could have chosen the outcome to their dilemma by arriving with a hundred armed men to make the Duc de Guise consider well before moving against them — the princes of the royal blood!

He bowed and limped from the chamber, looking neither right nor left, though he felt that some of the glances he received were of pity.

So they knew already that Fabien was involved in the sinking of the Duc de Alva's ships. This would be dangerous news upon his return to France. That Guise was aware showed his close workings with the Spanish envoy. Sebastien had seen the ambassador's dark eyes flashing with indignation when Guise had mentioned the galleons set to fire.

The wind tossed the leaves on the trees in and around the palais-château of Fontainebleau. Sebastien rode out of the courtyard with the royal chamberlain toward the Bourbon princes.

The entire avenue through which the two princes would ride was lined shoulder to shoulder and pike to pike with royal soldiers; not to welcome, but to intimidate. Once the princes began to ride down the street between the pikemen, there would be no altering course. They could only go forward.

Sebastien sat astride his horse at the head of the line — the pikemen on one side of the avenue, while the chamberlain led the other pikemen. Sebastien heard the wind fluttering the uniforms, causing the tassels on the spears to tinkle ominously.

He watched in a spirit of sobriety as the princes rode their black horses slowly along the cobbled street. The two men's faces were grim. Did they finally recognize their true predicament? Prince de Condé saw him, and their eyes met.

They were garbed in elegant finery with velvet cloaks, and their horses were robed with jeweled harnesses, but they were alone and vulnerable.

But now! The trap was unashamedly in the open. The Guises must believe they were in control and no one could stop them — not even the Queen Mother, who appeared to be one with them. This was often her deliberate way, to play one side and then the other, maintaining a precarious balance that preserved her power.

Antoine and Louis rode through the double line of pikes and through the gate to Fontainebleau, where Sebastien and the royal chamberlain fell in beside them.

"Did you not receive the duchesse's message?" Sebastien hissed, looking straight ahead.

The horses' hooves clopped smartly.

"Yes, mon ami, we received the warnings. But let no Frenchman ever say that I, Condé, am afraid to show my face at Court. I will go and proclaim my innocence. I have no cause to fear."

"Ah, Monseigneur Louis! The most courageous among us have reason to beware when the shrewd ploys used by the Guises are hatched."

"This summons from the king cannot be ignored," Louis said. "All would declare us guilty if we refrained from going to Court now. The Guises would assuredly claim to the young king that we are plotting a new rebellion and should be apprehended, by an army if necessary."

"As the messieurs, the duc and the cardinal, know very well. They have planned this, I assure you."

"Yes, but there was small choice," Condé said. "To not take heed to a royal summons is an act of rebellion."

*If the princes had been under any impression that they would be treated as "royal cousins" when they arrived, they must see now how they erred in coming alone.*

Sebastien now rode quickly ahead of the princes to prepare their way.

When he returned to the audience chamber, all were waiting, their faces alert.

Sebastien bowed his head. "The Bourbon princes have arrived. They will be here within minutes."

Those assembled took positions either along the walls or behind and to the side of the seated Queen Mother and King Francis.

Sebastien, in self-preservation, kept his feelings masked.

❅

CATHERINE SAT ON HER throne beside her son Francis. *The mock king*, she thought with both scorn and pity. *The duc has him wrapped in his fingers, and the cardinal smirks at him. Ah, that would never have occurred in the days when my husband was King of France! And the Bourbons! What fools to pay heed to the suggestion that they come peacefully without armed men.* Were it not that she needed them to counter the Guises she would be rid of them for their idiocy. But alas, they would both be useful.

The double doors of carved wood opened, and Antoine de Bourbon, King of Navarre and first prince of the royal Bourbon blood, walked forward toward her and Francis. He was King of Navarre only through his marriage to Queen Jeanne d'Albret. It was their son, Henry of Navarre, that Catherine was considering for her daughter Marguerite.

Antoine knelt on one knee to King Francis, but Francis, as planned by the Guises, did not move or make one conciliatory step toward him. Instead, he silently indicated that Antoine's first obeisance should have been to Catherine.

Her scorn matched her secret amusement. One bow was not enough for Antoine, he would bow twice, and contrary to custom knelt on one knee to Francis. *Yes, Monsieur Antoine would do well for her plans to thwart the duc's power.* Antoine, the popinjay, was so submissive he would never claim his superior rights to the throne. The Guises should be bowing to Antoine! He was a far cry from the character-driven Marquis Fabien! Fabien was out dueling Spaniards while Antoine was bowing when he should be indignant over the offensive way he was being treated by the Guises.

Francis, close beside her, had one eye on the duc and the other on the cardinal to see what they expected of him.

*Ah, my son Francis, your weakness is a danger to me and to the Valois name.*

Next Prince Condé came forward. Catherine knew well enough what the Guises thought of him. They feared Condé. Condé was aware that he was a royal prince. He was cool and arrogant and did not look at the Guises or their niece, Mary, who, like Francis, obeyed their every call. Nor would he trouble to speak to them first, though he smiled at Catherine. *Louis has a comely smile,* she thought.

*Ah yes, this is the clever one.* Her mind raced, ever awake. *Too clever for me to permit the Guises to kill him. If Condé is dead, I will be left alone to oppose the sneering cardinal and the scowling fanatical duc. Ah yes, I know. But I too have a plan.*

Catherine, keeping her face emotionless, slid her unblinking gaze over to the Guises. They were lounging against the high stone window behind their niece, Mary. *Ah yes, the family spy! I have not forgotten you. You will be going back to Scotland posthaste when the hour comes.* Wherever her oncles were, there was petite Mary, always ready to do their bidding, to woo her husband, Francis, into complying with their every whim.

Duc de Guise caught Catherine's gaze, the arranged signal. She went along as planned, allowing him to believe she was cooperating. She stood and looked pleasantly at Prince Louis de Condé, which she found was not difficult to do.

"Monsieur le Prince, step this way, as I wish to speak with you alone for a moment on an important matter."

Condé showed slight surprise, but he bowed elegantly and followed, his dark eyes suggesting he found her the only interesting person at Court. *Ah, that was like him.*

Catherine walked toward her private chamber, Condé followed. She smiled briefly to herself and raised a hand to signal the guards hiding in the antechamber. They were ready as planned. After a brief moment she bid Condé to enter her chamber. His expression was curious, his eyes showing a flicker of wariness. Yes, this one was clever. She turned her back toward him. There came a start of surprise from behind her as quick steps sounded. The guards had surrounded him.

"Your Majesty—" Prince de Condé said in injured outrage.

Catherine kept still. She was surprised that the moment of victory brought her no personal pleasure. She rather liked the romantic figure of the Bourbon prince. She even allowed herself a few romantic fantasies where he was concerned. She was no womanly fool though; she would not put herself in a position of subservience to a man again. She had known humiliation enough while enduring the pain of watching her husband, King Henry, with that old piece of baggage, Diane de Poitiers.

The guards under Duc de Guise arrested Condé, taking his private sword and dagger. He was led away under dignified protest to the prison dungeons.

Antoine must have heard the disturbance, for he appeared, wearing a twisted look of shock. She kept her cool distance.

"Your Majesty, I beg to be Louis' guard," Antoine cried. "There is no need for the dungeon. We have come freely, and freely we will stay until our reputations are cleared of this wicked lie of treason hurled against us."

She need not reply, for she was not ready to move on her private plans as yet. Duc de Guise and the cardinal, who had also entered her private chamber, looked triumphant.

*They think matters have gone as they have planned, and they are very smug.*

King Francis mustered a stern royal expression while he stood beside the cardinal. But even then it was the duc who spoke for him.

"Your brother, Louis, is under arrest," the duc told Antoine coldly. "He is thoroughly implicated in the rebellion at Amboise against the king. He will stand trial, and if found guilty, will be condemned to die."

*Ah yes, you are most anxious for his death, are you not? His removal puts you closer to the throne.*

Antoine too was under arrest but was at liberty to wander the corridors and gardens. Catherine had her reasons for leaving him here at

Fontainebleau where, on secret occasions away from Duc de Guise, she might walk with Antoine alone. Sometimes a serpent did not wish to kill its victim, but keep it alive as needed.

❖

A SHORT TIME AFTER Prince Condé was arrested for treason, Catherine quietly made the decision to have him taken from the Orléans prison at Fontainebleau and moved by night to the more secure dungeons of Amboise. Her reason for doing so was due to a whisper that reached her by way of Madalenna that the Guise faction was plotting to have Condé assassinated in the dungeon before the trial, rather than risk his being declared innocent and set free. This proved their true goal: to remove the Bourbons in order to strengthen their own rights to the throne. This would put her position at risk. Francis was getting older, and Mary would come into maturity and reign as Queen of France. Where would that leave her as the Queen Mother? Mary did not like her. She never had, even when Mary was a spoiled schoolgirl under tutorage in the palais when Catherine's husband was alive as king. And Mary would still be dominated by the cardinal. *And my son, Francis, is moving from me, trusting me less by the day as Mary and her oncles fill his mind with treachery against me . . . Ah yes, I know.*

No, the petit galant Prince Louis Condé must be kept sealed within the dungeon away from assassin's plots.

*If anyone shall devise an assassin's plot, it will be my sovereign right for the gloire de la France!*

Catherine made many visits to see him, oftentimes ordering a stool brought in for her to sit and converse with him pleasantly for an hour or so. She took pleasure in whispering promises to him that he would live.

On a certain afternoon not long after one such visit with Condé, Catherine sat in her royal bedchamber at Fontainebleau looking over the correspondence brought to her on a gold laver by her chamberlain. While she enjoyed melons from the garden, one of her favorite foods, she leafed through the envelopes from far and near, and came upon a lettre sent to her by Sebastien's inane sister, *Comtesse* Francoise Dangeau-Beauvilliers, the doting mère of the conniving Maurice Beauvilliers.

Now what could this fluttering woman want from her?

Catherine read the lettre with contempt. Once again the comtesse was flattering Catherine and begging help for her son.

How many pleas for favors of one kind or another had there been through the years? The woman was wearisome with all her schemes to promote Maurice to a high position at Court. Catherine mused that she might arrange to promote Maurice if she thought she could use him. He was easily bought, and she would have little trouble training him as her petit monkey on a chain. Would Maurice be a bon assassin?

No. Maurice was undisciplined and would easily talk under threat of torture and incriminate her. She best remain committed to her plan of using Marquis Fabien to rid her of the Duc de Guise. If only she could lure him back to Court. Fie! He had slipped out of France before she could snag him to her cause. And where was he now? Sinking Spanish galleons! Ah yes, she knew. *And perhaps I could offer him "protection" from the wrath of Spain in return for his cooperation in the elimination of the Guise plague.*

In the lettre, Francoise wept over her poor petit Maurice who was stricken in amour over the belle Mademoiselle Rachelle Macquinet. He had even taken to his sick bed, pining for her presence. Ah, but her son would not eat, nor could all the chère mademoiselles in or out of Court console his woeful heart. She feared her son might waste away to nothing, so aggrieved was he. Therefore it was her prayer that Her Majesty, the bonne Queen Mother, would aid her in solving her dilemma.

The comtesse had first appealed to Princesse Marguerite to recall Mademoiselle Rachelle to Court, but while the princesse had been sympathetic, she affirmed that Rachelle was home with her family at the Château de Silk in mourning over the death of her grandmère and her petite sister. But now, Comtesse Francoise affirmed, Princesse Marguerite was concerned about her wardrobe for the upcoming journey to Spain and was anxious for Rachelle's return. So would the Queen Mother appoint Comte Maurice to escort Mademoiselle Rachelle to Paris?

Catherine hardened her lips. What effrontery this woman had! She sneered and tossed the lettre aside.

Her eye caught the particular lettre she was waiting for, from her personal spy, Monsieur d'Alencome, the French Ambassador to the English court of Queen Elizabeth.

Catherine, who always carried a personal dagger on her person as a caution against assassins, used the gold-handled knife to open the seal. She read:

*Your Majesty,*

*In regard to your last lettre, I have now received confirmation from a lofty source on the subject of which you recently inquired as to its accuracy. I am told by a personage of grand position who is near the English queen that Marquis de Vendôme's ship,* Reprisal, *is due to anchor at Portsmouth to take on supplies before voyaging on to Florida within the next two weeks — even one Fort Caroline as founded by the Huguenot Admiral Coligny. The information I have received confirms that le marquis will journey from Portsmouth here to St. James Palace with some of the queen's privateers who are to be commended for sinking the war galleons of Duc d'Alva near the Netherlands.*

*Awaiting your further instuctions.*

*Your servant for la gloire de la France,*

*Monsieur Ronsard d'Alencome,*
*French Ambassador to the English Court*

Catherine tapped her finger against the side of her temple as she leaned back in her gilded royal chair. Her mind schemed. She had intended to gain the service of the marquis, but her women of the *escadron volante* had utterly failed her in this matter. She had grown so impatient with Madame Charlotte de Presney that she had dismissed her from Court upon learning that the marquis had slipped through her clutches and left France. The last she had heard of Charlotte, she was at her husband's estate, soon to have a child.

Ah, but la *belle des belles*, Rachelle Macquinet. Maurice was not the only monsieur interested in her charms. Catherine had seen the fire in Fabien's eyes when he looked at the daughter of silk.

Catherine smiled as a cunning thought filled her mind. Ah yes. There was a way to use this passion for her purposes.

She looked over at the missive that the Spanish ambassador, Chantonnay, had flaunted before her earlier that morning. He had told her with self-righteous glee in his dark eyes that the Duc d'Alva himself was on his way from the Netherlands to see her over the sinking of his galleons.

Alva! That incorrigible iron-booted commander! When Alva arrived, he would show his scorn with such veiled threats, that she would have to assure him of her deepest loyalty to Spain and its wise and religious King Philip. Alva would behave aggrieved. Ah yes, he would tell her that his morbid, sullen master of Spain might be forced to invade France and depose the House of Valois and replace it with the House of Guise if she did not urge her son, the king, to move with greater strength against France's heretics.

*Ah! If I did not need that audacious beau marquis, I would dispose of him in a moment!*

She snatched up Duc d'Alva's missive and crumpled it into a wad. He demanded her son, the king, send Duc de Guise to destroy the French privateers joining forces with the English queen's heretic corsairs. But he wanted Marquis de Vendôme alive and transported to Madrid.

Her lip curled downward. Ah yes, King Philip would assuredly think up some horrific treatment for the marquis. But that must not happen; he was too useful to her.

It would not be a light thing to excuse the marquis's buccaneering ventures. Spain was also angry that the Huguenot Admiral Coligny and Queen Jeanne d'Albret of Navarre, defenders of the Huguenot middle class, walked freely. Rome, too, wanted them put to death.

But now was not the time to move against the stalwart admiral. At present she needed the Huguenots.

If they want Coligny and Jeanne's heretical heads on the religious platter, they would need to arrange for her daughter Marguerite to marry the chief son of King Philip. She would make this clear to Philip's emissary when she went to Spain next year.

At present, Catherine's main interest was in securing her rule and the rule of the Valois sons, and that meant the meddling of Duc de Guise must end.

She threw the wadded missive from Duc d'Alva into the hearth. How her hand itched to use poison against this most feared and hated enemy. And yet she could not risk using poison again so soon, or could she? She must go to Paris and visit the Ruggerio brothers. Perchance they now had what Cosmo long promised her, a new poison that left no trace.

She paced.

The various parts of her plan were here before her — and would bring the primacy she craved — if she could merely arrange them in the right order. Patience and time were needed, she had little of either. Under the present circumstances it would be difficult to bring Marquis Fabien back to Court. And she must not threaten him. Not yet.

*Marriage.*

Quite suddenly, Catherine laughed gustily. She pushed her kerchief to her mouth to silence her amusement, her shoulders shaking.

Francoise's lettre was not to be scorned after all. The request that her son, Maurice, marry Rachelle may hold the means by which to bring the marquis back to France, and to his knees, whereupon his hope of survival would depend upon his secret service in the matter of the Duc de Guise. If any cause would bring him to her in submission, it would be the threat of losing Rachelle in marriage, or even a possible arrest for heresy and the fiery stake ... Yes, bien sûr! Oh why had she not thought of this sooner?

Catherine went quickly to her writing closet and dipped her golden quill into the inkwell.

First she wrote her summons to Rachelle. She must come at once, bring all her silk equipage, and begin Marguerite's wardrobe for use in Spain next year. Sebastien's neveu, Comte Maurice Beauvilliers, would be sent by Catherine to escort her here safely.

She would not yet tell Rachelle about the threat of marriage to Maurice. This would only upset the Macquinet family. She could easily tell them it was the right of the king to arrange Rachelle's marriage, and none could intervene. But why make problems now? It was sufficient that Marquis Fabien and Comte Maurice both knew.

Next, she wrote a missive to Comte Sebastien ordering him to see that her wishes in regard to Rachelle were carried out without delay. Then she wrote Marguerite:

*My daughter, I know how much you want the Macquinet couturière, Rachelle, to set her full attention to your wardrobe for our upcoming journey to Spain. I am sending a summons to Comte Sebastien, through his neveu Maurice Beauvilliers, to arrange for Rachelle's journey from Lyon to Fontainebleau.*

Catherine struck the gong. Almost immediately Madalenna appeared.

"See that these missives are delivered tout de suite."

"Oui, Madame."

After Madalenna left, Catherine again dipped her quill into the inkwell and wrote a lettre to another of her daughters, Elisabeth, the Queen of Spain, to let her know that she and Marguerite intended to visit her in the future.

*Give my most honoré greeting to my son-in-law, His most Christian Majesty, King Philip*, she concluded. Her lip curled with secret malice. *That carnivorous reptile*, she thought.

I would enjoy seeing the look on the marquis' handsome face when he learns that the Macquinet belle des belles may be given in marriage to Comte Maurice Beauvilliers.

# Far Horizons

## CHÂTEAU DE SILK

THE SWEET ESSENCE OF LATE-BLOOMING FLOWERS DRIFTED UPON THE MID-afternoon breezes as Rachelle walked through the mûreraie orchard on her way to the silkworm hatcheries. Red-breasted birds were trilling in chestnut trees lining the path of rich brown loam beneath her slippered feet. Her fine-woven linen dress of cool blue cotton billowed softly.

The workers were on ladders, men, women, and girls, pulling leaves from the white mulberry trees and placing them in large softly woven baskets dangling from branches, to be carried to warehouses where other workers chopped them for the silk larvae.

When she neared the outbuildings she saw Arnaut with Madame Clair near the "nurseries" where the larvae were hatched. Inside the buildings the "silkworm mothers" were spoon-feeding the chopped leaves to the larvae. There were many thousands of pastel-hued silkworm cocoons that filled the tiny dry cubicles set in wooden frames.

Most of the cocoons would not be permitted to hatch, since emerging moths would damage the cocoons that provided the unbroken filament for the finest silk thread. To transform the cocoons into silk, they were soaked in hot water to release the sticky sericin, or roasted, and then spread out to dry. Other workers were in the delicate process of unwinding the cocoons. The individual silk thread was so fine, that as many as a dozen cocoons were needed, sticking them together to form one long thread and wound together, to fill each reel. From there it was taken to the weavers' huts with special looms and woven or knitted into a variety of textures and designs. The dying and tinting was an art in itself.

Madame Clair was sitting in an open *calèche*, in discussion with Arnaut, when Rachelle joined them.

"It will not be an easy operation to accomplish, for the ship must sail at the right time, while the eggs are in incubation. If they hatch before we arrive at Canterbury, the larvae will die without enough of the right mulberry leaves. Then there is the trip by wagons to Spitalfields from London. Hudson assures me there is land to buy outside London that will make a very nice plantation for sericulture."

Clair frowned. "This will be difficult, and you will be gone for several months at least, and with Idelette ... I do not see how I can possibly go with you as you wish."

"Idelette insists she is in fine stead for the journey. Many a woman has taken a voyage while enceinte."

Rachelle had heard all this before. She was aware that her père was considering the preparation of a shipment of mulberry tree cuttings, silkworms, and eggs to take to London. He was also concerned about the growing persecution in France, and he felt an urgency to build a stronger alliance with Cousin Bertrand at Spitalfields.

"We cannot transport the château de Silk to England," Clair said wearily. "We do not even know if our tree cuttings and the silkworms will thrive in England's weather."

"That is what concerns me most." He looked thoughtfully around them at the beloved estate, and Rachelle felt a pang as she saw the sadness in his face.

"If we should ever be forced to leave Lyon ..."

"It will never be the same, Arnaut. The château is our family's lifeblood."

"True enough, but we must plan for the worst, Clair. The day may come when we will be forced to seek safety, at least for a time," he said when her face bore grief as she looked back toward the white château.

"We were all born here," she said, "and to leave with naught but cuttings and some larvae is most dismaying."

"It may not come to anything that drastic yet, mon amour. It is a precaution. After what happened to Avril and Idelette, and then Sebastien — I would be unwise if I did not take heed of Bertrand's suggestion to gain land in England."

"What does Bertrand think of England's climate?" Clair asked dubiously. "So much fog, and the cold."

"Spitalfields is a small, but growing weavers' center, but England has much farmland where the mulberry trees may flourish. We must try."

Rachelle kept her peace. Arnaut must indeed be troubled about the future if he was thinking of moving the growth and harvesting of silk cocoons to England. What did this mean for the family?

"Bertrand has mentioned Admiral Coligny's colony in Florida," Arnaut said thoughtfully. "Bonne climate, to be sure. But such a voyage would be a great endeavor, and we could not be certain of success. If I left on such a journey, I would be gone for over year."

"How would you keep the silkworms alive?"

Arnaut sighed and shook his head. "It could be done, but it would be most difficult."

At the mention of Florida, Rachelle became alert. "Admiral Coligny has tried to start several colonies in the Americas. The marquis spoke of them to Bertrand when he was here."

Rachelle felt her père's alert gaze.

Her tone indifferent, she said, "I believe there was also a colony somewhere in the Caribbean, or was it the West Indies?"

"Excellent climates, I hear. There is no ice or snow in Florida or the West Indies." He lapsed into thoughtful silence, staring off into the distance as though he could see these faraway lands.

An uncomfortable expression crossed her mère's fair face. "But so very far away, Arnaut," she said in a tired voice. "It is across the world, is it not?"

Arnaut smiled at her gently. "England is closer, and their queen accepts Huguenots."

Clair laughed suddenly and laid her hand to the side of Arnaut's handsome face. Their eyes held and Rachelle smiled, watching. *They are still lovers; that is the manner of marriage I want.*

"Bonne weather in Florida," Arnaut repeated. His gaze turned to Rachelle. "The marquis impressed me as being a man of much adventure when we met briefly in Calais. Did he not tell Bertrand he was going to Florida?"

"I believe it is his intention," she said, loathing the heat that came to her face. "He once said he had financially assisted Admiral Coligny's colony there."

"Yes, Fort Caroline," he said, still studying her.

"He will be bringing a relief ship of supplies."

"But now he is engaged in a venture with Queen Elizabeth's privateers against Spain," he said.

There was no accusation in his voice, Rachelle noted, just a statement.

She remained silent. So he had told her père as well as Bertrand about it .

"A very dangerous venture," Clair said uneasily, her fair brows creased. "Does he have his own ship?"

Arnaut spoke before Rachelle. "He does. A fine one; I caught sight of it at Calais. The *Reprisal*, I believe he calls it."

"I do not think the marquis will be settling down anytime soon," Clair said. "He is likely to become another of Queen Elizabeth's buccaneers. He may never return to France."

Rachelle tightened her mouth and kept silent. She knew her père was watching her.

"He must come back sometime, Clair. He is a royal Bourbon with a *marquisat* in Vendôme, and he has duties to fulfill to his serfs." He rubbed his chin, frowning. "What was it Sebastien wrote me recently about Florida ... It escapes me, but I will read his lettre again."

Rachelle wondered too, her interest keen. What about Florida?

Arnaut looked at Clair. "Did I tell you that Bertrand is on the marquis' ship?"

There was a gasp from both Clair and Rachelle. "Bertrand?" Clair said. "But did the marquis not voyage out with other privateers to attack Spanish war galleons?"

Arnaut chuckled. "And sank them, so Sebastien wrote. Spain has brought the matter before the king and Queen Mother."

"The marquis is in a most risky position," Clair said. "And Bertrand, if he is aboard, why, he could be held accountable."

"So he could," Arnaut said thoughtfully. "Yet it was his deliberate choice to go aboard the *Reprisal*."

"And the Bibles?" Clair arched her brows.

"Will be delivered to Portsmouth. The marquis promised him. Bertrand should have a most interesting tale to impart when next we see him in London."

*So, Fabien did aid Bertrand with transporting the Bibles.*

Rachelle was still thinking of Cousin Bertrand aboard Fabien's buccaneering ship when she accompanied her parents in the calèche back to the château for the afternoon dinner.

She had a suspicion that Bertrand may have had as much spiritual interest in the marquis as in delivering his Bibles. Perhaps he had decided his mission to the marquis was just as important?

Rachelle's hopes grew brighter. If Bertrand's interest in Fabien was enough to prompt him to risk a buccaneering venture against Spain, then what did this tell her except that Bertrand knew of her love, was on her side, and hoped to win over Arnaut and Clair?

In the days and weeks that followed, Arnaut pursued his urgent endeavors of research on how he could manage a voyage to England with mulberry plantings and silkworm larvae and eggs. He worked late into the evenings and made several short journeys to Paris and Fontainebleau to discuss these matters secretly with Sebastien. Sebastien had shown a great interest in the project, and with his contacts at Court and in the university, found men who met with Arnaut to discuss his project. When Arnaut returned to the château he seemed much more convinced that the project could be successful. He hoped to receive a message from Cousin Bertrand about land in a sunny location near Spitalfields.

When Arnaut returned from one of his meetings with Sebastien and a certain group of like-minded monsieurs at Fontainebleau, Rachelle heard him telling Clair that grave difficulties loomed ahead for the Huguenots in France. He related what Sebastien had learned at Court, that their only hope for new freedoms rested with the upcoming colloquy in the fall.

A few days later as Rachelle came down the stairs, she heard her parents in the grand salle speaking in worried tones. They were speaking of a religious civil war led in part by Huguenots on behalf of their gentry and serfs who were under great hardship and increased suffering for practicing their faith.

Arnaut told Clair he now felt it imperative to make a trip to London to see the land near Spitalfields and to make plans for starting a silk plantation.

"By now Bertrand should have returned to England."

There was also mention of the Hudson family's help in the matter of securing land suitable for such an enterprise.

Rachelle did not intend to listen to her parents' conversation, but as she entered the atelier and began work on a gown, her parents continued their conversation in the next chamber with the door open.

When next Clair spoke she did not seem enthused, though Rachelle knew she fully understood the growing need and supported her husband's decision.

Arnaut continued in an earnest tone, "Lady Hudson is most keen to meet you and our daughters. The gown for Queen Elizabeth has enthralled Lady Hudson. Sir James has not yet been able to see the queen, but the opportunity may come soon."

"What about Idelette? I cannot go away and leave her now with the child due in December. And Rachelle should not be laden with all the duties here."

"There is no reason why they should not come to England with us."

"Idelette would rather die than see James Hudson in her delicate position, Arnaut. The child shows now, as you have seen. It would be most shameful for her."

"Yes, by all means. Then she will do well with Madeleine and Sebastien. We will be back in France before the child is born. She will be among family and friends there, and Madeleine will know how to keep her well and comfortable."

"I admit that a visit to Madeleine would do Idelette well, and I do not want her to lose contact with the young monsieur, Andelot. A finer young man I have yet to meet, and now he has taken so much interest in Geneva."

The mention of Andelot Dangeau pricked up Rachelle's ears. This was not the first time Clair had stated openly how much she liked him. She had been fond of him even as a child, but his religion had interfered. Recently he had written to Arnaut about Geneva and asked if he might read Calvin's *Institutes*, which were first written as an apology to King Francis I in defense of the Reformation. Since then Calvin had expanded his work on doctrine and theology, and Andelot had written that he was hungry for learning after discovering a French Bible in the forest near Fontainebleau.

The news of Andelot's enlightenment had been received by the family with enthusiasm. Rachelle, because she thought of Andelot as a brother, was pleased for him. But Clair had taken the news with an interest in Andelot as a possible match for one of her daughters, and it appeared as though it was Idelette that Clair had in mind. Idelette knew little of Clair's thoughts, but Rachelle felt Idelette might be secretly pleased.

"I will write Madeleine and Sebastien about Idelette," Clair told Arnaut. "But I think Rachelle should come with us to England. She has wanted to go since working on the gown for Queen Elizabeth, and I think she should spend time with Sir James Hudson. He is committed to the same faith as we, and is a couturier. With the merging of our family name, what better young man for Rachelle than James Hudson?"

"I have high regards for James. And I think he may already have an interest in Rachelle. But what about the marquis? We both know, Clair, that she is love with him. I have seen it from the beginning in Calais."

"But Arnaut, he is a Bourbon, and a marquis. He is attracted to her, I could tell that when he was here. But he cannot marry her. The Bourbons will no doubt insist he marry a princess. I see no hope of such a romance working into marriage. Rachelle will be hurt if this goes on much longer. And beside that, he is a Catholic."

"Perhaps he is, Clair, though his ventures at sea against Spain, as well as his support of Admiral Coligny, speak otherwise. However, I agree that James Hudson would be more suitable for our Rachelle, simply because of the marquis's position."

"Then I shall speak to both our daughters this night about our plans."

In the atelier, Rachelle found that her heart was beating so fast she had to sit down. She gripped her scissors. Dismay filled her vision. James Hudson! She had naught against the comely young monsieur, in fact she had enjoyed his pleasant company.

Even so, it was the marquis she wanted! Thoughts of marrying any man other than Marquis Fabien de Vendôme left her cold. *If I cannot have him, I shall not marry.*

Where was he now? Would she ever see him again?

*If only I had been wiser and not thrown myself at him, demanding he swear his allegiance to me now. If I had let him go — and his love proved genuine, would he not have more easily come back?* And that moment in Calais — her eyes moistened, and her heart was sick with love as she smelled the sweetness of jasmine coming through the window, remembering their almost-kiss, and how she had come alive to his touch. Now — gone, like everything else.

*Oh, where is my faith in God, in His guiding hand, in His good plans for me, for all of us who are His, including Fabien, for surely Fabien is as strong a believer in Christ as any of us.*

The mulberry leaves rustled like an orchestra awakening to the conductor. She leaned her head against the side of the open window that looked onto the arched colonnade of colorful patches of flowers in the garden. She prayed, again recommitting herself to His purposes.

She prayed for Fabien. He must come back. She could not bear it if he did not!

# A Net Is Cast

## FONTAINEBLEAU PALAIS

INSIDE THE ANTECHAMBER THAT CONNECTED WITH ONCLE SEBASTIEN'S appartement in the castle of Fontainebleau, Andelot prepared the herbal medicine that le docteur had prescribed for Sebastien's weakened health. Once the quintessence of heartiness, Sebastien, since his months in the Bastille, now suffered from headaches and pains throughout his body. *It is ungodly what they did to him in the name of religion*, Andelot thought, revolted.

As Andelot was measuring and mixing the medicine, the outer door opened from the public corridor and a guard looked in. Andelot recognized the young chevalier in service to Comte Maurice Beauvilliers. The guard, appearing satisfied that it was safe for his seigneur, stepped back to permit the comte to enter the antechamber and closed the door.

Andelot had recently discovered that Maurice's mère, Francoise, who was Sebastien's sister, had been urging Maurice to cultivate his relationship by marriage to Marquis Fabien, since association could elevate Maurice and Francoise as well.

Maurice, however, was so jealous of the marquis that they remained at odds. For a season at Amboise, it had appeared that Maurice and the marquis might come to a peaceable camaraderie, but Maurice's growing interest in Mademoiselle Rachelle had put an end to it.

Andelot had heard one of the younger ladies-in-waiting to Madeleine say that Maurice had "ostrich eyelashes." Now, whenever Andelot looked at Maurice he noticed his long lashes and looked away to keep from grinning. He would be in much trouble if Maurice knew that he found it *très amusant*.

"Bonjour Cousin," Andelot said, taking enjoyment in belaboring the point of relationship.

Maurice made a generous display of his superior position by offering a laconic lift of a slender, jeweled hand to his feathered cap.

"Bonjour, Andelot. Is mon oncle yet awake?"

"Oui. I must take him his medicine. Then he will retire."

Maurice straightened the pink lace at his wrists. "I wish to speak with him. Have you not heard? Our Antoine de Bourbon may soon be in the favor of the cardinal and King of Spain."

Andelot was aware that while Prince Condé remained in the Amboise dungeon awaiting execution for treason, his brother Antoine, King of Navarre, was gaining favor at Court through his compromise. He was often seen in the company of the duc and the cardinal, and more recently with the Spanish ambassador. There were whispers that Antoine was about to give up his Protestant beliefs and attend Mass.

"Has Prince Antoine unmasked himself as *L'Echangeur*?" Andelot asked. "Yesterday a Huguenot, today a Catholic, and tomorrow? Who can say?"

"Ha, so you have heard what the Huguenots in Navarre are calling Antoine. That infuriates him, I assure you."

"The truth should convict his conscience rather than infuriate him."

"He vacillates, still," Maurice said, his expression a mix of cynicism and amusement. "I am most sure he will eventually decide in Rome's favor with la belle Rouet convincing him to cooperate with the Guises."

The belle Rouet, as she was called, was a chief member of the Queen Mother's escadron volante. Sebastien had intimated that the Queen Mother had used her to lure Antoine into cooperating with her plans.

Andelot felt sympathy for Antoine's good Huguenot wife, the respected Queen Jeanne of Navarre, who remained wholly committed to the Huguenot cause. Her husband's fall from marital faithfulness would grieve her deeply and injure the Protestant Reformation in France.

"If Prince Antoine has compromised and exchanged one outer religious garment for another, it is a dishonor to both Catholics and Huguenots," Andelot said, disliking Maurice's amused smile. "But true faith, Monseigneur Maurice, cannot be shed like snake skin to humor kings or belles dames."

"Do not trouble me with religion, Andelot, for I find the squabbling between Catholics and Protestants most distasteful. It makes me wish to stay far from either of them. As for you," Maurice continued, "you are sounding more and more like a heretic. You best be cautious, I swear it. You could not ask for a more dangerous flirtation while under the shadow of the cardinal than to be caught doing something heretical — like reading a French Bible." He gave a dismissing flick to a piece of lint on his coat of brocaded red and black.

Andelot glanced at him while mixing the herbal powder in Sebastien's cup. *Now why did he mention that? He could not possibly know about the copy he kept hidden among his things.* As yet he had not been able to return it to the Huguenot pasteur. Or was it because he did not wish to give it up? He told himself he would, eventually.

With an amused quiver of his lip, Maurice watched him stirring. "Still serving mon oncle Sebastien, I see? I pity you, Andelot. He can be a tedious man to please, of that I am certain."

"I have not found him to be so."

"Andelot, the loyal page," he said with a small smile.

Andelot passed over the mocking tone. "I hope so, Messire-Comte, as I am also a loyal cousin. Comte Sebastien has done much to aid me at Court. There is little more I would rather do than pursue my studies under a scholar like Thauvet."

Maurice waved a hand to show he had enough of the conversation. "Announce me to mon oncle, if you will."

"At this hour? The day, it has been long for our weary oncle. He is not strong, as you are aware — "

Maurice waggled his fingers. "The lettre I bring is worthy of his attention. He must see it tonight."

Andelot saw a gleam of smug satisfaction in his eyes. Something was afoot, and most likely unpleasant, coming from Maurice.

"Shall I tell you my secret?" Maurice tilted his dark wavy head with a smile.

If he showed his interest, he knew Maurice would deliberately hold back.

Andelot pursed his lips. "I am certain mon cousin will say nothing unless he wishes to."

Maurice's mysterious smile deepened. "My lettre," he stated, "is from Princesse Marguerite Valois — who wishes most ardently to recall Mademoiselle Rachelle Macquinet back at Court posthaste. She wishes for a new wardrobe for her journey with the Queen Mother to Spain."

*So, Maurice had managed somehow to fan the flame of Rachelle's return.* This, as Andelot saw it, was disturbing. After the attack on the Huguenot assembly at Lyon and the strange death of Grandmère and sickness of Madeleine, how could Maurice want her where danger stalked?

"You frown like an aged wood chopper bending over his log, Andelot." Maurice smirked, then waved a conquering hand. "You will see. Enough now, announce me to Oncle. It is important, as I have said."

Andelot swallowed his mottled pride and bowed his head, then entered a door into Sebastien's apartments.

Sebastien was at Fontainebleau alone, for Madame Madeleine and petite Joan were in Paris where he had wished them to remain, unless Madeleine decided to visit the Château de Silk. Although Sebastien had not said so, Andelot believed that Sebastien feared to have Madeleine here, so close to the Queen Mother. He appeared to tense each time she asked about them, wearing a strange amused smile. It made Andelot's blood turn cold. Sometimes the Queen Mother played with Sebastien like a cat with a mouse. Andelot wondered why. She must have favored him at one time, and even after Amboise and the Bastille dungeon, she had reinstated him to her privy council.

Andelot was with Sebastien enough to become convinced he did think the Queen Mother had poisoned his wife and Grandmère. Andelot had tried to introduce the topic of his own suspicions, but Sebastien had made it clear from the beginning that he would not discuss it, not even with Duchesse Dushane who had broached the matter when he and Andelot first arrived. Sebastien had rejected the notion of poison, but Andelot was now sure it was because he fully understood the danger.

If Rachelle came to Court, would the matter remain hidden in the shadows? He thought not. This was yet another reason why Andelot was worried. Maurice was behaving most smugly, which meant to Andelot that his desires in having her at Court were on the verge of fruition.

Andelot, disheartened, opened the door into the comte's blue and gold apartment with Italian tapestry hangings and brocade furnishings of deeply carved, dark wood.

Sebastien stood near the hearth, hands behind his back, staring into the glowing coals sending off a warm and pleasant pine fragrance. Andelot noticed the stoop of his shoulders and disliked bringing him more burdens, especially at this hour when he was soon to retire after taking his medicinal tea. He deserved a restful night's sleep, for tomorrow would have trouble enough. Andelot cleared his throat politely to gain his attention. It had become a signal between them whenever he needed to interrupt Sebastien's thoughts.

Sebastien lifted his dark head streaked with gray and looked across the chamber.

Andelot had learned to keep his expression unobtrusive, as though he had no opinions of his own, but he always experienced satisfaction when a look of family fondness lightened Sebastien's face upon seeing him. Having been raised without a father, Andelot had a special fondness for his oncle. Andelot once thought a family relationship would develop with the Cardinal de Lorraine and the Duc de Guise, but that had swiftly dissipated. At first he had been disappointed, but recently he had found that he was relieved. His recent interest in the Reformation would be almost impossible to pursue if the cardinal had taken him under his wing. Andelot was beginning to see the working of God in the events of his life.

Not that Sebastien was demonstrative. *Au contraire.* Sebastien was pleasant but precise, and Andelot felt genuinely liked.

"Monseigneur," Andelot said quietly, and bowed his head in deference as formality required, for even in families, respect was given to titled members. Andelot took pleasure in showing respect to Sebastien and Marquis Fabien, but it goaded him to bow to Comte Maurice.

"Yes, Andelot? You have that revolting herbal medicine prepared?"

Andelot smiled. "I am afraid so, but you may not wish to drink it yet. Your sister's son is here. Comte Maurice Beauvilliers awaits most anxiously to speak with you about a lettre from Princess Marguerite Valois."

At the mention of the flamboyant princesse, Sebastien groaned. "Now what? More woes, to be sure. Speaking of woes — it pains me to say so, but I had just been thinking of that rapscallion nephew of mine, and see how he shows up to plague me?" His eyes showed faint amusement. "Do you agree that your cousin is a rapscallion, Andelot?"

"Mon oncle, I would forget myself if ever I disagree with you."

Sebastien chuckled. "A fair answer and a diplomatic one. You will go far among your titled superiors. As for Maurice, I am in no mood for him . . ." He tossed up his hand. "So the princesse brings him here at this hour? And in the rain?" He sighed. "Ah, but send him in." Sebastien rubbed the tired frown from between his heavy brows. "Francoise would not forgive me if I ignored her golden lad."

Andelot smiled, stepped back into the antechamber where Maurice waited, looking bored as he lounged his lean frame against the wall, picking at his polished fingernails.

"Le comte awaits to receive you."

"It is past time."

Andelot stepped aside and held the door wide to allow passage.

Maurice ambled past him into the chamber and bowed. "Ah, mon cher oncle. I will not detain you long." His melodious tenor voice rang smoothly throughout the chamber.

Andelot was about to close the door on their privacy and return to his own chamber to his studies when Sebastien said: "Non, Andelot, do remain. It is not often that I have more than one neveu together with me."

No one could have been more surprised than Andelot, except perhaps Maurice, whose languid eyes sharpened into a speculative once-over.

Sebastien limped across the Aubusson rug toward Maurice.

Why did he wish him to remain? Andelot moved away from the door to stand near the window, wondering what to do with his hands. He finally put them behind his back and looked on with a practiced immobile face, though his mind was alert.

Maurice shrugged and pursed his lips. "Just so, mon oncle, and as you suggest, why should Andelot not join us, I ask?" He gestured toward Andelot with a show of disinterest. "Andelot is a blood relation — is he not?"

Andelot snapped awake. Now what was the doubtful emphasis on blood relation meant to suggest? Andelot shot a look at Maurice, then to Sebastien, but while Maurice looked sleepy, Sebastien showed only irritation.

"I am sure you did not come here at this hour to talk about Andelot." Sebastien lifted his brows.

Maurice spread a careless hand as though it were all in passing and of no interest. "A taste of wine first before I am sent away, Monsieur Oncle, at least. A few pleasant words."

Andelot stood straight, hands behind him. *So*, he thought, *he is reluctant to tell him about Princesse Marguerite demanding to have Rachelle back at Court. He knows Sebastien will be displeased, for he too prefers to have his wife's younger sister stay in Lyon.*

Maurice sauntered to the long, waist-high table inlaid with the fleur-de-lis where there stood a Florentine decanter of renowned French wine. He poured himself a goblet of the ruby liquid. A ruby of another sort encircled with diamonds hung from his left earlobe and danced. Andelot had seen him adorned with all sorts of gold bracelets, diamond pins, emerald pendants, and even pearls. Where does he come by all of these jewels?

"Wine, Oncle?"

Sebastien shook his head. "Non."

Maurice draped his lithe figure against the wall beside a gilded cage holding a linnet. He clucked his tongue and offered the tiny bird a bit of fruit from which it fled to the far side of the cage.

"You go to bed early, mon oncle."

"These days have been trying. You should know that, Maurice."

"It is most troubling, I assure you. The burnings throughout Paris sicken my sense of smell, and the storming of cathedrals and smashing belle statues of the saints is also appalling." Maurice made kissing sounds at the bird.

Sebastien slowly lifted his head. "That you lament so sincerely, neveu, over the recent arrests of your fellow Frenchmen who are Huguenots, touches me deeply."

Andelot felt satisfaction at the bitter jab. Sebastien then began his limping pace, hands behind his back, head bent in thought.

"Arrests ... ah oui, pardone! The Bourbon princes ... a pity." Maurice frowned and gave a toss of his dark head suggesting sympathy. The gesture did not convince Andelot. Maurice was indifferent to all but his present concern, getting Rachelle back in his presence.

Maurice settled leisurely into a brocade chaise lounge with gold fringe. He sipped his wine and crossed his ankles. His lips turned upward as though his mind were in some distant reverie. One hand trailed along the rug where he played absently with the fringe.

"Princesse Marguerite boasted to me of how Mademoiselle Rachelle does the finest and brightest work with the silk and the little needle, taking over the couturière work of her grandmère. Marguerite knows about this Englishman Hudson who has transported Macquinet silk to Spitalfields. She knows all about the land too that Monsieur Arnaut wishes to acquire to start a new plantation like the Château de Silk."

Sebastien ceased his pacing and turned sharply to Maurice.

"Did you mention Arnaut's plans to la Valois?"

"Oncle!" Maurice lifted his head from off the fringed gold satin pillow. His eyes widened. "Would I do such a thing? Why should I?"

What was this about? Andelot had not heard of Arnaut Macquinet's interest in England before. Why was Sebastien looking distressed, even angry?

"If I thought it was you who spoke of this to the Queen Mother's daughter—"

"*Saints*, why should I?"

"You keep saying that, but you might have, Maurice."

Maurice shrugged. "It matters not to me that Arnaut has ties in England and wants to strengthen them ... As long as Mademoiselle

Rachelle does not go there with him. Ah! That I cannot endure, Oncle. You had best tell him so."

"It is none of your concern, Maurice."

"Non, Oncle! Nor should Messire Macquinet's interest in going to England bring trouble to you. You are sure to remain at Court serving the Queen Mother." Maurice sipped his wine, studying him over the rim of his goblet.

Andelot could not keep his frown restrained. It sounded as though Maurice were indirectly telling Sebastien he was aware of a matter that Sebastien wanted kept secret.

"Fabien's recent venture of sinking Spanish galleons is known by Madrid."

"You think that is news to me? I have been shuffling papers back and forth from Madrid to the Queen Mother for weeks on the matter. The question is how you know, mon neveu."

"Chantonnay talks freely."

"Chantonnay, that Spanish spy! You are too much in his company of late, Maurice. He badgers me, as he does the Queen Mother."

Maurice shrugged. "They both spy upon each other. I do not feel sorry for either."

"That be as it may, I would ask that you not speak of Marquis Fabien around Court. He has problems enough without anyone enlarging upon his dealings at sea."

Maurice did not appear the least sympathetic. "I should be surprised if, upon his arrival, he is not immediately summoned before the king and made to explain his actions to the Guises. The Spanish king is most distraught over the English privateers, and now the marquis and other French buccaneers have joined them. They make a formidable force, I assure you."

"What else might the Spanish ambassador have told you?"

"That Marquis Fabien has done some business with English privateers, sinking several galleons on their way to the Netherlands. The Duc d'Alva lost his supplies as well as the gold he was bringing for his soldiers' wages." He smiled and sipped his wine. "Mademoiselle Rachelle will not wish to keep company with such a ruthless corsair."

Andelot was annoyed. With Maurice's lusty eye on Rachelle, he had most likely convinced himself he could get Fabien out of the way.

Sebastien's voice warned: "You concern yourself too much with the future of Madeleine's younger sister. And as for the marquis, he can speak well enough for himself to the king."

Maurice's mouth turned with boredom. He put his arm behind his dark head and held the goblet in the other, studying it.

"I wish to marry Rachelle."

The statement, though mentioned lightly before, now seemed more determined.

Sebastien made a snarling sound, lifted a hand of rebuff, and turned away to the fire.

Maurice was swiftly on his feet like a panther ready to leap. "Mille diables! You fret too much, Oncle, I swear it. And you, Andelot, do not look like a frog swallowing an egg. I am devoted to la Macquinet. I shall go posthaste to her père Arnaut and beg for her hand."

"And be denied. You are never more cunning than when you use lofty words to justify your dubious ways," Sebastien said wearily. "How many demoiselles in the last two years have you sworn to adore unto your utter loss?"

"Ah Oncle, those were all different."

"Regardless, you will not involve yourself with Madeleine's younger sister."

Maurice looked at him over his goblet, his gaze turning angry.

"I will have my way, Oncle. I always do. And why should she not be pleased with me, I ask? One would think I was a barbarian. I attend Mass daily. I have even braved le Cardinal de Lorraine and gone to *le prêche* as a Calvinist, now and then."

"Now and then," Sebastien repeated with a wry glance his way.

Maurice placed his palm against his ruffled silk shirt above his heart. "Because Rachelle stirs my heart, am I now marked as a man of dubious intent?"

*Précisément!* Andelot thought.

"Too many mademoiselles stir your heart, Maurice. Your intentions are well established at Court," Sebastien said.

Andelot wanted to nod agreement.

"You fret like an old hen," Maurice said. "It was long in the planning for Rachelle to come back to Court to resume her place as Princesse Marguerite's maid-of-honor. I do nothing that was not already agreed upon in the past. All I do is awaken the sleeping little bird. Now, Rachelle will come as a couturière instead of her grandmère's grisette. She will enjoy herself. The wardrobe Marguerite desires for her Spanish trip will fill Rachelle with delight. Ma mère will talk to you about this."

"Francoise need tell me nothing."

"Oncle, be reasonable; it is she who was sent the summons to bring Rachelle back to Court. I have it present with me to give you, for I should marry la Macquinet at once."

Andelot displayed outward indifference, but his fingers twisted together in anger behind his back.

"It is dangerous for Rachelle to be at Court," Sebastien said, shaking his head firmly. "Francoise should have come to me first about your schemes instead of appealing to Princesse Marguerite."

"Andelot, more wine." Maurice held out his cup. He snapped his lean fingers against the gold shining goblet.

Andelot went for the decanter and came back to his cousin who was lounging once more.

"Ah, mon belle amour has the most intriguing of eyes, the hair …" Maurice sipped. He sighed. "Oui, perhaps I will have my wedding at the colloquy. It will be most religious."

Andelot gripped the decanter.

Maurice held the goblet to the light, and with a little sensuous smile, watched the ruby liquid as Andelot poured. It was a smile Andelot loathed. He relaxed his grip on the decanter so it tipped downward just slightly, spilling wine down the front of Maurice's frilled shirt and onto his satin doublet —

"Ehh!" Maurice jumped from the lounge attempting to brush off the spilled wine. "I am drowned in it! You did this vileness, Andelot, on purpose! I declare you to be false and disloyal!"

"*Mille pardons*, Monseigneur." Andelot hastened to say with the right amount of humility and rushed to bring cloths to soak the wine from Maurice's wardrobe. "It was most clumsy of me," he added.

"Clumsy? Non! It was deliberate. Give that cloth to me — I shall do it myself." Snatching it, Maurice blotted his garments. "They are ruined." He threw the cloths down with aggrieved disgust.

"I am most apologetic, Monsieur Cousin. I — "

"Do not call me cousin!" Maurice turned to Sebastien who looked on with a curious glint in his eyes.

Maurice, his arm rigid, pointed at Andelot. "You saw what he did!"

"Calm yourself, Maurice," Sebastien soothed. "It was but an accident. You have dozens of like finery. We have more grave matters with which to be concerned."

Andelot bowed toward Maurice and moved away, gently now, avoiding those once deceptively languid eyes, and set the half-empty decanter back in its place. *It was worth it.*

"Well?" Sebastien's voice showed a strain of impatience. "What is this missive you speak about from Princesse Marguerite?"

Maurice, with narrowed gaze following Andelot across the chamber, said stiffly: "It is important, I assure you, else I would not have troubled you at this hour." He reached beneath his stained doublet and produced an envelope with an impressive gold seal that alerted Andelot. Sebastien's expression changed.

Maurice noticed and looked satisfied with his disclosure. "The missive is not from Princesse Marguerite, mon oncle, though she was the means of bringing the request to the attention of the Queen Mother."

Maurice handed the envelope over to Sebastien.

"From the Queen Mother herself," Maurice said. "The Macquinet couturière is to be summoned here to Fontainebleau for audience with the queen."

Andelot bit back his grumble of defeat.

Sebastien took the envelope, scowling his worry. "A mistake. A dreadful one. So Francoise went through Princesse Marguerite to get you what you want. It was clever of my sister, but unwise and dangerous."

"Dangerous? You must exaggerate, mon oncle!"

With the royal missive in hand, Sebastien limped to the hearth where a crystal lamp in a silver base burned on a gilt-edged marble table.

"The Queen Mother is behind this. But why would she want Rachelle here at Court now?" Sebastien murmured, frowning thoughtfully.

A sullen expression came to Maurice. "I swear, mon oncle, beside Marguerite's gowns, there is no motive except my desire for her in marriage."

Sebastien looked at him with a dark countenance. "Marguerite would have no power to recall Rachelle if Catherine had not given permission. And I ask, why? Maurice, one must not forget that Catherine de Medici is in the shadows — always in the shadows."

Andelot shifted his stance, still watching Maurice.

Maurice fell silent. After a moment he refilled his wine goblet and stared into it.

"Francoise should have told me of her plan to go to Princesse Marguerite. In this foolish game of yours to get Rachelle to Court, you have put her at risk."

"La belle will be busy with her silk," Maurice said sullenly. "If it is her religion you worry about, it will not come before the cardinal."

Sebastien turned. "You speak glibly. With the attacks on the Huguenots all across France, Prince de Condé imprisoned, and Antoine de Bourbon morally defeated? The Guises have more power now than ever."

"Sainte Denis! You cannot think that the Guises would turn on Rachelle."

"No? Who then do you think turned on her two young helpless sisters with their brutish soldiers at Lyon?"

Maurice scowled. He banged his empty glass down. "That was loathsome. If I had been there, I would have drawn sword, to be sure. I and the marquis both could have laid many of them low. But it will never happen to Rachelle here at Fontainebleau."

"I do not expect it will. The danger here is more subtle, but just as ruinous."

"If Princesse Marguerite heard of any danger to Rachelle, she would stop it. Did she not send her away from the danger at Amboise during the Huguenot rebellion?"

"The Princess Marguerite must please the Queen Mother. And I! I can do nothing." Suddenly Sebastien wavered on his feet.

Andelot rushed to his side, leading him into a chair. Maurice appeared shaken and brought wine to Sebastien, pleading for him to drink it for strength.

"I will not let anything happen to Rachelle, I swear it. Nor will harm come to any Macquinet," Maurice said, so that even Andelot looked at him.

"You will stop it?" Sebastien said. "With what authority do you think to match wits with the Guises?"

Maurice fingered the Alençon lace waterfall at his throat, grave thoughtfulness showing on his lean, dark, saturnine face.

"Ma mère has bonhomie with Princesse Marguerite, as do I. And Marguerite has influence on Henry, son of Duc de Guise. The duc will do whatever Henry may ask him. Anyway, I do not believe in this danger you insist upon where Rachelle is concerned."

*Because you are selfish and do not wish to see it*, Andelot thought angrily. He could keep silent no longer.

"Monsieur Oncle, if Mademoiselle Rachelle comes back to Court, let us remember Marquis Fabien has bonhomie with Princesse Marguerite, King Francis, and even Prince Charles. Perhaps we should appeal to the marquis?"

Maurice flushed and his lips tightened. "The marquis, if he turns up at Court, will find his friends have turned their heads." He pointed a jeweled hand toward Andelot's face. "Why do you mention the marquis? Is there not trouble enough with the Bourbons?"

"Enough ... enough ... both of you," Sebastien said wearily. He pushed himself up from the chair. "I need peace to think this matter through. Go now, Maurice, I wish to study this summons."

Maurice snatched up his dove-hued cloak. The orange and gold threads glittered in the light as he walked briskly toward the door. As duty demanded, Andelot reached the door first, opened it, and bowed.

Maurice glanced over his shoulder toward his oncle who stood at the hearth, studying the parchment and scowling.

"*A bientôt*, mon oncle," he said with agitation. "For despite your displeasure, I am on my way with my entourage to Lyon, for it is the order of the Queen Mother, as you will see." He bowed. "By your leave." Maurice passed through the doorway. Andelot followed, closing it behind them.

In the antechamber, Maurice faced him, his eyes sparking. "Do you think I do not know you have a foolish heart for ma chérie Rachelle?"

"Your chérie? If she has a heart for any, it is the Marquis de Vendôme. She will not have you."

"So you think! Non, non, she will have no voice in the matter!"

"Her Huguenot parents will have much to say about whom she marries!"

"One way or another, I will have my way!"

"What selfish scheme brews in your mind now?"

"I need not explain to you." Maurice pulled at his wine-stained silk shirt. "This, I will not forget. Of this, you have not heard the last. One day—I shall demand the slap to my honneur be repaid. Ah, you had best learn the rapier, Andelot, I promise you." He turned on his polished heel, cloak floating behind him, and jerking the door open, swept out into the common corridor, and strutted away.

*Now I am in for more misfortune*, Andelot thought wearily.

# The Unwanted Suitor

## CHÂTEAU DE SILK

RACHELLE HEARD GALLOPING HORSES APPROACHING.

She turned toward the diamond-shaped windows that formed the wall facing the front of the atelier. She rushed across the floor, pushing aside the crisply frilled white lace curtains. They came thundering up the road toward the Château courtyard, horsemen, an entire retinue on black and brown muscled horses with Spanish leather saddles adorned with heavy silver. The men-at-arms were archers and swordsmen, wearing dark hose, and blue vestments embroidered with gold.

*Who are these?* No self-appointed revengers, surely. These men rode under the flag of—Beauvilliers.

The atelier door opened in a rush. It was Nenette. "Mademoiselle Rachelle, horsemen!"

Rachelle, still standing at the window, now recognized the seigneur in charge. *Non, not him!*

"Ooh, it is Comte Maurice Beauvilliers," Nenette whispered, excitement and awe in her voice. "And so many men."

"And so much trouble, I assure you. Now why is he here?"

"Maybe he brings news from his oncle, Comte Sebastien Dangeau?"

Rachelle narrowed her gaze. Maurice was the last monsieur she wished to see now. The young comte had become Rachelle's bane ever since their meeting in Paris. He had made several attempts to capture her amour; the more she resisted, the more persistent he became. *Would he ever give up?*

"Why is it always the messire you do not want who shows such determination?"

Nenette giggled. "Maybe he knows Marquis Fabien is far, far from France!"

Rachelle's gaze skipped over the seasoned faces of the men-at-arms, hoping against all reason she would see Andelot among them, though she had no sane cause to think so.

The men were strangers, though she remembered having seen some loitering about with Maurice at Chambord and Amboise. Her gaze stopped on the sensuous face of Maurice with his saturnine dark looks and almond-shaped, pearl-gray eyes. He wore slashed hose with a coat of purple satin, engraved with the Beauvillier family armorial in rose and silver thread. A light blue velvet cap dipping saucily toward one ear bore a sprig of verdant greenery. A ruby earring encrusted with diamonds swayed from an earlobe and caught the sunlight. He carried a puppy in one arm in a bag of cloth-of-gold; he kissed its floppy ear, speaking to it, then handed it over to a lackey. Maurice slid down from his ornate saddle in a lithe movement as graceful as a panther. He looked toward the Château, a little smile on his lips.

Rachelle, interpreting that smile, narrowed her lashes. She released the curtain to fall into place and turned toward the atelier archway, hands on hips. Had she not troubles enough without this wolf's arrival?

Nenette was still gazing out the window at him with a dreamy little smile. Rachelle's mouth turned. She propelled her away from the window toward the door.

"Go, and find Messire Arnaut or Madame Clair. Tell them we have company — unwanted, in my opinion. Hurry."

"Monsieur Macquinet is down at the weavers' huts, and Madame Macquinet left to join him in the calèche only ten minutes ago."

Rachelle released a breath and glanced hopelessly about. She must receive him. Idelette would be of no help. She would not come down, of that she was certain. Idelette had hardly gotten out of her bed this morning to sip warm quinine water to settle her nausea.

"Go anyway."

"It will take me a long time on foot."

"Then have Pierre take you on the horse. And don't linger to watch the comte." The family kept a gentle horse tethered under a chestnut tree near the back smokehouse to run quick errands about the estate.

"The way he smiles with that little curve of his lip — " Nenette tried to mimic it, arching one brow — "it is most cute."

Rachelle took hold of Nenette's shoulders, turned her around, and marched her toward the door. "Out and away with you, you shameless flirt."

Rachelle smiled as she watched Nenette fly to the task, her curls bouncing from her cap.

Rachelle turned away, slapping a palm to her forehead. *Such trials as these — I am surely undeserving of.*

She cast another look through the window. Maurice was coming up the court toward the veranda steps. *Look at him, moving like a king. Can there be anyone more conceited than he! It is hardly conceivable that he does not know of all that has befallen us in recent weeks. Perhaps he is here to offer his sympathies for the recent death in the family. Could Nenette be right about him knowing Fabien is away at sea? Or was he still at sea? The battle of the galleons must surely be over. Where was he now? Had he voyaged on to resupply Admiral Coligny's colony, Fort Caroline, in Florida?*

Rachelle left the atelier and passed through the outer salle. The front door stood open, and she could see the servingman Laurent out on the porch bowing a greeting to the comte.

Rachelle walked briskly through the doorway onto the front porch, dipping a small curtsy of her dark blue cotton weave skirt as Maurice saw her, his eyes lighting up. A jeweled hand went to his frilled bosom as though her appearance made his heart flutter.

"Ah, Mademoiselle Rachelle, we meet again. How long the year has been without seeing your loveliness!"

Laurent cleared his throat.

"Monsieur le Comte," she said with all the grave formality she could muster to keep him at bay. She must keep her servingmen close at hand as well. The lean-faced Laurent and the hefty Pierre should chill the most presumptuous of men.

Maurice was up the steps like a springing feline and swept up her hand. Not content to merely bend over it, he pressed his lips, mustache tickling—not the least disheartened by the presence of the servingmen.

Maurice's languid eyes crept over her, a smile on his sensuous lips. She lowered her eyes to hide a glare. She managed to release her hand from his long, intertwining fingers, weighty with rings.

"Mademoiselle Macquinet, I bring you my deepest condolences. So much heartbreak befalls you. I grieve for your losses, I assure you. If there is anything I can do . . ." His tone conveyed his desire to open the door to his treasure house—leaving her to imagine what it might be like to enter.

She bowed her head. "Merci, Monsieur de Beauvilliers."

His lips turned upward. "Pardon Mademoiselle, if I have failed to permit you to call me Maurice."

"As you wish, Monsieur Maurice," she said primly. "You have graciously called upon my family in our sorrows, but how unnecessary and burdensome for you to come this far from Paris."

Maurice did not appear to notice her intimation, as he rearranged the lace at his wrist. His eyes found her gaze.

"Non, Mademoiselle. And though my sympathies are extended to one and all, what has drawn me so far from the delightful pleasures of Fontainebleau, is you alone."

She widened her eyes with innocence. "I, Monsieur? But why? I was not injured—as were my sisters and my père's cousin, Monsieur Bertrand—in le Duc de Guise's attack on the innocent Huguenots in the barn church. Had it not been for the intervention of God, we should all be dead."

He bowed his head, hand at heart. "A woe, Mademoiselle, surely.

"Princesse Marguerite sends her greetings, for it is she who is part of my reason for coming to see you."

Marguerite? She had not officially released her from serving as one of her ladies-in-waiting. Nor were Marguerite's additional summer gowns and accessories finished. Rachelle also knew both the Queen Mother and Marguerite wanted to have the Macquinets create Marguerite's wedding trousseau, if that time ever arrived. There had been several princely men from various kingdoms Marguerite was to have married, until they became offended by her notorious flirtations at Court.

As yet, the Queen Mother had not been able to arrange another marriage with Spain, which was her preference. Duchesse Dushane, in her last lettre, wrote that there was again talk of Marguerite's marriage, and that the Queen Mother was keeping her wayward daughter out of the public eye, hoping the scandals over young Henry de Guise would fade. But Marguerite, as usual, complied in the Queen Mother's presence, but continued her secret *amoureuse* with Henry de Guise.

Maurice tweaked his fingers at a page who turned over a sealed lettre. Maurice bowed and extended the lettre toward Rachelle.

"This, Mademoiselle," he announced with triumph, "bespeaks the most stimulating of news for your future. A royal trip to Spain is being planned by the Queen Mother and Marguerite, and you are summoned to Court to design and create the gowns for both to wear."

His gray eyes did a victory dance. "And I am under royal orders to escort you and your grisettes and equipage to Fontainebleau. I am sure the Queen Mother explains all of this in her correspondence."

She stared at the lettre with its gold seal, seeing the unexpected call not as a bane but a boon. Gowns for both Catherine and Marguerite! An opportunity to discover the Queen Mother's workings with poison.

"The court will be richer to have gained such a fair jewel as you, ma chérie."

"You must not call me your chérie, Monsieur Maurice. I beg you to remember that I intend to remain unattached."

"Ah yes, the renowned Marquis Fabien still holds some enchantment for you perhaps, but you will forget him soon. He is in disgrace at Court. Duc de Guise has brought the matter of the marquis' piracy before the king, and I assure you, Mademoiselle, it is no light matter to be so charged."

She looked at him in pretended offence. "A pirate? The marquis! But what an outrage. Surely the duc must be mistaken. Why would a marquis, well supplied with gold and rubies of his own, need to plunder Spain's treasure ships to pay his debts?"

"Not treasure ships, but war galleons—the Duc d'Alva's galleons —bringing soldiers and supplies to the Spanish Netherlands. Shall we say the marquis' hatred of Spain compelled him to take such drastic actions on behalf of his fellow Protestant Dutch? He is a secret Huguenot. Surely you know that?"

"The Marquis? Oh non, Monsieur Maurice, I hardly think so. He is most loyal to Rome, I am sure of it."

"Ah? Then how can one explain the cause for which he devotedly kept one of Lefèvre d'Étaples' Bibles in French at his estate in Vendôme?"

She could not keep back her genuine surprise. "A Bible? How do you know that?"

His little smile was full of mischievous self-satisfaction. "It was my hap to have come across such a forbidden book when I was at Vendôme, when I so gallantly took you there to safety from Amboise. It was signed by his mère, Duchesse Marie-Louise de Bourbon, an amie of the Huguenot sister of King Francis I. You are surprised?"

Indeed, but she did not want to react under his gaze. What was Maurice up to? Was he a spy for the Queen Mother or the Guises? Her irritation sharpened. "It would not please the marquis, I am certain, to know you were sneaking through his personal belongings!"

He shrugged. "It was fairly by accident, I give you my surety."

His tongue seemed dipped in oil when it came to giving a pledge to anything concerning the marquis, of whom he was resentful. She was confident he had not merely come upon a French Bible. Fabien was too careful to have left such a forbidden treasure lying about casually. Especially one from his deceased mère.

*What happened to Fabien's family Bible?*

She studied Maurice's smug face for a moment with a fearful suspicion that he may have removed the Book as future evidence against him. Would Maurice have done so? Maurice altered his conduct, and he was once more full of attentiveness. He needed to meet with her parents, he said, and assure them of her safe passage to Fontainebleau, for he would as soon fall upon his sword as ever allow the slightest mishap to befall their belle daughter and her petite grisettes.

Rachelle left Maurice to the nurture of Laurent, assuring Maurice that Monsieur and Madame would be there momentarily. In the meanwhile she told the dour Laurent to take him to a bedchamber where Maurice might refresh himself before the evening dinner, and to presently send up tea, fruits, and wine until he could meet with her parents about his royal mission. Food and drink must be prepared for his retinue, and all the horses and donkeys in his train must be tended for the night, and perhaps even longer, for it would take a day or more to prepare. Rachelle and her family would need to oversee careful preparations for storage of the bolts of silk and lace and the entire equipage for the journey from Lyon to Fontainebleau. She had no doubt but that she would go; for not even Arnaut and Clair, no matter how dismayed they may be, could say no to royalty.

She did not mention to Maurice that her parents were also planning a journey of their own to London and Spitalfields for business with the Monsieurs Hudson, father and son; or that Idelette would be going with them as far as Paris to be taken in by Madeleine and shielded until the birth. Idelette would not show herself in public in the village, and no one except the immediate family and Docteur Lancre knew that she was enceinte.

"Mademoiselle is too kind," Maurice said after Rachelle had made sure of his comforts, and he bowed his gratitude.

Rachelle, still holding the royal summons in hand, excused herself and went up the stairs to tell Idelette of Maurice's arrival.

As she climbed the staircase she frowned, for while she considered her call to Court to be fortunate, it would not seem fair to Idelette, who would enter a time of voluntary isolation. Rachelle would have the opportunity to make gowns for both Catherine de Medici and Princesse Marguerite Valois, but Idelette's task was to persevere under trial while feeling unappreciated. Rachelle worried that by displaying her own sense of excitement for her purpose at Court, she might add to her sister's sense of loss.

Their sisterly paths were separating, veering away into far different journeys. Would Idelette resent the open door the Lord apparently was giving Rachelle at Court again?

*But I am walking into a field of thorns, and who can say whether roses will bloom by the wayside? It is not only the work of a couturière that beckons me, but Catherine de Medici's poison closet and her secret poisoners — who were they who did her evil bidding? I intend to find out.*

※

A GOWN FOR CATHERINE de Medici! Rachelle's nerves tingled with alarm, though her imagination was kindled as she thought of the possible style and color that would befit the Queen Mother.

"Rachelle?"

Rachelle turned toward the anxious voice of Idelette who stood in her chamber doorway further down the corridor.

"The retinue that arrived, do I recognize the banner of Beauvilliers?"

"Yes, Sebastien's neveu, Comte Maurice has arrived from Fontainebleau. Idelette! I have been summoned to Court again by the Queen Mother. I will have no choice except to obey."

Idelette's fingers tightened around the collar of her bodice, and she took several steps toward her.

"Catherine de Medici asked for you? Rachelle, do not go. Go to Spitalfields with Père instead. I have a horrid feeling she means ill toward you."

Rachelle was swiftly beside her, trying to calm her. Usually Idelette was the composed one. This time her cheeks were flushed and the lashes on her pale blue eyes twitched nervously.

Rachelle took her arm and led her back to her chamber.

"Do not worry, sister. She has no idea that I suspect her. This summons should come as no surprise. I never finished the gowns Princesse Marguerite wanted me to make for her at Amboise. The dreadful rebellion and massacre took place and stopped everything. Now there is a journey to Spain."

"Spain!"

"Oui." Rachelle restrained a shudder. "There is to be a meeting about Marguerite's marriage. The Queen Mother also wishes for a gown to wear when she is received by King Philip. Not that he appreciates such things, I have heard. He is dour, always wearing black. Perhaps it is his conscience. He is responsible for so many deaths in the Inquisition, he looks as though he is at a perpetual funeral."

For a moment, the brightness in Idelette's pale blue eyes reminded Rachelle of her old spirit as she must have envisioned the creation of a gown for the Queen Mother of France. Then the look faded to concern.

"When will this journey to Spain take place?"

"She did not say in the summons. I suspect it will not be until after the colloquy this fall. Probably next spring."

"Our parents will be most upset over this. You will be at Court alone."

"Not entirely. Sebastien and Duchesse Dushane are at Fontainebleau, as is Andelot."

At the mention of Andelot, Idelette's mouth tightened.

"I will be able to visit you in Paris," Rachelle continued. "You will be with Madeleine. And should she ever come to Fontainebleau, you could come with her. It is not often we can gather as three sisters."

"I should rather die on my bed than show myself enceinte to — to anyone who knows me at Court." Her breathing came hurriedly with emotion. "I shall never be able to look them in the eye."

"It is not your shame. This came to you uninvited. You did not willingly play the fool."

"It matters not to me. The results are the same. I am enceinte. Even if I went to stay with Madeleine, what then? In a few months everyone will see. Should I walk about Court growing big with a beast's child?"

Idelette ran her palm over her stomach. "I used to dream of having enfants of my own, but little did I know it would end like this for me." She looked up, firming her mouth. She entered her chamber and walked to her bed and sank onto the edge. There was an urn on the table, and she poured herself a glass of water and sipped it.

Rachelle stood in the doorway, entered, and closed it. She stood for a moment, lost for words.

"Nenette has gone to the weavers' huts for Père and Mère," she said quietly. "Will you come down to greet the comte?"

"Non. He does not like me. I remember the way he looked at me when we were at Chambord. Undoubtedly, I am the only woman at Court he did not like. Why that was so, I cannot say, but I do not wish to be in his conceited company."

"Perhaps you misunderstood Maurice's look, sister. There is not a woman with fairness he does not appreciate."

Idelette shook her fair head firmly. "Non, there was dislike in his eyes. I remember it well, and it was most unpleasant, I assure you."

Madame Clair was right. Idelette did need to get away from the location of her ordeal, but she would never appear in public now, not even if she went to stay with Madeleine until after the birth. Idelette had begun wearing somber colors which made her skin appear sallow. Her once soft mouth was too often seen drawn into a tight molded line, pinched at the corners.

Rachelle's anger festered at the thought of the selfish beast who had brought this change upon her sister. But then, if she began raising difficult questions about her own loved ones, why not also inquire why God allowed thousands of Huguenots to die at the stake, be torn limb from limb on the rack at the Bastille, or languish in a hundred other painful situations? Indeed, why only the Huguenots, why not also inquire of the Protestant Dutch? She could not pick and choose the situations that troubled her just because it was *her* sisters. They were all somebody's sister, somebody's brother.

She remembered what Pasteur Bertrand said. The earth was in rebellion against God, Satan was still loose, prowling about seeking whom he may devour, and the fruits of sin were rampant and would run their course until the final judgment. And God's redeemed were not yet removed from the results of sin. As God's rain and sunshine fell on the just and unjust alike, so the sufferings that were the result of man's rebellion came to all. But there the likeness ended and the great divide began; for God gave a promise to His redeemed, that as their loving heavenly Father, He would make all things, good and bad, dark and light, work together for good for those who were His own.

"Where is the comte now?" Idelette asked.

"Hmm? Oh. Downstairs. Look, Idelette, he expects to speak with you while he is here. Can you not merely show yourself at dinner tonight?"

Idelette sank into the chair, pale and rigid. She shook her head firmly. "How can I? How can I possibly explain?"

"There is nothing to explain. He has no idea. How could he? And besides that, is it not better that the true facts come out about what happened than to allow ugly whispers that will surely come instead? Even if you hide away for nine months, you will not be able to hide the enfant once it is born."

Idelette dropped her forehead into her hand. "I do not know. I am confused, afraid, so very angry—" She clenched a fist. "My life is ruined."

Rachelle hurried to her and dropped to her knees beside the chair. "If I were in your place, I would be more than angry, ma chère sœur. If you do not wish to see him, you need not do so. But is it not wiser to speak the truth of what happened? Let the shamefulness of the Duc de Guise's men come to light."

Idelette closed her eyes. "I cannot escape that shame. But there are ways for a child to be born in secret I have heard. They do it at Court all the time—a king's mistress will have a child under a secret name away from Paris. Oh, why should this happen to me? It is unfair. Did I not pray every day? And did I not read our Bible in French, though I risked death?"

"Bien sûr! But yes, you were more faithful than I, sister. Oh, do not think such hurtful things against yourself as though God allowed it to happen because you had sinned against Him. What happened had naught to do with your lack of dedication to the Savior, but because we live in a time when Satan has great wrath against us. He wants to ruin those whose faith remains steadfast in Christ."

"You are right. Oui! But oh, what will become of me, of this enfant? Should I not just end my life and be done with such shame?"

"Idelette!" Rachelle rose to her feet and looked down at her sister. "You are not well. That is why you are saying these things. It will turn out, you will see. The Lord will help you. Somehow, someway, He will."

"How can this turn out for good? How?"

"I do not know. But God's Word can be depended upon in the darkest circumstances of life."

"What of my ruined honneur?"

"Your honneur is not ruined. You were violated. Your honneur remains."

Idelette dropped her head against her hand again and let out a frustrated, angry breath. "What man will ever have me in marriage now?"

Rachelle folded her arms. "Many, unless they are fools."

Idelette smiled ruefully. "My loyal sister." She wiped her eyes and smoothed her ashy blonde hair away from her cheek.

"Andelot Dangeau is twice the galant as any at Court," Rachelle said.

Idelette turned to her with a strange look. "Andelot … Oui, a fine boy."

"He is no longer a boy, sister. He is quite handsome and dependable. If a woman were looking for a husband, then Andelot would be a fine catch."

"But, he is yours."

"No, he is not."

"He is too young for me anyway."

"Only younger by a few years. Once you have the enfant and time passes, by then he would make a wonderful husband!"

Idelette actually smiled at her. "Ma chère sister, the matchmaker. Non, he is yours. He has always been yours. He is most attached to you."

She was not the matchmaker, but her parents. She wondered what Idelette would say if she told her their mère wanted Andelot to marry Idelette.

"I confess, I want another," Rachelle said wearily.

Idelette looked at her. "You ask far more than I, ma sœur; you ask for the moon and stars too."

"Since we like to discuss impossible things, why not?" Rachelle smiled.

Idelette dabbed her eyes with her gathered handkerchief. "I am feeling sorry for myself, that is all."

"I am hoping you will see how God has not changed just because your circumstances have. If God was faithful, true, and good a week ago — then He is so now. Bertrand always says God is not capricious. Remember, Jesus Christ is the same yesterday, today, and forever. Things turn out far differently than our plans, and there is naught we can do but trust and go on."

Idelette was the calm, stoic daughter, the sensible one, the prayer warrior, the Bible student, the daughter who could sit with Père and the Geneva minister who came to call and discuss doctrine sensibly when they asked her. How often she had seen the pride in Père's eyes as he looked at Idelette, and the minister showed his admiration. When Père had brought theology students home from Geneva, it was to Idelette he introduced them first. Idelette, who sat with them carrying on discussions about Calvin's *Institutes*. It was sober Idelette who surged ahead in the spiritual race, growing in patience. How many times Rachelle had heard Père say that "Idelette will marry a pasteur, wait and see. The finest pasteur in all Geneva's theology school."

And now Idelette was the injured lamb, the perplexed saint who cried out in confusion and doubt.

"I thought I knew my Lord ..." Idelette crumpled her handkerchief and passed it from one hand to the other as she frowned. "Then something like this happens, and suddenly I am a ship torn from its moorings, tossed by wind and storm. He allowed this nightmare to come upon me. If anything more happens to us, I shall swear we are all related to Job."

As she mentioned Job, Idelette turned toward her. Her eyes burned with an intensity Rachelle had never seen before. "Why did not the Lord protect me?"

Rachelle was struck by the rage in her question.

Rachelle spoke after several minutes of silence, not facing her but watching the curling flames destroying the wood on the hearth, oddly thinking that it was in the wood's ruin that warmth came to her.

"You ask me to answer so profound a question? I cannot. I will ask a question of you."

Idelette looked up at her with a puzzled look. "Ask me a question?"

"Yes."

"What question?"

Rachelle faced her soberly. "You are grieved because you say God did not protect you. Why did our Lord not protect them all? If you can answer why He did not send angels to protect them all, you may have your answer why these things happened to you."

Idelette wrinkled her brow.

"Monsieur Lemoine used his fields to allow God's people to meet, knowing it could mean his arrest. He even built a new barn to keep us from the weather. Yet the Lord permitted him to die by the sword. Now his wife is a widow. She will lose the fields unless she and her son recant. Children died, and Madame Hershey — and our petite sister Avril." She said her name with a small choke. "And what of Cousin Bertrand's injuries, and James Hudson who arrived from England just in time?" She turned toward the thin, drawn face of her sister. "And *me*."

Idelette looked at her and widened her eyes. "You? What befell you?"

"Nothing."

"You just implied — "

"That naught happened to me. And it is what troubles me. If I had not been late in arriving, if it had not been that Mère asked me to wait a few minutes longer to bring the scarf to Madame Hershey, what happened to you may have happened to me, or I might be dead like Avril. Sometimes I feel guilty I was not there ... As if it should have been me instead of Avril."

Idelette closed her eyes and shook her head showing disbelief. "I vow, you are hard to understand, Rachelle. You should be counting yourself favored. God's Providence. That is why you were late."

"Yes, but I would not say I was favored. It may be that, unlike you, I could not endure such a trial, so I was kept from it."

"Who can answer such questions?"

"Did you not say just minutes ago that we are all like the offspring of Job? Then perhaps part of the answer is that your faith is being tested — and it is much more precious than silver or gold."

Rachelle thought it wiser to urge Idelette to speak, for she was not ignorant of the truth.

Idelette dropped her head into her hands and shook it silently.

The silence grew, the dry wood cackled like an old witch, its sparks going up the chimney into the black, starless night.

Finally she spoke, her muffled voice uttered: "I would tell you God does not change with the winds of adversity. He is not capricious. He is good and faithful today, as He was yesterday, and He shall be tomorrow. The events of our lives are as the roaring wind upon a feeble leaf, but God holds the wind in His fist. I would tell you that evil will hound our steps until the moment of our death, but that our Savior is greater than all the hosts of evil that Satan can hurl against us."

Rachelle remained a moment longer, pondering her words, then, feeling there was nothing left to be uttered, turned and went to the door. She looked back. She was remembering the verse from Ephesians 6:14 that had come to be used as a motto for suffering Huguenots after a woman prisoner had carved the words into the wall of her cell.

"*Tenez ferme*," she said softly.

Idelette turned her head and their eyes met. A smile came to her lips. She nodded. "Merci, ma chère Rachelle."

Rachelle left her sister to wrestle with her trials, with a faith sorely tried, but in Rachelle's mind, standing firm in the faith.

✻

WITHIN TWO DAYS, RACHELLE was ready for her journey to Fontainebleau. Her personal trunk was packed with her finest Court frocks and slippers, while the bolts of Macquinet silk and velvet and lace were arranged carefully within the enclosed coaches.

Nenette was going as her grisette, and twelve-year-old Philippe, who had lost his mère in the barn attack, was now with her as an aide who would also run her errands.

On a sunny morning, the coaches were lined up and ready for departure. Comte Maurice had his men-at-arms in stately position as though the caravan were bringing royalty itself. Dressed grandly as ever, he was bidding Père Arnaut adieu and vowing his life would be exchanged for the safety of Rachelle should so great a sacrifice be in his fortune to make. It was not at all clear to Rachelle whether her père believed him. She knew that he was not impressed with Sebastien's neveu and was not pleased to be sending Rachelle off to Court, while he and Clair went to England, and Idelette to Paris.

A lettre arrived from Madeleine which finally helped to decide the matter for Idelette. She would not remain at the château as she had wished, but would go to Paris to stay with Madeleine and petite Joan until Père Arnaut and Mère Clair returned from England with Cousin Bertrand to attend the colloquy.

Arnaut and Clair would not yet be leaving for Calais and England, for there was yet much preparation to ready the silkworm eggs and leaves and new mulberry seedlings for the voyage. It was deemed wise that Idelette should travel with Rachelle as far as Orléans and then go on to Paris, while Rachelle would go to Fontainebleau.

It was clear that Madame Clair was troubled about separating from her daughters at such a time. Both Rachelle and Idelette tried to assure her they were able to care for themselves.

Rachelle walked toward the coach holding her hand case of burgundy velvet with her name inscribed in gold, which contained all manner of sewing equipment: special needles and pins, cutting instruments, and spools of colored silk thread from Italy, Spain, and the Netherlands. She also carried Grandmère's gold thimble as a reminder of whose steps she followed—which affected the other mission on her heart at Court.

She did not pause long enough to consider what she would do if she could prove the Queen Mother had poisoned Grandmère. Even so, she was bent on knowing the truth.

As Rachelle came down the veranda steps she saw that Idelette was being helped inside the Macquinet family coach by Maurice himself. Idelette wore a loose-fitting cloak, unusual for such a warm day, and she wondered if Père Arnaut had spoken to Maurice of his daughter's condition. She had noticed a solicitous behavior toward Idelette that he had never shown before.

Now, as Idelette entered the coach, having said her adieus to her parents, Rachelle bid her mère au revoir.

Clair drew in a breath, but her dignity and elegant composure remained. Taking Rachelle's arm, she drew her aside.

"You will not mention Grandmère's death or Madeleine's frailty, Rachelle. Do not give her cause to suspect for a single moment that you look upon her with even a butterfly lash of suspicion, understood?"

"Mère, do not worry; I have been in her presence many times, and I know what to do. But if I always avoid mention of their illness, and what befell them, she may grow suspicious."

"This is most distressing. I had longed to bring you with us to England to meet the Hudson family, and James writes that he hoped you could be there when the gown is presented to Queen Elizabeth."

"Oh, Mère, and I as well. It seems that all our paths are leading us in different directions."

Rachelle put her arms around her and kissed her cheek.

"The separation will not be long, God willing. We will all meet again for the colloquy at Fountainebleau. I shall pray that the trip to Spain does not come this year. So be wise at Court, and give no cause to the fickle gallants to think of you in their frivolous ways. Keep your faith to your own heart and count much on Comte Sebastien and Duchesse Dushane. Ah, but we must not live in fear but trust in the good hand of our Father through all uncertainty. His presence is with you, ma petite, and His angels, may they keep your steps."

Rachelle squeezed her mother's hands. "Adieu, ma mère."

"Then take care. Adieu, ma chère."

They looked at one another, for despite the words spoken with forced cheer and confidence, Rachelle felt her heart quaver as she saw the beginning of tears in the corners of her mère's eyes as she hastened to blink them back. With a firm smile, she reached over with concern and straightened a strand of Rachelle's hair.

Madame Clair stepped away, with her back and shoulders straight. Rachelle walked to the coach where Idelette already waited, having said her good-byes. Rachelle was helped inside by Père Arnaut.

"Au revoir, daughter. Remember the words we discussed in Paris after our return from Calais." He kissed her forehead.

Rachelle knew what words he meant. Again, there was the warning that she tread softly where the gloves were concerned.

"Au revoir, mon père. God speed with the precious cargo of silkworm eggs and leaves."

He smiled and reached over again to clasp Idelette's hand. "Be strong. Your mère and I will see you in a few months."

Madame Clair came up beside Arnaut, and there were more repeated good-byes. Then the coach door was closed, and Rachelle felt the coach moving along the courtyard and through the gate toward the road to Fontainebleau and Paris. She and Idelette looked out the windows and waved and smiled for a last time.

Rachelle watched the white château slip away into the morning. She embraced a last memory of her parents standing together arm in arm, smiling and waving at their daughters.

The moment was soon gone, and she leaned back in the seat and prepared herself to meet further winds of change.

# Omens from a Far Country

## LONDON, ENGLAND

MARQUIS FABIEN, GARBED IN THE COLORS OF THE HOUSE OF BOURBON, accompanied the queen's privateers to a meeting at Whitehall for a subdued celebration after successfully preventing the Duc d'Alva from resupplying his armies in the Netherlands.

The queen entered. She was dressed entirely in purple velvet, with much gold, pearls, and jewels. There were others there who received audience with Elizabeth, and Fabien stood with Bertrand and the other privateers waiting their turn.

The piazza under the long gallery was draped with gold and silver brocade, and the air hung with the diffusing scent from wreaths and garlands of fresh flowers. The reach of the river in front of Whitehall palace was covered with swans, and in the palace garden were thirty-four columns, each surmounted by the effigy of a heraldic beast.

Queen Elizabeth seemed a most interesting woman. She had very white skin and red hair. She did not look strong, or all that well, but there was a fiery determination in her eyes that bespoke her will to serve and defend England. Fabien liked her at once. How different was this young woman than the dark, sinister, scheming Catherine de Medici. He noticed a different spirit altogether. What was the difference? One seemed satanic, while the other seemed open to the light.

Fabien, standing with Bertrand Macquinet and Capitaine Nappier, noticed a vaguely familiar young man who was now having his audience with Elizabeth. He headed up a small party of what appeared to be couturiers, showing samples of their cloth and drawings of gowns and other articles of fashion to the queen's silk-woman, Mrs. Montagu, who was also receiving gifts. There were numerous gifts for the queen. Fabien caught sight of "loose-bodied gowns" in blush pink, known in Paris as a negligée; there were handkerchiefs, night smocks, and night coifs, and hairnets knitted of gold and silver thread, all from the famous couturiers.

Fabien brought his hand to his chin and pretended to look at the floor to keep from grinning. Nappier caught his eye and wore a wry twist to his lip. This seemed rather a strange group for ruthless privateers to follow — all were rugged men boasting swords, leather, and a thirst for Spanish blood; while the couturier was brandishing not steel but silk, flowering the English queen with feminine dainties, all the while hoping for her favor and business.

Fabien cocked a brow, as several pairs of new "silk" stockings came out and were handed with grand fanfare to the queen's lady.

Queen Elizabeth seemed to take it all with casual indifference until the presentation of the new stockings. Her pleasure could not be hid. She had never seen silk stockings before, she said, but had heard about them flourishing in France.

Hose were usually cut out of taffeta or worsted wool, and were only partially elastic and fitted only as leg covering reaching from the instep to mid-calf or knee. The clinging quality of the knitted silk stockings was something new for the *haute monde*.

The queen's voice carried across the gallery. "I like silk stockings well. They are pleasant, fine, and delicate. Henceforth I will wear no more cloth stockings. You may tell your couturière Mademoiselle Rachelle Macquinet that I am most delighted, Sir Hudson. Have her make many more for me."

Fabien came fully alert. *Rachelle?* He was suddenly interested in silk stockings and looked sharply at the young Englishman who was giving these gifts. Yes, the Englishman looked familiar. He limped as he turned and spoke to his page, who helped him open a larger container. A minute later they brought forth a stunning silvery-pink gown that shimmered and rustled as though alive and purring. Even the queen was delighted and smiled her pleasure.

"Is that not the Englishman I saw at Château de Silk?" Fabien asked quietly of Bertrand.

"It is. And if I am not mistaken, that gown is the one Rachelle and James were working so arduously on at the château. He is representing the new English silk enterprise of Dushane-Macquinet-Hudson. I take it he is trying to earn the queen's blessing for support of the new silk enterprise here in London. Arnaut wants to open an estate near London, and he needs the queen to agree. These gifts, rather extravagant, I admit, are from the Macquinets to woo Her Majesty to their cause."

"The silk stockings alone may do it," Fabien said wryly.

This was the first time Fabien had heard of any such enterprise as the Macquinet-Dushane-Hudson company of couturiers opening in England. Fabien now recalled James Hudson from the morning of the barn burning. With the circumstances as they were when he was last at the château, he had not known why Hudson was there.

Fabien studied Hudson. He was speaking about the gown —

"Your Majesty, it is with great delight that I bring you the workmanship of one of the finest young couturière's in France, Mademoiselle Rachelle Macquinet. She and your humble servant — " he paused to bow lightly — "worked on this gown for a month of days in order to have the privilege to bring it to you just as we join forces with the famous name in silk in France, the Macquinets."

The gown looked to Fabien to be made of silk and satin and was embroidered in silver and pink, with pearls on the long, narrow waistline and puffed skirts, and a pink feather fan as an accessory.

"Such splendid silk. Some of the finest I have seen ... the workmanship is exceptional, Sir Hudson. The French couturière, is she here in London?" the queen asked.

"Mademoiselle will be coming to London very soon now. She will be working with me as we open our own shop together. It is our desire to offer splendid gowns ready-made to be sold. This is our plan, to work as partners."

*What was this?* Fabien tried to not scowl. *Rachelle coming to London? To work hand in hand with James Hudson?*

He measured James Hudson more thoughtfully. How long had this Englishman been staying at the château?

Fabien leaned toward Bertrand. "You never told me Mademoiselle Rachelle planned to leave France to work with Hudson."

"I believe the matter was briefly discussed when I was there, but without a decision. As I recall, Madame Clair was not pleased with the idea of her daughters being in London alone, though staying with the Hudsons, a fair family of Reformed conviction."

Fabien was displeased. James Hudson was well dressed in black and white with some gold ribbon to his coat. There were several clothiers standing behind them.

Bertrand said, "With circumstances as they are for the Huguenots in France, Arnaut thinks it wise to have an open door into England. I fully encourage him in this enterprise. For some period of time he has thought to open a second silk production estate outside France. The question of concern is the damp, cold weather."

And the enterprise would mean the uniting of the Macquinet family of couturières with the family of the Hudson couturiers . . .

"Marquis de Vendôme?"

Fabien turned. At his elbow there stood a silver-haired man elegantly attired. "Monseigneur, permit me to introduce myself, s'il vous plaît. I am Ronsard d'Alencome, King Francis's ambassador to England. My secret condolences, for the arrest of your kinsmen, the Bourbon princes."

Fabien sharpened his gaze. "The arrest of the princes? Let us hope you are in error. Do you not mean Comte Sebastien Dangeau? But there is news that he was released and is again serving the Queen Mother."

"Oui, most fortunate for Comte Sebastien. I knew him in Paris. But non, I meant the Bourbon princes, Louis de Condé and Antoine de Bourbon. However, I see you do not know. My apologies, I did not intend to be the bearer of dark news." He bowed his head a moment. "Then, I fear I must proceed to inform you."

"Feel assured that I wish to hear the truth."

Ambassador d'Alencome glanced toward the queen who was now speaking to some privateers and expecting Fabien afterward. D'Alencome whispered, "If you will, can we speak alone after your meeting with Her Majesty? In the garden, perhaps?"

As soon as Fabien had exchanged pleasantries with Queen Elizabeth, he slipped away and found the king's ambassador down near the river.

The swans were farther out on the water now, and the moon was trying to shine through the London mist and failing. D'Alencome paced on the bank. Seeing Fabien, he hurried toward him and bowed lightly.

*Why do I feel uncomfortable with this fellow?* Fabien thought. He was behaving in the customary manner expected of him, and yet, something was not right. Was he a spy for Catherine? She had her spies everywhere in the courts of Europe and especially in the court of Queen Elizabeth, whom Catherine did not trust, for in the queen she had met her match. Elizabeth was a far better woman, but she was also shrewd and discerning. Queen Elizabeth was no fool.

Fabien was wearing his cloak and sword, permitted by Queen Elizabeth and considered part of the dress of the privateers. He rested his hand on his jeweled scabbard and met d'Alencome's light blue eyes evenly. But the ambassador looked back clearly, as though he had nothing worthy to hide.

"Monseigneur, I had to speak with you alone. I have a message for you from the Queen Mother of France."

Fabien said nothing for a moment. The breeze stirred about them. The water lapped softly in the distance.

"A message for me?"

"Yes, from our queen — "

Fabien stepped back, his hand still on his scabbard. Alarm spread across d'Alencome's face by the gesture.

"Monseigneur, I beg of you! I am your loyal ami, and the news from the Queen Mother is also conciliatory. She bears no animosity over the sinking of the Spanish galleons; indeed, secretly she is pleased, for she is no true lover of Spain, I assure you. King Philip has plagued her cruelly. The Guises, also her enemies, and the enemies of the House of Valois, are the legates of Philip, not the Queen Mother. If she could be free of the Guises, she might be free of Spain and free also to deal more sympathetically with the Bourbon-Huguenot faction in France. Surely,

Monseigneur knows she thinks well of the Huguenot Admiral Coligny, and of yourself also, Monseigneur."

Fabien listened without comment. He knew better than to believe these words at face value.

"What does the Queen Mother want of me?"

"Monseigneur, I do not know."

"I would not call you a liar, Monsieur Ambassador," he said. "But I think you do know. Where is the Queen Mother's lettre? Hand it over slowly, if you please."

"Marquis de Vendôme, if I attempted to use a dagger against you, I should be a madman."

"Let us hope you are not. Merci," he said with a faint smile as the ambassador handed him a lettre with Catherine's impressive gold seal.

"Before I read this, tell me of my Bourbon kinsmen, if you please."

"The news is not good for them, though Prince Antoine fares better. He is under palais arrest at Fontainebleau. He will not be executed. The Guises hope to use him to further their ambitions with Spain, which wants the Huguenot kingdom of Navarre."

"What are their plans?"

"To turn Prince Antoine over to the Roman Church and exchange his wife's rule of Navarre with Antoine's, thereby placing Navarre in a hand loyal to Rome and Spain, which would bring the arrest of the Huguenots in Navarre."

A Catholic? Would Antoine change religions for favors from Spain? Fabien did not have confidence in Antoine. His kinsman was known to waver, to change his mind often, and to compromise. But Louis —

"And Prince Louis de Condé?"

"I fear Prince de Condé is now in the dungeons of Amboise."

"Amboise!" The very mention of the fortress castle brought back all of the treachery and murder Fabien had seen there last March.

"He was arrested in Orléans as he and his brother rode of free will to Fontainebleau where they had been summoned by King Francis to answer for the treason of the Amboise rebellion."

As Fabien heard all that had happened, his anger boiled. The Guises were behind the treachery, of course. They would have convinced King Francis to cooperate with whatever they intended.

*Louis convicted of treason. What could he do to free him?*

Fabien read the lettre from the Queen Mother, taking every word with suspicion and trying to discover falsehoods.

He learned little more than what d'Alencome had told him. She hinted vaguely that should he return to France for the long desired colloquy sought by his ami and ally, the grand Admiral Coligny, that she would have no cause to arrest him for sinking Spanish galleons, although the irate Duc d'Alva demanded her action against him.

*"I assure you my intentions remain peaceful and cooperative."*

His mouth turned. He wondered if she had given promises of peace and friendship to the Bourbon princes.

*I am not so trusting, Madame,* he thought, and continued to read ...

> *There has been much discussion between myself and your cousin the Comte Maurice Beauvilliers and Mademoiselle Rachelle Macquinet. The comte is most smitten with her and has begged for her hand in marriage. Who am I to stand in the way of true amour? I hover on the verge of allowing this sacred union soon after the colloquy. Her parents, Messire Arnaut Macquinet and Madame Clair, would not oppose the will of the king in this matter, for all loyal daughters and sons of France will do what is best. Should you desire to return to France, I am open to discussing this matter with you in private, even as I am willing to discuss the death sentence against your kinsman, Prince Louis de Condé ...*

Fabien crumpled the lettre and met the surprised gaze of Ambassador d'Alencome.

*Maurice! That nefarious pariah!*

"Monseigneur, I fear not all is well?" d'Alencome said meekly.

Fabien stepped toward him; d'Alencome backed away, unsure, his hand shining with sapphires in the moonlight.

"Monseigneur, I beg of you, remember I am but an ambassador for our beloved Queen Mother, Catherine — eh! Messire, non, non — "

he sputtered as Fabien latched hold of his shirt collar and gave him a shake.

"Beloved Catherine, is she?"

"Monseigneur—"

Fabien released him with a small shove. "When did you receive this lettre from her?"

He cleared his throat and looked behind him at the waterway as though he might end up in its embrace. "I confess, Monseigneur, whatever the news, it was none of my doing. I am but a humble servant."

"Just another of her many spies, only a novice would not think so, I assure you. How did you know I would be here this night?"

"I overheard Queen Elizabeth's privy counselor, Cecil, mention it to her one evening. He was against permitting the privateers in the channel and advised her to move against them, but she refused, saying they were an extension of her Royal Navy. I heard your name mentioned with those who scuttled the Spanish vessels, and also that you were involved in taking the gold from the Genoese ships meant for the Duc d'Alva's mercenary soldiers. It is of utmost concern to my life, Monseigneur, that these little matters are sent by circuitous routes to the private chambers of Catherine de Medici; though I hasten to add that she already knew from the Spanish envoy of these particular matters. I tell you the truth, Monseigneur, that secretly she is not concerned, but publicly, like Queen Elizabeth, she must be cautious. Both queens fear the might of Spain upon their own countries. So, Monseigneur, when the Queen Mother knew you would arrive as planned to be received by Queen Elizabeth, she wrote the lettre you now hold and had it delivered to me by the visiting Portuguese envoy who left France to come to England."

"And Maurice Beauvilliers?"

"Ah, I know naught of such a one."

"A marriage to Mademoiselle Macquinet was being planned by the Queen Mother. Why so? To lure me back to the viper's den?"

"I know naught of it, Monseigneur. But she planned for your return, to be sure. Yes, yes, the marriage, as you say, must be some manner of plan to bring you back to France."

"Even so, it does not mean she will not force the matter. Is this a trap? Does she have soldiers waiting?"

"I swear I know naught of that. I do not think so, for she wishes for your help in a certain unspeakable matter."

*Unspeakable matter? What could it be except more intrigue over her hatred for Duc de Guise?*

There were voices coming from the palace and footsteps of the guards. The privateers were leaving the audience hall. Fabien saw Bertrand and Capitaine Nappier waiting for him on the grassy lawn. Fabien turned to the French ambassador.

"Say nothing of this, or I shall need to see you again to make known my hearty displeasure."

"Monseigneur," he bowed, "in my precarious position both here in the English court and with the Queen Mother at France, I am not fool enough to wag the tongue, except when it furthers the will and pleasure of the king."

Fabien looked at him long and hard, and did not like the glimmer that deepened in his eyes.

"Monsieur Ambassador, I do hope for your comfort you have not chosen to lie to me for the pleasure of the Queen Mother."

Ambassador d'Alencome said not a word, but bowed deeply. Fabien gave him a measuring glance, then turned on his heel and walked toward Bertrand and Nappier. Fabien knew his countenance must have been noticeably affected, for neither man spoke to him as they boarded the coach and returned to the King's Way Inn.

*Rachelle, ma chère, this I cannot allow. You belong to no one but me.*

He must go to her. Deceptive trap or no, he dare not risk the year's voyage to Coligny's colony and back again only to find her the wife of Maurice or James Hudson.

THE LONDON STREETS, SOME cobbled, most not, were crowded with vendors crying their wares. Apprentices stood in the doorways of shops calling out their master's specialties. There were men and women of nobility moving about in fancy carriages, and beggars: the old, the dirty, and the infirm. Ragamuffin children ran as undisciplined as feral cats and dogs. Everywhere there were church spires on the skyline, with bells tolling for one event or another at frequent times.

The streets were dirty and the odor foul. Rats moved in and out of refuse piles raked into mounds to be set on fire. Houses were plentiful but cramped together, two and three stories high, as if for protection. Creaking signs swung overhead, and the fog was moving in, mingling with smoke from cooking fires.

Inside his room at the King's Way Inn, Fabien paced across the quality but worn floral carpet, his buckled boots making no sound. His leather scabbard, with family jewels, hung within easy reach on the hook beside his royal blue plumed hat and matching coat with gold, worn for the English queen. Elizabeth had flirted with him. He would swear to it. The Earl of Essex had not appreciated it, though Fabien knew that with Queen Elizabeth it was always, and only, a flirtation from a distance.

The treachery heaped upon his Bourbon kinsmen, and the news of a possible marriage arrangement of Rachelle to Maurice, left Fabien no choice except to return to France and take his risks with the scheming Queen Mother.

Across the room watching him, Pasteur Bertrand in Huguenot black and white, stood with grave dignity, arms folded. His white brows were lowered over his dark, piercing eyes. Tall and thin, he gave the impression that if he raised his hand and pointed with a scowl, a lighting bolt might strike.

Bertrand would be returning to Spitalfields at dawn. He was anxious over possible important correspondence from Arnaut about the land he wished to buy outside London. He also expected an important lettre from Sebastien.

Fabien had already arranged for wagons to carry the French Bibles to the Spitalfields community of Huguenots and Protestant Hollanders, using several of his men as guards. By now they would have returned to the *Reprisal* anchored at Portsmouth, and awaited him there.

Capitaine Nappier and the crew anticipated a voyage to the Florida colony, but Fabien could not set sail now, nor could he release the ship to Nappier. He thought it wise to bring the vessel to Calais until he knew how matters would affect him and Rachelle.

Fabien sat down opposite Bertrand and glanced restlessly about the wooden table where their upcoming meal of kidney pie would soon be delivered. His rank mood was such that neither the pie, nor the ale appealed to him. *Maurice, you conniving little fox. I will have your head this time, I promise you.*

He snatched some grapes from the large urn and concentrated on their purple color. "If I sailed for Florida, I would return a year from now to find Rachelle either bearing Maurice's child, or in the dungeons!"

"I fear the spoiled young comte will not relent peaceably," said Bertrand. "And remember, the danger coiled in the vipers' den at Court may not be for Rachelle alone, but also for you."

"The Queen Mother is a deadly entity that I must handle with wisdom. Unfortunately, she wants something from me, Bertrand."

Bertrand's eyes flickered, alert. "What are your suspicions?"

Fabien reached for his scabbard, took it down from the hook, and unsheathed his rapier. The long, thin blade of steel glimmered with deadly precision.

"This," Fabien said in a low voice. "Madame le Serpent wants Duc de Guise dead. She is likely to offer me proof that he arranged for the assassination of Jean-Louis near Calais. I believe it of him. She will expect me to assassinate the man she feels is the greatest threat to keeping the throne of France for the Valois, or she will use her authority with King Francis to arrange Rachelle's marriage to Maurice."

Alarm spread across Bertrand's face. "You would not do so murderous a deed!"

Fabien looked at him grimly. "Would I not? I tell you, Pasteur Bertrand, there is a part of me that would take pleasure in doing so. I have long planned for it, and after his attack on the Huguenots and Macquinet family in Lyon, I could bring my form of justice down upon his head and sleep well for doing it. For the brutal death of Rachelle's little sister alone I could do so — and Idelette."

Slowly, Fabien replaced his rapier. "But I am no fool, though a sinner. And because I know my heart, I will be cautious when the Queen Mother meets with me, giving both fair promises and dark threats."

Bertrand rested his chin between thumb and forefinger. "This is more dangerous than the face of things as I first saw them. You must beware, Marquis, mon ami. Satan is most cunning. Temptation is not a matter you wish to treat gently. If the Queen Mother provides you a cause for revenge, you will face a great struggle. Apart from God's sustenance, you will not be able to resist. I had not realized the duc was responsible for the death of Jean-Louis de Bourbon." He studied Fabien for a moment. "By returning, you risk more than your physical life; you now put your character at risk."

"There is no other way. I must go. She was shrewd enough to make it so. If I refuse the summons to meet with her, I have no doubt of her vindictiveness. I have seen such in action before with others. She would see to it that Rachelle was given in matrimony to my selfish cousin."

"Then what will you do? What are your plans? You cannot agree to assassinate Duc de Guise."

"I will hear her words. But all the while I will be making plans to see that Rachelle is taken to some safe refuge where she is not easily reached by Maurice."

"That may work for a short time, but that too will eventually prove futile."

"I will take matters as they come." He gave Bertrand an even look. "If all else fails, I shall marry her at once. That would end matters for Maurice."

Bertrand's mouth turned faintly. "It would. It may also end matters for you where the Queen Mother is concerned—and perhaps with Arnaut and Clair as well."

"I will need to take my chances, mon ami Bertrand."

"Let us not trust in our bon fortunes, but in our God and give ourselves to intercession and petitions."

"You speak well there, Bertrand. Do so for me and I will be grateful to you, and our Savior."

"I have, and will continue to do so."

LATER THAT NIGHT, WEARY and in need of sleep, many thoughts raced through Fabien's mind: of possible religious civil war in his beloved France, of treachery and love, of his future as a Bourbon. Soon now, if war did come, how would he declare himself? As a Huguenot? Joining the admiral with his own retainers?

He thought longingly of Rachelle and of the precarious situation that would surround her at Court, and once more considered how he might safeguard and keep her for God, and for himself. Just how did she feel about Sir James Hudson? He frowned.

*If she would have me, we can marry at Vendôme.*

Would she accept? Was marriage still too soon for them? Was he acting in desperation because he was so sure a civil war would come?

He would know soon enough if her heart had kept beating for him in his absence, for he would be in Paris within a few days. Would she be pleased to see him, or as unreachable as she had been when they met at the Languet lace shop?

He recalled walking with Rachelle amid the fragrance of flowers at the Château de Silk and at Vendôme. He could feel her in his arms even now, and remember the softness of her lips beneath his, and how her eyes had told him she wanted him. She had loved him then; did she love him still?

*I will propose marriage when I see her. If she agrees, she will be mine alone.*

No more need to trouble himself over Maurice, or over her service at Court among wolves and serpents. He would make a bargain with the Queen Mother. Rachelle was his. But at what price?

He narrowed his gaze. Yes, a bargain, but what would be her terms, and how would he fulfill them? And if he could not? What then?

Fabien thought the impossible, of something he had told himself he would never do for the honneur of the name of Duc Jean-Louis de Vendôme and of his mother, Duchesse Marie-Louise de Bourbon. He may find it necessary to turn his back on everything he had, his title and lands, and leave France for England, Geneva, or perhaps even a new colony in the Americas or the Caribbean.

Even now, the thought of leaving his beloved France was painful, but for the first time, he considered it. Others, like John Calvin, had been forced to leave, and why not himself? Perhaps the more he considered the notion of leaving, the more he could adjust to the idea.

Could he walk away? He decided that he could, but only if he had Rachelle, which meant children growing up in security. For the first time, the thought of the Bastille, the torture rack, and the burning stake took on a more personal meaning. Yes, he could walk away from his title and leave France, if he must.

The colloquy and the chance of civil war took on a new urgency. Matters had to change in France. The life he wished to live there with Rachelle and with any children God might give them was worth fighting for.

Had it come to this then? Civil war, or leaving France to establish their Huguenot roots elsewhere?

In his mind he seemed to hear the thunder of war horses and the clash of swords. War, sorrow, and death. In exchange for what? Freedom of worship, peace, and love.

*Yes, it was worth it. Rachelle was worth it. Vendôme was worth it — if he decided he could stay.*

He left the bed and walked to the window. He looked out, but London was draped with fog and he could see nothing. Somehow, the lack of sight brought to mind the words he had been reading in Scripture, *"For we walk by faith, not by sight."* Faith in the words of Scripture alone, and in Christ alone. Not in his own wisdom, nor in his own abilities, not even in the exercise of prayer, but *in* God.

These Spirit-breathed words would guide his future and Rachelle's along the treacherous road that lay ahead for all Huguenots who remained in France. The road would be rough, but they were not alone. They were not to be pitied for being chosen to represent Christ in such a time as this, for Christ declared that the suffering church was rich and not poor, and well favored in His love.

*Fear none of those things which thou shalt suffer ... I will give thee a crown of life ...*

Fabien anticipated telling Rachelle that he would openly declare that he was a Huguenot. He would publicly take Communion at the colloquy with Bertrand, Beza, and John Calvin.

And he hoped she would welcome him into her heart.

He would leave London before sunrise. In a few days he would be in Paris to see his belle amie Rachelle again.

*This time I will vow my enduring love through marriage.*

# *The Secret*

RACHELLE'S JOURNEY FROM LYON TOWARD FONTAINEBLEAU PROCEEDED without difficulty. Near Fontainebleau Comte Sebastien and his guards rode out to meet them, and they pulled off the road among the pine trees for a short rest. When Rachelle first saw Sebastien she was momentarily stunned by the change in his appearance, and Idelette caught her breath. He now looked as elderly as Pasteur Bertrand, but even frailer. Her heart went out to him. *What Sebastien must have endured! I am heartily ashamed of myself. I shall never again entertain a single tainted thought about his recantation.*

She was so moved that when they met on the side of the road she embraced him. "Cher brother," she said, and for lack of anything worthy to say, lapsed into silence.

Sebastien, his manner as fatherly as Bertrand, patted her shoulder. "I am doing well, ma petite sœur. I am cheered to see you again, but grieved that you have come to Court at this time. I worked against it for more reasons than one, for I may not always be there, but at least Duchesse Dushane should be. If ever in the future you find yourself in dire need, go to her immediately. These are precarious times for us all. You must behave most wisely before the Queen Mother, as I have confidence you will."

*He also suspects Grandmère and Madeleine were poisoned. Was he expecting his own arrest again?*

Rachelle tried to reassure him to alleviate his worrisome burdens. He surprised her when he announced that he would attend them both on the remainder of their journey, and that they would be going to Paris.

Sebastien was to spend a few days with Madeleine and his bébé Joan before returning to Fontainebleau with Rachelle.

Rachelle had not expected this. She was journeying with all of her sewing equipage.

Sebastien rubbed and straightened his black velvet glove with fidgety fingers. *Was anything wrong? Was he perhaps not given permission to go to Paris?*

"And where is the Queen Mother?" she asked in a low voice.

"She has gone for a short time to Chambord to keep a meeting with the Duc d'Alva."

Rachelle shuddered at the thought of the Spanish military commander of the soldiers in the Netherlands, recalling the brutality Fabien had told her about. She thought also of Fabien, and worried. Surely the duc was here to make complaints against the sinking of his galleons.

Rachelle did not mind going on to Paris, for there was the matter of the gloves that she had not been able to search out, and now she may have the opportunity. She wished to see Madeleine again and bébé Joan.

Idelette helped Rachelle down from the coach to walk about and stretch after such a long ride from the château. Maurice Beauvilliers rode up to his oncle.

"What is this, mon oncle? Paris, you say? But non. I am under orders by the Queen Mother to bring Mademoiselle Rachelle straight to the palais-château at Fontainebleau."

"The Queen Mother is at Chambord entertaining the Duc d'Alva. We will be but a few days at the Louvre. Mademoiselle Rachelle will return with me to Fontainebleau then. Do continue on with the sewing equipage. Make certain all of the goods and bolts of silk are secured in an atelier."

Maurice looked from Sebastien to Rachelle. "There is something odd about this, mon oncle."

"Do as I say, mon neveu," Sebastien said impatiently. "It is getting on toward afternoon, and I wish to be in Paris before sunset. Madeleine is expecting us. I sent word ahead to her."

Maurice studied him for another moment, his lips forming a tight line, then he barked orders to his men to turn the wagons toward

Fontainebleau. His languid eyes roved back to Rachelle. Suspicion showed on his face. Rachelle stared back evenly, vexed by his possessive demeanor. Since his arrival at the château he had treated her as though she were his belle amour.

He swung down from his black horse and sauntered up to where she stood. He swept up her hand and pressed it to his lips. She snatched her hand away and narrowed her gaze.

"I beg of you, Comte Maurice, that you cease such behavior. Everyone is watching."

"Would you permit me then, if they were not?"

"I have given you no such right."

"Ah, but I have that right, mademoiselle," he said stiffly, "and none shall deny it on the word of the king." A satisfied smile drew over his sensuous mouth.

*The king?* Maurice's confidence irritated and alarmed her. "Whatever do you mean?"

"The Queen Mother has written you and explained."

"I beg to differ. The Queen Mother has explained nothing except that I am wanted at Court to create Princesse Marguerite's wardrobe for her visit to Spain. You, mon comte, were not even mentioned," she said with a taste of her own satisfaction. His pride was insufferable.

"Hah, *ma belle*, but you are most mistaken. I shall soon have you as my own princesse."

"You imagine more than shall ever be, I assure you. I wish for no interest from any messire at Court, or otherwise. All I want is to be left in peace to do my work for Marguerite."

"It is you, Rachelle, who imagines you have more rights than you are entitled. You and I will be married. The Queen Mother has promised me."

Astounded, she stared at him. His eyes were bright and passionate and his determined expression alarmed her. He believed it!

"Messire, I think you are sadly mistaken. The Queen Mother could not have made you such a promise. My parents will not hear of it, I assure you."

"They will have nothing to say about it," he said flatly. "It is what the king will say that matters. If he wishes us to marry, we shall marry.

I suggest you be pleased you have won my devoted heart and begin to make plans to make me a happy and contented husband."

Rachelle glared. "Ah, you are conceited, Maurice. I tell you I will not marry you. Now do step aside; my sister is waiting to board the carriage for Paris, and I am going with her. You have the orders of your oncle, and I suggest you honor him by carrying those duties to completion. I bid you adieu—and please do not permit the lackeys to soil one inch of my bolts of silk or they shall hear from me." And she swept past him to the carriage, holding her breath, half expecting to feel his hand grab her arm or throw a tantrum over her rejection. Maurice kicked a rock across the road and shouted angrily at his lackeys.

"What was that all about?" Idelette was seated across from her as the coach proceeded once more toward Paris, Sebastien and his guard of a dozen armed men in the lead.

"I do not know, but he has some inane notion that the Queen Mother will arrange my marriage to him by going to the king about it."

"Marriage to Maurice? But that will never be permitted by our family, I assure you."

"So I told him, but he only insisted the king could force the marriage to take place if he wished."

"I suppose he could. So could the Queen Mother, but why would they? Such enforcement is kept for high nobility and princesses like Marguerite."

Rachelle made no further comment, but she was perturbed and growing more uneasy. What if the Queen Mother had promised Maurice her hand in marriage for some scheming reason? Was it possible she had done so? Maurice had oozed with confidence.

*Things are not as they should be*, she thought as the horses trotted along the unpaved road to Paris. She looked out the window at the speckled sunshine filtering through the chestnut trees along the roadway.

Sebastien had behaved oddly. She wanted to mention it to Idelette, but she was resting her head against the back of the plush velvet covered seat, her eyes closed.

Rachelle mulled over the events. Yes, matters were not as they should be. Something was in the wind. There was a certain mood that told her life as she had known it was changing, even perhaps, coming to an end.

*Marriage to Maurice Beauvilliers? Never!*

Her heart turned toward Marquis Fabien. The longing became overwhelming and tears soon dampened her cheeks. She blotted them away, glad that Idelette did not see them and feel worse than she already did.

She turned her heart to her heavenly Father, remembering, *I am not alone.* God stood in the shadows of life's providence, keeping vigilant watch over His very own.

⁂

RACHELLE HAD BEEN AT the Louvre for several days. She set about almost immediately to search Grandmère's chamber once again to see if the gloves might have fallen behind a piece of furniture, or got pushed under the canopied bed. The chamber had been swept clean.

On occasion she sought out each of the servants, asking questions, but again no one knew a thing about the missing gloves. They remembered seeing Grandmère wearing gloves, but they could not say where they may have disappeared.

Rachelle's only glimmer of new information came from the serving maid.

"There was only one thing odd, Mademoiselle."

"And what was that?" Rachelle urged.

"I saw a very small ghost in the grand madame's chamber the day before she died. First I thought it was a boy child, but then I saw his face, and he looked old, Mademoiselle. And when I blinked and rubbed my eyes, thinking I was seeing a vision, well next thing I looked again, and whatever it was, it was no longer there. And now that I have thought it over, Mademoiselle, I am sure he was a dwarf."

A dwarf!

The Queen Mother had several dwarves who served her as loyally as did Madalenna. It would have been possible for one of them to hide during the emotional comings and goings, when Grandmère became so ill.

Had they been clever, they should have left an untainted likeness of the poison gloves in the belle red box. They would have been tested for poison and found harmless.

"Did anyone else see this dwarf?"

"If they did, no one said so, Mademoiselle. They were all so busy with Grand Madame. It was those petite apples, Mademoiselle. They made her most sick, so that she succumbed."

Later, Rachelle spoke to Madeleine about the Queen Mother's dwarves.

Madeleine frowned in distress and was still unwilling to discuss anything that had to do with the gloves, Grandmère, or her illness.

"You do not understand, Rachelle. I have Joan to think of."

"I do understand, but if Grandmère —"

"If you discover something — then what? Take the matter before King Francis, who is only a weak boy controlled by the cardinal? Or burden Sebastien with it? He needs a long rest away from the demands and fears of Court that lash his conscience. He disagrees with much that the king is allowing the Guises to do in France, but how can he stop it?" Madeleine straightened her shoulders and wore a determined face. "All I want is to go away from here."

Rachelle, understanding the weariness in her eyes, kept silent. Joan began to fuss in the next chamber and Madeleine went there. Her face changed, a sparkle came to her eyes, and she smiled as she took her daughter from the nurse. She held her possessively close.

On that same afternoon she accidentally overheard Sebastien speaking urgently to Madeleine: "Nothing else matters, just ..."

"But Sebastien —"

"I must take them to him now. Do as I say, chère."

"He will take nothing else?"

"Non."

Rachelle bit her lip, backed quietly away, and returned to her chamber. Did Sebastien have debts?

When Rachelle came to the table for the evening dinner she noticed Idelette whispering vehemently to Madeleine. Upon seeing her, they drew apart. Sebastien did not show for the meal, and Rachelle noted that both of her sisters appeared tense.

After dîner no one spoke much. Sebastien did not come back to the appartement. Soon, Madeleine stated that she had a headache and was going to retire, and Idelette had correspondence to catch up on.

Rachelle, left alone, watched them leave, wondering. As Idelette turned the corner to her chamber, she looked back over her shoulder, and Rachelle caught her looking at her.

"A bonne nuit, petite sister," Idelette said.

Early in the morning, Rachelle was awakened by Nenette shaking her shoulder.

"Wake up, Mademoiselle, wake up. Philippe was with the boys at the stables when he saw the Queen Mother and Madalenna arrive secretly."

Rachelle sat upright, wide awake. "Secretly?"

"She came without fanfare—no trumpets and flags, and with an unmarked coach. And Mademoiselle, that is not all." Nenette lowered her voice to a bare whisper. "Philippe has something to tell you."

Rachelle threw on her loose-bodied gown over her night smock. "Quickly, then."

Nenette beckoned for Philippe to enter.

His dark eyes reflected like pools, brimming with excitement and fear.

"Mademoiselle, I saw the girl that the stable boys call Madalenna creeping about, so I followed her. There is a secret passage behind the palais. She waited there. Then an old market woman came out, and they went to the river. Then I realized it was not a market woman but the Queen Mother. I followed them to the wharf. There were strange shops and some houses. The Queen Mother went inside a house behind the apothecary shop. And the name said 'Ruggerio Brothers.'"

Rachelle gripped his arm. "When was this?"

"Only a little time ago. Then I came to Nenette."

Her heart beat faster. "Can you point out the house and shop on the wharf?"

"That is why I ran here. But we need to hurry."

"Wait for me in the courtyard. I shall be there in a very few minutes."

When he had gone, Nenette was breathing quickly with excitement. "Is it safe for you to go? What if she sees you? Oh, Mademoiselle, do not do this."

"She will not see me. Quick, hand me the dark dress and the cloak."

"If the Queen Mother learns of your suspicion, she will poison you!"

The truth was so bluntly put that Rachelle was speechless for a moment.

Nenette wrung her fingers. "Oh, Mademoiselle, one faux pas and — "

"Hush. I will not be seen. Make excuses for me should my sisters ask. Do not tell them I have gone to the wharf."

Within a brief time Rachelle slipped from Comte Sebastien's chambers and entered the back courtyard nearest the river Seine. The dawning sun had not yet burned away the mist over Paris. Philippe was waiting out of sight and took her to the dark river and the wharf.

They hurried in the mist, the boats creaking. Farther down the wood walkway, Philippe pointed toward fish and fruit shops. Behind them stood the many cramped and narrow houses. In the early mist they looked like wooden crates facing toward the town, but a few had oil lamps lit, showing golden windows.

"Over there, Mademoiselle. That is where she went — to that house, the tall one. There are shops too. See? The lamps are lit early for business."

She turned to him, trying to look stern. "This is far enough for you, ami Philippe. Go back now and wait for me in the courtyard."

"Should I not hide and keep watch? Where is the spy, Madalenna?"

Madalenna worried her, but she feared involving Philippe even more than she worried about the Italian spy or the dwarves. As Philippe went back, she walked toward the markets. They were already opening for a busy day's work. The noise and babble on the wharf was breaking like the sunlight through the mist. She came to the shop that Philippe had pointed out. In the window there was an assortment of fine leather gloves and jewelry. A wooden sign tossed in the breeze: "Ruggerio Brothers."

The shop was closed. Rachelle looked up and saw the house above the shop. This must be the residence of the brothers from Florence.

The "market woman" was nowhere to be seen. Could she have left already?

Rachelle decided to conceal herself and wait to see if she departed, then talk to the brothers, pretending to want to buy gloves.

Foul smelling breezes tossed her cloak and mantle. She hesitated, then circled around the shop to the side of the house. A window was drawn open and silhouettes moved about inside the room. Then Rachelle caught sight of her. The Queen Mother was dressed as Philippe had said. Catherine was standing in front of two men with stooped shoulders. She was making blunt gestures with her hands.

"I need something that will work on a seigneur. Most shrewdly devised, and untraceable. No gloves or rings. I want something that leaves no evidence."

"Come in back, Madame. We have something never used in France. It leaves no trace. Cosmo tried it on his rats and cats and it worked."

"There was no trace?"

"Non, Madame."

"But will it work on larger specimens?"

"Cosmo used it on a branded woman, and it worked quickly."

A branded woman was a poor creature who had once been arrested as a thief. Rachelle shuddered. Why should she be surprised? Did she not suspect Grandmère's death to be murder? But even as fear goaded her to flee, she heard a rustle in the bushes to her right. She turned her head to see the dark eyes of Madalenna meeting hers.

Horrified, Rachelle fled through the shadows and back along the busy wharf. She looked over her shoulder but did not see Madalenna.

Rachelle ran, reaching the small swaying bridge, where she paused, grabbing hold of the rail and trying to calm her heart.

*She saw me. She knows it was me. She knows I was listening — She knows I understand that the Queen Mother is a murderer!*

Frightened and angry with herself for having taken such a risk, she hurried across the bridge and back along the walkway into the courtyard. Here she paused again to look over her shoulder toward the murky Seine, gray and mysterious in the misty morning, where small boats were plying up and down the waterway.

Once inside the palais she entered Sebastien's appartement.

There came a breathless cry from Nenette who met her with wide eyes and clasped hands. "Oh, Mademoiselle Rachelle. Look!"

Nenette turned her head and stared into Madeleine's bedchamber. Rachelle rushed to the door and looked inside.

"They are gone," Nenette cried.

"Gone? How can they be gone?"

Philippe burst in, his eyes large with excitement. "Mademoiselle, it is true. Mademoiselle Idelette is gone too. Her bedchamber is empty."

"That is not possible," Rachelle cried. "They cannot simply disappear."

Though the wardrobe contained clothing and shoes and hats, the bureau drawers that had held items for travel were empty. Still refusing to believe it, she hurried over to the box where Madeleine kept the treasured bébé blanket that Grandmère had made here at the Louvre for Joan just before Grandmère's death. Madeleine would never leave it behind.

Rachelle lifted the lid of the box. *Empty.* The treasured blanket was gone. She looked further and discovered that Joan's bébé clothing was missing as well.

*Then it was true. They had departed silently during the night.* Rachelle felt as though she had swallowed a brick. She looked around her with a sense of loneliness and loss.

*So this was the secret Sebastien had kept to himself and Madeleine these months. How long had Idelette known? Probably not for very long. Their escape beneath the very nose of the Queen Mother was also undoubtedly the cause for Sebastien taking Madeleine's jewels. He was telling her not to take anything but the jewels and essentials. Evidently he had been packing priceless goods elsewhere and preparing them for travel, but travel to where? The château? Non, that was not far enough away to satisfy Sebastien.*

Then Rachelle saw the note at the bottom of the box where Joan's blanket had been stored.

*Chère sister,*

Idelette told me to put our *lettre* here in the box where she knew you would look. Please burn it as soon as you are finished reading. By now you understand we have departed from Paris. We are on our way to freedom, and England. We will write from London when safely settled at Spitalfields with Cousin Bertrand. We kept this from you for two reasons; Sebastien insisted that if anything went wrong and we were caught, he did not want to involve you. Your ignorance of the plan would spare you. Secondly, we knew you would not be coming to England, that your calling from God yet remains in France. The decision to leave France at this time is Sebastien's and mine alone. *Père* Arnaut knows of our decision, for he and Sebastien discussed this secret plan and how to enact it soon after Sebastien's release from the Bastille. Idelette's decision to come with us was encouraged by our parents because *Mère* thinks it will be better for our sister to give birth in England. We will all be staying with Cousin Bertrand until we become settled. We will, with God's speed, be meeting *Père* Arnaut and *Mère* Clair in Spitalfields when we arrive. As you already know, *Père* is trying to buy some land outside London. When they return to France to see you, they will tell you all that will have happened. Pray for our safe voyage, especially for Idelette, that the voyage is not too difficult for her. Duchesse Dushane knows of our plans, as Sebastien discussed these matters with her at Fontainebleau. Andelot does not know. You will see the duchesse there in Paris soon, and our *bon ami*, Andelot. Stay close to them.

Adieu, *ma chère sœur*. Our *amour* as ever. Until we meet again,

Madeleine, Sebastien, Idelette, and petite Joan
Jeremiah 29:11

*How long until the Queen Mother calls for me to explain my presence at the Ruggerio brothers' shop?* She will return to the palais soon, by the secret way she had departed disguised as a market woman. *How long before Madalenna informs her about Mademoiselle Rachelle Macquinet the spy. Oh, how the Queen Mother detests spies when they spy on her.* Rachelle paced across the Aubusson rug in the salle de séjour of

Sebastien's appartement, her perfumed skirts of blue and ivory silk rustling softly with her tense movements.

*She is too shrewd to believe I was there by coincidence. Ça alors! Now what? Oh, why did I take such a foolish risk? She will know I followed her.*

The pit in which Rachelle found herself trapped at the Louvre was closing in about her. If her own situation were not enough to take her to the Bastille, what of the Queen Mother's response when she discovered Sebastien took his family and escaped France while in service to her?

Rachelle shuddered at the thought of facing the serpentlike eyes of Catherine. Her family had departed and now she must face the woman alone! They could not have guessed her dilemma, and she had no one but herself to blame for her adventure on the wharf.

*Non, I am not alone.* She ceased her pacing and placed a hand to her forehead, momentarily closing her eyes, trying to remember details from Scripture of individuals in grave circumstances … Daniel for one. Daniel in the court of heathen kings … Daniel walking circumspectly amid his duties, serving with dignity, yet remaining faithful to God.

She resumed her restless pacing. The chambers were still. Not even Madeleine's ladies-in-waiting were anywhere to be found, which caused Rachelle to wonder what Sebastien may have told them. It was not likely they would have left for England with Madeleine, for several were married and they all had their families in France. Perhaps the Duchesse Dushane had aided in the ruse in some way. Had they been told to wait for Madeleine at Fontainebleau believing she would go there?

Nenette and Philippe huddled together in the archway adjoining the servant's antechamber, speaking in urgent whispers.

Rachelle ceased her pacing and looked across the chamber. "What is it, Nenette?"

Nenette's eyes were round and glinting with fear. "Philippe says someone nears the chamber. Oh Mademoiselle!"

Rachelle's impulse was to flee for the opposite door, but what good would that do her when guards were everywhere? Even if she made it as far as the courtyard, she could never escape if the guards were alerted.

"Shh, quick, into the antechamber and close the door. You will say you know nothing about what I have been up to, *c'est bien compris?* When you can—find your way to Duchesse Dushane and take shelter there."

Nenette burst into tears and knelt beside Rachelle, wrapping her arms about her skirts. "Non! I will not leave you! If you go to the Bastille, I shall go with you!"

Rachelle stooped and threw her arms around her. "I love you dearly for such a thought, but if I am imprisoned, they will not keep us together. The best thing you can do for me now is to protect yourself and Philippe."

The door from the outer corridor opened into the antechamber; there were footsteps. The summons had come. Rachelle stood, clutching the sides of her skirts, but she was determined to keep her dignity.

A formidable figure in black paused in the doorway of the antechamber, then entered the salle de séjour.

A little moan nearly escaped Rachelle's lips. *Fabien!* She wanted to cry with joy, and fought back the desire to run with relief into his arms. If anyone could help her now, it was the marquis, but she dare not run to him to show the delight she felt at his presence, for that would assume the familiarity she had so boldly discarded. Still, she could not help the growing excitement in her heart that maybe she was the reason he had chosen to return to Paris. But was she rushing to conclusions? His unexpected presence was no proof he had come for her, nor that he would not be leaving again.

Was it possible that Sebastien and her sisters were escaping to England on *his ship?* Her hopes sprang anew. But how would he know that Sebastien even had plans to escape the palais of Catherine de Medici? He could not—unless Sebastien had contacted Fabien in London.

The marquis swept off his hat and bowed. "Mademoiselle," he said too gravely.

She dipped her head with restrained dignity. "Monseigneur."

She read a challenge in his violet-blue eyes, one that she could do without under the circumstances. A suggestion of a sardonic smile showed on his lips before he turned and spoke to Nenette and Philippe. They bowed and scattered into the next chamber. As Nenette was closing the antechamber door, and Philippe was peeking from under Nenette's arm, a look of relief and excitement showed in the glance she cast to Rachelle. *This is your opportunity*, Nenette seemed to say, *ask him for help!*

Rachelle was alone with the marquis. She saw that he stood watching her with affected seriousness. "Are you not going to ask the reason for my unexpected arrival?"

"That, Monseigneur, is assuredly your private concern."

"How cool and indifferent you are, Mademoiselle." He tossed his hat and cloak aside, taking her in with a glance that suggested he did not accept it.

Rachelle looked away, turning her shoulder toward him. She pressed her palms together tightly. This was maddening. Her nerves curled inward.

"I have risked my head, left my ship and buccaneers to come to Paris, and this is your response, Mademoiselle? I am gravely disappointed. Which sorely tempts me, Mademoiselle, to prove your manner false!"

She slipped behind the crimson velvet chair with gold tassels and held to its back with a dignified stare.

His smile was disarming. He folded his arms.

"Your head, Marquis?" she asked with raised brows. "I wonder who would wish to have your most noble head?"

He bowed. "Philip of Spain, to name one. But as he remains at *El Escorial* in Spain on his throne, he has sent the Duc d'Alva here to France demanding action from the Queen Mother against me. I will doubtless hear from her soon on the subject of the duc's galleon. We sent the scoundrels of the sea to a watery grave."

She was alarmed. "You sank the Duc d'Alva's galleon?"

"Among others. It was gloriously satisfying, I assure you. We gave no quarter. You may be heartless enough to take some satisfaction in the fact that I honorably drew sword against those who empower the Duc de Guise to war against your fellow Huguenots."

Rachelle's alarm was now not for herself but for him. He was in more danger than she, and yet he had risked coming to Paris.

"Do you not know that Duc d'Alva is in France and will be entertained by the king and Queen Mother at Fontainebleau? He may be there now."

"I have word that he is."

"You have walked into a trap!"

"One that I entered with full understanding. Sebastien also knows about it."

"Oh! Then you know about Sebastien?"

He lifted a brow. "Know what?"

"Not now, please do go on with what you were saying."

"It is indeed a trap, plotted by the Queen Mother to lure me here. I sometimes think Catherine de Medici is the greatest intriguer in all Europe."

She was appalled, but perhaps she should not have been by anything Catherine did to further her aims at Court. "Then did the Queen Mother lure you here to hand you over to the Duc d'Alva?"

"Non. I have come to duel your fiancé."

She stared at him. Was he serious? From the hard gleam in his eyes, he appeared so.

"Where is the dashing Comte Maurice Beauvilliers?" he asked wryly. "I went to his chamber, but the fastidious rogue is not there. A pity, for I should have had him pinned to the wall then and there and been done with it."

Shaken, her lips parted and she stared at him. How outlandish — her whirling thoughts came to a crash. Duel Maurice!

She came swiftly from behind the chair. "Surely you do not think that Maurice and I — "

He stepped toward her, caught her hands, and lifted one to his lips, kissing her wrist. The romantic challenge in his violet-blue eyes did not relent.

She stepped back, hands behind her skirts. "Did Sebastien tell you the Queen Mother promised Maurice that she would arrange my marriage to him?" The very thought left her appalled.

"He mentioned it in his lettre. The facts were brought to me by the French ambassador to the English court. Before the Queen Mother flagrantly arranges the marriage, I will have an understanding with her that will disappoint Maurice. He will become so angry he will demand of me an *affaire d'honneur*. And then?" He sighed with mock regret. "I will need to grant his boastful request and teach him some humility."

"And I have nothing at all to say about this absurd situation?"

"Non. You are like all the daughters of nobility at Court, to be bartered for the best political prize to enhance the power of the throne of France."

"I see. And who does the Queen Mother wish to win this romantic battle?"

"Your servant, Mademoiselle, of course." He bowed lightly. "I am of more use to her than Maurice. He is but the unsuspecting pawn; so aptly used because of his vanity."

She felt the heat grow in her face. "I do not see what I possibly can bring the Queen Mother."

"It is not what you bring her personally, chère; it is what she wants of me. It is not a flattering thing to say of one so belle as yourself, but you are the bait for the trap, the one thing she knows will bring me back to deal with her. So perhaps I shall play along with her and make a bargain. I will tell her I want the silk couturière with the honey brown eyes and the dimple by her mouth . . . And she will say, 'Anything you want is yours, all you need do is murder the Duc de Guise.' " He stood back and looked at her gravely through narrowed dark lashes, one hand on his hip.

She trembled. So that was it. This was the horrid reason for Maurice's recent confidence toward her. The Queen Mother had indeed implied the marriage could come to fruition to lure Fabien to Paris. But that would imply she believed the marquis cared enough to take her bait. Rachelle glanced at Fabien, then turned away, distraught.

"It is atrocious — kill the Duc de Guise? And have the House of Guise forever plotting your death in revenge? It is unthinkable."

"It would fit her plans very well, I assure you. I would rid her of her chief enemy, and in turn be killed by the Guises. She would be rid of two enemies. Quite Machiavellian, her most cherished style of plotting."

She turned to search his face and found it momentarily inscrutable, deliberately, or so she believed. "You—would not cooperate with her. It is foolish of me to even ask."

"If I refuse, chérie, she will arrange your marriage with Maurice."

She tossed up her hands in frustration and paced. "I will not marry him."

"You will have little choice if she insists. King Francis will do whatever she expects of him. You cannot turn down the king's choice. So you see my dilemma, do you not?"

She paused and looked over at him. What was he thinking?

"Your dilemma?" she asked uneasily.

"The dilemma over cooperating with Catherine. Tell me, you have not led Maurice in any way to let him think you will oblige him in this marriage?"

"How can you imply I would be so foolish? I would never lead him on, nor want him for a husband!"

*As you well know*, she could have said but kept silent.

He folded his arms, and his direct gaze and slight smile brought a flush to her cheeks. She turned her head away with more indignation than she felt. She was hardly able to control her anxiety.

"As matters now stand for me, your dilemma, Marquis, may already be of no consequence. I have even more dangerous matters to contend with than Maurice and his notions of amour." She whirled and faced him openly. "I could be sent to the Bastille. Then what will become of your duel with Maurice?"

He looked at her as though trying to weigh whether she was serious. The look on her face must have alerted him. He tapped his chin thoughtfully, and something changed in his manner as his gaze became perceptive.

He walked up to her, taking her by the shoulders so she was forced to look up at him.

"What is it, Rachelle?" His voice was quiet, but not what she would call gentle; rather, it demanded the truth.

"It is Sebastien and my sisters. They escaped. They left France late last night or early this morning for England. No one knew of Sebastien's secret plans until Nenette brought morning tea for Madeleine and found them all gone. My sisters left me a message, but I've burned it as requested."

After she explained what Madeleine had written and about Sebastien's plans, she wondered that Fabien did not seem surprised.

"I knew of his plans to leave France," he said, "but I expected it in the fall, during the religious colloquy at Fontainebleau." He looked off toward the window, frowning to himself and apparently forgetting her for the moment. He said as if speaking to himself, "He must be nearing Calais now. His secret must be kept at any price lest Catherine discover it and send elite guardsmen to overtake him at the port." He looked at her. "Who else knows of this other than yourself and your maid?"

"No one that I know of, just little Philippe."

"The boy I saw?"

"Yes. He lost his family in the attack in Lyon and I — we have taken him in as an apprentice in my work. But Fabien, there is more, for me, the worst."

His fingers tightened on her shoulders. "Go on."

"I played recklessly with the Queen Mother — "

She paused and bit her lip. His jaw clamped. He was upset with her, and she loathed having to tell him.

"I was so sure she murdered Grandmère — that when Philippe told me about the poison shops on the wharves and how the Queen Mother is said to masquerade herself as a shopping woman, I knew I must follow her."

She heard his breath escape. His gaze narrowed. "Rachelle!" he gritted.

"I know, I know, and well, this morning the opportunity came and I followed her to the wharf, to the shop of the Ruggerio brothers. I overheard her demand poison from them. She plans to murder someone else now — "

He swiftly put his fingers to her lips, restraining her. He glanced toward the door. "Not so loud." He looked at her. "So she saw you?"

"Madalenna did. How did you know?"

"What else could go wrong?" he said fiercely. "Why did you do it? Did I not warn you to stay away from her? You are no match for her diabolical wits!"

Then suddenly he pulled her into his arms and held her tightly, stroking her hair gently. "This complicates matters. Tell me everything. Leave nothing out," he ordered quietly, his mood completely changing. "When did this happen?"

She tried to pull her thoughts out of the warm mesmerizing pool she found herself in with his arms around her possessively. She buried the side of her face against his fragrant jacket. "This morning, about an hour ago. It was Madalenna who saw me." She looked up quickly. "Do you think she will inform Catherine?"

"Without question, she has no mind of her own. She is naught but a slave. Are you sure of this? You are not exaggerating just a little out of alarm? Madalenna saw you?"

"Yes, yes! I mean she saw me, and I am not exaggerating." Her teeth chattered despite herself. "She knows I was there, that I overheard. I could be sent to the Bastille."

"Not if I have anything to do with your future. But we must leave here at once." He turned her loose, frowning, deep in thought. "Let me think . . ." He tapped his chin and paced, then looked at her evenly, scanning her. "Speaking of a disguise, that may aid us both at the moment. Can you make yourself— " he gestured with his hands, as if measuring her girth — "heavier, here and there?"

She looked down at herself. "Yes, I am sure I can."

"We will go straight to my palais at Vendôme."

Vendôme. Her thoughts rushed back to an earlier time when she had fled there for safety and remembered his promise of amour in the garden.

"But will she not send guards after me at Vendôme?"

"Undoubtedly. She may even come herself. That is good. I shall have her on my own terms." He let the drape fall into place, looked over at her, scowled, and came to her.

"We will need to leave your maid and the boy here until I can find a way to send for them. They should be safe. I'll tell them to admit that you ran away with me if she questions them. That will give her pause. She needs me to get rid of Guise. She will not do much to anger me until after the assassination. So I must delay." He walked over to the window and moved the heavy velvet drapery to look below in the courtyard. "Go and change. Do what you can to disguise your appearance."

Rachelle, heart thudding with excitement and fear, rushed to her bedchamber for a dark dress and cloak, stuffing lighter undergarments beneath the dress until she looked broadly rounded. She started to smile, but was sobered when she imagined the face of the Queen Mother peering at her. A few minutes later she came out and stood in the doorway expecting his approval.

He turned and took her in from head to toe. He put a hand to his forehead and closed his eyes. Rachelle smothered a laugh.

He gestured toward the door, bowing deeply, and she walked past him with dignity, head high.

CATHERINE DID NOT RETURN to the Louvre as expected but boarded the royal coach for the ride to Fontainebleau, content with what she had accomplished at the Ruggerio brothers' shop. As the horses raced along the wooded countryside of Orléans and Fontainebleau, she laughed to herself, for a message from one of her chief spies had reached her by rider. Marquis Fabien de Vendôme had docked the *Reprisal* at Calais and was on his way to Paris to stand against Comte Maurice Beauvilliers. There would most likely be a duel over the belle des belles Mademoiselle Rachelle, unless Catherine decided to stop it. She chuckled. She was in no mind to stop so entertaining a spectacle.

She would make certain they met at Fontainebleau, and she would rile them up first like two poisonous snakes and then arrange to have them meet by chance.

She pressed her kerchief to her mouth and chuckled.

Later that afternoon within her royal appartement at Fontainebleau, Catherine received another message, this one from Paris. A cold fury wrapped around her until she yelled: "Madalenna!"

The girl appeared at once from the shadowy recesses of the chamber. Catherine stalked toward her shaking the lettre in her pale, stoic face.

"Why did you not tell me this? You little fool. You have failed me. I should throw you to the snake pit, you worthless creature. How long have you known Comte Sebastien fled Paris, taking his family?"

The round dark eyes, empty, like deep pools stared up at her.

"I did not know, Your Majesty. I swear I knew nothing of this news until you just told me."

"Lies!" She slapped the thin girl, and she fell backward, bumping her head against the wall. "You fool," Catherine said again. "He is on his way to England. You will pay for this failure, Madalenna. I will have you beaten. What else do you know that you are keeping from me? Out with it, or I vow you will wish you had spoken all the truth to me."

Madalenna crawled to her knees, wiping blood from her lips. She looked up at Catherine.

Catherine scowled down at her. "Well? You had best tell me. I have all the truth here on this piece of paper. If you hold anything back I shall know it."

Madalenna pushed the lock of ebony hair away from her cheek.

"I saw Mademoiselle Rachelle at the wharf. She followed you to the Messires Ruggerio. She saw me and ran away."

Catherine felt her heart turn to ice. She could not speak. She stared, unblinking, down at Madalenna, then turned slowly away and walked with leaden feet over to the window. She looked out at the forest and gazed at the circling crows, cawing.

*She must suspect me of the grande dame's death.*

*Danger*, her mind whispered, *danger.* No one must know of her secret dealings with poison.

*Spying on me. Following me? She will pay for this indiscretion. Ah yes, she will pay a weighty price for this treachery.*

*So be it. Rachelle must die. But not before I use her lover, the marquis, to destroy Duc de Guise. Then I will alert the duc's devoted son to the fact that the marquis assassinated his beloved father. Young Henry will not rest until he reaps revenge on the marquis. I will be rid of two enemies and no one will suspect my involvement. After the marquis is no longer here to defend her, I will have my way with Rachelle the spy!*

# *Together . . . at Last*

## VENDÔME

AT THE GRAND BOURBON CHÂTEAU AT VENDÔME IT SEEMED TO RACHELLE that all the schemes to entrap her and Fabien for personal and political gain had been left behind in Paris.

In the grand salle Rachelle surrendered to Fabien's embrace, to his fervent lips on hers, and suddenly the world was no longer bleak, no longer fearful or lonely. Fabien was here, showing her how much he wanted her, and she felt safe. She was hearing his unexpected words of commitment—words that she had merely dreamed of hearing and thought she never would. He loved her . . . loved her, fully and completely, and—

"Say yes, Rachelle, because I will not give up until you agree to marry me here at Vendôme. Will you become my beloved marquise, Rachelle de Vendôme?"

"Yes, yes . . ."

"Do you love me, Rachelle?"

She laughed, throwing her arms around his neck, holding him ardently.

"Forever," she whispered, warmed by his gaze.

How safe she felt in his arms; how right it seemed to be here with him, hearing his words of amour, and forgetting all that was darkness and fear. She had awakened from a dreadful nightmare to light and hope again.

She sighed as she heard him whisper, "And nothing will ever be allowed to tear us apart again."

For this moment the summer flowers bloomed in rich abundance, their fragrance heavy and sweet; the gilded cup of amour overflowed, and the future was as golden as though it were written on silk.

End of Book Two

Book Three, 2008

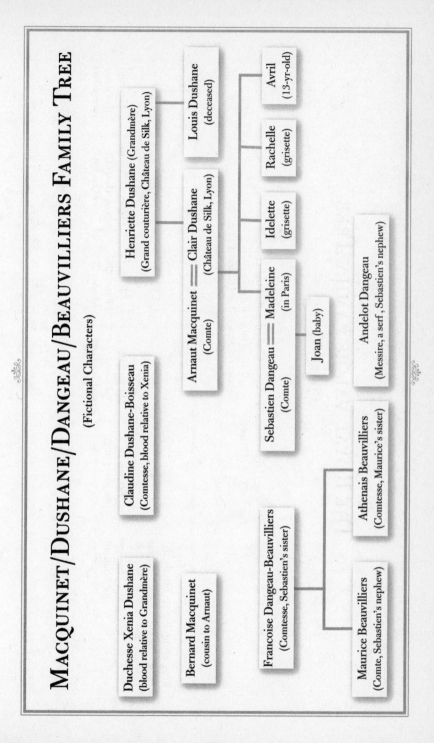

# Macquinet/Dushane/Dangeau/Beauvilliers Family Tree

(Fictional Characters)

**Duchesse Xenia Dushane**
(blood relative to Grandmère)

**Claudine Dushane-Boisseau**
(Comtesse, blood relative to Xenia)

**Henriette Dushane** (Grandmère)
(Grand couturière, Château de Silk, Lyon)

**Louis Dushane**
(deceased)

**Bernard Macquinet**
(cousin to Arnaut)

**Arnaut Macquinet** = **Clair Dushane**
(Comte)                  (Château de Silk, Lyon)

**Madeleine**
(in Paris)

**Idelette**
(grisette)

**Rachelle**
(grisette)

**Avril**
(13-yr-old)

**Sebastien Dangeau** = **Madeleine**
(Comte)

**Joan** (baby)

**Andelot Dangeau**
(Messire, a serf, Sebastien's nephew)

**Francoise Dangeau-Beauvilliers**
(Comtesse, Sebastien's sister)

**Athenais Beauvilliers**
(Comtesse, Maurice's sister)

**Maurice Beauvilliers**
(Comte, Sebastien's nephew)

# THE ROYAL VALOIS FAMILY TREE

(Historical)

King Henry Valois II ═══ Catherine de Medici
(King of France)      (Queen Mother and regent during
                      reigns of Francis II and Charles IX )

King Philip II ═══ Elisabeth
(King of Spain)    (oldest daughter)

Mary Stewart ═══ Francis II
(of Scotland)     (the young king)

Marguerite
(princesse,
second daughter)

Charles
(future King
Charles IX )

Henry of Anjou
(King Henry III
after Charles)

Hercule
(fourth and
youngest son)

# THE HOUSE OF GUISE FAMILY TREE

(Historical)

Anne d'Este ══ Duc de Guise (Francis)
(Marshal of France,
persecutor of Huguenots,
blood uncle to
Mary of Scotland)

Cardinal de Lorraine (Charles)
(younger brother of Duc de Guise
and a leader of the French inquisition
against Huguenots, blood uncle
to Mary of Scotland)

Henry de Guise
(the love of Princesse
Marguerite Valois)

# Daughter of Silk

*Linda Lee Chaikin*

Pursuing the family name as the finest silk producer in Lyon, the young Huguenot Rachelle Dushane-Macquinet is thrilled to accompany her famous couturière Grandmère to Paris, there to create a silk trousseau for the Royal Princesse Marguerite Valois.

The Court is magnificent; its regent, Catherine de Medici, deceptively charming … and the circumstances, darker than Rachelle could possibly imagine. At a time in history when the tortures of the Bastille and the fiery stake are an almost casual consequence in France, a scourge of recrimination is moving fast and furious against the Huguenots — and as the Queen Mother's political intrigues weave a web of deception around her, Rachelle finds herself in imminent danger.

Hope rests in warning the handsome Marquis Fabien de Vendôme of the wicked plot against his kin. But to do so, Rachelle must follow a perilous course.

Softcover: 0-310-26300-X

*Pick up a copy today at your favorite bookstore!*